THE
BOOKLOVER'S
LIBRARY

Also by Madeline Martin

The Last Bookshop in London
The Librarian Spy
The Keeper of Hidden Books

MADELINE MARTIN

THE BOOKLOVER'S LIBRARY

A NOVEL

HANOVER
SQUARE
PRESS

**HANOVER
SQUARE
PRESS™**

Recycling programs
for this product may
not exist in your area.

ISBN-13: 978-1-335-00039-2

The Booklover's Library

Hanover Square Press
22 Adelaide St. West, 41st Floor
Toronto, Ontario M5H 4E3, Canada
HanoverSqPress.com

Printed in U.S.A.

To my girls

Thank you for making me a mother—it is truly the greatest and most beautiful gift. I will always cherish the memories we've made, and continue to make, from family fun nights to silly inside jokes, and, of course, breakfast faces.

PROLOGUE

Nottingham, England
April 1931

JUST ONE MORE CHAPTER. Emma lingered in the storage area on the second floor of her father's bookshop, Tower Bookshop, with Jane Austen's *Emma* cradled in her lap. Sadly, not her namesake—her parents had named her Emmaline for an aunt she'd never met, who had died on Emma's seventh birthday ten years ago.

Still, the book was one of Emma's favorites.

"Emma." Papa's voice rose from somewhere in the bookshop, sharp with irritation.

She frowned. Papa was seldom ever cross with her.

Perhaps the smoke from the man who had come in with his cigar earlier still lingered in the shop.

She settled a scrap of paper into the spine of her book.

"Emmaline!" Something to that second cry snapped her to attention, a raw, frantic pitch.

Papa was never panicked.

She leaped up from the seat with such haste, the book dropped to the ground with a whump.

"I'm in the warehouse," she called out, racing to the door.

The handle was scalding hot. She yelped and drew back.

That's when she saw the smoke, wisps seeping beneath the door, glowing in the stream of sunlight.

Fire.

She put her skirt over her hand and twisted the knob to open the door. Thick plumes of smoke billowed in, black and choking.

She sucked in a breath of surprise, unintentionally inhaling a lungful of burning air. A cough racked her and she stumbled back, her mind reeling as her feet pulled her from the threat.

But to where? This was the only exit from the storeroom, save the second-floor window.

"Papa," she shouted, terror creeping into her voice.

All at once, he was there, wrapping a blanket around them, the one she kept in the shop for cold mornings before the furnace managed to heat the old building.

"Stay at my side." Papa's voice was gravelly beneath the blanket where he'd covered the lower part of his face. Even as he led her away, a great cough shuddered through his lean frame.

Beyond the wall of smoke was a vision straight out of Milton's *Paradise Lost* as fire licked and climbed its way up the towering stacks of books, devouring a lifetime of careful curation. Emma screamed, the sound muted by the blanket.

But Papa's hand was firm at her back, pressing her forward. "We have to run." Not slowing, he guided her to the winding metal staircase. She used to love clattering down it as a girl, hearing the metal ringing around her.

"It's hot," Papa cautioned. "Don't touch it."

Emma hugged against his side as they squeezed down the narrow steps that barely fit the two of them together. It swayed beneath their weight, no longer sturdy as it had once been. The blazing heat felt as though it was blistering Emma's skin. Too hot. Too close. Too much.

And they were plunging deeper into the fiery depths.

The soles of Emma's shoes stuck to the last two steps as rubber melted against metal.

What had once been rows of bookshelves was now a maze of flames. Even Papa hesitated before the seemingly impassable blaze.

But there was nowhere else to go.

The fire was alive. Cracking and popping and hissing and roaring, roaring, *roaring* so loud, it seemed like an actual beast.

"Go," he shouted, and his grip tightened around her, pulling her forward.

Together they ran, between columns of fire that had once been shelves of books. An ear-shattering crack came from above, spurring them to the front as fire and sparks poured down behind them.

Emma ran faster than she ever had before, faster than she knew herself capable. Papa's arm at her side yanked her this way or that, navigating through the fiery chaos. Until there was nowhere to go.

Papa roared louder than the fire beast and released her, running toward the blazing door. It flew open at the impact, revealing clean sunny daylight outside. He turned toward her even as she rushed after him and grabbed her around the shoulders, hauling her into the street.

Emma gulped in the clean air, reveling in the cool dampness washing into her tortured lungs. A crowd had gathered, staring up at the Tower Bookshop. Some came to Emma and Papa, asking in a frenzy of voices if they were hurt.

In the distance came the scream of emergency sirens. Sirens Emma had heard her entire life, but had never once needed herself.

There was need now. She held on to Papa's hand and looked behind her at the building that had been in her family for two generations and was meant to become hers someday. Her gaze skimmed over the bookshop to the top two floors where their home had once been.

The fire beast gave a great heaving howl and the top floor crumpled.

Someone grabbed her from behind, dragging her back as the rest of the structure came down, ripping her hand from her father's. She didn't reach for him again, unable to move, unable to think, her eyes fixed on the building as it crashed in on itself in a fiery heap. Their livelihood. Their home.

All the pictures of her mother who had died after Emma was born, all the books she and her father had lovingly selected from bookshops around England on the trips they'd taken together, everything they'd ever owned.

Gone.

Emma choked on a sob at the realization.

Everything was gone.

"We need a doctor." A man's voice broke through her horror, pulling her attention to her father.

He lay on the ground, motionless. Soot streaked his handsome slender face, and his thick gray hair that had once been the same shade of chestnut as hers was now singed in blackened tufts.

"Papa?" She sagged to the ground beside him.

His eyes lifted to her, watery blue and filled with a love that made her heart swell. The breath wheezed from his chest like a kettle's cry. "You're safe."

Once the words left his mouth, his body relaxed, going slack.

"Papa?" Emma cried.

This time his eyes did not meet hers. They looked through her. Sightless and empty.

She shuddered at how unnatural he appeared. Like her father, and yet not like her father.

"Papa?"

The wailing sirens were still too far-off.

"I'm a doctor." A man knelt on the other side of her father. His fingers went to Papa's blackened neck and the man's sad brown eyes turned up to her.

"I'm sorry, love. He's gone."

Emma stared at the man, refusing to believe her ears even as she saw the truth.

It had always just been Emma and her father, the two of them against the world, as Papa used to say. They read the same books to discuss together, they worked every day at the book-shop together, friends and colleagues as much as they were father and daughter. Once Emma had completed her schooling, she'd even traveled with him, curating books like the first editions they were still waiting on to arrive from Newcastle.

Now that beautiful light that shone in his eyes had dulled. Lifeless.

It was no longer Papa and her against the world.

He was gone.

Their shop was gone.

Their home was gone.

Everything she knew and loved was gone.

1

Nottingham, England
August 1939

EMMA TAYLOR HUGGED the first-edition copy of *Alice's Adventures in Wonderland* against her chest and strode determinedly down Pelham Street, finally arriving at the pawnshop.

The book was one of the precious five delivered from Newcastle a month after her father's death.

Eight years had passed since then. Just after the shop burned down, a young gentleman from her father's solicitor's office named Arthur had tucked her under his wing. She'd allowed herself to be pulled in, drawn to Arthur by loneliness and grief.

The wedding was quick, too soon to realize they weren't compatible, both too young. Too different. There had been fights, tears, expectations that were impossible to fulfill. And after yielding to the pressure around them, there'd been a baby. Olivia had been born with Emma's deep blue eyes and Arthur's chocolate brown waves. Beautiful, happy, and perfect.

But everyone was wrong. A child hadn't fixed their problems, but made them worse. And when Arthur didn't come home one night five years ago, Emma had assumed he'd been out at a pub again. He had, but apparently, upon weaving his way home, he stepped out into the street and had been struck by a car.

In all her years raised by a single father, Emma had never anticipated she too would become a single parent.

She stopped and looked at the sign with three golden balls announcing Pelham Pawnbroker. Her courage wavered.

Rent for the small flat in Radford was due and Olivia needed a new pair of shoes before school started next month. Already she had worn her shoes from last year too long. No doubt they pinched, though she'd only mentioned the discomfort once.

Seeing how easily her daughter had adjusted to a life with so little money pulled at a place in Emma's chest.

It's only a book, Emma.

Resolve thoroughly in place, she pushed through the door. A jangle of bells sang merrily overhead, and she couldn't help but wonder how many others teetering on the brink of financial desperation had been subjected to that mocking, cheerful tinkle.

A man stood behind the counter, his gaze feasting on the parcel in her hands before dragging up to her face. "May I help you?"

The array of goods beneath the glass counter taunted her, treasures sold cheap under the pressure of time and need. Amid the glittering gemstones were several solid gold bands. One of those was hers, sold while it was still warm from her left finger only six months prior. A cheap band replaced it, something to keep her respectable in the eyes of society.

The money had run out quickly.

"Are you interested in purchasing?" the man prompted, his focus flicking back to the book in her arms. "Or selling?"

A shelf behind him displayed a pair of small leather shoes, not unlike what Olivia needed.

"Selling." The word caught slightly. Her hands trembled when she set the book on the counter and gently—reverently—peeled off the paper wrap.

Excitement flashed in the pawnbroker's eyes before dulling with practiced disinterest. "Which edition is this?" he drawled, as if he didn't know.

Emma stared down at the red cover, recalling how the gold-embossed spine had stood out among a row of old books at the shop in Newcastle, and how her father had held it in his hands, a prize both wondrous and precious. Perfect for their collection. "First edition."

"Well." The man reached for the book and everything in Emma screamed for her to snatch it back, to cradle it against her chest and run home.

But that wouldn't keep the electricity on, or put food in their larder, or keep them in the decent home they'd managed to find for such an affordable rent.

It's only a book, Emma.

But it wasn't just a book. It was part of her father's legacy, one of the few remaining pieces that hadn't gone up in a fiery blaze.

The man examined the book carefully—pristine save for a dent at the bottom of the cover that he made a point to tsk over. "I wish I could say my clients have an appreciation for first editions," he murmured sympathetically. "They won't be willing to pay what it's worth and I *do* still have to make a living."

After a round of haggling, Emma pushed out of the shop several minutes later with a quarter of the sum she'd anticipated. The opening notes of a headache pounded at her temples. She had hoped the funds from the sale would cover expenses for at least several months. At most, this would last three, maybe four.

And what then?

She walked several feet and stopped, leaning her back against the brick wall as she tried to breathe through the dizzying rush of anxiety.

Her widow's pension was ten shillings a week combined

with Olivia's government support of five shillings. Though it was just the two of them and they lived as frugally as possible, fifteen bob went fast.

The ache in her temples edged around to the backs of her eyes. A groan rasped in her throat as she remembered they'd run out of aspirin tablets several days before.

More money to spend.

Already the measly sum in her handbag was getting lighter.

At least she was near the chemist. She pushed off the wall and made her way toward Boots', the sprawling chemist that took up a full corner of Pelham Street. The hand-painted letters scrolling over the wide plate glass windows was posh, displaying goods within that she could never afford. She went in through the corner entrance just below the ornate clock and strode past various wares in their glittering cases.

A variety of items were laid out, from thermometers and medications to bottles of perfume, stationery, and handbags. She ignored it all and picked up a tin of aspirin, setting the little tablets inside rattling about.

The woman at the register lifted her thin brows. "Will that be all?" Before Emma could reply, she rushed on, shimmying her shoulders with excitement. "The Fancy Department is having a sale on handbags, today only."

Emma tucked her purse behind the counter to keep the woman from seeing its sorry state. The once neat corners were now slightly dented and the entire thing resembled a discarded paper sack. "This is all for now, but thank you."

A crack of thunder boomed outside and the young woman leaped in surprise. "That's quite the storm coming in."

It was a storm Emma might be walking in. After all, she was only about a dozen blocks from home, and walking saved her the cost of the bus fare. If she hurried, perhaps she could—

Lightning flashed outside, immediately followed by torrential rain that came down in veritable buckets.

"Maybe a bit of tea?" the woman suggested, eyeing the rain whipping against the windows. "The café is just upstairs beside the Booklover's Library."

Tea was more money Emma didn't need to spend. But then, wearing out the last bit of her own shoes in a downpour would be far more expensive. Even sprinting for the bus would do little good at this point. At least Olivia would see the storm and know why Emma was late.

There was nothing for it but to wait. And at least a cup of tea meant Emma could take the aspirin and receive relief sooner rather than later.

She climbed the stairs, and turned toward the café opposite the exclusive lending library as she inhaled the comforting aroma of freshly baked scones and the earthy, spicy scent of tea. Her stomach snarled with longing.

The moment she sat down, a waiter approached and took her order—a single cup of tea. Once it had cooled enough, she withdrew three of the five-grain tablets from the tin and downed the bitter medicine with one swift swallow.

The tea was heavenly, strong and bracing with a bit of milk and sugar.

She leaned back, surveying the café as the tables filled with patrons eager to wait out the rain.

This had been her life for a brief spell when she'd been married to Arthur, enjoying the income of a solicitor's wife. She'd sat among tables covered in crisp linens and fine china without a thought about the cost of a cup of tea. Or a scone for that matter.

But money didn't buy happiness. She knew that well and good by now.

There may not be much money in the box in her wardrobe, but she had the purest joy there ever was. She had Olivia.

As Emma sat, she caught a familiar aroma in the tea-and-scone-scented air—the fragrant pull of paper and ink, of books.

Her gaze wandered unbidden to the grand entrance of the Booklover's Library just steps away from the café, where stained-glass windows welcomed cheerfully colored light to splash across the rows and rows of books. The lending library had been as much a fixture in Boots' as the glass counters exhibiting the costly purses and makeup downstairs. Being a subscriber was just as prohibitively expensive.

She pulled in a pained breath.

Books had once been such a comfort to her, helping her through life's difficult moments as well as the struggles of a motherless childhood. Her father and their shared love of literature were so closely linked, imagining one without the other was quite impossible.

Outside, the rain had eased to a bearable drizzle. She drained the last of her tea, desperate to flee before memories could settle over her.

The ache in her head was beginning to subside and her spirits were somewhat bolstered by the tea. Emma stood and nudged the chair back under the table with her hip when a woman's voice sounded from a cracked door several feet away. "You've only just completed your training."

"I know, and I'm terribly sorry," another woman replied, her voice younger, her tone almost pleading. "Tommy said that with the last war, his parents almost didn't get married for want of a pastor. We must have our wedding before the war starts, so we can do it how we want."

There was a pause.

"I understand," said the older woman, resigned. "Felicitations on your nuptials."

"Thank you, Miss Bainbridge."

The door opened fully and a pretty redhead wearing the lending library's green overalls tied over her dress swept from the room, buoyant with youthful optimism and the promise of a bright future.

Both things Emma had been lacking leading up to her own marriage all those years ago.

The older woman who emerged from the office had her feet firmly planted on the ground, a line of concern etched on her brow. Her hair was more gray than black, swept neatly away from her austere expression.

She stiffened when she caught sight of Emma. "I'm sorry you heard that. I didn't realize the door wasn't closed."

"You needn't concern yourself." Emma squared her shoulders. "Though I'm assuming this means you have a position open?"

The query hung in the air long enough to make her tamp down the urge to squirm.

"I might," the older woman replied carefully. Miss Bainbridge, that's what the young bride had called her. "Are you seeking employment?"

Was she seeking employment?

The question would be scornfully funny if it weren't so very serious.

Emma had been looking for a job going on two years. Ever since the money box had become distressingly light. At one point, the combination of her father's and Arthur's inheritances had seemed a king's ransom. But after five years of living expenses, the fortune had become little more than a pauper's life raft—a swiftly sinking one at that.

The marriage bar restricted wives from remaining employed or seeking employment. It was not supposed to extend to widows. Unless, of course, there was a child involved.

Respectable shops wouldn't hire her. Being a single mother made her too much of a liability.

She'd applied everywhere, including factories, which were usually less fussy about such things, but even there she'd been turned away. The industry hired girls straight out of school at fourteen, ones with swift hands and young, bright eyes. An untrained woman over the age of twenty was not worth the effort. At twenty-five, Emma was far too old to start a factory job, even if she did look young.

"I am indeed seeking employment." Emma stuffed her left hand into her pocket and slid off the cheap tin band.

The woman considered her for a long moment. "Very well, if you've the time, step into my office and I'll conduct the interview this very moment." She hesitated. "Miss..."

Emma didn't think twice as she stripped away the *Mrs.* from her name. "Miss Taylor."

2

EMMA LISTENED PATIENTLY as Miss Bainbridge pontificated on the finer details of what duties the job of a Booklover's Librarian entailed. They included dusting the books and waxing the handrails while Emma began her training, then eventually she would be on the floor assisting patrons.

"You'll have to recommend books, primarily to our Class A subscribers," Miss Bainbridge added. "While the Class B may receive a nudge of a suggestion from time to time, our Class A subscribers pay significantly more for the pleasure of having a curated list of books recommended for them personally." She folded her hands over the neat stack of papers in front of her. "Does that seem like something you could do?"

"Yes," Emma answered earnestly. "I used to work at a bookshop. At Tower Bookshop in Beeston." A familiar pain twinged when she spoke of her father's bookshop, even all these years later.

"Tower Bookshop?" An inscrutable expression passed over the woman's face, but cleared quickly. "That has not been around for...what? Five years?"

"Eight." But sometimes, it seemed like only yesterday, while simultaneously feeling like a life someone else had lived.

"You aren't as young as I'd assumed then." Miss Bainbridge tapped her finger on the desk thoughtfully.

Emma expected that. She had a youthful face like her mother, enhanced with her father's large blue eyes. One man she'd interviewed with at the stocking factory advised her to slip a few years off on her next interview and that no one would be the wiser.

Except that Emma hated to lie.

Miss Bainbridge tilted her head. "Why haven't you married?"

There was a directness to Miss Bainbridge Emma appreciated. She had never understood women who danced and prevaricated around saying what they intended.

Emma clenched her hands in her lap and forced her thoughts on Olivia, who patiently awaited Emma's return to their flat. The rented space was small but offered an en suite washroom and a living area, and had a cozy kitchen with enough room for a table and a few chairs.

If Emma didn't acquire a job soon, they wouldn't have enough money to keep them there.

And yet her tongue would not work to speak the lie.

"I was married," she confessed on an exhale. "I'm a widow."

Miss Bainbridge nodded. "I see."

Emma swallowed. "And I'm a mother."

Miss Bainbridge's face fell and the excited hum in the air went flat.

"I have sufficient experience for the position," Emma rushed. "More than enough. My father owned Tower Bookshop. I was raised in that shop and remained there until it burned down."

Miss Bainbridge straightened. "Mr. Williams was your father?"

"Yes. I married a year after the fire and had a little girl. But my husband was struck by a car, leaving me alone with Olivia—

that's my daughter. I've tried everywhere, but no one will hire a widow with a child. Aside from factories, but I'm too old…"

The regret already hovered in Miss Bainbridge's gray eyes, a preliminary rejection on the cusp of being spoken.

"Please." Emma sat forward in her seat. "I know books."

"Miss Taylor." Miss Bainbridge closed her eyes and corrected, "Mrs. Taylor, you must understand that by you having a child—"

"A daughter," Emma corrected, disliking the anonymity of the general word *child*. Olivia was so much more than just a child. She was Emma's whole heart.

Miss Bainbridge remained quietly pensive for a moment. The fine lines at her forehead were more pronounced than those at the corners of her eyes, which said a lot about how the woman perceived the world. "Your father was a good man. What happened to him, to you, was a shame."

A shame.

Deficient words for the most devastating day of Emma's life. She looked down, focusing on the small oval callus under her naked ring finger and the slight band of discolored skin from the cheap ring.

"If you were to recommend a book to me, what would you suggest?"

Emma looked up.

Miss Bainbridge settled back and her chair gave a low creak. "Take your time."

Emma shifted her perspective of the older woman from potential employer to reader. Once upon a time, Emma could deduce a person's book preference in seconds, a sixth sense that guided her to the part of their soul that was missing, a gap that could be filled with the perfect story.

She'd had a gap in her own life for far too long. A chasm really. The ability to discern a reader's preference felt weak as she tried to flex the anemic skill. Instead, she considered the woman in front of her.

The weight of the world rested on Miss Bainbridge's squared shoulders, but despite her stern expression, she had offered benevolence to the soon-to-be newlywed who had quit, even though doing so clearly put Miss Bainbridge out. Then there was her style—ageless with her simple updo and her tailored black dress.

Miss Bainbridge seemed the sort to prefer the Everyman's Library classic reprints rather than a contemporary novel.

Before Emma could second-guess her choice, she replied, *"Jane Eyre."*

Miss Bainbridge blinked and narrowed her gray eyes. "Why would you suggest that book?"

"You seem the pragmatic sort," Emma replied. "Intelligent, but also kind. After all, I'm still here talking to you despite my circumstances."

A smile stretched over Miss Bainbridge's thin lips. *"Jane Eyre* happens to be my favorite book. How far do you live from here?"

The abruptness of the second question was jarring. "A ways. I'm on Moorgate Street in Radford."

Miss Bainbridge tapped at her chin with a short, immaculate fingernail. "That's far enough away..." she murmured to herself.

"I'm sorry?" Emma scooted to the edge of her chair, not wanting to miss a single word.

"Would you be willing to be addressed as Miss Taylor and refer to your daughter as your sister instead, should your relation come into question?"

Emma blinked, incredulous. Was she really being offered the job?

"It's crude to ask, I know, but you're aware of the rules..." Miss Bainbridge hedged.

"Yes," Emma said quickly. "I mean, yes, I agree to the terms. Please, I need this job."

The lines running across Miss Bainbridge's brow deepened and perhaps she was second-guessing her decision. Regardless, she said, "Welcome to the Boots' Booklover's Library, Miss Taylor."

She stressed the word *Miss*.

"Arrive tomorrow morning promptly at seven, prepared for your training to begin. Do bear in mind that your employment will be dependent on passing the necessary exams."

The word of caution did nothing to dampen Emma's soaring spirits. After all, she had always received excellent marks in school. "I won't let you down."

3

BY THE TIME Emma exited Boots', the rain had stopped, leaving the air heavy with moisture and the threat of more to come. She rushed the distance to the tenement house on Moorgate Street and unlocked the door to her flat on the second floor.

Olivia was exactly where Emma had left her, sitting at the dining room table with an array of colored pencils and a series of masterpieces ranging from the flowers in the garden out front to happy drawings of Tubby, their landlady's little white dog. The sandwich Emma made before she left had been eaten, the crumb-filled plate resting beside Olivia's drawings.

"Mum." Olivia leaped out of the chair and rushed to Emma, throwing her arms around her waist in an enormous hug. "You were gone so long."

Guilt nipped at Emma. She *had* been gone for a while.

However, the time would be nothing compared to how long Olivia would have to be home alone while Emma was at work. At least for this final month of summer before school resumed.

"Something came up." Emma brushed Olivia's silky hair back while her daughter began sorting through the drawings.

She showed them one by one to Emma, taking care to point out each detail.

"Are you still hungry?" Emma asked after having thoroughly praised the collection of masterpieces, fully aware lunch time had long since passed.

Olivia nodded and put aside her drawings.

Emma went into the kitchen to make sandwiches for both of them. "How was it today on your own?"

Olivia sat on a stool by the kitchen counter and shrugged her narrow shoulders. "Not as fun as when you're here."

Emma concentrated on the sandwiches so Olivia wouldn't see the remorse in her expression. This job was unfortunately necessary, a godsend Emma knew she should be grateful for. And yet she hated how much she would be away from home.

"Olive." She tried to keep her tone light, referring to her daughter by the nickname she'd used when she was little. "I have news."

Olivia watched her with wide blue eyes. So like Emma's own. A spitting image, Papa would have said.

"I had an interview for a position at Boots'." Emma set the sandwich in front of her daughter.

"The chemist?"

Emma nodded and set to work on her own sandwich. "I'll be working at the lending library there."

Olivia was silent for a long moment. "When?"

"Starting tomorrow. I'll be there weekdays, with weekends off." Two days off a week was a benefit indeed, one many employers did not offer. Yet another aspect of the job to be grateful for.

When Olivia didn't respond, Emma looked up and found her daughter's head bent over her plate.

"Olivia?"

But still her daughter remained staring at her plate. Olivia was like this when she encountered news she didn't want to hear. She did not have tantrums like other children, or rail at the unfairness of life. No, she tucked her head down and processed her thoughts internally. Keeping any opinions or concerns from Emma.

"I know you're upset," Emma started.

Olivia lifted her head. "Can we still go to the pictures on Saturday?"

Emma put a hand on her hip. "Would I miss a date at the cinema with you?"

The morning children's shows were offered at a reduced price, allowing them to become an affordable luxury Emma had started when their savings felt limitless. This job would mean they could continue their Saturdays at the cinema.

Her daughter broke out in a grin, revealing a gap where her left eyetooth had recently fallen out.

"I'll leave before you wake in the morning and be back by the afternoon," Emma said. "And when school resumes, I'll be home about an hour after you. I doubt you'll even miss me."

Olivia snorted. "I always miss you when you're gone."

There was the guilt again. A hot flash in Emma's stomach.

She was glad now for the activities they'd done together that summer—taking the bus to Forest Park for ice cream beneath the sun-flecked shade of the various elm and oak trees, going to Highfields Lido to swim in the icy water pumped in from the lake and eating warm jam sandwiches on the grass, or looking through the vendor's wares while strolling over the cobblestoned streets at Market Square.

"Having this job means more trips to the cinema." Emma winked. "And this weekend, I think we should find you some new shoes."

"Yesssss." Olivia pressed her tongue over her teeth, letting the air hiss from the gap in her smile.

Emma laughed and ruffled Olivia's hair. "What am I to do with you?"

Olivia beamed up at her. "Take me for ice cream?"

"On a Wednesday?"

Olivia waggled her brows.

And got exactly what she wanted.

Emma woke to a tangle of nerves the next morning. Olivia slept soundly as Emma prepared lunch for her daughter, depositing it in the larder with a note.

The idea of having Olivia remain home alone for so long was not a welcome one, but Emma had little choice. With no family in Nottingham and no close friends, there wasn't anyone to ask for assistance. Not that Emma had been one to ask for help.

Before leaving, she slipped into their shared room one last time and pressed a kiss to Olivia's sleep-warm forehead.

Olivia's eyes squinted open against the light streaming in from the kitchen. "Are you going?"

"Yes, but I made lunch for you. Make sure to open the blackout curtains when you wake up."

Olivia nodded. "What if there's another air raid?"

Emma had worried after the same thing. "The last one had only been a test."

England was on the brink of war. No matter how much she wanted to ignore the impending strife, it was evident in the palpable excitement of men preparing to enlist in the military, in the shelters being hastily built around the city, and the signs plastered everywhere calling for volunteers and safety alike.

And in the letter she'd received the month before.

No. She wouldn't think of that.

Instead, she brushed her daughter's rich, chocolate brown hair from her face and pressed another kiss to her brow.

"They ran the air raid testing times in the newspaper then, remember?" Emma asked. "There was nothing mentioned about today."

The tension drained from Olivia's face and she nodded.

"I love you, Olive."

"I love you too, Mum."

With those sweet words in Emma's mind, she left the flat, ensuring she locked the door behind her before heading to the Booklover's Library for her first day.

Emma arrived fifteen minutes early, the ring off her finger and the small band of greenish gray against her skin covered with the powder remnants from an old compact she had from years ago when she wore makeup for Arthur's work dinners.

Miss Bainbridge welcomed her with a cup of warm hot chocolate. "Mrs. Boot has long since retired, but still likes to have all her girls receive a cup of hot chocolate or tea every morning and lunch every afternoon. Not everyone can always afford both and she won't have her girls going hungry."

Immediately Emma tabulated the savings such generosity would afford. This meant her pay would stretch even further. A way to refill her dwindling money box more swiftly.

Oblivious to Emma's mental calculations, Miss Bainbridge went on. "While you are in training, you'll need to dust the books every morning, then attend lessons throughout the day until you pass. Today will be the Understanding of Publishing Trade course as well as the Knowledge of Best Sellers."

She waved her fingers in silent indication for Emma to follow and led her into the Booklover's Library.

Whatever might have resembled a chemist's shop fell away, as did the boutique facade and the shelves of gifts available for purchase and even the café behind them. The library transported its subscribers to a place of cozy comfort with large stained-glass windows that overlooked the street below, plush rugs underfoot, and the lingering perfume of freshly cut flowers from the small bouquets in elegant glass vases throughout the open space.

Then, of course, there were the books. Neat shelves, perfectly arranged, pristine from Emma's vantage point, each spine punctured with a small eyelet at the top for a subscriber's badge to be threaded through.

This marked Emma's first time wandering into a lending library or bookshop since her father's death. The familiar scent hit her like a blow.

That evocative fragrance of books, of paper and ink, of dust and leather and linen bindings. Once that smell had been her world. It was a piece of her past, one she had shoved away, intending to leave dormant.

Now it began to awaken, carrying a note of excitement and the surprising longing to run her fingers along the neat row of spines.

Unaware of the complex emotions raging through her newest employee, Miss Bainbridge strode toward one of the two ornate wooden desks in the room, the one with *Class B* written on a placard, and withdrew a feather duster from a cabinet beneath. This she handed to Emma.

A pretty blond strode in, sporting her youth and confidence the way one would a mink coat.

"Ah, Miss Avory, do come and meet our newest librarian, Miss Taylor." Miss Bainbridge waved the woman over.

Miss Avory sauntered toward them, red lips curling upward as she approached. A small diamond engagement ring glittered on her left hand. "It's so lovely to meet you, Miss Taylor. Welcome to the best job in all of England."

"Miss Avory loves her position here so much she's been engaged for a year and a half." Miss Bainbridge's gaze narrowed in thought. "That might be a record."

"We tend to have notoriously long engagements here at the Booklover's Library," Miss Avory added conspiratorially. "A love of books, or the love of a man…" She put her palms up and alternatively raised and lowered them, like scales. Then she gave an unapologetic laugh.

"Will you be a dear and show her around?" Miss Bainbridge asked Miss Avory.

"Of course," she replied even as Miss Bainbridge was already walking away in clipped strides.

"She's all efficiency," Miss Avory warned. "But she's really very kind."

Emma nodded, quite aware of how very magnanimous Miss Bainbridge could be.

Miss Avory whipped a compact and lipstick tube from her purse and swept a bit of rich red over her lips, touching up lipstick that hadn't even begun to fade. In fact, there was not a bit of Miss Avory that wasn't perfect, from her heart-shaped mouth to her high cheekbones and glossy blond hair swept back in a fashionable roll.

Makeup had never appealed to Emma. Nor had fashion. Perhaps it was the byproduct of growing up without a mother, but the entire act of always touching up lipstick seemed altogether time-consuming and exhausting.

Still, she didn't want to miss an opportunity to connect with a coworker, not like she had in missing so many chances for friends in school.

"That's a lovely shade, Miss Avory." Emma hoped the compliment sounded less awkward than it felt.

"It's called Firefly." She snapped her compact closed. "From our Number Seven collection. I just refilled my lipstick tube with it and simply adore the color."

Emma nodded, knowing very little about the Number Seven cosmetic line that Boots' often advertised. While it meant to offer a luxury product at an affordable price for the middle class, the frivolity was one Emma couldn't fathom spending money on.

"And do call me Margaret." She tucked her purse under the counter. "I'll show you where to get started. Make a note of where the books are located while you're dusting so you'll know where to return them to later." She paused by a vase to adjust the thick stems of several dahlias before nodding in satisfaction and leading Emma to the far shelves.

When Emma was finally released from work that afternoon, she spared the money for bus fare to get home as quickly as possible. The frenzy of the tour of the library and a litany of manuals and training folders had filled her day. Though busy, her thoughts had remained on Olivia. She'd been alone before, of course. But not for an entire day. Not like this.

Heart racing, Emma now rushed into the tenement house. No sooner had she entered the stairwell than the landlady's door flew open. The older woman braced her leg at the crack in the door as she closed it to keep her little white dog from squeezing out alongside her.

Emma offered a cheerful hello to Mrs. Pickering while secretly hoping the older woman wouldn't want to talk. The landlady was a widow as well, one Emma gathered was rather lonely.

In all honestly, they were likely one another's closest friends. Mrs. Pickering because she did little more than go out to the grocer or to walk her dog. And for Emma, because she was far too busy with her life with Olivia.

"I do hate to overstep, except I couldn't help but notice…" Mrs. Pickering pressed her lips together, as though trying to piece words together in her mind. "You left quite early this morning and you are home rather late."

Emma tilted her head, unsure how to respond to such an unnerving observation of her comings and goings.

"And your daughter..." Mrs. Pickering smiled apologetically. "Well, she's here. In my flat."

"You have Olivia?" Alarm shot through Emma as her mind spun in all the ways her daughter being home alone could have gone so horribly wrong.

4

"WHY DO YOU have my daughter?" Emma asked, barely concealing the fear creeping into her tone.

"I was worried when you were gone so long." Mrs. Pickering's brow creased and she studied a small crack at the corner of a tile on the floor. "With the war so close, I thought Olivia might be scared and figured I'd offer to let her come downstairs for a spell to play with Tubby." Whatever unease played over her expression now shifted to a smile that set her pale blue eyes twinkling. "The two had such a day romping about in the garden. They were both knackered after. Olivia is sleeping on my sofa now. And until you came in the door, Tubby lay right beside her. They were a sight, the two of them." Mrs. Pickering chuckled softly to herself.

Perhaps Emma ought to have been upset at Mrs. Pickering's interference, but the idea of Olivia playing with Tubby rather than sitting alone in the flat all day eased some of her guilt for having to leave.

"I've recently become employed," Emma confessed. "At the Boots' Booklover's Library on Pelham. Today was my first day."

The mirth dissolved from Mrs. Pickering's face. "On account of the rent?"

Heat flooded Emma's cheeks. "I beg your pardon?"

Mrs. Pickering folded her hands anxiously in front of her. "Is the rent too high?"

It was. And it wasn't.

The sum was next to nothing compared to what most landlords charged for half the space with a shared water closet for the entire tenement house. And yet even that minimal cost chipped away at Emma's savings that had no way of growing.

That Mrs. Pickering assumed she couldn't afford the rent, however, was untenable.

"Not at all," Emma exclaimed through her burning mortification. "The opportunity for employment presented itself and school will resume soon, so I knew I would have the time on my hands."

The lie was bitter on her tongue, but the truth was far more caustic.

Mrs. Pickering waved Emma into her flat. This time Tubby was not trying to break through the widening gap in the door, but was on the couch, nestled next to a sleeping Olivia, her cheeks flushed and mouth open. Mrs. Pickering's living area was lovely, with polished mahogany furnishings and two stuffed chairs of a plum-colored velvet set beside a full bookcase. Tubby's pet-safe, gas-resistant kennel was off to the side, next to Mrs. Pickering's gas mask box. The entire room carried the delicate fragrance of roses Emma so often associated with her landlady.

A smile tugged at Emma's lips. It had been years since Olivia napped. But then, she'd never been one for playing outdoors all day the way she clearly had with Tubby. She'd never connected with the other children at school enough to join them outside in their games. In fact, attending school was what had made her become more subdued. Whatever unfettered and carefree delights she'd enjoyed as a girl had slipped away not long after her lessons began, leaving her more reserved when outside the home. Her marks reflected that same unhappiness with her lessons, but one couldn't simply not go to school.

Emma followed Mrs. Pickering into her cheerful kitchen, the all-white cabinets and appliances set off by rose-printed wallpaper that matched the curtains draped over the windows in the room. The kitchen in Emma's flat was nearly identical, though the walls upstairs were a buttery yellow with a green trim that reminded her of mushy peas. And the appliances were not nearly as well appointed.

Mrs. Pickering filled the kettle. "Tea?"

"Please."

"Olivia still has a little more than two weeks before school resumes, I believe." Mrs. Pickering spoke as she moved about the kitchen. "How many days a week will you be working?"

Warmth burned in Emma's cheeks once more and she knew the stain of her guilt was scorched across her fair skin. "Five days. I'm off on weekends."

"I can watch her, if you like." Mrs. Pickering busied herself pulling two teacups from the shelf, the fine porcelain painted with a similar rose motif as the wallpaper.

Emma waved off the offer. "That isn't necessary."

After all, she and Olivia had gotten by these seven years without help. And Papa had never needed assistance with seeing to Emma. They had been a team the way she and Olivia were now.

The two of them against the world.

"Oh, having Olivia here would be a great favor to me." Mrs. Pickering turned to Emma. "Tubby has more energy than I can handle, the rascal. I haven't seen him so happy as he's been today playing with your Olivia. And she'd be wonderful company for an old woman."

Before Emma could reply, Mrs. Pickering put up a hand to stop her from protesting. "No need to answer now. Have a think on it."

The following morning, when Emma left the flat, she wrote a note for Olivia telling her she was welcome to go to Mrs. Pickering's if she liked. The decision would be best made by Olivia. After all, she was the one most impacted.

The coursework at Boots' Booklover's Library was far more intense than Emma could ever have imagined. What she thought would likely take only a few days turned into two weeks' worth of instruction. In that time, she learned how to properly offer advice to the Class A members who required the experience of having their books curated for them, how to handle potentially difficult patrons, the procedures for ordering books from other Boots' locations and warehouses, and so, so much more.

Every afternoon she arrived home to find Olivia at Mrs. Pickering's flat, either playing with Tubby on the floor or enjoying a bit of lemonade in the kitchen with some new baked item that left the elegant kitchen smelling like a confectioner's haven.

But Emma was never one to accept anything without offering a form of payment in return. In this particular case, it cost her a penny to purchase a copy of *The Protection of Your Home Against Air Raids*. The thirty-six-page manual contained a litany of precautions one might enlist to prevent damage in the event of an attack.

"Do you think we have enough sand on the floor?" Mrs. Pickering pressed her hands to her lower back and regarded the empty attic late Friday afternoon, its floor layered with a hefty sifting of sand.

They'd spent the last few days after Emma came home from work clearing out the attic per the manual's instructions. The boxes, trunks, and spare furniture now resided in Mrs. Pickering's flat, cluttering the formerly neat space.

Once the attic had been divested of its inventory, they had poured an inch of sand over the scuffed wooden floorboards. The manual had suggested two inches, but its warning of "if the floor can withstand the weight" had given them both pause.

Olivia held up her trowel with a grin. "I can add more." She'd been a little sand pixie, dashing about the place while sprinkling the grains like fairy dust. Her jubilant demeanor at home now extended to any time she was in the presence of Mrs. Pickering and Tubby, a bond of trust drawn tight by their time spent together.

"More sand might be risky," Emma warned.

Mrs. Pickering pursed her lips and met her gaze with a look of concern. "I think we should leave it as is. And I doubt we'll have need of the precaution in any case. I'm sure there won't even be a war and we'll be lugging Mr. Pickering's desk back up here by Christmas."

Emma gave a playful groan, though truly she was not looking forward to hauling the unwieldy mahogany piece upstairs when taking it down had nearly done her in.

Mrs. Pickering laughed, a dry, husky sound. "Or perhaps I might be able to find a place for it in my flat. Permanently."

"Now can we have lemonade?" Olivia asked hopefully.

Though Mrs. Pickering owed Emma nothing at all for her help with the tenement house, she had promised cold lemonade after each day of their labor. The task of emptying the coal vault below the stairs to transform into a refuge had been the hardest. The filthy work had left a fine dusting of stubborn black silt in its wake. Emma was still finding dark smudges throughout her flat. A good coat of whitewash helped make the former coal vault less messy, but the task was one Emma had no interest in ever repeating.

At least the space would serve as a makeshift shelter in a pinch. If war came.

Or, as the urgency of the government's insistence on preparations implied, *when* war came.

Goose bumps prickled over Emma's arms despite the oppressive heat of the attic.

"Now we will have lemonade." Mrs. Pickering swept a hand over her gray hair, dusting away grains of sand. "Leave one of the buckets. We'll need to keep sand on every floor just in case."

She didn't add the reason, but she and Emma both understood why after having read the manual from cover to cover. In the event of a bombing, there would be so many in need that the limited rescue services would be overwhelmed. Nottingham's residents had to be prepared to fight their own fires. Literally.

The prospect was terrifying, but one they had to be prepared to take on.

Mrs. Pickering paused on the third floor on the way down and set a bucket of sand by Mr. Sanderson's door. Not that the third-floor resident had done a bit of work to help them with their efforts.

As they were turning to continue their descent, the door flew open. Mr. Sanderson prodded the heavy bucket with the toe of his old brown slipper. "What's this?"

"Sand to douse flames if need be," Mrs. Pickering replied matter-of-factly.

Mr. Sanderson scoffed, his face lined heavily under his sparse gray hair. "'Twon't do no good if a bomb hits directly."

"The odds of that are very slim," Emma said quickly and cast a reassuring smile at Olivia, who grinned back, full of childish trust.

Mr. Sanderson glanced at Olivia and scrubbed a hand over the top of his head where the pink pate of his scalp showed glossy beneath a halo of thin hair.

Just as he'd opened his mouth to offer some other thought-less invective, Mrs. Pickering quickly added, "Might I remind you that this building belongs to me, and I would like to ensure the protection of my investment."

At that, Mr. Sanderson grunted and closed his door on them.

Mrs. Pickering rolled her eyes heavenward and led them down the stairs to her flat. Her usually tidy living space was a sight to behold, now more of an attic than the fashionable home it had been only days before. While likely something of a fire hazard, Tubby enjoyed the clutter as a playground and enthusiastically ran around the abundant chair legs and over piles of boxes.

Olivia dropped to her knees and scrabbled after the dog.

"What do you plan to do with all of this?" Emma asked as she followed Mrs. Pickering into the kitchen.

The late Mr. Pickering's desk abutted the dining room table like a misplaced appendage and several boxes with *Harold Pickering* written in neat print on their sides covered the desk's surface.

"I haven't the foggiest." The landlady skirted around the desk with ease, as if it had always been blocking most of her kitchen, and pulled open the larder.

"Do you want some help going through everything?" Emma offered.

"I confess, I don't even know where to begin," Mrs. Pickering replied from behind the door before appearing with a pitcher of opaque yellow lemonade. "It's rubbish mostly, but I can't bring myself to get rid of it. Like the old slippers he wore every day, shuffling about the house. I was always on him to lift his feet properly when he walked. But now with him gone, I'd give anything to hear that lazy scuttle over the floors again."

Her marriage to Mr. Pickering had lasted a good thirty

years, but he'd been gone over a decade. She had sold the fine house they'd lived in, opting to remain in the tenement house he'd purchased early in their marriage as an investment. Emma suspected the change in residence had everything to do with fending off loneliness. No doubt the act of Mrs. Pickering sorting through the boxes would be both difficult and painful.

"If you need help, I'm always here," Emma offered a final time.

"Thank you, dear." Mrs. Pickering poured a glass of lemonade and Olivia came running as if she'd been summoned by the sound of liquid splashing in the glass. Her sudden appearance was a good reminder of that age-old idiom that little pitchers have big ears.

"Why don't you take Tubby and have your lemonade outside, Olivia?" Mrs. Pickering suggested, obviously having the same thought.

Olivia carefully carried the glass in one hand and grabbed a small red ball with the other. Tubby leaped into the air in acrobatics of elation.

When the door closed, Mrs. Pickering clicked on the radio. She didn't like to listen to the wireless when Olivia was nearby in case any terrible war news came on.

News exactly like what was being conveyed now. Through the crackle of static, they listened in horror as the announcer declared Germany had attacked Poland, bombing cities and towns.

"Those poor people," Mrs. Pickering whispered under her breath.

Yes, indeed those poor people. Had they prepared for bombings like Emma and Mrs. Pickering, doing so out of duty without ever expecting to truly have their efforts tested?

And with an ally so brutally attacked, what would this mean for England?

5

THE ROUND GLASS goggles stared up from the cardboard box like something alien. Emma lifted the gas mask, the bulky respirator ungainly where it dangled from the flimsy face. The sharp odor of rubber and disinfectant assaulted her senses.

"Well, this is exciting." She bobbed the mask in the air, dancing it toward Olivia. "These look very...official."

"Mine doesn't look official." Olivia withdrew her gas mask from the cardboard box, a slightly smaller version of Emma's.

The start of school had been postponed as the buildings were being used as coordinating centers for various purposes such as distributing housing supplies and enlisting soldiers. Olivia was delighted with the delay, but the country's preparations hung over Emma like a heavy cloud.

And then there was that letter.

Emma set aside her concerns and waggled her mask, making the wide glass eyes clack together. "This isn't official-looking to you?"

Olivia giggled and her nose scrunched up the way Arthur's used to. "No."

"Are you sure?" Emma pressed, wriggling the mask emphatically. Olivia squealed with laughter and shook her head.

Those giggles were all Emma wanted to hear, sounds of joy to blot out the horrors she'd read about in Poland. The *Evening Post* had been full of terrible stories.

Small villages were bombed to oblivion, major cities had their schools and hospitals targeted. Too many atrocities to wipe from her mind.

Word was, Britain would be at war if Hitler didn't pull out of Poland. But a madman like Hitler who was set on killing civilians likely wouldn't care about threats from across the Channel.

She glanced toward the window, the light outside muted by a beige mesh pasted over the glass to prevent splintering in the event of a bomb. The sun rose high as late morning slipped into afternoon. There was still time before the sky darkened to night and brought the interminable hours filled with nightmares of bombs and war.

"Shall we try these on?" The smile on Emma's mouth was forced. But Olivia's wasn't, and that was all that mattered.

Olivia brought the mask to her face, paused, and wrinkled her nose. "It smells."

"On the count of three." Emma held up her mask. "Take a deep breath."

They both inhaled, chests puffed out in exaggeration. Together they caught the head straps with their thumbs and thrust their chins into the masks, per the directions.

Cold rubber clung unpleasantly to Emma's face and suctioned against her skin as she inhaled. The stink of the thing was enough to make her eyes water. Through the round goggles, she could clearly see Olivia in her gas mask.

Olivia exhaled and the mask fluttered around her cheeks, mimicking the sound of flatulence. Emma did likewise, producing an even louder effect as the rubber vibrated against her skin. They both erupted into a fit of laughter. Their gasping inhales made the rubber suck harder on their faces and their explosive exhales sent the masks reverberating. The goggles fogged.

They could stand those awful masks only for a moment before both ripped them off their heads, eyes damp with mirth and the aftereffects of the noxious chemical smell. The cool air on Emma's face was immediate and wonderful.

Olivia dropped her mask into the box, her smile fading. "That was funny, but I don't like it."

Emma didn't like it either. "Good thing we only need them for emergencies."

"Emergencies, like what?" Her daughter gazed up at her, a note of wariness evident in the fathomless blue.

A child's innocence was such a fragile, ephemeral thing. Unable to be pieced back together once shattered. Emma knew that well enough from her own experience after her father's death.

This was the part of motherhood she'd been least prepared for. How was a parent to be honest with their child while still safeguarding that precious innocence?

When school did resume, Olivia's schoolmates would not be so gentle in sharing the news of the war, especially those whose parents or older siblings had been brutally honest with details of Poland's devastation.

But then, not all children were as sensitive as Olivia.

"There is a possibility England might go to war if Germany doesn't leave Poland," Emma said carefully. "If that happens, Germany may try to attack us with gas."

"Gas?" Olivia scrunched her face in disgust.

Emma nodded. "Gas makes the air hard to breathe. That's why we all have masks. To keep us safe."

Olivia slid a glance at the little cardboard box containing her mask as though assessing if it was indeed within arm's reach.

"And why we need to have them with us at all times." Emma smiled, trying to look at ease with the situation when she was decidedly not.

There had been many publications on the preparation for war, including what to expect. She had read them all, reasoning that the more she knew, the better she could protect her daughter.

But filling her mind with such things also meant that every night she lay in bed with Olivia sleeping peacefully at her side, she was haunted by what could be. Thinking of what a gas attack could do to the body, the carnage wrought by dropped bombs, the terror of the enemy swooping down on their quiet little street in the event of an attack.

Such possibilities were too horrific and had her pulling her daughter closer into her arms. As if love could be enough to shield Olivia from war's harm.

No, Emma was not at ease with any of this, but she could be strong for her daughter.

A shout sounded in the corridor just outside the front door of their flat. She knew the time to be nearly eleven before she even looked at the clock.

The time Chamberlain would declare war on Germany. The time when life would change for them all.

Chills raced over Emma's skin.

She had to hear for herself, to have the solidity of those words cement the truth. Her body moved of its own accord, carrying her toward the door to their flat and out into the hall. Mrs. Pickering's voice filled the stairwell once more, this time calling for Mr. Sanderson as Emma rushed down the stairs, drawn toward the burbling drone of Mrs. Pickering's radio.

The older woman waved her into the apartment. Olivia was at Emma's heels, caught up in the moment of excitement.

Should she be there?

Emma hesitated, locked once more in the perpetual maternal battle of trying to decide what the correct course of action regarding her child. The gentle touch of Mrs. Pickering's hand on her forearm interrupted the back-and-forth vacillation.

"Better she hear the truth herself than through the nattering of her classmates." The older woman nodded sagely and tilted her head in silent invitation to Olivia, who remained anxiously waiting at the threshold. "But mind you keep quiet, love. We need to hear this."

Mr. Sanderson entered the flat, his expression cross. "I have my own wireless."

"This isn't the kind of thing one should hear on their own," Mrs. Pickering replied. "Now hush and come into the kitchen."

They all shifted to fit around Mr. Pickering's desk as the wireless crackled and emitted Chamberlain's distinctive voice. Germany had declined the order to withdraw from Poland.

England was officially at war with Germany.

The air in the warm room was suddenly too heavy to breathe.

"Here we go again," Mr. Sanderson muttered.

Emma sank into one of the cushioned chairs and Olivia nudged against her, a silent request all mothers knew well. Though Olivia was far too large to be held, Emma scooted back slightly, allowing room for her daughter to climb into her lap.

The comfortable warmth of her daughter nestled against Emma, the familiar clean scent of Olivia's soft wavy hair was almost more than Emma could bear. She wanted to wrap her arms around her daughter and never let her go.

Not when Emma faced such a terrible decision.

Mrs. Pickering put her hands on her hips. "We pulled through for the Great War, and we'll do likewise for this one."

She was of a generation who had endured rations and terror and loss. Despite Mrs. Pickering's determined speech, her gaze was haunted.

A chill rattled its way down Emma's spine.

She had been born just days before the war broke out. Though she too had lived through the Great War, she had little memory of her life then. Perhaps that was for the best.

She held Olivia closer. The girl was quiet amid the reception of such unwelcome news, processing what had been said in that silent way of hers. Perhaps Emma ought to offer words of comfort, a more detailed explanation, something to assuage any burgeoning fear.

Except that she couldn't speak, not when she was reeling, not when she knew the time had come for her to make the worst decision a mother had to face.

"I'm sure all will be well." Mrs. Pickering's shaky smile was no more convincing than the uncertainty of her tone. From the floor below, Tubby gave a low whimper and edged closer to rest his muzzle on his mistress's feet. Mr. Sanderson grumbled something under his breath, as though the declaration of war was a personal affront, and left the room, closing the front door firmly behind him.

Emma rose from the chair, pulling Olivia along with her, cherishing her daughter's weight in the brace of her arms, the reassurance of Olivia's head resting in the crook of her neck.

"I think we should go," Emma said softly.

Mrs. Pickering's expression pulled down into one of sorrow. "The letter?"

Emma drew in a pained breath and nodded.

The letter she received in July indicated Olivia was eligible for relocation to the country, stating Nottingham was too dangerous. She'd run into the immensely perceptive Mrs. Pickering not long after having read the upsetting letter, after knowing what choice she would have to make.

That Nottingham would be considered a potential target for Germany seemed ridiculous when they were more than a two-hour train ride from London, where Hitler would likely set his sights. But then there were the factories, the ones like Raleigh, whose bicycle creation turned to munitions, and the Royal Ordinance Factory churning out explosives and massive gun barrels.

Yes, their quiet little city practically smack in the center of England would indeed be a target.

Emma nodded now.

"I have a Sunday joint in the larder," Mrs. Pickering said. "It's far too much for me to eat on my own if you'd like to join me." She gave a mirthless chuckle. "Might be the last of our meat for a while."

Emma adjusted Olivia's weight in her arms. "We would like that very much, thank you."

Mrs. Pickering smiled sadly and led them toward the door.

Before dinner could be served, the *Evening Post* distributed a rare Sunday newspaper with only four pages, proclaiming that Britain was at war with Germany and noting that all public entertainments had been canceled to prevent large gatherings. Not only were schools closed until further notice, but there was a note about evacuations.

Emma gripped the paper so hard, the pages crumpled against her palm. Evacuations would proceed Tuesday with details to come in the morning.

As promised, instructions were in the paper the following day, along with an ominous message: "Parents must make up their minds today whether or not they wish their children to be evacuated."

Emma had thought of the possibility of sending Olivia away, but some quandaries were so awful that no matter how many times one turned them over in one's mind, there was never a satisfactory resolution.

Olivia could be sent away to an undisclosed location to live with people Emma didn't know for an unknown length of time. Or she could keep her daughter close in Nottingham, and knowingly place her in direct danger.

The time had come to finally decide.

6

THERE WAS AN alternative for Emma regarding Olivia's safety: the option to send her to rural Chester, where Emma's in-laws lived. She flicked the consideration away as soon as it wandered into her thoughts.

Arthur had been an only child, eager to flee the harsh rules of his parents and the grueling work on their farm. Emma and Olivia had lived with them briefly after his death and found not only a cold reception, but the same uncaring, disapproving attitude Arthur had endured in his life with them.

No, Olivia would be better off going with her classmates—with children she already knew—than being sent to grandparents who had never bothered to pursue a relationship with their only grandchild.

But if Emma kept Olivia with her in Nottingham...

The thought brought such comfort that Emma curled around the idea and let the warmth of Olivia's sleeping form against her lull her into slumber.

The wail of a siren cut through the night, wrenching Emma out of a deep sleep. Her heart slammed against her chest.

Air raid sirens.

They were going to be bombed.

Just like Poland.

Whatever cry rose to her lips was unintelligible. A fresh dose of adrenaline shot through her as she grabbed for Olivia in the dark, pulling her daughter and part of the coverlet with them toward the door of the bedroom.

"What's happening?" Olivia howled, a rawness to her voice Emma had never heard.

Fear.

The hair on Emma's arms stood on end.

"We must get to the coal vault." Though she'd tried to speak calmly, there was a slight pitch to Emma's tone.

How long did they have before the bombing started?

She wrenched open the bedroom door in the blackout-regulation darkness, not bothering with the lights.

Together they stumbled their way to the front door, the blanket trailing behind them.

The infernal shrilling siren continued, urgent, a warning to hurry, hurry, *hurry*. Together, they flew out of the flat, tripping in their haste to get down the stairs.

Mrs. Pickering opened the door to the coal vault as they arrived downstairs and waved them in. "Come on, come on."

A candle flickered in a brass holder in the center of the cramped space. To one side was a box marked in Mrs. Pickering's neat handwriting: *Bomb Shelter Treats*, with Tubby sniffing eagerly at one corner. The box had been something of a joke, citing being sequestered in the coal vault as a logical excuse for a few toffees and some crisps.

Olivia had been excited at the prospect then.

Now she wasn't even looking at the box of goodies. Instead, she was clinging to Emma, her body shaking. Emma drew the coverlet around them both in an attempt to share her body heat with her daughter.

Within the small coal bin, there were no windows, no clocks. The siren fell quiet, filling the room with the weight of an ominous silence.

Unease trickled like ice water down Emma's spine. She suppressed a shiver and gave a nervous laugh. "I don't even know what time it is."

"Two thirty in the morning," Mrs. Pickering replied. "Or at least it was when the siren went off."

Olivia whimpered and pressed closer to Emma.

"Where is Mr. Sanderson?" Mrs. Pickering demanded in irritation, looking upward as though she could see through the floors to his whereabouts. "If bombs come crashing down—"

"Which they won't," Emma rushed to reassure.

Mrs. Pickering's eyes widened with the realization of what she nearly said in front of Olivia. "You're right. They won't. In the meantime, I intend to go collect the man myself."

With a huff, she extracted a spare candle from the treats bin and left the room.

"Be careful," Emma cautioned.

Mrs. Pickering harrumphed. "If I die, I'll come back to haunt him for leading me to this nonsense."

The door slammed shut and Olivia pulled back slightly to look at Emma, her eyes big and frightened in the candlelight. "Are we going to die?"

"Of course we aren't." But even as Emma said the words, she wondered how many Polish mothers had promised their children the same thing.

Those lies, she realized suddenly, were flimsy. No matter how well-intentioned.

The idea of their being bombed also brought to mind how very vulnerable they were in the basement. Yes, the windowless room might shield them from shards of glass or the sharp bits of rubble in a blast, but if they sustained a direct hit, the house would be obliterated. The entirety of the structure would collapse into itself.

On top of them.

Her heart jolted up into her throat.

"If we do die," Olivia said softly, "we can join Papa."

Her words took Emma aback. Olivia never discussed Arthur.

"We won't die." Emma secured an arm around her daughter, so her head rested against Emma's chest. "Now try to get some sleep. Who knows how long we'll be here."

Olivia didn't go to sleep, but she quieted down, her gaze distant as Emma rubbed soothing circles over her back. As she did so, her ears strained for the low hum of an engine, expecting the blast of a bomb.

Her body tensed against the silence, in dread and in anticipation.

How long until the bombs came?

The door flew open and in walked Mrs. Pickering with Tubby at her side. His tail was more quivering than wagging with the nervous energy vibrating in the stale room.

"Mr. Sanderson won't come, the stubborn old blighter." Mrs. Pickering swatted her hand in the air dismissively. "I won't be wasting my life for his sake again."

"Why won't he come?" Emma asked.

Mrs. Pickering scoffed. "Who knows with that one? Always keeps to himself, muttering about this or that."

Olivia began to relax in Emma's lap.

"You don't know anything about him?" Emma pressed, encouraging Mrs. Pickering to keep up the distraction of her chatter.

"Not really." Mrs. Pickering settled on the floor by Emma while Tubby nestled between them. "All I know is that he's lived here since the house was built. I inherited him with the property, as much a part of the building as the iron fence out front. Who was I to force him out?"

She paused and smiled down at Olivia, where she sagged against Emma's chest in exhausted slumber. Between them, Tubby slept as well, expelling raspy little snores. "I think the excitement has been too much for these two."

"It's for the best," Emma replied. "I know she's trying to put up a brave front, but she's terrified."

"And you?" Mrs. Pickering asked quietly.

The ground was cold and hard beneath Emma, the whitewash muddied with flecks of coal dust. She imagined what bombs dropping would be like—a possibility that still might become a reality until the all-clear siren could reassure them of their safety.

A shiver prickled over her skin.

"I still am terrified," Emma answered slowly, "that something like what happened in Poland could happen here."

Rather than disregard her fears, Mrs. Pickering nodded. "It well could. At least Olivia will be safe with you sending her away." She closely regarded Emma. "You *are* sending her away, aren't you?"

In reply, Emma looked down at her daughter, and even though she had not wanted to, Emma knew then she'd already made up her mind. Her daughter's reaction to the air raid warning had been the deciding factor.

Olivia would have to leave.

7

THE FOLLOWING DAY, Emma received two important pieces of information. The first came from the newspaper, informing Nottingham that the air raid siren had been a precaution for an unidentified plane that turned out to be one of Britain's own.

The next came from Olivia's teacher who showed up with a luggage tag, an identification card on a string necklace, and instructions for drop-off for the impending evacuation. That night, sleep was impossible, knowing Olivia would leave the next day. Giving up on the idea of getting any rest, Emma instead lit a candle and studied her daughter's face in the flickering glow.

Olivia's nose, which had been round as a baby, had straightened to a little point at the end, like Emma's. And there was a slightly petulant thickness to Olivia's bottom lip, so like Arthur's, which she used to her advantage when pouting to get her way. Something she didn't do often.

Emma was lucky in that regard.

Olivia was an obedient girl, with a smile at the ready and a heart eager to love. Such traits left her open to kindness, but also made her vulnerable. The latter was a terrifying thought when she was soon to be sent to live with strangers.

★ ★ ★

When morning finally came, Emma's mind was hazy with exhaustion, and overwhelmed with the impossible task ahead of them. She put a hand on her daughter's shoulder to gently rouse her. Olivia jerked, eyes snapping open and immediately finding Emma's. "It's time already?"

Emma nodded and the small muscles at Olivia's neck tensed. Despite her obvious apprehension, she obediently set about her morning routine, donning the jumper and skirt Emma had set out for her and tackling her messy waves with a brush.

Parenting involved many difficult things. Punishing wrongs, saying no when Emma wanted desperately to say yes, forcing Olivia to do her schoolwork through her tears, and many times acting as both mother and father. Preparing Olivia to be sent away for an indeterminate amount of time, however, was by far the hardest and most painful moment of being a parent that Emma had ever endured.

The scant time remaining together slipped away in a flurry of activity as Emma prepared a small bag for Olivia containing two ready meals of buttered bread with jam, several sweets, and some leftover cottage pie—Olivia's favorite. They were not allowed to include liquids. Surely some would be provided for the children en route.

She also dipped into the money from selling the first edition of *Alice's Adventures in Wonderland* to give Olivia two pounds. The very dear amount was the maximum allowed for children to carry with them on this venture. No matter what Olivia encountered, money would always help.

Wasn't that the way the world worked?

Emma plaited her daughter's hair into two braids to control the riotous waves, then set the suitcase in front of Olivia, a relic that had once belonged to Arthur. Essentials were carefully packed within: several changes of clothes, a brush, even stationary with preaddressed and stamped envelopes for Olivia to write home upon her arrival and let Emma know where she was.

How disconcerting to send her daughter away to an undisclosed location.

"Can you carry it?" Emma asked.

Olivia lifted the case, her considerable height offering her a necessary advantage. "Yes."

"Your gas mask." Emma snatched the box from a brass hook by the door.

Had only two days passed since they'd laughed over the crude sounds the masks made?

The sweet moment of carefree laughter felt a lifetime ago.

Olivia stood by the door, her new leather shoes gleaming. Thankfully the income from Emma's new job provided the extra money needed to purchase the sturdy footwear lest Olivia be sent to the country in flimsy plimsolls.

While on that shopping trip at Woolworths, Olivia had stopped to admire a beautifully knit red jumper. One with a considerable price tag. Olivia didn't ask for things she knew Emma couldn't afford. But now Emma regretted not making the purchase.

Tears burned in her eyes. Not for the jumper. For her daughter. For the undeniable ache in Emma's chest at having to send her away.

The purpose of gathering the items concluded and left only the acceptance of what was to come. Emma had preferred her hands to be busy, her thoughts racing, rather than focused on this frozen moment of ineffable pain.

"Well, then, we should be off," Emma declared awkwardly.

Olivia nodded, her eyes luminous and large in her pallid face. But she didn't exit the flat right away. Instead, she paused and let her gaze skim around the room, taking everything in with a slow, methodical measure. As if it might be the last time she ever saw her home.

"You'll be back," Emma said gently—almost as a reminder to herself as much as to her daughter. Still, she waited patiently, allowing Olivia all the time she needed.

Finally, Olivia nodded in silent satisfaction before squaring her shoulders and exiting the flat with the determination of a soldier going to battle. And in a way, she was. This was a child's lot in the face of war. Painful and terrifying despite her brave facade.

Mrs. Pickering's door swung open as they reached the first floor landing.

The older woman's hair had been hastily pulled back, a blue robe wrapped tightly around what looked suspiciously like a nightdress. "Tubby wanted to see you one last time." She smiled though tears shone bright in her eyes. "And so did I."

Olivia threw her arms around the landlady with all she had, then knelt to Tubby, solemnly reminding him to be well-behaved in her absence, which earned her a head cock from the little dog. As they had their brief, but serious conversation, Mrs. Pickering reached out and gently squeezed Emma's arm. A much needed show of support.

Olivia straightened upright and swept at her neat skirt. "I shall likely return soon."

"I hope you do, sweet girl." Mrs. Pickering patted Olivia's cheek with tender affection before they turned to leave.

The walk to school was a quiet one, Olivia's damp hand clasped desperately around Emma's in a tight squeeze.

How would Emma's life be without the warmth of Olivia's fingers against her own? To sleep alone at night without her daughter? To return to an apartment knowing Olivia wouldn't be there?

The careful construction of Emma's control began to erode

under the tide of such thoughts, but she quickly buffeted them away.

Several children at the school milled about, waiting for the bus that would bring them to the train station. Only ten evacuees would be transported at a time to ensure crowds of children would not be impacted in the event of an attack. Mothers offered overly bright smiles and made promises for a swift return, the end of the war, a happy second home, all things of which they had no control. Some children remained locked at their mother's sides while others gamboled about in play, eager for an adventure without any thought to the ramifications.

"Don't leave yet." Olivia used both hands to hold tight to Emma, causing her name tag to twist on its string around her neck.

"I will stay until the bus arrives to take you to the train station," Emma reassured her, not even caring that she would be late for work that day.

Kneeling in front of her daughter, Emma tried to find the right words. She wanted to tell her how lonely she would be without her, that sending her away was like cutting out her still-beating heart, that life would be lacking color and light in her absence. But those words were too dangerous. Those were words that would crack the fragile shell of Emma's strength. "Be good while you're there," she said instead.

Olivia's chin notched up a little higher, her chest puffed with a similar bravado. "I'm always good."

"I know you are." Emma nodded. "I know. But maybe try a bit harder in school for me too."

Olivia scrunched her face, giving Emma a glimpse of the playfulness they shared together, then pinched her fingers together. "A bit."

"That's my girl." Emma offered her widest smile, stiff on her lips and feeling entirely wrong. Likely that smile was as false as those of all the other mothers.

Olivia grinned back, revealing the gap beside her front tooth. How many teeth would she lose in the time she would be gone? How many other little pieces of Olivia's life would Emma miss in that unknown span of time?

The rumble of an engine sounded outside and Emma's heart dropped. The buses had arrived. Too soon.

This moment had come far too soon.

Emma pulled Olivia to her and cradled her daughter, breathing in the clean scent of soap from her hair, a fragrant milk-and-honey perfume as she savored the feel of her child in her arms.

One last time.

"I love you to the end of the world," Emma said fiercely.

Olivia trembled. "I love you too. I promise to be good and to make you proud." The quaver to her voice was nearly Emma's undoing.

A teacher called for the children to board the bus and Olivia pulled from Emma's grasp, jaw clenched.

"I'll visit as soon as I'm able." Emma gathered Olivia's luggage, lunch and gas mask.

Olivia nodded mutely in a way Emma understood, her own throat too tight to speak another word.

Outside in the brisk September morning, the sun was slowly rising over the city. The dawn of a fresh day with new possibilities, all of which seemed endlessly bleak at this present moment.

The children were carefully, but efficiently, parted from their mothers by several uniformed women with the Women's Volunteer Service, and made to queue for the waiting bus, which now sat quiet to preserve petrol.

Olivia's hand slid from Emma's as she looked up a final time. "I love you, Mummy."

Immediately the warmth where Olivia's fingers had been went cold, leaving Emma wholly and completely bereft. "I love you, Olive."

For her part, Olivia remained intrepid. She didn't cling desperately to Emma as some children now did with their mothers. Nor did she bawl with protest. Not Olivia. She mustered her dignity and self-respect and strode onward. The twin braids hung parallel down her ramrod-straight back. But Emma knew her daughter. Her actions were all a show of bravery. For Emma's sake.

The woman beside Emma began sorrowfully weeping and somehow that strengthened Emma's own resolve. The line of small, tearstained faces inched forward. Emma's gaze remained fixed on the tallest one with hair in plaits, watching Olivia shuffle toward the open door of the bus.

All at once, Olivia spun around, her eyes locking with Emma's, bright with tears. "Mum." Her face crumpled as she began to weep. She did not depart from the queue, ever the rule follower, but she mouthed the words *I love you*, over and over, until she was next to disappear into the bus.

Emma repeated those same words back long after Olivia took her seat. Still Emma remained standing where she was, waiting to wave to her daughter one final time. Olivia's face pressed to the window and the glass immediately fogged. The bus rumbled to life, expelling a burst of exhaust, but Emma scarcely noticed as she waved frantically at her daughter. As if the force behind the gesture could convey the full extent of her love.

The bus lurched forward and drove away, carrying the children toward the train station. Away from home.

The mothers who had begun to weep earlier now sobbed with abandon as they pressed damp handkerchiefs to their eyes. Several others had held their tears until that very moment.

And the rest, like Emma, had remained carefully bridled in their composure. Surely if she cracked even the slightest bit, she would shatter completely.

Instead, Emma rushed home, knowing she must prepare for work. The busier her mind remained, the less chance her broken heart would consume her. Her resolve did not buckle once. Not until after that brisk walk home, when she pushed open the door to her flat, alone and empty. Only then did the dam truly break.

She had been home alone many times before, relishing a quiet sliver of peace while Olivia was at school. But this was different. There would be no cheerful walk home together when school let out. There would be no chatty companionship at dinner. There would be no comfort of a sleeping child beside her.

The loneliness in the apartment rang out and resonated deep inside Emma, snapping something loose she had managed to hold in check until that very moment.

The force of that emptiness, that loneliness, that loss hit Emma like a pugilist's fist. The pain crumpled her, sending her sagging to the floor, as she finally, miserably, began to cry.

Olivia was gone.

8

EMMA WAS NEARLY an hour late to work once she finally managed to stifle her tears. As it was, she didn't even know how she'd managed to right herself from that pathetic puddle on the floor.

Though her face was puffy and her eyes red, at least her striped shirt dress was neatly ironed and her hair sufficiently styled into a neat updo.

Fortunately, she did not run into any customers upon her entry into the Booklover's Library, but she did nearly crash into Miss Bainbridge as she rushed to put her belongings in the back room and wrap her green overalls over her dress.

"I believe you were supposed to be here an hour ago, Miss Taylor." The manageress's gaze raked down Emma, disapproval emanating from the older woman.

Emma stared down at the tips of her scuffed shoes to keep her boss from clearly seeing her distress.

"Forgive me, I..." The words clogged in Emma's throat. She couldn't very well say she had just sent her daughter away. Someone might overhear.

And she was not supposed to have a daughter.

"Go into my office at once," Miss Bainbridge commanded in a hard voice.

Resigned, Emma turned away, doing as she was bid, passing Margaret on her way. Though Emma didn't look up at her coworker, the other woman reached out a hand and gave her arm a gentle squeeze.

"Her bark is worse than her bite," Margaret whispered.

Once in the office, Emma sank onto the hard wooden chair opposite Miss Bainbridge's desk, awaiting her fate.

If what Margaret said was true, then hopefully Emma was in for a dressing-down rather than being sacked.

What would she do if she lost her job? If she couldn't afford the six shillings a week the government charged for billeting Olivia in the country? If Emma didn't have the money to travel to see her daughter?

Emma would sell off the last four books in that meager collection of beloved first editions before she let that happen. But the money from the books would only last so long.

No, she couldn't lose this job.

She waited for what felt an interminable length of time, locked in a dizzying mix of anticipation and misery.

Finally the door opened and Miss Bainbridge entered, her stern expression melting. "Miss Taylor, I heard. About the children, I mean."

"I'm sorry for being late." Emma swallowed. "I had to see Olivia off, to say goodbye…" That ache was back in Emma's throat, threatening to choke away her words.

"I imagine seeing her off was not easy." Miss Bainbridge walked to her chair and sat down. "You appear to have calmed down. Are you quite all right?"

Emma parted her lips but found herself uncertain how to answer.

She could lie, of course, say that she was perfectly fine, thank you. Or there was the truth, to admit that the chasm inside her chest had broken open with such agony that even breathing was painful. That every part of her dreaded going home in the evening to an empty flat and enduring the enormity of terrible loneliness.

"What a foolish question." Miss Bainbridge glanced down at the desk. "Of course you are not. If you need the day——"

"No," Emma said quickly. "Please, the work will be a good distraction."

Miss Bainbridge studied her for a moment, gray eyes sharp. At last, she gave a sigh. "Very well, but if you become distraught, you must leave the floor at once. We cannot have our subscribers witnessing your distress. And do ensure you arrive on time going forward. Am I understood?"

"Of course."

"And for heaven's sake, please distract yourself." Miss Bainbridge leaned over a box on the edge of her desk and produced a book, which she lay before Emma.

A gray face stared up at her from a blue-and-black cover. *The Mask of Dimitrios* by Eric Ambler. Emma glanced up at the manageress.

Miss Bainbridge smiled warmly. "One of the benefits of working for the Booklover's Library is the opportunity to read incoming books before they go out on the floor for our Class A subscribers."

The Class B subscribers would have to wait a full year until they could borrow this book, and now Emma had the opportunity to read it even before their most exclusive clientele.

Still, Emma hesitated. After her father's death, she hadn't read a single book. She had tried, of course. Many times before Olivia was born. And after, when Olivia was very little, Emma was successful only in the small children's stories she read to her daughter.

But after Olivia's birth and following Arthur's death, there was no time to indulge in the pastime of reading, not that Emma had managed to summon the desire.

Not with how much books reminded her of Papa. Of their conversations on shared reads, of their recommendations to one another, of how they could sit in agreeable silence as they were each lost in their own literary world. The loss and the hurt had been far too fresh.

Where once reading had been a great comfort, it became far too painful.

Sensing Emma's hesitation, Miss Bainbridge tutted. "Oh, do go on, Miss Taylor. You must read these books to recommend them."

Indeed Emma must. It was a consideration she hadn't thought of until that moment. She lifted the book and hugged it to her chest in gratitude as she rose from the chair.

Miss Bainbridge opened a ledger and peered up once more. "The Bespoke Room has a new box to be sorted out. The task will allow you the opportunity to fully recover."

On the floor, Emma passed an older woman deep in conversation with Margaret. "Oh, she was truly scandalous, wasn't she?"

"Indeed she was," Margaret answered in a conspiratorial tone. "The way she manipulated men and did anything necessary to pull through."

"Scarlett O'Hara was a deplorable woman and yet I couldn't wait to find out what happened next." The woman gave an indulgent chuckle. "But I'd have that Melanie Hamilton to tea any day of the week. What a good soul."

Though Emma hadn't read *Gone with the Wind*, one would have had to live in a cave over the last several years to be ignorant to its existence. The conversation about the characters reminded Emma of her father, of the way he would speak about characters as if they were real people, including his running list of protagonists who he would join for a pint.

Emma hadn't thought of that in years.

But the sensation the memory elicited wasn't one of pain. No, the reminder of those precious moments was warm and comforting, a gentle, soothing heat that washed over her wounded heart like a balm.

Bolstered for the task ahead, Emma pushed into the Bespoke Room, ready to tackle the waiting box.

Class A subscribers were allowed to request certain titles, some of which had to be obtained from other Booklover's Libraries all over England. Upon the books' arrivals, they waited in the Bespoke Room to be paired with the subscribers who requested them.

The door opened and Margaret appeared. "Miss Bainbridge wasn't all that bad, was she?"

Emma attached a note to a copy of *A Tale of Two Cities* and carefully added the requesting subscriber's name. "You were right."

"Then there's no more reason to be so glum." Margaret reached into her pocket and produced her gold compact, which she extended toward Emma. "Pat your face and no one will even know you've been crying."

Emma wanted to protest that she hadn't been crying, but there was hardly any point in denial. Especially when her red-rimmed eyes and pink-tipped nose were reflected back at her in the small mirror. She did as Margaret suggested and dusted some powder on her blotchy face. The result was remarkable as the telltale ruddiness of her tears all but disappeared.

Giving her friend a grateful smile, Emma returned the compact. "Thank you."

Margaret slid it into the pocket of her overalls. "Do you have a son or a daughter?"

"I beg your pardon?"

"You've been at least fifteen minutes early ever since you started working here. Being over an hour late the first time you're delayed must have been caused by something drastic, especially considering how upset you are. Something like sending a child off to the country as they all were this morning." Margaret indicated the narrow strip of indented skin on Emma's left hand where the cheap ring had been just that morning. "You were either engaged or married."

The implication hovered in the air between them, silent and without judgment.

Emma shifted slightly, uncertain how to answer. Perhaps she ought to prudently tiptoe around the question. But there was a part of Emma that wanted Margaret as a friend, and a true friendship required trust.

"Married," Emma replied at last. "I've been a widow for over five years. With a daughter. Olivia."

"And we can't hire women who are married or widows with children." Margaret scoffed. "I'd have married my Jeffrey a year ago if I could be with him and keep my job. That we have to choose is absolute rubbish."

"It is." Emma lifted another book from the box and found the title on the list to assign to the requesting patron.

"I'm sure your girl will be back soon." Margaret peered into the box in front of Emma. "Oh, is that *Lady Chatterley's Lover*?"

"*Lady Chatterley's*—what?"

"*Lover*." Margaret bent over the books and retrieved one of them. "Surely you've heard of *this* book?"

Emma's mouth opened, but she didn't have a ready reply to offer. She wasn't supposed to know *every* book in their inventory, was she?

Margaret laughed, the sound warm and friendly rather than mocking. "I was actually just coming in here to retrieve it for one of our Class A subscribers. Books like this can only be procured through personal request, as I'm sure you're well aware."

She turned the cover, revealing a red label on the spine and tapped at the mark with a crimson lacquered nail. Emma swallowed her gasp just in time to keep from looking prudish.

Books with red labels were far too risqué to be placed on the floor. A considerable amount of material in Emma's training had to do with those sensitive "red label" books. They were locked away in the main headquarters warehouse and only brought out upon personal request, then they remained in the Bespoke Room until asked to be retrieved by the patron. Emma regarded *Lady Chatterley's Lover* with renewed interest.

"Oh, it's very good," Margaret said with a saucy laugh. "It made my cheeks burn so bright, I didn't need cosmetics for a week. Still, every woman who came in asked what color rouge I was wearing." She laughed.

The middle-aged female subscribers had a tendency to flock to Margaret for her romantic book curation and her sage cosmetic advice. That was something Emma noticed about the patrons of the Booklover's Library. They were drawn to specific librarians for certain reasons. Like how the more studious subscribers found their way to Miss Crane, their moody co-worker only several years older than Emma who often recommended classics.

"Women seem to enjoy asking you for beauty tips," Emma complimented.

Margaret shrugged. "My father told me I wasn't good for much else but looks and books. Just playing to my strong suits." She winked. "Shall I set *Lady Chatterley's Lover* aside for you to borrow when it's returned?"

"It must be put into the Bespoke Room as soon as it's returned to go back to headquarters." Emma frowned, more at Margaret's awful father than the idea of breaking a rule.

"For normal subscribers." Margaret waved the book in the air, the red slash at the spine titillating against the otherwise bland cloth cover. "What do you say?"

Miss Bainbridge did suggest Emma give herself to distraction, and this indulgence would surely be that. Emma grinned. "Yes."

Margaret tilted her head, a silent acknowledgment of her victory, then spun around and departed with the salacious book in hand.

In for a penny, in for a pound, and all that.

Otherwise, Emma would be left to her own devices, to wrap her worry for Olivia around her shoulders like a heavy blanket, and tumble over the rough edges of all the worst-case scenarios until they were worn smooth.

Still, the niggling thoughts in the back of Emma's mind had her stopping by Woolworths on the way home, to purchase the red jumper despite its very dear cost. Only the item was no longer available.

Instead, in an act of extreme desperation, she selected a skein of brilliant red yarn. Her skills at knitting had always been somewhat lackluster, but she'd seen the basket next to Mrs. Pickering's chair with several balls of yarn thrust through with knitting needles. Likely she could help Emma through the harder parts.

Perhaps even in time for Christmas.

How surprised Olivia would be to finally receive that red jumper she'd so longed for.

The thought of Olivia's joy at such a gift kept the darkness at bay when Emma entered her flat, her bag filled with the yarn for Olivia's jumper and the copy of *The Mask of Dimitrios*. She pulled the latter out of her handbag and considered the pristine cover before setting it aside on the counter.

This would be her first book read since her father's death. Surely that required something poignant, something cherished to guide her back onto the path of being a reader. Her pulse quickened with an unexpected eagerness to return to the world she'd abandoned for far too long—the world of reading.

And she knew just the book that would call to her in the loudest, clearest voice.

She went to her wardrobe and pulled out the small box of precious books that had arrived after the bookshop had burned down, and withdrew the first-edition copy of *Emma*.

With great care, she carried the book to the sofa where she settled in and ran her fingers over the stiff leather cover. Her head nestled into the cradle of her palm the way it had for so many years when she'd tuck in on the left side of the sofa to read, the action still a well-formed habit despite having been dormant for years. Then she opened the cover and began to read.

9

THE NIGHT SWEPT Emma away as she tipped into the story that had always been the cornerstone of literature for her. *Emma's* protagonist was a young woman who'd grown up without a mother, with a father who bestowed every affection upon her. Was it any wonder such a heroine had appealed so greatly to a young Emmaline?

The book was an altogether different read now, through the lens of a parent rather than a girl. The fascination of her new understanding of the tale combined with the familiarity of a story Emma could once recite by heart, kept her turning the pages until her eyes could no longer remain open.

Which had been the precise goal—to be so tired she wouldn't notice Olivia was not there with her. But when the lights clicked out and the Regency world of Highbury village filled her thoughts, they were crowded out by concern for Olivia.

Was she sleeping well in her new home? Was she terribly lonely? Perhaps she was given a grand billeting location where the beds were comfortable and she was happy. The latter thought was the one Emma clung to so that sleep could finally claim her.

★ ★ ★

She woke at her usual time the next morning with gritty eyes and a mental fog of exhaustion. Olivia's pillow was in her arms, a sad substitute for her daughter.

As Emma readied for work, her thoughts were fixed once more on her daughter. On where in all of England she might be. And for how long.

Emma sucked in a pained breath, the sound audible in the unnatural quiet of the flat. That was the thing—without her daughter, everything was too large, too quiet. Dare she say it…too clean.

There was no trail leading from the front door to the table where Olivia stripped off her shoes and jumper and bag. No errant socks strewn on the chair or shoved between the cushions of the sofa. No dishes flecked with crumbs left on the counter.

Emma had spent much of her life chasing after Olivia's messiness, and wondering at a house that would one day be neat and orderly when Olivia was older.

Now Emma would give anything to trip over a hastily removed shoe.

The silence, the immaculate flat, the intense absence of Olivia, was more than Emma could bear. She shoved her feet into her shoes and donned her jacket before rushing from the flat, unable to stand another second of loneliness.

She arrived at work nearly an hour early that day.

Miss Bainbridge lifted her brows when Emma entered the small back room for the Booklover's Library employees. "I told you not to be late, but I didn't mean you had to arrive quite this early."

"I needed a distraction." Emma hung her handbag and gas mask on the hook and swapped out her jacket for the green employee overalls, tying the coat-like covering over her plain yellow dress with care.

Miss Bainbridge lifted a blue teapot into view. "Would you like some tea?"

The scent of brewing tea leaves filled the air, the spiced fragrance humid and pleasant. And with Miss Bainbridge's mention, Emma acknowledged that she *had* left the flat in such a hurry, she hadn't even thought of tea. "Yes, please."

Miss Bainbridge brought over an extra cup and set it in front of Emma. "I was thinking today would be ideal for you to start on the floor. Not simply organizing as you've done, but helping patrons with their selections. Getting to know them, so you can eventually move on to assist the Class A subscribers."

Being assigned Class A subscribers was what all librarians aspired to at the Booklover's Library. Emma knew she was being asked onto the floor as a special favor from Miss Bainbridge, another source of diverting Emma from the pain of Olivia's absence. And Emma was markedly grateful.

Once they'd finished their tea, Miss Bainbridge went to her office and Emma assumed her usual morning routine of dusting and polishing.

Margaret came in not long after the tasks were complete, wearing a larger smile than usual. "Miss Bainbridge says I'm supposed to guide you on the floor today and introduce you to the patrons. Are you ready?" She paused and tsked. "You poor dear, you don't look like you slept a wink. This will be good for you. Come here."

She whipped out her trusty compact and dabbed some powder under Emma's puffy eyes before touching a bit of lipstick on her fingertips and rubbing the waxy substance over Emma's cheeks, explaining, "It works like rouge in a pinch." Margaret stepped back and nodded approvingly at her handiwork.

Before the patrons could begin to arrive, Margaret showed Emma how to remain off to the side until a customer seemed to be struggling to find a book. "We're here to answer questions and offer general suggestions to our Class B subscribers. You can tell who is a Class A by their green tags and Class B by their red ones. Or by the Class A subscriber standing about, waiting to be served." She rolled her eyes playfully. "You won't be tasked with this yet, but all Class A subscribers are to be greeted by name and then you are to retrieve their personal notebooks from the Class A desk where they can record the books they wish to borrow."

The lending library opened and several people began to trickle in, perusing the shelves with interest. A gentleman in a tweed jacket with pads on the elbows walked by, his head cocked thoughtfully as he stopped beside a group of women.

"Good morning, Mr. Beard." Margaret smiled at him and added in a quiet voice, "He's a Class A subscriber who likes mysteries, despite his claims."

"His claims?" Emma asked.

Margaret chuckled. "You'll see once you deal with him. Just remember, he likes mysteries."

The man pulled a notepad from his breast pocket, then removed a small pencil from inside, licked the tip and began to write.

"He's always on with that thing, scribbling furiously like he's recording our conversations," she added in the same hushed tone.

"That seems rather rude," Emma ventured.

Margaret shrugged. "He's a Class A subscriber. They can't get away with murder, but they can squeeze by with just about anything else." She inclined her head toward a middle-aged woman who accepted her journal from Miss Crane and stopped to regard a section of books with a basket slung over one elbow. Inside the basket was a small black Scottie dog curled up on a cushion. "See what I mean?"

"She has her dog with her?"

"Class A subscriber," Margaret said by way of explanation. "That's Mrs. Chatsworth and Pip."

"How can you remember all these names?" But even as Emma asked, she knew precisely from her memories of working at Tower Bookshop. Life had been so much simpler then, when her thoughts weren't crowded with a mother's ceaseless worry and an endless list of tasks to be done.

"Remembering all their names is easy. You just play on words." Margaret's gaze shifted to the gentleman in the tweed jacket with the notepad. "His name is Mr. Beard, but he doesn't have a beard."

Sure enough, despite his thick white hair slicked neatly back with pomade, his face was clean-shaven.

"And the woman with the dog?" Emma asked. "What was her name again?"

"Mrs. Chatsworth." Margaret smiled indulgently. "Her name is easy to rememer too. You'll see. Come with me, but don't say anything." She strode forward with that enviable confidence. "Good morning, Mrs. Chatsworth." She turned toward the dog. "And Pip."

An unfriendly growl emanated from the basket as Pip's upper lip curled back to reveal a row of sharp teeth.

"He's so very charming," Margaret cooed. "Can I help you both with anything today?"

Mrs. Chatsworth tipped her chin with pleasure, making the plum-colored feather in her hat quiver. "Well, I was wondering about a new book I saw in the Class A catalog soon to be coming out, *The Mask of Dimitrios*…"

What started as an inquiry somehow spiraled into a lamentation about the air raid wardens and their obtuse attitudes toward fashionable window dressings, which quickly became a memory about the Goose Fair back when Mrs. Chatsworth had been a girl. This was followed by a story about the neighbor's daughter and how children these days were so very un-disciplined.

Half an hour crawled by as Mrs. Chatsworth nattered on, affording Margaret a scant moment to issue a polite hum of acknowledgment on extremely rare occasion.

Pip lay his head down five minutes into the one-sided conversation and began to quietly snore.

For Emma's part, the exhaustion of two nights of poor sleep left her lids feeling heavy and she found herself envying the dog in his little cushioned basket.

As Mrs. Chatsworth lived up to her moniker, Emma's thoughts drifted where they were wont to go so often these days—to Olivia. How much longer until Emma heard from her daughter?

"I'll get that for you now." Margaret's smile was just as bright and genial as at the start of the conversation and melted away once she and Emma entered the Bespoke Room.

Despite the weight of her worry, Emma couldn't help but chuckle. "I see why it's easy to remember Mrs. Chatsworth now."

Margaret issued an exasperated sigh. "I don't even think she breathes between sentences."

They both laughed quietly. Such mirth was a reprieve from Emma's sadness, no matter how short-lived.

"But truly, she is very kind. I suspect she's lonely." Margaret selected the book Mrs. Chatsworth had ordered—since *The Mask of Dimitrios* was not yet available even to Class A subscribers—and Emma followed her back onto the main floor.

"You can practice on a Class B subscriber, if you like." Margaret nodded to a young woman in the classics section.

"May I help you find something?" Emma asked.

The woman looked up, blinking with her mink-like lashes and wide doe-brown eyes. "I'm in the mood for a classic, but am not quite sure which one. Something gothic, perhaps. I do prefer female authors as the men can be so disparaging of their heroines. Something thrilling and..." She bit her lip, considering. "Passionate."

With each description, the mental catalog of books in Emma's mind filled the request, cycling out ones that no longer matched the woman's criteria until that last word was uttered.

"How about Emily Brontë's *Wuthering Heights*?" Even as Emma spoke, she knew the book was precisely what the woman sought.

The woman's eyes lit with excitement. "Oh, I haven't read that in years. Yes, that sounds perfect."

Emma pulled the book off the shelf and handed it to the subscriber, who hugged it in her arms like a cherished gift. "I do love rereading books when it's been a while since I last read them," she said excitedly as she followed Emma and Margaret to the checkout desk. "Isn't it remarkable how the same story can be so different depending on when you read it?"

The day before, Emma might not have fully understood what the woman meant. But now, after having spent the entire evening before lost in her rediscovery of Jane Austen's *Emma*, the woman's words struck a special note in Emma's heart.

"Indeed, it is remarkable," she replied in earnest.

As the day progressed, Emma found the rhythm of inter-acting with the customers. Her conversations and suggestions recalled those early memories of working alongside Papa at Tower Bookshop in a way that felt like puzzle pieces fitting into place amid the chaotic jumble of her life.

The familiarity of handling readers brought a connection to her father she hadn't experienced in far too long.

Miss Crane approached Emma, her face set in its usual pinch-lipped scowl. "I'd like to speak with you in the Be-spoke Room immediately."

She didn't say anything until the door to the room was closed, sealing them off from customers. "*The Death of the Heart* was in the mystery section."

Emma hadn't even seen *The Death of the Heart* while returning the books to their shelves earlier. "I didn't—"

"I know the title does sound like a mystery, but it is not." There was not a shred of patience to Miss Crane's tone.

Though Emma was well aware the book was not a mystery, she simply nodded.

"We cannot incorrectly shelve books, Miss Taylor." Miss Crane folded her arms over her chest and straightened an inch taller, as if making Emma feel small were not enough. "This isn't some basement lending library like W. H. Smith's or Mudie's. We are an elite lending library and following a strict set of guidelines is how we set ourselves apart. We are Boots' Booklover's Library." The last part was hissed.

"It won't happen again," Emma said by way of apology.

Apparently her acquiescence was sufficient to placate Miss Crane, who gave a quiet scoff as she turned away and left the room.

At home later that afternoon, there was still no letter from Olivia. Emma sagged back against the wall with disappointment. Her gaze fell on the ball of red yarn and the old pair of knitting needles she'd procured from a knitting box abandoned long ago. So much time had passed since her last attempts at the endeavor, she couldn't recall where to start.

Likely Mrs. Pickering would know. She might even have a design for the jumper. Emma plucked the ball and needles from the counter and exited her flat in search of Mrs. Pickering.

On the way downstairs, Emma nearly ran headlong into Mr. Sanderson, who simply gave a grunt at her hasty apology.

Emma hesitated. "Did you receive a letter for me perchance?"

Mr. Sanderson lifted a steely gray brow.

"Olivia has been sent to the country for her safety. I know it's a bit soon, but I'd hoped maybe a letter arrived letting me know where she is. Where I can write to her."

Mr. Sanderson's brow crinkled, etching the grooved lines in his skin even deeper. "You sent her away?"

The response was so disarming that Emma could only stammer her reply. "For her own safety, with all of Nottingham's factories… I did it for her."

His eyes narrowed slightly, but whatever emotion passed there was gone in an instant, buried under his usual glower. "I didn't receive no letter."

Emma thanked him all the same as he brushed past her on his way up the stairs. Seconds later, she was being welcomed into Mrs. Pickering's crowded flat.

"What is this?" The landlady indicated the yarn.

"I want to make a jumper, but it's been so long since I last knitted, I don't know where to start. It's for Olivia. They didn't have the jumper I know she wanted at Woolworths—I should have bought it when I first saw it…" Emma was rambling, her pain coming out in the rush of an overly long explanation. "I want her to have something special because…"

Her words choked off.

Because she missed her. She loved her. She wanted her daughter home desperately even though she'd really only just left. The flat wasn't the only thing altered without Olivia. Life was not the same.

Mrs. Pickering put her hand on Emma's shoulder. "We'll sort it out, dear." She welcomed Emma inside amid Tubby's excited yips and closed the door. "And your timing couldn't be better. I've just put the kettle on."

The boxes, trunks and random pieces of furniture still cluttered every available space within. Mrs. Pickering considered the bookshelf, then shook her head, and went to a chest of drawers that she had to squeeze around a stack of boxes to get to. "I have a pattern here somewhere," she mused to herself.

Emma saw to the tea while Mrs. Pickering unearthed a pattern exactly like what Emma was looking for.

Together they sat down on the sofa with their tea, and under the landlady's careful guidance, Emma began knitting Olivia's jumper.

The lovely diversion lasted an hour or so, with each stitch becoming easier and easier. Perhaps life without Olivia would be that way as well. Hard at first, but more bearable as Emma pressed on.

At least, she could only hope. For now, despite the entertainment of friends and books and—yes—even knitting, the ache of missing her daughter seemed impossibly painful.

10

EMMA STRODE INTO the Booklover's Library a week later, eager to begin her shift. Life had not become easier without Olivia, but Emma managed to muster through one day at a time.

After finishing a very satisfying reread of *Emma*, *The Mask of Dimitrios* had been an excellent way to pull her mind away from real life. She'd read the new mystery in just a couple days, losing herself in the pages. For those few precious moments, she didn't have to think. She didn't have to feel.

The jumper for Olivia, however, was not coming along with as much success. The ball of yarn and the modest beginnings of a jumper were in a tote in the employee's room at work, packed alongside a flimsy promise to work on it while on break.

Her recent attempts at knitting, however, reminded her of exactly why she'd given it up. There were dropped stitches, ones that were too tight when she forgot to loosen her grip, and even two times when she'd accidentally started working in the wrong direction. Truly, she was rubbish at knitting.

Yet every time she pushed the project irritably aside, she saw Olivia's face in her mind. The way her daughter's eyes had lit with longing, the way she obediently did not ask for something she knew they could not afford. Emma's heart would wrench anew and she would resume the task with more care, shoving away her frustration and instead imbuing the unwieldy task with love.

Emma checked in her copy of *The Mask of Dimitrios* at the Class A subscriber desk and made a mental note to thank Miss Bainbridge for the wonderful suggestion. Across the room, Margaret caressed her own cheek by means of demonstrating her soft skin as she spoke to a middle-aged patron.

Miss Crane stopped beside Emma and regarded Margaret with an irritated glare. "She's such a halfwit, always falling for the latest beauty advertisements." At Emma's appalled face, Miss Crane amended, "She is a pretty halfwit though, I'll give her that."

"She's not a halfwit at all," Emma retorted sharply. "She's actually quite clever. What she says to those women builds trust with them. They come to her with problems they'd like addressed and she offers advice, and when she recommends books, they immediately accept her suggestions. The patrons love her, and her beauty advice is part of that affection." Emma looked hard at the other woman whose irritation had now shifted toward Emma. "And Boots' is rather clever as well—to hire a woman who can sell their makeup so effectively. As these women leave, many stop by the cosmetics counter on their way out."

Miss Crane gave a saccharine smile. "Well, I'm sure her efforts are appreciated by the shop, but we're here to provide books for our patrons. Nothing more."

Emma wanted to add that they provided so much more than simply books with their recommendations, but Miss Crane was already off, sailing toward a tall man with broad shoulders and dark hair that was just a touch too long.

Margaret finished speaking with her subscriber, who left with a book in her hand and a smile on her face.

The library was relatively empty, save for the man Miss Crane spoke with. Margaret sidled over to Emma and casually picked at the small arrangement of daisies. "That's Mr. Fisk. Every woman who comes in here can't keep her eyes off him."

"You're engaged," Emma teased.

"But I'm not blind." Margaret winked. "I'm not sure why he's not signed up like the other men, though." She shrugged, as if it was of little consequence to her. "Poor Miss Crane trips all over herself every time he comes in."

As if on cue, the book Miss Crane was pulling off the shelf tumbled to the floor. Mr. Fisk bent and grabbed it for her, handing it back to a red-faced Miss Crane.

When he left some time later with the book Miss Crane had suggested, he caught Emma's eye and gave her a casual smile that caught her somewhere in the chest. Yes, it was easy to see why the women of the Booklover's Library were all drawn to Mr. Fisk.

The sensation that smile had summoned was one she hadn't felt in a long time. Not that she cared to dwell on such trifling emotions.

Instead, she selected *The Lady of Red Gables* by Elizabeth Carfrae for herself, preferring to relegate any romance in her life to books rather than people.

Through the remainder of the day, it did not escape Emma's notice how Miss Crane peered toward women who departed the Booklover's Library after speaking with Margaret. And how many of them truly did stop by the cosmetics counter.

That night—to Emma's great relief—she found she had received not only a postcard from Olivia, citing her location somewhere in East Anglia, but also a letter. Emma opened the letter with hands that shook, making her movements clumsy as she pulled the papers free of the envelope. Her eyes darted over the pages quickly, absorbing the longest letter Olivia had likely ever written, all done in her messy writing. The usual misspellings and grammatical slips in excessively large lettering made Emma smile with their familiarity.

As she read, the band that had formed around her chest squeezed tighter and tighter, drawing out a pain only a parent could know.

Olivia described how the children had been on the train for a considerable time, long enough for some of the younger children to have wet the seats they sat in. They were given an orange, chocolate and some milk, which she had liked very much.

When they finally arrived, they were told to line up at the station while men and women chose which children they wanted to bring home.

There was a note of shy embarrassment in the letter as Olivia confessed to having not been chosen.

All the pretty girls with blond curls were picked. But you know I'm not blond. And not pretty neither.

Emma released a hard breath at that last line.

How appalling that people went through these children like they were selecting prime stock. But Olivia's low opinion of herself struck the deepest blow.

Every mother thought their children were beautiful. And Olivia *was* beautiful, with her soulful, ocean-blue eyes and long, thick lashes, especially when coupled with her overzealous gap-toothed grin. While she was taller than most, and perhaps still learning grace with her long limbs, Olivia was endearing and lovely and the best kind of beautiful there ever was.

How dare those people pass her up as though she were less than perfect?

Heart in her throat, Emma read on.

A woman had come to the building late and went to Olivia when she found out no one else wanted her.

No one else wanted her.

Those words sliced into Emma's core.

The woman—whom Olivia referred to as Aunt Bess—offered to billet Olivia, and now she lived in a large house with a shed of animals in the backyard.

The rest of the letter went on to say how very much Olivia missed Emma and Mrs. Pickering and Tubby and how she hoped Emma would write soon. There was a happy cadence to Olivia's words, infusing the letter with a quiet joy that soothed the rougher parts of Emma's fears.

She immediately wrote back, filling pages with how much Olivia was loved and how grateful she was for "Aunt Bess." And while Emma ended the letter with *Miss you tremendously*, she didn't delve into the depths of that loneliness.

If Olivia knew how truly difficult this separation was for Emma, she would likely fight her way back to Nottingham.

A few days later, Emma received a government form to complete, listing each member of their household, to be turned in near the end of the month on a date dubbed National Registration Day. And though Olivia was not there in the home with her, Emma had to declare her daughter's information so Aunt Bess could receive Olivia's identity card and ration coupons.

Which meant that after Christmas, the ration would soon begin.

11

PRIDE AND PREJUDICE sat stubbornly in the mystery section, its spine camouflaged with the other books, lined up so perfectly, one might never suspect a misshelving had transpired until they read the title.

Everything in Emma tingled to snatch the book from the incorrect location and hide it behind her back to reshelve. But with Mr. Beard at her side, she could not risk him catching the error.

"Mysteries are the bane of the literary world." There was a slight ruddiness to his cheeks as he continued with his invective. "And I won't even mention romance, which is sullying every woman in Britain's expectation of love."

And though he said he wouldn't mention romance, he went on to demean the genre for another five minutes. As he did so, a specific romance was on Emma's mind—Pride and Prejudice—in its incorrect location.

"What we need are classics," Mr. Beard continued. "True literature written by the learned, the elite. In writing these flighty novels that are meant only to entertain, the intellect of our country is dropping." His face went a shade redder. "Dropping, I say."

"This one is truly awful." Emma pulled the book directly

beside *Pride and Prejudice*. The empty space left the book to tilt awkwardly, taunting her.

Mr. Beard's eyes sharpened on the book. "Dare I ask what that atrocity is about?"

"*Death on the Nile*, by Agatha Christie, is a murder mystery that must be solved while on a steamer on the Nile River before the killer can strike again."

Mr. Beard studied the book more closely. "Sounds truly dreadful."

"I scarcely slept because I couldn't stop turning the pages."

"You don't say."

"Oh, I do say. I'm sure you'd loathe it."

He held out his hand, his palm lined with age. "I should like to take a look for myself."

"Of course." Emma passed him the book.

"For research," Mr. Beard added gruffly.

"Of course," Emma repeated with a smile.

She knew this game. They played it once every week or two. The first time he'd ridden in on his high horse, she had foolishly led him to the classics section, where he proceeded to declare there wasn't a classic he hadn't read and that he wanted something new. The more he berated the mysteries, the more his gaze had wandered toward the section like a child eyeing a sweets shop. Ever since, she was the only librarian he would approach.

"Shall I check this out for you, Mr. Beard?" she asked.

"Yes, but hurry. I have much to do today and must read through this drivel first." Without waiting for her reply, he scuttled over to the Class A subscriber counter and presented her with his Class A membership token.

The metal token was attached to a ribbon that went through the eyelet at the top of the spine, intended to be a bookmark.

Emma jotted down his information, then looped his token through the hole and handed him the book.

"I shall deliver a full report once I'm done." Mr. Beard slipped the book into the soft leather bag he held at this side. As he did this, he glanced surreptitiously about as if anticipating his selection to be publicly judged.

"I would be disappointed otherwise," Emma replied easily.

But he was already turning away, heading out the door.

"Why doesn't he just admit he loves mysteries?" Margaret asked when he was gone.

Emma shook her head, her own mystery heavy on her mind. Who was moving the books?

Miss Crane breezed by the mystery section. Emma tensed, but fortunately the other woman didn't pause to look closely at the shelf where *Pride and Prejudice* still tilted at a jaunty angle, merrily mocking Emma.

Margaret lifted a stack of books from under the counter where they'd been placed upon their return. "Are you going to the event next month?"

From what Emma had been told, the day-long get-togethers for the Boots' chemist and the Booklover's Library employees were previously excursions done farther away in more coastal cities. But with the war on and petrol being rationed and trains needed for troops, such a trip would be unpatriotic. Fortunately, Boots' still wanted their employees to know they were valued and instead planned for a picnic along the River Trent with the promise of delicious food before the ration set in.

"I think attending would provide a nice distraction," Emma replied.

Margaret's face immediately softened. "How are you getting?"

"I've finally had a letter from Olivia and she seems well." Emma didn't add how the children had been selected by adults or how her daughter had been passed over, though the anger at the incident still burned.

"I think I'll be in need of distraction as well." Margaret looked down at the floor. "Jeffrey has signed up and will be leaving for training soon." She pressed a finger to the corners of her eyes to blot her tears without smearing her makeup.

Miss Crane passed through the main area of the library once more, heading toward the mysteries. As she strode by, her gaze caught on Margaret.

While it was well and good that Miss Crane didn't see the misshelved book, she'd likely report Margaret's overt display of emotion to Miss Bainbridge. Turning her back on Miss Crane, Emma stepped in front of Margaret, putting herself between her friend and the sharp-eyed employee before the latter could witness a single tear.

"Jeffrey said he wants to marry before he goes." Margaret sniffed and dabbed at her eyes again.

Miss Crane's direction shifted, beelining her toward the mystery section.

Blast.

"Let's go to the Bespoke Room." Emma put a hand on Margaret's elbow and led her into the private room.

"If I marry him, I'll have to quit and I won't have a thing to occupy my time." Margaret covered her face with her hands. "Emma, I can't."

Before Emma could open her mouth, the door flew open and Miss Crane entered, *Pride and Prejudice* brandished in her hand. "Misshelved again," she snapped. "This never happened until you began working here, Miss Taylor."

Margaret cleared her throat. "Oh goodness. That was my fault. I put that away this morning and could have sworn I tucked it in the classics section."

"You?" The heat went out of Miss Crane's glare. "Clearly

this is not a mystery." She pinned Emma with a warning glare that said she suspected Margaret was lying before turning on her heel and leaving.

"Thank you," Emma said. "I don't even recall having seen that book in the return pile this morning."

Margaret shrugged. "It happens. Miss Crane is always looking for something to grouse about. I think she has a miserable life and that's why she treats others as she does."

No more books turned up in the wrong location through the rest of the day, not that it spared Emma any of Miss Crane's scowls. Emma stayed later that evening to do some tidying and walked home hurriedly to ensure she avoided the blackout. October was sweeping in, shortening the days and leaving them chilled with the promise of a hard winter.

Along the walls and billboard columns were posters rallying British support in a time of war. Men were asked to sign up for the army; women were called upon to become members of the Women's Volunteer Service. And mothers were told to keep their children safely in the country. The image of Hitler whispering into a mother's ear as she cradled her children struck Emma. As if a mother who kept her children home was welcoming Hitler onto their shores.

There had been another letter from Olivia in the days following. This one detailed life at Aunt Bess's farm. How there were chickens with eggs to gather every morning, a cow that made milk, and a goat that jump about like his hooves were made of springs. The house was large and grand, with a piano that they played every night after a fine dessert with clotted cream.

No more letters followed in the next couple of weeks.

When Emma's concern became an insistent distraction, she sat down to pen a letter to Aunt Bess. First Emma thanked her for taking in Olivia, then asked about the possibility of a visit. Inviting oneself to someone's home was rude, yes, but surely this was an extraordinary situation where such formalities could be overlooked.

In the absence of any letters to read, the ball of red yarn and knitting needles on the table by the sofa called to Emma. Nearly a third of the jumper's trunk had been knit, mostly with Mrs. Pickering's help. The more Emma performed the action of twisting the yarn over the needles, the more proficient her slow, awkward fingers became. She would never be as adroit as Mrs. Pickering, whose needles moved with such speed they blurred with a click as rhythmic as that of a machine, but Emma was pleased with her progress.

With their shared enthusiasm, the jumper would be ready by Christmas, a perfect gift for Olivia.

12

SCONES WERE LAID out in a starburst pattern of various flavors—from black-flecked vanilla bean to blueberry dotted with purple lumps, and even a pumpkin ginger, evidenced by its persimmon hue. They were stacked neatly around a large pot of clotted cream, whipped to perfection. Beside those stood a carafe of tea and a bowl of lemonade.

The warm coziness of the presentation, however, was dashed away by the brisk wind lashing off the River Trent.

It was not an ideal day for a picnic, but a good effort had been put forth.

Music rose jovially in the air before being whipped away by the stiff breeze, carried off from the band that had been hired to play. All around Emma, other Boots' employees and their families were enjoying the festivities.

Despite the frivolities, Emma was painfully aware of the distinct lack of children at the family-themed event.

"Are you planning to sign up for the Women's Volunteer Service?" Margaret pulled her charcoal-gray coat tighter around her slender frame and nodded toward the red, white, and blue table. The women there were stationed with clipboards hugged in their arms and wore the smart WVS gray-green herringbone coats and red-banded hats.

Margaret's attempt at cheerfulness did not hide the maudlin note in her voice. There was a dimness to her smile, a faraway look to her gaze, an errant sigh here and there that pulled too deep, as if dredged up from the bottom of her soul.

Jeffrey was supposed to attend the picnic with her that day, but had been called up earlier than expected.

"I considered joining…" Emma admitted. And she genuinely had, ever since she'd seen the women of the WVS shepherding the children at the school during the evacuation. She'd been seeing the posters to volunteer ever since, as if they'd been speaking to her.

If she worked alongside those women, she might have a better understanding of the children's evacuation. She might have advance notice on when they would return home.

Beside Emma, Margaret was looking morosely down at her engagement ring. The diamond had belonged to Jeffrey's grandmother and now the ancient stone winked in the weak stream of sunlight that was trying to fight its way through the heavy clouds.

Emma settled a hand on her friend's forearm in comfort.

Margaret looked up and gave a sad smile. "He had so hoped to be married by now. But I can't just sit at home all day with my trousseau unpacked, and nothing better to do than wait for the post for a new letter to reply to."

Emma nodded, understanding on a deeper level than she cared to confess.

"Why are married women unable to work? It's ridiculous." Color rose in Margaret's cheeks that had nothing to do with the nip in the air. "If there are no children to tend to at home, why must they have to put their energy into cleaning an empty house and setting a lonely dinner table? And even if a woman has children, why can't she work? Are we not allowed to derive joy from our careers as men do?"

Several people turned to look at them.

Margaret blinked and considered Emma with soft brown eyes. "But you know perfectly well how I feel given your own situation. Forgive my thoughtlessness."

"I think the WVS will be a good distraction." Emma guided Margaret toward the colorful table.

The last thing she needed were other Boots' employees wondering what Margaret meant by Emma's "situation."

The smart-suited WVS women spied them coming and straightened in anticipation, their smiles growing broader with each step that brought Margaret and Emma to them.

"Let's bring our loved ones home sooner." Emma looped her arm through Margaret's. "By doing our bit for Britain and helping to end this awful war."

Margaret nodded, making her blond curls roll against her chic coat. "Let's."

The women at the table were more than eager to take down their names and addresses.

"We will be meeting this Friday afternoon at the Council House to assemble care packages for the soldiers," the shorter of the two women said with an apple-cheeked smile. "Until then, we're doing all we can to help promote the Comfort Fund to provide each soldier with cigarettes and chocolate and other goodies."

"We're also collecting aluminum," chimed in the other woman, who seemed all business and little pleasantry.

"Turn your toaster into a Spitfire," the apple-cheeked woman added with a grin.

The idea was a curious one, but Emma was willing to do anything to help.

Margaret accepted the pamphlet they handed her. Behind them, the band struck up a cheerful tune.

As they turned away from the WVS, her smile fell once more. "I think I'd like to return home for the rest of the afternoon."

"Will you be all right?" Emma regarded her friend with concern.

"I just need a day or two to rally." Margaret lifted a shoulder. "That's how I've always been. My mother's kidney pie will also help. Mum's cooking can solve any problem or heartache." The optimistic look she gave seemed genuine.

Emma never had the solace of a mother's kidney pie, or a mother's comfort or counsel at all for that matter. Not when her own had died days after her birth and Arthur's parents had proved unwilling to offer any warmth.

But then, Emma had had a supportive and loving father, and she was eternally grateful for the time they'd had together, for the beautiful memories they'd created.

She hugged her friend and took comfort in the embrace as well.

After Margaret walked off from the field, Emma remained, awkwardly glancing about, debating what to do in the way one does when suddenly finding themselves alone in a crowd. Just as she considered leaving as well, she spied Miss Crane standing off to the side, looking as out of place as Emma felt.

Everyone deserved a chance. That was what Papa used to say.

Emma joined the other woman whose startled expression at her approach melted into something pleasant. Miss Crane was actually rather pretty when her face wasn't so pinched with disapproval.

"Group events like this have a tendency to make me rather uncomfortable," Miss Crane said with a nervously exhaled laugh. "I'm so out of place."

Emma looked around at the faces of other men and women who worked at Boots'. "At least mostly everyone is familiar."

"It does help to know a friendly face."

Miss Crane's comment rang with an earnestness that took Emma aback. Had Miss Crane thought Emma friendly?

Her attitude in their previous interactions suggested otherwise.

"I know I'm not as welcoming as the other women at Boots'," Miss Crane said, as if reading her mind. "Women like Margaret who melts everyone like pats of butter in her palm. Or like you, who exudes such kindness, people can't help but like you."

"Not at all," Emma stammered, unsure how to reply to such a statement.

"I see how the customers react to you both," Miss Crane said. "And how they react to me. I assure you, I'm aware of my deficiencies."

"You shouldn't say such things," Emma protested, the mother in her balking at any person resigned to such defeat.

Miss Crane smiled, though the action looked as if it hurt. "You truly are kind, Miss Taylor."

At that moment, their conversation was interrupted by one of the head chemists as he thanked everyone for coming, implored them to bring several scones home, and to ensure they were all doing their part to aid in the war effort. After a sharp look from the stiffer WVS woman, he hastily added a reminder to contribute to the Comfort Fund and gather spare aluminum for donation.

When the speech concluded, Emma turned to Miss Crane, and found she'd gone.

Emma thought of what the other woman had said the whole way home, realizing that perhaps this entire time, she had truly not given Miss Crane a proper chance.

Once inside the tenement house, Emma stopped by Mrs.

Pickering's flat. The older woman appeared in the doorway with Tubby eagerly pawing at her side.

"I have an idea for some of those boxes," Emma said. "The WVS is asking for aluminum collection. I wonder...do you think there might be some goods in Mr. Pickering's effects that contain aluminum?"

Mrs. Pickering didn't speak for a moment, pulling a blue cardigan around her body, clearly cautious about the idea.

"I could help. And you'll be aiding the war effort..." Emma encouraged. "Turn your toaster into a Spitfire."

Mrs. Pickering laughed at that. "A Spitfire indeed. Very well. When would you like to start?"

"I'm free now. You know I have nothing to do but bungle my way through knitting that jumper."

Mrs. Pickering laughed again and widened the door, edging Tubby back gently with her calf as she allowed Emma inside. She led Emma to a tower of boxes to the right of the living space and settled her fists on her hips as Tubby glanced between them. "Now where to begin?"

13

IT TOOK WELL over a week to go through Mr. Pickering's boxes, but they were successful in excavating items to donate. Likewise, Emma had collected a box of her own household items, including an old teakettle with a dented side, a pan that was too big to be practical and thus never used, and several other kitchen items that did little more than take up space.

Her donations were piled in a box by the door for her to take to the WVS at the Council House on Friday with Mrs. Pickering.

The following day at the Booklover's Library, Margaret seemed back to her usual cheerful self.

"It was Mum's kidney pie," she said with her usual beaming smile. "That and a cup of milk always sets me to rights."

Miss Crane strode past as they were talking and scowled at Margaret. "You're far too old to be coddled so."

The skin under Margaret's rouge reddened.

"I think it's quite nice." Emma almost added that she hoped Olivia would always look to her for comfort the way Margaret did with her mother. "That's what good mother's do, isn't it?"

"I wouldn't know," Miss Crane said coolly.

Margaret shot Emma a grateful look. "What was your favorite meal your mother made?"

Emma was quiet a moment, her mind racing for an answer before finally admitting the truth. "My mother died when I was a baby. It was only my father and I."

Margaret covered her mouth, her expression displaying her sorrow. "Your father raised you? I imagine the two of you are thick as thieves now."

"Yes…" Emma floundered for words then. It was curious how one's vocabulary could be so extensive, complete with the knowledge to string the words together appropriately, yet one could still be utterly at a loss in moments such as these.

"I'm sorry you didn't know your mother either," Emma offered to Miss Crane in consolation.

"Oh, I know her." She scoffed. "And she's perfectly alive still." Suddenly she straightened, the plaster smile she offered guests firmly in place once more. "Mr. Fisk. May I help you?"

Before he answered, a cheeky woman who'd been appreciating his appearance spoke up. "Oh, you should find this young man a nice romance."

Mr. Beard lingered nearby and snorted. "A man reading a romance. What nonsense." He wandered over, fully involved now as he tucked his notepad and pencil into the breast pocket of his jacket.

Mr. Fisk appeared entirely unruffled. "I have been known to read a romance from time to time."

"You? Read romance?" Mr. Beard snorted again, gazing incredulously up at Mr. Fisk, who stood easily three heads taller.

"I find the best way to understand a woman's mind is to delve into the books they love best." Mr. Fisk's explanation came readily and without hesitation. And likely made hearts flutter for every woman in earshot.

"Ah, a man for the ladies." Mr. Beard smirked, satisfied with himself for having deduced the core of the situation.

"Actually, to understand my mother and my aunt." Mr. Fisk's face remained impassive.

"Your mother and your aunt?" A laugh erupted from Mr. Beard as he looked about in an obvious attempt to garner support for the ridiculousness of the situation.

"The way you say that suggests you've never had a relationship with the women in your family," Mr. Fisk said. "They can appear to be rather mercurial—"

"They *are* mercurial," Mr. Beard exclaimed, rudely cutting him off.

"Unless you understand who they are and why life affects them as it does." Mr. Fisk shrugged as if this was a perfectly obvious answer. "With such knowledge, you can help lessen their stressors and offer proper support for whatever they might need."

"Indeed." Mr. Beard chortled, eyeing Mr. Fisk as though expecting the other man to deliver a punch line.

None came.

Miss Crane cleared her throat. "I'm afraid romances aren't my strong suit."

"You could try *The Death of the Heart*," Emma offered. "I read it recently and rather enjoyed it."

"Why not *Lady Chatterley's Lover*?" Mr. Beard muttered derisively.

"I believe I'm receiving that one next, am I not?" Mr. Fisk asked, an acceptance to the challenge thrown at his feet.

Emma clenched her jaw to keep it from dropping open as she recalled the scandalous red label book. Even she had not worked up the temerity to read it yet.

"I...do not recall that being on your list," she sputtered.

Class A subscribers were given a catalog of available titles from which they composed the list of books they intended to read in their journals kept at the lending library. Even red label books written in their journals were overlooked in favor of more socially acceptable reading material. Or so Emma's training had indicated.

"Please do put it on my list." Mr. Fisk gave a charming smile.

"Are you quite sure?" Miss Crane asked, her cheeks so brilliantly scarlet, Emma could practically feel heat radiating off them. "It is a book that must be ordered specially...because... because..."

"Quite sure." Mr. Fisk nodded and waited for Emma to bring him *The Death of the Heart*.

She always had admired readers who ventured outside of their natural genres. Those were often the people who had the greatest empathy, the most understanding of others around them, and the broadest appreciation for the world.

Mr. Beard pulled out his notebook and licked his pencil before scribbling furiously, pausing from time to time to chuckle and shake his head.

"Does he have any other books on his list?" Emma asked.

Miss Crane shook her head, unable to tear her gaze from Mr. Fisk.

That was it then. There would be nothing to prevent him from receiving the red label book.

The incident appeared to pique Miss Crane's ire, souring any goodwill that had begun to mend the divide between her and Emma. As Miss Bainbridge was out that day for an appointment, Miss Crane was in charge and set Emma to task after task, working her beyond her allotted time and well into the evening.

Books were sorted, banisters waxed to a high shine, immaculate countertops were dusted—twice—and the water in all the vases was changed, with the flower stems nipped to ensure the longevity of the fragile blooms. When all was done, Emma was left weary from her efforts.

By the time she pushed out of the grand building on Pelham Street, the sun had already set and the streets darkened with the full effect of the blackout. She had a torch for just such an occasion, complete with a fresh change of number 8 batteries procured from a delivery just that morning at Boots'.

Not that the torch was particularly helpful. The slitted covering over the lens allowed for scarcely any light to see by. She left her jacket untied to ensure her white jumper beneath showed to keep her visible, especially to passing cars.

Though the speed limit had been lowered for vehicles, there had been many reports in the *Evening Post* of people struck by drivers who did not see their victims until too late.

Thankfully the newly painted white curbs helped her navigate her way home. She had just turned down Mooregate Street when a car rushed by, nearly swiping her off the pavement.

Wind from its wake left her skirt swirling around her knees and her heart knocking against her ribs as the vehicle careened onto the walkway and corrected back onto the street, tires squealing.

Emma set her hand over her chest to calm her heart and gather her wits.

That could have been tragic.

The thrumming of her pulse stopped in a moment of petrifying fear. If something happened to her, what would become of Olivia?

Before the thought could plague her further, the meager light of her torch caught a dark shape against the sidewalk.

A person.

The car had struck someone after all, the sound likely obstructed by the screech of the tires.

Emma rushed over. "Are you hurt?" She crouched as the man pushed up to a sitting position, muttering in confusion.

That was when she realized she knew him. Not by his appearance—she could scarcely see even with her torch—but by the man's irascible grumbling.

Mr. Sanderson.

14

"MR. SANDERSON, are you hurt?" Emma helped the older man to his feet and the whole of his weight sagged against her. Hugging his bulk to her side so he didn't crumple to the ground, she led him up the short path to their tenement house and up the three steps leading to the front door.

She paused by Mrs. Pickering's flat and knocked. The sound reverberated through the stairwell. Tubby's shrill barking came from the other side. Emma waited for what felt like several long minutes, but Tubby's yips were not interrupted by Mrs. Pickering's shushing or footsteps.

Emma hesitated a moment more until it was obvious the landlady was not home.

Mr. Sanderson's weight seemed to intensify and her hold slipped. He leaned harder on her, groaning. "I can walk."

"Don't strain yourself." She tried to make her voice sound easy and casual despite the effort to keep him upright.

There was nothing for it but to haul him upstairs. Any thought she had to get him to his own flat, however, was dashed by the time she managed to help him up a single flight. Her muscles ached with the effort and he swayed dangerously.

If she attempted one more landing, they might both come crashing down.

"We're going to nip into my flat so we can both catch our breath," she said between pants of exertion. He didn't complain as she fumbled with the lock and managed to get her door open before leading him inside.

She flicked on the lights without thought. Outside, a sharp whistle from the ARP Warden reminded her to close the curtains.

"Please, have a seat." She guided him quickly to the nearest chair at the dining room table and rushed about the flat, pulling the heavy curtains closed completely to ensure not a wink of light showed at any window.

Once the house was sealed enough to ensure the ARP Warden wouldn't come knocking, prattling on with threats of a citation, she saw to Mr. Sanderson. She filled a cup with water from the tap and brought it over to him.

His elbows were propped on the table, his head resting in his palms. The halo of wispy hair was rumpled, jutting up at parts, and it took everything in Emma not to carefully smooth the strands back into place.

"Are you injured, Mr. Sanderson?" she asked again. "Shall I see if there is someone at the Red Cross station?"

The medical aid stations had begun popping up around the city in preparation for the war, in the event of a bombing. There were several within walking distance.

While there had not been bombings or attacks, the proximity of first aid had been beneficial and used by many in Nottingham for random injuries. Especially ones sustained during the blackouts. People ran into walls and into each other. They fell off curbs and docks. Cars crashed into other vehicles, and—in cases like tonight—into people.

Mr. Sanderson scrubbed his hands over his face and along

the top of his head, making his sparse hair stick up even more. When he met her gaze, his eyes were bloodshot. "Just took a good knocking. Bounced the wind right outta me, it did." His hands dropped and he blinked, bewildered. "Bloody car came outta nowhere."

"It nearly hit me as well." Emma sat down next to him and nudged the water closer. "Did you hit your head at all?"

He frowned in a way that seemed to fill his entire weathered face, causing even the wrinkles at his brow to tug downward. "Dunno." He lifted his hand and gently prodded the pate of his head with his fingertips. "Nothing hurts. It was just the fall that took it out of me."

"Are you certain?" Emma asked. "I can bring the ARP Warden round."

In addition to telling the people of Nottingham to put out their lights, the wardens were also trained in first aid and had been of some help. Even though, in general, they were rather a nuisance.

Mr. Sanderson grunted. "Don't be looking at me like that, like I'm some fragile old man in need of cosseting."

"Not at all," Emma rushed. Though she was indeed concerned for his well-being due to his age and apparent frailty.

His nostrils flared and he pulled in a deep breath, surveying the flat around him. The irritation melted suddenly from his features. "You've a lovely home, Mrs. Taylor."

"Oh." Emma regarded the room with the tired sofa that had once been elegant when purchased just after her marriage to Arthur. The faded blue rug beneath it served only to protect the hardwood floors and keep their every move from echoing off the yellow walls. Olivia's drawings were hung throughout the flat, crooked and dangling by bits of scrim tape. One of these artistic renderings displayed the two of them at the Goose Fair one year; another was of them at a sweets shop when she'd let Olivia pick out whatever she'd wanted on her last birthday; several were of them at the cinema and there were even a few of Olivia and Tubby in the front yard. Truly, there was little to commend the flat, especially as his layout above was likely a mirror of her own. "Well, thank you."

A smile touched his face, just barely notching up the corners of his lips. "I know your girl is in the country, but this…" He nodded, as if in confirmation to himself. "This is a home where a family lives. You're a lucky woman, Mrs. Taylor."

The earnest note to his flattery warmed Emma's heart, making her thanks as genuine as his praise.

Mr. Sanderson pulled the water glass closer and took a noisy slurp before setting it on the table with a muted thunk. "I think I'm about as right as I'm bound to feel at this age. I'll see myself upstairs." He pushed to standing. "Thank you for your hospitality, Mrs. Taylor."

Emma shot to her feet. "Let me walk up with you."

"I'll be fine."

"Please. I'll feel better ensuring you've made it home safely."

Mr. Sanderson waved his hand dismissively. "Ach—fine, fine, fine…"

Emma eagerly accompanied him, not ready to release him from her care until he was upstairs with a hot cuppa. Thankfully he had not lied about being able to walk and could make his own way up the stairs without having to rely on her. She waited as he unlocked his door.

He hesitated. "Do you mean to come in?"

"I'd like to make sure you're properly settled and don't need anything."

"I'm fine."

She tilted her head, a silent indication she had no plans to leave.

Huffing a sigh, he pushed into his dark apartment and

flicked on his lights. The blackout curtains had already been pulled, sparing them another whistled reminder, and likely a visit from the warden as well. Two infractions in one night would certainly warrant a dressing-down.

Emma entered the flat behind Mr. Sanderson and was taken aback by the stark furnishing. With being at the tenement house for so long that Mrs. Pickering considered him a permanent fixture, Emma had anticipated the space to be bursting at the seams with the contents of life. Books and pictures and bits and bobs from vacations and memorable moments with mates and all the things in between.

The flat appeared as if Mr. Sanderson had only just moved in.

She blinked in surprise at the lack of personality in the home. There was a dun-colored rug under a serviceable brown sofa, a wooden dining table with two chairs and a copy of *David Copperfield* resting beside a pair of spectacles. And the bland endless white of empty walls.

This was the flat of a man whose life was not being lived.

Mr. Sanderson cleared his throat. "It's not much to look at, I know."

"It's so very clean," Emma said quickly with a ready smile. "I always appreciate a tidy home, especially since mine never feels that way." She laughed, and the sound came out as nervous as her prattling. "Have a seat, I'll put together some tea for you."

"Don't worry after it."

"Please let me do this for you."

He sighed. "I haven't a kettle."

She blinked. Didn't everyone in England have a kettle? The very idea of not having one was...well, it was not British.

Mr. Sanderson's blunt fingertips tapped lightly on the table in front of him. "I take my tea at the shops."

Suddenly, Emma recalled the teakettle she was planning to

donate to the WVS for scrap metal. "I have an extra. I'll be back in a tick."

Before he could protest, she was out of the pristine flat and rushing down the stairs.

Her own flat seemed cluttered by comparison. Olivia's mac, wellies and plimsolls crowded in the entryway beside Emma's coat and handbag. An abundance of dishes and appliances covering the countertops in the kitchen due to the limited cabinet space. Emma reached for the donation pile of aluminum to retrieve the dented kettle and stopped.

Mr. Sanderson had nothing. Not even a kettle. And here she was about to bring him a damaged item. She pivoted toward the stovetop and removed her newer kettle, its round-bellied shape gleaming. Within a few seconds, she was back up to the third floor with the kettle and a tin of tea, relieved to find Mr. Sanderson's door handle unlocked.

"You can keep this kettle," she said as she moved about the kitchen, setting the water to boiling and preparing the tea. "And the extra tea. In case you want some in the morning without having to go out."

Mr. Sanderson nodded his thanks and said nothing more except to agree to a lump of sugar and grunt at her request to call if he needed anything else.

Secure in the knowledge he was well and secure, Emma returned to her flat once more. Only then did she realize how nice it had been to be needed—even just for a moment.

Life over the last seven years had revolved around caring for Olivia—mending and washing clothes, preparing meals, reassuring her, listening to her, cherishing her.

Emma's gaze fell on the red jumper, now nearly halfway done. And not a moment too soon now that it was November. She had to hurry to have the gift ready in time for Christmas.

But first, Emma could do with a cup of tea herself. She retrieved the dented kettle from the donation pile and filled it with water.

A steady stream dribbled from the bottom rim.

Frowning, Emma lifted the kettle to investigate. Sure enough, a trickle of water ran from a pinprick of a hole where the aluminum bottom ought to have been sealed together.

With a sigh, she set the kettle in the sink, remembering that the reason for her purchasing a new kettle had not been due to the dent, but on account of the leak.

Her cup of tea would have to be boiled in a saucepan that evening, a perfect accompaniment to her slow going efforts at knitting.

15

IT WAS LUCKY for Emma she had the opportunity for tea at work the following morning, lest she be forced to begin her day without. After a strong cup, she set about the quiet routine she'd fallen into, dusting the shelves to ensure all was orderly before opening hours began. As she did this, she paid special attention to the placement of the books, ensuring not one was out of order. It did not escape her notice that Miss Bainbridge eyed her in this task.

When the manageress strode in Emma's direction, an uneasy knot tightened low in her stomach.

Miss Bainbridge stopped before Emma and folded her hands in front of her. "Miss Crane informs me there has been misshelving."

"There were two that I'm aware of," Emma said.

"I was under the impression there was only one." Miss Bainbridge's mouth thinned into a hard line. "We have a certain standard here at the Booklover's Library, one our subscribers expect us to uphold." She stopped speaking for a moment, drawing Emma's full attention. "Miss Taylor, if there were indeed two, that is simply unacceptable."

"I don't know how it's happening," Emma confessed. "I

don't even recall having shelved the books that ended up in the wrong location."

"If you are under duress at the absence of your daughter—"

"That is not the case," Emma rushed, interrupting the other woman.

Miss Bainbridge tucked her chin into her neck, evidently irritated. "Be mindful, Miss Taylor. I took a great risk with you. I hope you prove worthy of the opportunity."

Emotion ached in the back of her throat and Emma was embarrassed to find her eyes stinging with tears. She lowered her head to shield her reaction. "Yes, ma'am."

After all, what could she say? She'd defended herself to no avail. How could she prove the misshelved books were not her fault?

After work, Emma stopped by Mrs. Pickering's door with the box of aluminum to collect her to attend their first WVS meeting. Mrs. Pickering's contribution hadn't made much of an impact on the clutter in her home, but at least the donations meant one less box.

Margaret was already at the Council House, sitting in one of the folding chairs with her handbag and coat on the two beside her, clearly saving the seats. Looking at the packed room now, Emma was glad for Margaret's foresight. She and Mrs. Pickering deposited the boxes next to a tower of gleaming aluminum items framed by posters of splendid Spitfires in action, then Emma made the introductions between her two friends as the remainder of the women coming in found their seats.

Apparently, every housewife in Nottingham had heeded the WVS's call for volunteers.

The straight-backed woman from the WVS table at the Boots' luncheon was at the front of the room and clapped her hands. The chatter quieted.

"Thank you for coming this evening. I am Mrs. Stark." She paused, as if waiting for people to acknowledge who she was. Several women nodded, but Emma had no idea as to the significance of her name.

"Nottingham appreciates your efforts in joining the Women's Volunteer Service," Mrs. Stark continued. There was a note of austerity to her voice, very different from the laid-back dialect of most people who lived in Nottingham. If she wasn't an important person, she clearly thought herself as one.

Mrs. Stark paced in front of the room, looking at the women as she spoke. "You'll notice the previous poster we used to entice women to the WVS is no longer being utilized despite its attractive appearance. It has been removed on account of the model being German."

There was a collective gasp in the room.

The model had been the most striking thing about the poster, with a determined glint in her eye coupled with her classic beauty.

"We like to face any controversy head on here at the Women's Voluntary Service," Mrs. Stark announced above the murmur of women's voices so they quieted once more. "You can always expect the truth from me. We have important work to do here, ladies. I'm glad to have you at my side."

The lecture continued on, offering various ways each woman might be able to help. The uniform was presented, a lovely herringbone jacket with six large buttons on the lapels and a gray-green felt hat with a red band. Not only did they look expensive, they *were* expensive—with a fee that the women volunteering were to cover on their own.

Certainly the cost was beyond Emma's budget.

As with many other women that evening, she simply purchased the armband at a price she could stomach.

"Can you believe they're making us pay for the uniforms?" Margaret hissed as she pocketed her own arm band.

Very few women lined up to purchase the jacket and hat, Mrs. Pickering being one of them. She emerged several minutes later with both in her arms and a wide smile on her face.

"Have you already filled out what positions you are willing to help with?" Mrs. Pickering asked excitedly. "I confess, I checked every one except the bit on driving."

Margaret was bent over a clipboard, filling out her information as Emma had just done.

There had been a checkbox to indicate if they knew how to drive. Emma had driven the Austin 7 Arthur purchased after the second year of their marriage. He'd saved for over a year for the "Baby Austin" and insisted Emma learn how to drive.

"I did," Emma replied. "And I checked every box but knitting."

Several hours passed before the meeting concluded. In the end, they all went home with several pamphlets and detailed instructions for their next meeting the following Friday evening, to assemble care packages for their boys who had been shipped out to fight. Emma and Mrs. Pickering bid farewell to Margaret, who walked home in the opposite direction.

"Well, that was delightful." Mrs. Pickering's eyes sparkled and her cheeks were flushed. "Thank you for inviting me to join you. I confess, I didn't think I would enjoy it—what with a bunch of busybody women. But I rather had a grand time. I can scarcely wait for our next meeting."

"It's nice to do something to help," Emma agreed.

"And if they see the work you're doing on that jumper for Olivia, they might just ask you to knit after all." Mrs. Pickering nudged Emma's elbow.

Emma laughed, feeling more buoyed than she had since

before Olivia left. As if the camaraderie among women who had sent their children away to the country as well as sons and husbands to war somehow loosened the band of tension that usually remained locked around her chest.

"I'm serious." The older woman scooted closer to make way for a young couple walking toward them. "You're quite good."

"That's because I'm making it with love." Emma smiled, pleasure warming her cheeks.

"Well, our boys out there need all the love from us they can get. You just keep right on knitting with your heart."

They turned down their street, passing the large, boxy partially-built structures to be used as shelters in the event of an air raid.

Tubby's delighted yips met them as they made their way up the front walk. Emma worked the key in the lock of the main door while Mrs. Pickering rubbed her hands over her coat sleeves. "This will be a cold winter. I can't wait for a nip of tea."

Tea. Emma almost groaned. "My kettle is broken. With the excitement of the WVS meeting, I forgot to pick one up."

Mrs. Pickering waved her hand. "Just come join me for a cup."

Emma murmured her thanks and opened the door for her landlady. Before following her inside, Emma reached into the mail and plucked out the day's delivery. There was one envelope from a name she didn't recognize, an Elizabeth Mason.

Frowning, Emma walked through the doorway. She moved too slowly and the door bumped impatiently behind her, shooing her inside the stairwell.

Emma slid her finger under the seal, gently tearing the envelope open with curiosity.

A quick skim to the bottom of the letter revealed the neat

signature of a woman named Mrs. Elizabeth Mason, also known as Aunt Bess.

Ah, that was it, then.

"What's that?" Mrs. Pickering asked as Emma followed her into the flat.

"A letter from the woman who is minding Olivia in the countryside. I've been eager to hear from her. Olivia's letters don't come often, but when they do, they are filled with wonderful things. I wanted to see if I might come by to visit, to meet the woman she calls Aunt Bess."

Mrs. Pickering swept her hips around the desk in the middle of the kitchen and patted the back of a chair on her way to the range. "Well, you have a seat here and read while I put the kettle on."

With a grateful smile, Emma slid into the seat Mrs. Pickering had indicated and did exactly as instructed.

Aunt Bess had delightful compliments to bestow upon Olivia. She was well-behaved, perceptive without being overly chatty, and reminded Aunt Bess of the girl she'd once been. Emma's brow furrowed as she got to the part of the letter where Aunt Bess cited some concern over Olivia's education and her lack of focus on her lessons. But aside from that, all was well.

What's more, there was a generous invitation extended to Emma to join Aunt Bess and Olivia for Christmas that year at Aunt Bess's home.

Relief flooded Emma at the invitation. Christmas had been weighing on her thoughts. In Olivia's last letter, she had indicated her excitement to decorate Aunt Bess's tree and go caroling in the square. But Emma had considered bringing her daughter home, especially as the war had not amounted to anything worth being frightened over—aside from that lone, misguided air raid warning they'd endured.

At this point, the blackout was their greatest danger. That and a citation from the ARP Warden for violating said blackout.

At least now Emma would be able to enjoy Christmas with Olivia without making her abandon all she'd been looking forward to.

"You're smiling, lovey." Mrs. Pickering set the tea tray in front of Emma.

"Yes." Emma sat back and beamed up at Mrs. Pickering. "I'll be going to East Anglia for Christmas. To see Olivia."

Mrs. Pickering put a fist on her hip. "Well, we had better ensure you have that jumper done in time, hadn't we?"

16

THE NEXT MORNING, as Emma rushed about to prepare for work, a knock resounded through her flat.

She had only just fastened her simple tweed skirt, and was still plucking at her shirt to ensure the fabric was not twisted about when she pulled open the door to find Mrs. Pickering in a bathrobe and curlers with Tubby sitting at her side. "We wanted to make sure you knew to come down for morning tea. Isn't that right, Tubs?"

Tubby's tail whipped back and forth and his mouth fell open in a tongue-lolling smile.

Emma had expected to grab tea at Boots' before work started, but this was certainly preferable. "Let me finish here and I'll be down in a moment."

Mrs. Pickering nodded with finality, the way one did when all was right in the world. "A moment is all I need."

Emma pinned her hair back from her face, grabbed her purse and toed on her low-heeled loafers. When she entered Mrs. Pickering's flat, she found the older woman still in her bathrobe and curlers. "Don't go telling anyone you saw me like this."

"Of course not." Emma accepted a cup of tea, opting not to let the other woman know she received tea before her shift. Because instead of arriving early to sit in an empty room after an evening of being in an empty flat, Emma wanted to enjoy every last moment of Mrs. Pickering's chatty company, right down to the last drop. After all, tea was better taken with a friend.

Because that was what Mrs. Pickering had become in these months with her care for Olivia, her assistance with knitting, and these lovely talks over a steaming cup of perfectly brewed tea—a friend.

The lending library had been uncommonly busy with Christmas soon upon them. Not only were there more sub-scribers than ever putting their names down for Charles Dickens's *A Christmas Carol*, but people were purchasing sub-scriptions to the library as Christmas gifts. An annual subscrip-tion was costly, even for Class B subscribers—ten shillings and sixpence for one book at a time—especially with everyone conserving money on account of the war.

While Emma and the other librarians received a discount, they still had to pay a subscriber fee.

As the darkness of winter pressed in on them, the days grew shorter and her shifts seemed to fly by faster. She welcomed the swift passing of time that edged her closer and closer to being able to see Olivia.

While Emma's earlier hours were consumed with work, her afternoons were busy with whatever the WVS needed of her—collecting aluminum from neighbors, rolling bandages, packing box after box so British soldiers away from home might have a Christmas parcel to open, and, yes, even knitting the occasional scarf from time to time. To be fair, she did find scarves to be much easier to manage than jumpers.

Even still, she took Mrs. Pickering's advice and infused all the love she could into the items she made.

The week before Christmas, she sat in Mrs. Pickering's cluttered kitchen for their usual cup of tea with the red jumper set before them on the table. Having added the little finishing details around the hem and neck, Olivia's gift was finally complete.

Mrs. Pickering examined the jumper with a nod of approval. "You've done well, Mrs. Taylor. I suspect your daughter will be immensely pleased with the result."

"I do hope so." Emma studied the construction with a critical eye.

The many mistakes that occurred through the creation were now seamlessly blended and imperceptible. The jumper appeared identical to the one at Woolworths—or at least as far as Emma could recall.

"I can't wait to hear about your visit to East Anglia." Mrs. Pickering tucked her burgundy cardigan more tightly around the plain dark wool dress she wore. They were all cold these days, with the winter being just as brutal as anticipated.

She handed a small parcel to Emma. "Will you give this to Olivia for me? It's just a bit of chocolate. To let her know we're thinking of her."

Tied to the brown paper was a note card stating the gift was from Mrs. Pickering and Tubby.

Emma set the item beside the jumper. "She'll be delighted. Thank you for the consideration."

"Not a day goes by that we don't miss your girl."

Emma didn't stop thinking of Olivia either. The week before the visit to finally see her daughter crawled by with the expediency of a tortoise despite the chaotic business at the Booklover's Library. Books were being taken out for vacation, as they could be returned to any Boots' location, and in preparation for the upcoming holiday closures. No one wanted to be left without a book, especially when most homes likely had at least one member of their family missing that year.

While Emma packed for her trip, she hummed the new song by Vera Lynn, "We'll Meet Again." Though ostensibly written for sweethearts like Margaret and her fiancé, separated by the miles put between them due to the war, the lyrics took on a different note for Emma. The words of missing the one she loved, of not knowing when or where she might see her again, they stretched deep into Emma's soul and touched the place that had been unsettled since Olivia's evacuation.

But while Emma didn't know when Olivia might come home, she at least did know when and where she would see her daughter again. Tomorrow was Christmas Eve and she would be there in East Anglia with her daughter, finally meeting the oft-mentioned Aunt Bess.

There had been warnings in the paper that trains would be running slow due to civilians and soldiers alike trying to get home to loved ones, but Emma was still caught unaware. People rushed this way and that, the massive crowds very much resembling an anthill that had just been kicked by unruly children.

Men in uniform hurried by with their heavy kits slung over their backs. Women and children clustered on platforms, some crying out in delight as their loved ones returned home for the holidays, and others packed up to depart elsewhere. And women—mothers—waited anxiously for children who arrived on their own, returned for Christmas.

The latter squeezed at a wounded place in Emma. Perhaps she was wrong in agreeing to the visit with Aunt Bess. Perhaps having Olivia return home would have been better, to remain in Nottingham going forward.

There was nothing happening with the war- a "phoney war" they called it. There were no threats, no attacks, no reason to keep her daughter away.

Emma's heart ached to have Olivia's presence in the flat again, the thump of her feet dashing across the wooden floor despite Emma always telling her not to run, the sweet sound of her laughter when she and Emma joked together, the way Olivia would draw and chatter on while Emma made dinner. How Emma longed to have it all back again.

Down the platform, a man in uniform approached each person with a ticket clutched in their hand. Each shook their head and he moved on to the next.

Until finally he arrived in front of her.

There was a desperate widening of his sky blue eyes as his gaze caught the ticket in her hand. "Please, ma'am, can I have your ticket?"

Her stomach knotted.

"Please." There was a pleading note to his deep voice. "I've been given special leave to see my mum. She's in hospital and terribly sick."

Emma swallowed, the "no" stuck in her throat.

The man's eyes watered and the muscles in his jaw worked, as if he were clenching his teeth to hold back his tears. "I don't know if I'll have a chance to say goodbye." He held out a ticket, the thin bit of paper trembling in his grip. "The closest I could find was a ticket for this afternoon, but every moment that goes by might be too late."

Emma took the ticket from him, examining the print. The departure time listed was half past four, delaying her arrival by several hours, especially accounting for having to change trains midway through.

"Please." The man's voice cracked.

He was young, twenty if he was a day. Ready to sacrifice his life to keep England safe in a time of war.

Emma knew the impact of missing a child. What must it feel like to send one to war, to know they were going into a place of nightmares—of danger and terror and death? To know they might never come home?

This young man before Emma was that mother's son.

How could Emma possibly deny him? Especially when she herself had never even known her mother, let alone had the chance to offer a proper goodbye.

She extended her ticket toward him.

He blinked, incredulous, then gave a hard sniff and swiped the heel of his hand against his watery eyes. "Thank you," he said thickly. "Thank you."

The train pulled up as he wished her a hasty happy Christmas and climbed aboard with the rest of the passengers. If nothing else, an individual from the outgoing wave of people vacated a seat on the platform for her.

She settled in and opened Barbara Cartland's latest novel, *Love in Pity*, knowing she'd be there for another four hours.

But four hours turned into five with unforeseen delays. Then five became six.

Her growling stomach had her buying a soggy dill-and-egg sandwich from a vendor with a bit of lukewarm tea. She'd eaten the sad meal quickly to ensure she didn't miss her train.

She hadn't.

The signposting indicated another hour's delay. At least.

When her train finally came to a stop at the station, the clock reflected nearly midnight. But the journey would likely be about five hours if what she'd overheard from fellow passengers was correct. But she refused to allow her spirits to dampen. At least she would still arrive by Christmas morning.

She gathered her suitcase, keeping its bulk close to her side as she joined the throng of passengers boarding the train. Several people jostled, pressing ahead of others when they might be polite under normal circumstances.

Even Emma, who was often calm, found her own patience pulling like a taut string ready to snap. Especially once finally inside the cabin and realizing there were no available seats. With a sigh, she stood at the back of the cabin with her suitcase braced between her feet.

The train lurched forward, launching them into the darkness of the blackout. A small blue light had been installed in the interior of the train, offering limited visibility and casting everyone in a grayish-blue hue.

Emma began to nod off, waking abruptly with either her head snapping forward or her knees buckling. Five hours had passed and they still were not at the transfer station.

Finally the train began to slow, but the station was impossible to discern with all the location names blotted out. What had originally been done to prevent Germany from spying now created a nightmare for travelers.

"Do you know where we are?" Emma asked the man next to her. Even as she did so, the question echoed through the cabin. No one seemed to know where they were until a conductor boarded the train and announced the location in a loud voice.

The tension in Emma's shoulders relaxed somewhat. She was at the halfway point. There would still be time to arrive by Christmas.

There was one seat available at the train station, freshly vacated by the rush of men and women who clambered onto the train from which she'd just departed. Before she could sink wearily into it, a man plunked down ahead of her and leaned his head back, closing his eyes.

Not that it mattered, really. She needed to approach the ticket office anyway. Exhausted, she followed the signs. Each step made her regret the low heels she'd worn for the journey. Somehow her most comfortable pair of shoes had become her most miserably torturous pair and left her feet feeling like the bones were grinding against the hard floor.

She rounded the corner toward the ticket office and drew up short. The windows were shuttered.

A man beside her turned to regard her.

"The ticket office is closed," she stated stupidly.

"Of course it is, love." The man eyed her curiously. "It's Christmas morning."

A lump rose in her throat. She wanted to shout that she knew it was Christmas morning, that she was missing her daughter after almost four months, and how after seven years of it being just the two of them, this was her first Christmas morning without her daughter. She wanted to rail about how exhausted she was, how rumpled she looked, and how bloody bad her feet ached from standing for so long.

Instead, she swallowed her rageful frustration down, right along with that lump in her throat and nodded her thanks.

The man lifted his hat and gave her an uncertain smile. "Happy Christmas."

At least the chairs near the ticket office were blessedly empty. She collapsed into one, propped her luggage longways, then curled her arms over it and laid her head in the comfort of her sleeves. There was nothing to do but sleep and wait for the office to open.

A crackling sound snapped Emma from her slumber. She jerked upright, her spine protesting the abrupt movement. The windows to the ticket office were open, revealing a man fiddling with a wireless set.

Several people milled around the window. Emma pushed to standing as pins and needles ran down the length of her legs.

How long had she been asleep?

It didn't matter. All that mattered was obtaining a new ticket. Boarding a train. Reuniting with Olivia.

She rushed to the counter, her heels striking hard at the ground as she did so. A woman in a red coat turned to her and put a finger to her lips to quiet Emma. "The king is about to address us."

Emma set her suitcase to the ground as King George's deep voice resonated from the wireless screen. "The men and women of our far-flung Empire..."

With her fellow countrymen, Emma listened with rapt attention as the new king's Christmas speech met their uncertainty with inspiration and hope through faith and love. The woman in the red coat dabbed at her eyes with a handkerchief. Emma might have cried as well were she not so desperate to be in East Anglia with Olivia.

The crowd dispersed and Emma snatched up her suitcase, hauling its weight with her to the window. "May I trade my ticket for a new time, please?" The pitch of her desperation was now as poignant as that of the soldier she'd aided.

The man behind the counter gave a broad smile beneath his perfectly trimmed mustache. "Anything you want, ma'am. After all, it's Christmas."

She nearly cried as she received her new ticket with an afternoon departure. Which meant she might still arrive in time for Christmas after all.

The trains, however, were desperately behind schedule and as the time of her train's arrival came and went, Emma had naught to do but rest her weary body in a chair and wait.

17

THE MORNING SUN teased at the horizon, reminding Emma that it was no longer Christmas.

Her breath came out in frozen puffs as she walked for what seemed like forever. Aunt Bess's instructions to her estate had made the location seem close to the train station.

It was not.

Emma's nose and fingertips were nearly frozen, though her body was uncomfortably warm and damp with sweat within her coat. If her feet ached before, they blazed with pain now.

Her plan had been to arrive stylishly dressed with a smile and a grand hug, a mother to make Olivia proud. Instead, she staggered up yet another blasted hill, having missed the most important holiday of the year, gritty with travel filth and miserably exhausted.

The home came into view, a whitewashed two-story building with a gray slate roof accompanied with a small red barn. At least she knew she was at the right place.

Thank heaven for small mercies.

Olivia was in that house. Only steps away. Emma quickened her pace, propelled onward by a mother's desperation to reunite with her child.

A flurry of emotions swirled in her, playing off her fatigue to heighten her anticipation—the heartbreak of missing Olivia, the thrill of seeing her soon, the hollowness of realizing their time together would be far too short. Emma had to blink several times to regain her composure before rapping on the front door.

When no one immediately answered, she hesitated before knocking again. The hour was indeed quite early.

And yet that wooden door was all that separated her from her daughter. Emma banged again, harder this time.

Eventually footsteps sounded on the floor and energy shot through her, bringing her to attention. The lock clicked and the door swung open to reveal a woman with white hair pulled back into a short braid no thicker than Emma's pinky.

Gray eyes screwed up tight with disapproval. "It is too early for guests."

The woman was already dressed in a blue shirt and skirt with an apron thrown over both. Clearly it was not too early for her to be awake and about. Just too early for her to have answered the door.

Emma pushed aside the irritable thought. "I'm terribly sorry." She looked behind the woman as she spoke, half expecting—and wholly hoping—to see Olivia rushing down the glossy wooden staircase. "I'm Mrs. Taylor, Olivia's mother. There was an issue at the train station. I've only just arrived."

The woman studied her in a way that appeared entirely without compassion. "You missed Christmas."

"As I said, I was unfortunately stuck at a train station with no way to arrive until now."

"Olivia was very disappointed."

Those words, stated so blandly and without a shield of kindness, struck Emma in the very rawest part of her chest.

"I'd like to see her." Emma's voice wavered with the overwhelming need for her child. "Please let me go to my daughter."

"She's asleep." Even as the woman spoke, she pulled the door open in what would otherwise be a welcoming gesture.

Emma's nerves hummed with eagerness. If the door hadn't been opened for her, she would have shoved in. A mother should never have to beg to see her own child.

"Upstairs?" she confirmed.

The woman's nod was barely perceptible, and Emma raced up the stairs. "Olivia?"

A door flew open and Olivia ran out, wearing a long-sleeved white nightdress Emma had never seen before, her hair a wild tangle of waves. "Mummy!"

Emma rushed, meeting Olivia halfway as she swept her into her arms and held her daughter for the first time in nearly four months. Every nerve ending in Emma's body sang with relief. The feel of Olivia's slender body still warm from sleep embraced in her arms, the softness of her hair, knowing she was safe and they were together again, it was more than Emma could bear in the most beautiful way.

Tears burned in Emma's eyes as she drew her daughter back. "Let me look at you."

Olivia blinked back her own tears and gazed up with so much love, Emma thought her heart might burst. As a smile spread over Olivia's face, Emma realized there was no longer a gap of space at her eyetooth.

"Your tooth has nearly grown in," Emma exclaimed.

"The other one is loose now." Olivia flicked her tongue over the tooth, and it wobbled precariously, exposing a ruby-red portion of gum beneath.

Emma gave an exaggerated shudder and Olivia laughed, knowing how Emma found those wiggly teeth so unnerving.

"Olivia, dear, why don't you get dressed while I make breakfast?" The woman's voice came from behind Emma. "You can see your mother downstairs when you're done."

Olivia's gaze went over Emma's shoulder. "All right, Aunt Bess."

So, the old woman *was* Aunt Bess. Given her rudeness, Emma had hoped the woman was simply a relative, or—given the fineness of the furnishings in the house—perhaps even a maid. The second floor alone was nearly twice the size of Emma's small flat in Nottingham.

Was it really just the two of them living there?

"Will you join me downstairs, Mrs. Taylor?" Aunt Bess asked.

Emma turned reluctantly from her daughter, wishing for nothing more than to hold her close once more. To never let her go this time.

But there would be time to spare for that in the next two days of her visit. Emma gave Olivia a kiss on the forehead and followed Aunt Bess.

"Forgive my rudeness at your arrival," Aunt Bess said as she led Emma to a kitchen with a large iron stove—likely the source of the pleasant warmth that made Emma's icy nose and fingers sting. The counters were free of clutter and the parted ivory curtains over the large sink revealed a stretch of land as far as the eye could see. "You see, Olivia was quite upset yesterday. I fear I'm rather protective of her."

Some of the tension knotting Emma's shoulders relaxed and she pulled out a chair at the small dining room table. "I'm glad to hear she's being so well cared for."

Aunt Bess's smile almost reached her eyes. "How did you say your train was delayed?"

A wary tightness threaded through the back of Emma's neck once more. She hadn't said how her train was delayed, as the sharp-eyed woman was well aware. While Aunt Bess moved around the kitchen, Emma patiently explained what happened with the soldier whose mother was ill and the un-expected events that followed.

At the end of the story, Aunt Bess smirked. "He pulled a fast one on you, didn't he?"

Emma stiffened. "I beg your pardon?"

The older woman set a steaming mug of tea in front of Emma. The brew was rich and dark, exactly what Emma needed after the ordeal of her travel. It almost made Emma like Aunt Bess.

Almost.

"The chap was likely off to marry his sweetheart or meet up with one of those tarts giving our boys a good send-off." The chuckle Aunt Bess gave clearly demonstrated how little she thought of Emma's intelligence.

Despite Emma's resolve that she'd done the right thing, her cheeks burned with humiliation. Even if she had been swindled, she'd like to think her sacrifice had been worthwhile.

Olivia ran suddenly into the kitchen and launched herself into Emma's lap where she lay her head on Emma's shoulder.

Her hair smelled different—no longer of the subtle milk-and-honey, but an herbal fragrance like lavender and rosemary. The scent was not unpleasant, but nor was it familiar.

"I'm happy to have you here." Olivia looked up with a grin, revealing that fully grown tooth once more, leaving Emma to wonder what else had changed about her child since she rode off on the bus with the other evacuees.

"After breakfast, you should show your mum all your presents." Aunt Bess broke a couple of eggs into a skillet and threw a conspiratorial look over her shoulder at Emma. "A lot of the evacuees here have been getting knitted jumpers and the like. Not really a proper gift, I say. I wanted to ensure my Olivia had a lovely Christmas."

Emma's stomach sank right down to her aching, blistered

toes. "Oh. How very thoughtful of you," she stammered. "Thank you."

It did not escape her notice that Aunt Bess referred to Emma's daughter as "my Olivia," and Emma's hackles rose.

Olivia was *her* daughter. No part of Olivia belonged to this woman who clearly found Emma wanting in so many ways.

Breakfast was a hearty assortment of sausage, eggs, bacon, thick-cut toast with a slab of fresh butter melting over the golden bread, and all the tea Emma could stomach. With such a filling meal, she found the weight of her exhaustion crushing her eyelids closed.

She squelched a yawn. "Forgive me, I believe I must have a lie down."

"After Olivia shows you her gifts." Aunt Bess nodded at Olivia. "I know how excited she's been."

"Yes, please just a moment more, Mum." Olivia pulled Emma's arm to draw her up from her seat.

Already smiling at her daughter's enthusiasm, Emma allowed herself to be tugged upstairs to Olivia's bedchamber. The room was grand, with a brass bed adorned with a pristine white coverlet, and floral wallpaper that made the paintings of peonies on the wall stand out with a lovely vibrant pink.

"She gave me a proper dollhouse, with furniture and dolls and the whole lot." Olivia sank onto her knees and gazed imploringly at Emma. "Will you play with me, Mum?"

"Your mum needs to rest," Aunt Bess said from the doorway.

Emma spun around in surprise. She hadn't even heard the other woman approach.

"But perhaps you'd like to receive your present from her first?" Aunt Bess nodded at Emma.

The elation of presenting Olivia with the red jumper Emma had spent so much time knitting now plummeted, weighed down by the flippant criticism cast by Aunt Bess.

Emma tried to wave off the idea. "That isn't necessary—"

"Nonsense. You want your gift, don't you, Olivia?"

"Please, Mum." Olivia turned her large eyes toward Emma. "May I have my gift now?"

Emma's full stomach churned. All she had was the jumper she'd knitted. What had seemed such a perfect present now felt paltry. At least Mrs. Pickering's chocolate would be well received.

A hollowness ached within Emma as she offered a tight smile. "It's in my suitcase by the door." She pushed up to standing, all stiff legs and sore feet, and went to retrieve the paper-wrapped parcel.

She took her time returning upstairs with her simple present.

But Olivia clapped when she saw the gift and bounced excitedly where she sat in front of the grand dollhouse. "Thank you so much, Mummy. I know I'll love it."

Likely Aunt Bess would be smirking when Olivia opened her present. But Emma wasn't looking at the old woman as Olivia carefully pulled back the printed paper; she was watching her daughter, the delight in her blue eyes and the anticipation on her face.

A flash of red came into view and Olivia sucked in a breath. The jumper came tumbling out of its wrap, the shoulders clutched in Olivia's hands.

"You bought the jumper at Woolworths," Olivia squealed.

"No," Emma confessed. "I went to purchase it and they had none left. So, I knitted it instead."

Olivia lowered the jumper and blinked. "You hate knitting."

"But I love you," Emma said tenderly. "I knew how much you wanted it."

Tears shone in Olivia's eyes and she hugged the jumper against her chest like something precious. "Thank you." She leaped up and rushed to Emma, nearly knocking her over with the force of her embrace. In Emma's ear, she whisper-breathed in perhaps far too loud a voice, "It's the best present I've ever had."

Emma held her daughter to her, grateful for every painstaking stitch and restitch she'd done on the jumper, and grateful Olivia was in a place that was loving and supportive.

She only hoped it wouldn't have to be for much longer and that Olivia could soon return home.

18

TWO DAYS WITH Olivia passed far too quickly for Emma's liking. All too soon, she was on the slow journey back to Nottingham on trains lit with that odd blue light and past stations with names hidden away. With each kilometer put between them, the ache in Emma's heart grew more palpable.

Seeing her daughter had been bliss and pain all at once. Not because of Aunt Bess, though the woman's interactions with Emma had been truly unkind. But having to leave so soon after being reunited tore open the wound in Emma's chest anew. What had passed for a tolerable life while Emma waited for Olivia's return promised to once more be excruciating.

Dread followed her onto the first train, then to the second, and on through the walk home to the tenement house on Mooregate Street. The hour was late due to the delays and she had only her hooded torch to guide the lonely trek home. The dark flat awaited her like a lurking monster, its vast emptiness ready to swallow her whole.

Her feet echoed off the wooden floors as she entered and went about in near darkness, flicking the blackout curtains closed with a precision created by months of the repeated gesture. She clicked on the lights and her mouth fell open.

There, on the dining room table, was a centerpiece made of pine boughs and gold ribbon along with three wrapped parcels. A note propped in front of the cheerful display had her name written in Mrs. Pickering's careful script.

Mrs. Taylor,
I hope your trip was a delight and cannot wait to hear every detail. We missed you at Christmas, and Margaret and I wanted you to know we were thinking of you. Welcome home.
   Tea tomorrow?
With great affection,
Mrs. Pickering
P.S. Mr. Sanderson questioned our going into your flat and insisted on adding something.

Mr. Sanderson brought her something as well? Emma smiled to herself, moved by the thoughtfulness of her friends.

She took each wrapped parcel in her hands, turning it this way and that before finally pulling off the paper, savoring every moment.

There was a new book from Margaret—a brand-new copy of *Lady Chatterley's Lover* with a cheeky note stating that if it was good enough for the likes of Mr. Fisk, it was jolly well good enough for Emma.

Mr. Sanderson's parcel was large and heavy. Emma didn't lift the item from the table for fear of it slipping from her hands through the paper. She pulled back the wrap and sucked in a breath of surprise.

A wireless set.

It was an older model, the face somewhat scuffed, but when she clicked it on and slowly adjusted the worn knob, the static crackling from the speaker cleared into the sound of a piano being played in a studio somewhere, the audio crisp and clear.

The music filled the silence of the flat as Emma drew Mrs. Pickering's gift toward her. Another book, by the heft and shape.

The note on the top indicated she would have purchased Emma a kettle, but she enjoyed their tea together far too much. Additionally, it explained that the gift had been suggested by Olivia.

When had they conspired this idea together?

Emma pulled off the paper and stifled a sob.

The first edition of *Alice's Adventures in Wonderland*, pristine save for a dent at the bottom of the cover.

This was *her* copy, the one she'd bought with her father before his death, one of the few books that remained of his legacy. The exact one she had pawned.

She hugged the book to her chest and embraced all the memories of her father—not only from when he'd found the book, but all the ones before that for as far back as she could remember.

She regarded the wireless set once more. Such a gift was truly a treasure. Far too much for her to accept from someone she didn't know particularly well. And while Mr. Sanderson claimed he already had a wireless set, she hadn't seen one in his sparse apartment.

The next day, she climbed the stairs and rapped on Mr. Sanderson's door. It opened to reveal his wizened face, his gaze narrowing with suspicion. "What do you want?"

"I wanted to thank you for your present, Mr. Sanderson. It was so immensely generous of you, but I really cannot accept such an expensive gift."

He grunted. "It was rubbish. Someone had it on the pavement to toss out. I only fixed it up for you. Not a halfpenny spent."

He had done that, for her?

"That was so kind of you. And you already have a wireless?" She peered around him to confirm he did have a set in his home. She could not take one and leave him without.

He shifted to block her view. "Hearing the radio downstairs will be better than listening to you cry all night."

His words were like a slap and she blinked at the sting of them.

"I'm terribly sorry, I didn't realize..." She searched the air as if the proper thing to say might leap out and present itself.

It did not, and she was left momentarily dumbfounded.

"Well. I'm glad you like the wireless. Keep it. Good day." Mr. Sanderson paused. "Mind your conversations. The government uses those confounded things to record everything you say." Then he tapped his temple and pushed the door closed. Not aggressively, but firmly enough to let Emma know she was not welcome.

But even as he did so, Emma couldn't help but notice that the draft of the door closing so swiftly carried the distinct aroma of fresh tea being brewed.

Emma was not put out that Mr. Sanderson had not invited her in for tea, not when she had a longstanding appointment each morning and then again after work with Mrs. Pickering. And while his words had been harsh, there was little truth to them. Yes, she had cried terribly that first month after Olivia was evacuated, but as life pressed on and she'd known Olivia was happy, her maudlin sorrow abated.

He'd simply said that...why?

To be unkind? To keep his prickly heart safely guarded?

Likely the latter considering the generosity of the gift.

Determined to keep the wireless, she would need to register the device with the government by law, as all wireless owners were required to do.

She was still puzzling over Mr. Sanderson's words when she swept down the stairs to Mrs. Pickering's flat. "Thank you for the generous gift. It's truly precious to me." She embraced her friend at the open doorway. "Your surprise made coming home alone so much less bleak." Her words caught and Mrs. Pickering squeezed her even more tightly, embracing her in the familiar rose perfume.

Tubby raced by Emma's feet into the hall as Mrs. Pickering turned toward the kitchen.

As she'd always done in the past, Emma pushed open the door to the tenement house for the little dog to run about in the gated garden while they had tea.

When Emma returned, Mrs. Pickering sank into her chair with a steaming cup in front of her, and propped her elbows on the table, chin in her palms. "Now tell me everything."

Emma did exactly as instructed, sharing about how much Olivia loved the jumper, and, of course, all about Aunt Bess.

"What a wretch of a woman." Mrs. Pickering set her empty teacup down with a hard clink. "It's a good thing she cares well for Olivia, or I'd be there myself with a thing or two to say."

The bell to the tenement house rang out in shrill notes.

Mrs. Pickering frowned. "Who could that be?"

Together they rose from the table and hurried to the main door.

Mrs. Mott from next door stood in the doorway with Tubby in her arms and a glower on her face. "Your dog has escaped again."

She shoved Tubby into Mrs. Pickering's arms. Oblivious to his offense, his whip of a tail swept back and forth as he excitedly bestowed flicking licks at his owner's face. She tried to pull away from the affectionate assault. "I don't know how he managed his way out of the flat."

"I let him out, I didn't realize the gate was open..." Emma trailed off as she looked behind the woman to where the gate was not left open, but missing entirely. "What happened to the gate?"

"Spitfires and ammo." Mrs. Pickering sighed. "They showed up while you were visiting Olivia and ran right off with the gate."

"And your dog has been roaming the neighborhood ever since," Mrs. Mott said in a churlish tone. "I don't know why you didn't put him down when pet owners were ordered to do so."

Mrs. Pickering blanched. The order had been appalling when issued several months back, citing the need for food for humans to be more important than what animals might consume. Mrs. Pickering had tossed the missive in the rubbish bin, her eyes blazing as she declared she herself would go hungry before she'd let any harm come to Tubby.

Emma stepped in. "Thank you for bringing him back, Mrs. Mott. The fault is entirely mine. I'll ensure not to repeat the mistake."

"See that you don't." Mrs. Mott sniffed and spun away on her heel.

Emma stared after the woman. Of all the children Olivia mentioned being cruel to her at school, Mrs. Mott's Edmund was the child Olivia spoke of most. Frustration and rage flickered to life in Emma's chest.

But she turned from the woman and put a hand to Mrs. Pickering's shoulder, leading her friend back into the flat, and apologizing again.

On the way to Boots' the following morning, Emma passed a woman pushing a pram who held the hand of a little girl.

On the next street, two boys were being rushed out the door by their mother with instructions for what to buy from the baker's. An older woman sat on a nearby stoop with several children gathered around. They were all bundled up against the icy, late-December morning air as they listened to her with rapt attention.

Not everyone had sent their children away for the evacuation, but enough had that seeing so many mites about the city was rather uncommon. Christmas had already passed and the new year was upon them. Perhaps parents were waiting to send their children back after the holidays.

Or perhaps the children were not going to be sent back.

Perhaps Olivia didn't need to be with Aunt Bess any longer. After all, the war had amounted to nothing so far. The fighting was relegated to Poland, those poor people. England had been left unscathed. Already they were almost four months into their declaration of war and still not a whisper of retaliation from Hitler.

Another woman strode past, holding the gloved hand of a girl who looked the spitting image of her and chattered on animatedly in the way that little girls do.

Emma's longing for her daughter hit with with a visceral pang, for the rapid-fire way she spoke, going so fast she almost stumbled over her own words like they were ready to run away without her.

Emma smiled to herself.

Maybe the time had come for Olivia to return home.

19

JANUARY BROUGHT LOWER temperatures to an already frigid winter as well as the enforcement of rations. Emma regarded the book of coupons with a sigh.

National Coupon Day made that Monday sound like a fun event. It would be anything but now that she could only shop at the corner grocery near work where she'd registered. She couldn't deviate from that shop if she intended to follow the rules, and Emma had always been a rule follower.

Morning tea wouldn't be the same with the sugar ration, but thank goodness the government hadn't rationed tea. Such a thought was truly appalling.

She passed the grocer on her way to work that morning and found a queue of women already waiting for their first week's allotment. Hopefully the crowd would be cleared in the evening on her way home.

Margaret was already in the library when Emma arrived and offered a gentle smile. "How did things go in East Anglia?"

The ache of missing Olivia crushed against Emma anew, so brilliant that it robbed her breath for a jarring moment. Emma nodded, unable to speak.

"I know. It's harder when they go after you've seen them."

Margaret looked down at her slender hand where the diamond glittered on her finger. "I saw Jeffrey, he surprised us all by coming home for Christmas. He said he wanted to set a date."

Emma sighed, understanding her friend's hesitation. "I'm sorry."

"It's so frustrating." Margaret's eyes glossed with tears. "I love him, I do…"

"Have you explained to him that you don't want to give up your position here?"

Margaret swiped at an errant tear and swiftly glanced to Miss Bainbridge's office to ensure the action hadn't been seen. "I've tried but he says that he wants to ensure I'll be cared for if…" She swallowed. "If he dies." She put a hand over the lower half of her face, as if her sobs could be physically held back.

The government took care of war widows in a way widows of men who were hit by cars were not. Jeffrey was correct in knowing Margaret would be seen to if he died after they wed. And yet, in garnering such security, Margaret would have to give up a job that would keep her financially stable as well.

The unfairness of what women endured blazed in Emma— that women had to sacrifice careers they enjoyed, being forced into the home simply because of marriage. Or women who companies refused to hire because they were widows with children, women who had done what society asked and married, quit their jobs, had children—only to be punished in the end.

Men weren't stifled by such restrictions, nor were they reduced to having to lie about their marriages or children to secure employment just to have enough money to put food on the table.

Emma stated none of this. Margaret needed support, not fire. "We would miss you terribly here, but you know I will stand by you either way."

Somewhere in the distance, a door closed and Margaret snapped upright as she swiped at her tears.

Miss Bainbridge entered the library floor and summoned them over with a wave of her hand. "I'd like to speak with you all."

Beside Emma, Margaret stiffened slightly, clearly thinking herself in trouble.

Miss Crane joined them, the three of them gathering around the Class A subscriber desk.

"I have something very serious I must discuss." Miss Bainbridge paused to meet each one of their gazes.

When her gray eyes landed on Emma's, a little chill trickled its way down her spine like a droplet of cold water sliding down the channel of her back. Perhaps the manageress had seen Margaret on the verge of tears. Or perhaps she had picked up Emma's own quiet suffering and feared how subscribers might feel about being assisted by England's saddest librarians.

"Boots' library detectives will be arriving later on today," Miss Bainbridge said. "They will be investigating a recent incident."

"Is it for all the misshelved books?" Miss Crane asked.

Emma didn't have to turn to know the other woman was sneering at her. Her scorn was evident in the nasty tone of her voice.

"Misshelved books...?" Miss Bainbridge spoke slowly, somewhat perplexed. Then the confusion cleared from her face in a dawning moment of realization. "Oh, good heavens, no. Nothing of that sort. No, there was a break-in at the warehouse. The detectives want to investigate to ensure nothing untoward is transpiring in the library as well.

"As I said, they will be arriving this afternoon, and be attired in civilian clothing to blend in," Miss Bainbridge continued. "The goal is to allow them to conduct their investigation without causing alarm or upsetting our subscribers. Likely they will speak to each of you in turn, so please do be cooperative and answer all their questions. Is that understood?"

They nodded.

"Good. You may resume your morning tasks."

When the library detectives did finally arrive, telling them apart from the usual subscribers was impossible. The only way Emma noticed one—a tall, thin man with a heavy mustache—was because he arrived that morning and then reappeared again that afternoon.

Should she approach him? Was she supposed to pretend he was invisible and ignore him? Or should she treat him like any other customer and help him blend in?

There was a crime afoot and these detectives were scrutinizing the details. Detectives who would be questioning her. It was rather exciting, really. Like being part of one of the many mystery books she read.

She regarded the man carefully as she approached. "May I help you, sir?" she asked, trying to sound casual.

"I'm merely looking, thank you."

Behind him, Mr. Beard snapped out his notebook and licked his pencil before jotting something.

The detective eyed Mr. Beard warily before stopping at the next shelf to inspect the books. But as thrilling as the encounter had begun, nothing seemed to come of it.

At least, not until that evening as Emma was preparing to leave for the day, when the mustached man entered the area reserved for employees. "Miss Taylor, might I speak with you a moment?"

Emma's stomach fluttered with anxious uncertainty to be so called out.

He must have read the nervousness on her face as he offered

a kind smile. "I simply need to ask after several subscribers. I'm Mr. Gibbs, library detective for Boots'."

Library detective—what an exciting-sounding title.

Emma allowed him to lead her to Miss Bainbridge's office. He took the manageress's seat and indicated the chair opposite. She settled in the familiar hard surface of the wooden seat.

Mr. Gibbs flipped open a small notebook not unlike Mr. Beard's. "Have you noticed anyone unusual in the library?"

"There are always unusual people from time to time…" Emma hedged, thinking of Mrs. Chatsworth toting Pip about in a basket at her arm.

The warm chuckle Mr. Gibbs gave surprised Emma. Weren't detectives supposed to be terribly serious? He seemed most genial.

"What about the man with the notebook?" he asked.

"That's Mr. Beard. He's been writing in it since I've known him."

"Do you know why?"

That was a great question. Emma hesitated, trying to recall the times she'd seen Mr. Beard write and guess as to what he might be doing. "I'm not entirely certain. It might be research on books. But I do believe he also records people's conversations."

Mr. Gibbs's eyebrows were as thick and dark as his mustache and they lifted up into his forehead. "Recording people's conversations?"

"Perhaps," Emma replied in a noncommittal tone. "I've never asked him."

Mr. Gibbs wrote something in his book and looked up. "Do you think you might?"

Did he suspect Mr. Beard of being the person who'd broken into the warehouse? Emma could scarcely imagine Mr. Beard, with his tweed jackets and rounded belly, smuggling himself into the warehouse.

Emma nodded. "Of course, I'll speak with him the next chance I have. Anything I can do to help."

After work, Emma stopped by the grocer with her new ration book, but though she had coupons and the money to afford the items, there was no sugar or meat to be had. With a can of tinned fish in her shopping basket and a loaf of day-old bread, she headed home.

Mr. Beard didn't come to the lending library for several days. No doubt affording him just enough time to read the latest mystery he'd been willingly badgered into borrowing.

When Emma finally caught sight of him, she strode over in the most casual manner she could muster.

"I imagine you've received more of these brain-rotting reads." He scornfully waved a hand to the mystery section, eyes bright with interest.

"There is one by Agatha Christie I recently read, *Murder on the Orient Express*." She selected the book from its place on the shelf. "A murder takes place on a train, then they become stranded when the engine blows and a blizzard hits."

"And they must uncover the murderer before he kills again, I presume?"

Emma smiled. "Precisely."

He leaned closer toward the book. "Sounds dreadful."

"So much so that I read it in one day." She tsked.

He reached for the book, but she drew it back slightly. "Do you record all the books you read in your notebook? Is that why you're always writing in it?"

He furrowed his brow and then glanced down at his breast pocket where the little notebook peeked out. "I...uh...actually, I'm with the Mass Observation."

"Mass Observation?"

"Yes. I'm to record the world as I see it as a means of charting life during the war. I write down prices of items, the general mood of people in regard to the events transpiring around them. And, of course, the weather."

Mrs. Chatsworth stood nearby and spun round suddenly. "Is that why you listen in on people's conversations?"

Mr. Beard cleared his throat. "Well, yes."

"Seems an invasion of people's privacy to me." Mrs. Chatsworth sniffed. It was quite a claim when most of her ramblings had to do with the affairs of those around her and neighbors she had never met.

"You do this every day?" she pressed.

Mr. Beard regarded her with sincerity. "Without fail, madam."

Secretly, Emma was glad for Mrs. Chatsworth's interjection into the conversation—it meant there would be less for Emma to ask. If nothing else, the other woman's interference helped to absolve Emma of any suspicion Mr. Beard may have at her random questioning.

"And why in heaven's name would you spend your time recording people's discussions and all these events with this... this phoney war." Mrs. Chatsworth adjusted the basket from one arm to the other as Pip continued to sleep on soundly.

"Historians will look back on this someday with keen interest." Mr. Beard puffed out his chest.

Mrs. Chatsworth chuckled and the dog in her basket pricked his ears at the interruption to his slumber. "You think they'll be interested in your diary?"

Mr. Beard's face flushed. "As a matter of fact, I do."

"I'm sure the information will be of value to people in the future." Emma smiled at Mr. Beard, feeling slightly sorry for the older man under Mrs. Chatsworth's assault. "Maybe even an author writing about this time period someday?"

"Why the devil would anyone do that?" Mr. Beard asked.

Emma simply shrugged and held up *Murder on the Orient Express.* "Let's get this checked out for you."

That evening at home, Emma found an official-looking letter from Mr. Boydell, the evacuation officer for Nottingham, who also served as the city's treasurer. Emma had heard nothing from Olivia in the last week and nothing from Aunt Bess since the visit at Christmas. Olivia's last letter hadn't indicated anything of concern.

Mr. Boydell couldn't be replying to her request for Olivia to return home, as Emma had not finished the letter yet.

Whatever information the missive contained, the sinking sensation in Emma's stomach told her the letter's arrival was indeed bad news.

20

EMMA STIRRED A bit of rationed sugar into her tea, the spoon clinking against one of Mrs. Pickering's rose-painted teacups.

"Sounds like Aunt Bess got a bit of what she deserves," Mrs. Pickering said bitterly as she added an extra lump of sugar to her own tea.

Somehow the ration had given Mrs. Pickering a taste for sugar she hadn't possessed before. As if scarcity made the commodity more desireable.

"Oh, Mrs. Pickering," Emma chided. "The woman is seriously ill. We ought to have kind thoughts for her."

"Bah." Mrs. Pickering batted a hand in the air. "She's a wretched person whose body finally caught up with her spirit. Anyway, she's the least of my concerns. What will you do about Olivia?"

Emma fingered the letter. "I'm going to bring her home."

Mrs. Pickering set her tea down just as she was prepared to take a sip and grinned. "It will be good to have her back. And anyway, there is nothing happening with this war."

★ ★ ★

After Emma reported her findings on Mr. Beard to the library detective at Boots', she notified the evacuation officer she'd be bringing Olivia back to Nottingham and secured several days off from work to collect her daughter.

Thankfully the trains were not as delayed as they had been during Christmas, though there were still more soldiers coming and going than civilians. This time, Emma didn't bother with fashionable style, opting for conventional flats rather than the low heels she'd ruined on her last journey.

When she knocked on Aunt Bess's door, a middle-aged woman with the same pinched face as Aunt Bess answered the door.

"Are you the girl's mother?" she demanded.

"Olivia? Yes, I'm her mother."

The woman opened the door. "Not a day too soon. We can't keep her, you understand. Not with Mum to look after these days."

Two children ran through the living room, their steps so hard that a lamp rattled on its small wooden table by the sofa.

"Enough," the woman called to the children, who chased one another into a different room rather than obeying her. With a sigh, she shifted her focus to the stairs and bellowed, "Olivia."

Olivia came down with a solemn expression. She wore the red jumper Emma had knit for her, arms crossed over her chest as if hugging it closer to her. Her face lit up as soon as she saw Emma.

They met midway on the stairs, where Olivia clung to Emma with a ferociousness that would make any mother's heart break. A shudder rippled through Olivia's small body and Emma realized her daughter had begun to cry.

Emma held her for longer than was necessary and added

cheerfully. "Why don't you lead me to your room so we can pack your things?"

Without waiting for her daughter to answer, Emma shepherded her upstairs. Olivia left her face pressed against Emma, clearly embarrassed by her tears. The few belongings the children had been instructed to travel with when evacuated made easy work of repacking.

"She can't bring the dollhouse."

Emma looked up to find Aunt Bess's daughter standing in the doorway with her arms crossed over her chest. "I need that for my children."

Olivia didn't protest, clearly resigned to the injustice.

"By all means," Emma replied as nicely as she could.

Olivia strode to the woman, and gazed up imploringly. "May I say goodbye to Aunt Bess?"

"She's not your aunt, but yes, you may," the woman replied.

Emma took the suitcase and followed Olivia from the room and down the hall.

Aunt Bess sat in a wheelchair, wearing a robe over her nightdress. Her white hair was unbound and flowed like pulled cotton around her shoulders. The woman who had been sharp with judgment and hard-flung castigation had softened with the illness. She looked old. Feeble.

Emma suddenly found herself sympathetic for the older woman who had opened her home to a little girl no one else had wanted and made her feel loved.

That little girl now spoke softly with Aunt Bess before giving her a gentle hug. Emma knelt by the wheelchair to put herself eye level with the other woman. There was a pallor of sickness to Aunt Bess's lined face and her eyes were moist with tears.

Emma took Aunt Bess's soft, dry hand in her own. "Thank you for caring for Olivia so well. She has loved her time with you and will forever have happy memories of your lovely home."

The older woman smiled and closed her eyes. A tear ran down her cheek.

Emma patted her hand and rose to leave. With a final glance back, she took Olivia's hand and they left the house to make their way to the train station.

Thankfully the journey home went quickly. When they reached their street, Olivia paused on the pavement, her gaze snagging on the large rectangular buildings meant to be shelters in the event of a bombing. The walls were constructed of two layers of brick, and their ceilings were made of thick slab concrete. Whatever caused Olivia to hesitate was short-lived and she raced past the shelters, barely bothering to look at the missing gates of the tenement house before sprinting up the three stairs.

Inside, Tubby's shrill barks were pitched with unmitigated joy. Within seconds, they were in Mrs. Pickering's flat, enjoying a tearful reunion peppered with exclamations of how lovely the jumper looked on Olivia. When enough hugs had been given—for the time being—and promises were made to come to dinner that evening, Emma led her daughter upstairs.

Finally, Olivia was home.

She stood at the threshold for a moment, staring at the flat, nearly a quarter of the size of the house she'd been living in.

A moment of apprehension passed over Emma. That their small flat might be disappointing by comparison. That maybe Olivia was heartbroken to give up the fine furnishings and fancy toys.

Olivia sniffed and Emma saw that she was crying.

"I'm sorry, my love," she said gently. "I know our home isn't as grand…"

But Olivia shook her head. "It smells the same, like toast and jam. Everything is exactly as I remember." She chuckled, even as she wept. "It's perfect, Mum, and it feels so, so good to be home."

Emma hugged her daughter to her. But even as she did, a niggling fear worried the back of her mind.

What had been a quiet start to the war could still very well become dangerous. She could only hope keeping Olivia home was the right decision.

21

WITH ONE MORE day off from work at her disposal, Emma took Olivia with her to queue for their rations. By going earlier, Emma was able to secure sugar and meat for them both for the next few days.

However, while they were out, Emma couldn't help but notice the way several women stared at her, their attention brimming with scorn.

Olivia was thankfully oblivious, but Emma was intensely aware of every mother who was without their child glaring in their direction. Rather than allow their anger to sink into her, she clasped Olivia's warm hand in hers and reveled in the knowledge that her daughter was finally home.

Much to Olivia's chagrin, she would be returning to school starting the following day. At least for the morning. Teachers were still in the country with evacuated students, which left very few remaining in the city to instruct the children. As a result, school was only in session for half the day, with some students taught in the morning and others in the afternoon.

Which meant Olivia would have to walk home from her new school on her own after lessons and would be alone in the afternoons now that Mrs. Pickering had become so involved with the WVS.

The following morning, Emma walked Olivia to school before her work shift and pointed out landmarks to ensure her daughter might easily find her way home afterward. Despite her careful details and Olivia having seemed to be paying attention, a number of fears raced through Emma's mind as she hurried to work.

Miss Bainbridge welcomed them all with her usual pot of tea and hot chocolate, which Emma now took advantage of in an effort calm her fraying nerves.

"I should like to inform you that the library detectives have taken their leave," Miss Bainbridge said.

"Did they find out what happened?" Margaret asked, worrying the diamond ring on her finger with the pad of her thumb.

Miss Bainbridge sighed. "They discovered the culprit to be a man who was far too eager to read a new mystery that was coming out and couldn't stand to wait another week to get his hands on it."

"Too bad we can't put that into an advertisement," Margaret quipped. "So good, you'll break in to read it."

Miss Crane rolled her eyes, but Emma laughed and even Miss Bainbridge chuckled.

"Still," the manageress chided. "We should be mindful to keep an eye on the Bespoke Room and our warehouse to ensure we don't have any overzealous subscribers trying to sneak in for an early peek."

With more subscribers to look after these days and many new faces, the request was entirely valid. The lending library had been excessively busy after Christmas with so many people having received subscriptions as gifts.

Even as work hummed with activity, Emma had half her focus on the clock. When noon came and went, her mind churned with worry. Had Olivia returned home safely? There were many corners to take on the way to the school. Had she remembered them all?

As Emma's concern fluttered around Olivia, her body moved in automatic motions, setting books on shelves almost without thought. At least until she realized the red label book that had been in her basket of return items was no longer there, and she had not been back into the Bespoke Room.

Her heart lurched.

A red label book should never be on the floor under any circumstances.

Emma retraced her steps, desperately seeking the mislaid item. To no avail.

"Are you quite all right, dear?"

Emma looked up to find Mrs. Chatsworth regarding her with concern. Pip slept soundly on his blue pillow in her basket.

Out of the corner of Emma's eye, she was relieved to see the brilliant red label against the row of green spines. "Just a book out of place." The classics, of all places. Emma swiped the book quickly from its errant location.

Thank heavens Mr. Beard hadn't seen it or she'd never hear the end of his tirade.

"A book out of place?" Mrs. Chatsworth's eyes widened and the feather on her scarlet pillbox hat quivered. "How could something such as a misplaced book possibly happen in the Booklover's Library?"

Emma tucked the book behind her back and opened her mouth even before she could come up with a reply.

Not that a reply was necessary. Mrs. Chatsworth was already answering the question herself with a dignified tilt to her chin. "I daresay the infraction was likely a subscriber."

Alarm shot through Emma. Subscribers were to be treated

with exceptional care, not decried as leaving the shelves disorganized. "No, I don't think—"

"I don't know how someone could do that." Mrs. Chatsworth tsked. "We all love an organized library where we can find the books we want."

"I don't think—"

Mrs. Chatsworth patted Emma's shoulder in a comforting gesture that left a powdery scent in her wake. "You're doing a wonderful job, Miss Taylor. Don't you dare let anyone else tell you otherwise."

Reassurances made, woman and dog turned away with a book in hand, heading toward the Class A subscriber desk.

At least this time, Emma did know the misshelved book to be entirely her fault.

That could have been disastrous.

For the rest of the day, she forced herself to focus, to ensure no more mistakes could be made. While Emma didn't have to pay the government the stipend for Olivia's billeting any longer—a shilling a week more than Emma received for her daughter's pension—they still needed the money from her job.

Once Emma was finally relieved of her daily shift, she ran out of the chemist shop so quickly, she almost forgot to remove the green overalls from her dress.

Though the winter day was a fine one, with a bit of sun to ease the bite from the frigid January chill, she took the bus to ensure she arrived home quickly. Pent-up energy vibrated through her as her mind flip-flopped at the certainty that Olivia was perfectly fine and catastrophizing over worst-case scenarios.

What if Olivia fell and was bleeding and in need of help?

What if someone forced their way into the tenement house and was trying to break into their flat?

Her blood ran cold and the leg she had been unintentionally jiggling went still.

What if there was a fire? What if Olivia was in a burning building too long, breathing in too much smoke? Like Papa.

If Emma hadn't been stranded on the bus, she would have run the rest of the way home. Now she was trapped, forced into a brutal wait.

The bus pulled up to Mooregate Street and the breath rushed from Emma's lungs in relief. The tenement house was still standing. No plumes of black smoke billowed from the aged building, no sirens blared in the distance.

How foolish it was, the way she spoon-fed her fears.

Emma had never been the type to envision every horrible scenario that might happen. Not until she became a mother. Not until she loved someone so completely, wholly, and wonderfully the way she did Olivia.

A child became a mother's world, filling her days and simultaneously filling her heart. Feeding, clothing, playing, laughing, living, cherishing, loving.

Emma exited the bus, feeling rather sheepish over her concerns, and entered the perfectly safe building. The click of her shoes echoed on the stairwell around her as she climbed to the second floor and unlocked the door.

"Olive," she sang out, a smile on her lips.

There was no reply.

Despite her self-castigation over her fruitless fears, terror once more curled icy fingers around her heart. Sunlight streamed in through the filmy screens covering the windows, highlighting dust motes as they lazily floated in the quiet, still living area.

There was no discarded bag from school, no toed-off shoes lying hazardously in front of the door, no coat slung over the sofa.

"Olivia, this had better not be a joke." But Olivia didn't joke. Not like this. Not when she knew how terrified it would make Emma.

Two years earlier, they'd been at the Market Square when Olivia ran off to look at a shop window displaying a doll she'd fancied. Emma hadn't known she was gone and raced round the entire square, screaming for Olivia like a madwoman. When they were finally reunited, Emma had been so distraught that Olivia promised to never give her cause for such fear again.

Emma rushed into their shared room now, her pulse coming faster as she found it empty. Calling again and again for her daughter, Emma ran from room to room in the small flat, heart thundering as each space met her with silence. As the horrifying realization dawned.

Olivia was not home.

22

EMMA SEARCHED THE surrounding streets at a frantic pace, hoping to find Olivia. Hoping that perhaps she had decided to play with some of the neighborhood children. With so many having returned home from the evacuation and school only being on for half the day, they'd taken to roaming the street.

Maybe Olivia had been persuaded to join them.

But Emma's gut reminded her how entirely atypical it would be of Olivia to do so.

After an hour of Emma's fruitless search and desperation settling in like a dark, ominous cloud, she hastened back to the tenement house to see if Mrs. Pickering had returned home to enlist for help. And possibly Mr. Sanderson.

She might even implore Mrs. Mott for assistance.

Emma's heart thumped harder with resolve.

She would ask the very devil himself if he would help her find Olivia.

As Emma tugged open the door to their building, the sound of voices echoed down the stairwell.

"When do you think she'll be back?" a woman asked, her

voice saccharine with barely concealed impatience as adults sometimes do when speaking with children.

"Soon." The uncertain reply was Olivia's.

Emma launched herself up the stairs. Her daughter stood by the door to their flat, her shoulders hunched forward, clearly displaying her discomfort. An older woman Emma had never seen before leaned over her daughter.

"Mum!" Olivia raced toward Emma, the echo of her clattering feet resounding through the narrow space.

Was it fear?

Emma hugged her daughter protectively to her and regarded the woman. "What's happened?"

"What's happened?" The woman had a slight underbite, causing her chin to thrust out with apparent disapproval. "You brought your child home from the country against the wishes of our government, and you cannot even properly care for her. I found this nipper wandering about the lace district, eyes as big as saucers and brimming with tears. Near broke my heart, it did. I had no choice but to take her in and try to find where her mam was. And here you are, just now returning home."

Emma's cheeks blazed. "I was out looking for her."

"I'm surprised she wasn't running about with the others whose neglectful parents kept them in Nottingham. Those wild packs of children." The woman fisted her hands on her hips. "Why weren't you at the school to collect her like a good mother ought to?"

Like a good mother ought to.

The words sliced deeper than Emma cared to admit.

"Instead you left this little one to roam about the streets, lost and alone," the woman continued. "Anything might've happened to her. Anything. Haven't you a care for her safety?"

Emma opened her mouth, but the words to defend herself stuck in her throat.

What was her excuse? That she'd been working? Mothers weren't supposed to work. They were supposed to stay home with their children.

To protect them.

"What's all this?" a gruff male voice demanded.

Mr. Sanderson strode stiffly down the last several stairs to the second landing.

Whatever had been roaring in Emma's ears had clearly blocked out the sound of his descent.

"This." The woman pointed a finger at Emma. "Is an inept mother."

Emma sucked in a breath. The woman had gone too far.

Mr. Sanderson took a step toward the woman. "Is that what this nattering on is about? Your bloody judgment?"

Color rose in the woman's cheeks and her underbite jutted out in stubborn defiance. "She shouldn't have her daughter here, not when the children are supposed to be sent away. It's unpatriotic."

Mr. Sanderson took another step closer. Despite his age, he cut an intimidating figure with his height well over a head above the woman and his face as ruddy as a rugby player's. "Your lack of support for a fellow neighbor in a time of war is unpatriotic. Now get out."

The woman opened her mouth to protest.

"Get out," Mr. Sanderson bellowed. "Or I'll call the constable to force you out."

"Some thank you." The woman drew herself up with a harrumph and glared at Emma as she passed. "And some mother."

Emma kept her stare level on the woman, refusing to drop her gaze. But she wanted to. With hurt. With shame.

Mr. Sanderson waited until the door to the tenement house swung open and slammed shut.

"Good riddance to that old pigeon." The brutish stance bled out of him, and he sagged forward, his shoulders wilting. He suddenly appeared a tired old man, defeated by whatever life had thrown his way.

"Thank you, Mr. Sanderson." Emma offered him a smile that seemed to wobble on her lips. "I—"

Mr. Sanderson waved a hand in the air and grunted, cutting her off. "I'm off to finish my nap."

Emma knew better than to argue or try to cajole him back. Instead, she shepherded her daughter into the flat and hugged her one more time, reassuring herself that Olivia was really there. Home and safe.

"Why did that woman say those horrible things to you, Mum?" Olivia blue eyes were sad with a wounded hurt that tugged at Emma's heart.

She knelt to be eye level with her daughter. "Some people have very strong opinions about what others should do with their children. And they're not always kind about what they say."

Olivia nodded, though Emma could tell she didn't understand.

And how could Emma explain what she herself could not fully comprehend how someone might so cruelly judge another without realizing their circumstances?

Emma was doing her best.

But what if her best wasn't good enough? What if *she* wasn't good enough?

"How was school?" she asked, desperate for a distraction.

"Edmund wasn't there, so I liked that." Olivia shrugged.

Edmund.

The very name made Emma clamp down her back teeth. Mrs. Mott's boy. The blight of Olivia's existence at school. There had been far too many days that she sobbed over things that boy had done. But every time Emma resolved to go next door and speak to Mrs. Mott, Olivia had blanched and begged her not to go.

Kids could be so brutally nasty to one another, and the inability to stop her daughter's bullying was a horrible, helpless feeling.

There had been far too many times Emma had seen Edmund playing in the street, kicking the ball too hard at other children and laughing when they fell, that she'd been sorely tempted to rush out and upbraid him for his boorish behavior. That was yet another thing Emma had never felt fully prepared for as a mother—how to handle those who hurt her child.

"What did you do today?" Emma carefully picked up Olivia's coat from where she'd dropped it next to the sofa and hung it on the hook by the door.

Olivia brightened. "We ran from the school."

"Ran from the school?" Emma paused as she bent to straighten Olivia's shoes.

"If a bomb comes, we don't have a basement to go into and there's no shelter near us, so we have to run."

Emma stood, giving her daughter her full attention. "I beg your pardon?"

Olivia pulled a glass from the drying rack next to the sink and went to the larder. "We're supposed to run to a house that has a basement. The teachers shout 'scatter' real loud and we all go, scattering about like ants."

Delight shone in Olivia's eyes as she spoke, but dread coursed through Emma. They were making a game of war.

If a bomb truly did come, what if there wasn't enough time for the children to properly "scatter"? And what of their safety once they were in a shelter or someone's home, away from a teacher's supervision?

"I'm glad it was so fun." Emma tried to mask the worry in her tone with a forced brightness as she opened the cabinet to withdraw a pan. They'd be having cottage pie with the meat she'd obtained the day before.

Not only was it Olivia's favorite dinner, the recipe was the first Emma had ever learned to cook and one of the three her father had known how to make. After over a decade of cottage pie, bangers and mash, and grabbing fish and chips from a corner stand—her father insisted that counted as a cooked meal—Emma had assumed the cooking duties for the household.

But even as Emma went through the motions of preparing a meal she could make in her sleep, the woman's words from that afternoon tumbled through her mind. They blended with the disdainful glares of other women and the appalling "scatter" method of the children running for safety in a school that was not prepared for an air raid.

And for the first time since bringing Olivia home, Emma's stomach twisted into a hard knot of regret.

23

A BOOK WAS MISSING.

Emma's gaze skimmed the spines in front of her. The new mystery had only just been put on the shelves the day before. There had been five copies. She learned four had been checked out after referring to the log.

She also knew with certainty that the title had not been mis-shelved by her. Over the last several weeks, she had been vigilant, going so far as to record the titles of each book she received to return to the floor. Truth be told, she reminded herself a bit of Mr. Beard, with a notebook tucked in her pocket and a little stub of a pencil that required a quick lick to get going.

"On second thought, I believe you might like a different book." Emma flashed a conspiratorial smile at the young woman. "Have you ever read *The Mask of Dimitrios*?"

The woman shook her head, and the wavy ends of her bobbed blond hair swept against her pearl earrings.

"It's a wild adventure," Emma gushed. "Not necessarily a mystery, but a page turner nonetheless. I read it a while ago, and still haven't been able to get the story out of my mind." Even just thinking of the spy novel and all the thrilling action made her pulse quicken. A good book could do that, and was one of the many things she was grateful to have rediscovered in her love of reading since working at the library.

"Oh?" The woman craned her neck with interest as Emma reached for the book. Properly shelved and available, thank goodness.

The woman accepted the item and ran her hand over the cover. "I'm recently married, you see. We were scarcely together three days before my husband was shipped out to some place he couldn't disclose. I've heard the post is slow to deliver and am not sure when I'll even get a letter." She looked down at the book again and swallowed. "I was a secretary, over at the Player's factory."

Emma nodded, recognizing the cigarette company's name. Player's was one of the prominent factories in Nottingham.

"But you know I couldn't keep my job…" The woman's gaze flicked to the wedding band on her left hand, the gold impossibly shiny, unscathed by the nicks of time and everyday use. "It's why my husband gave me this subscription for Christmas. He knew I'd be bored." She gave a nervous laugh that didn't reach her large, sad eyes.

"I think you'll very much enjoy this one." Emma smiled. "I found it a perfect diversion when I needed it most."

The woman brightened and the magic of finding just the right book for just the right person washed over Emma anew. She checked out the book for the young newlywed, pausing to loop the Class A subscriber tag into the small eyelet punctured at the top of the book's spine. "Enjoy."

The woman nodded her thanks and tucked the book into her handbag before departing.

Across the room, Margaret watched the woman solemnly and Emma didn't have to ask to know what her friend was thinking.

That young woman could have been Margaret.

Married and more alone than ever before.

After the new bride left, Emma discreetly scoured the shelves, seeking out the missing book. To no avail.

There was something amiss at the lending library. Nothing worth calling the library detectives over, but certainly worth investigating. Emma would get to the bottom of it.

On her walk home, she was still mulling over the puzzle of the missing book when she turned down her street to find a fire truck in front of the tenement house.

Fear clasped at her throat.

A fireman was bent over someone and stood to his full height, revealing Olivia at his side.

"Olivia," Emma cried, rushing to her daughter.

Olivia burst into tears. "I'm sorry, Mum. I'm so sorry. I only wanted to make some fried bread. I didn't know..."

"It's all right, love." Emma quickly examined her daughter, then hugged her tightly, allaying her own fears. "It's all right."

Emma didn't care about the toast or the kitchen or even the whole blasted building. In that moment, the only thing that mattered was Olivia being outside. Away from the fire.

Safe.

The man from the fire brigade turned to Emma. "There wasn't much damage, Mrs...."

Emma looked up from her daughter to find the handsome visage of none other than Mr. Fisk.

"Miss Taylor?" he asked, appearing suddenly hesitant.

No words or quick explanation came to her. Never had she thought she would run into one of the lending library's subscribers on her street, not when the clientele was the type who could afford a place far from the likes of Radford.

"Mrs. Taylor," Olivia corrected primly. "My father is dead."

Mr. Fisk blinked, unable to shield his surprise. "My condolences."

"It happened many years ago." Emma wasn't sure why she rushed to offer that explanation. The details were none of Mr. Fisk's business.

And yet the kindness in his brown eyes brought an inexplicable warmth to her cheeks and made her want him to think well of her. "The marriage bars, they apply to widows when it comes to finding employment..." Emma glanced at Olivia, indicating widows with children, but finished her sentence simply, "Widows like me."

"You'll get no judgment from me, Mrs. Taylor." He adjusted the brim of his cap, so the action doubled as a slight doff. "Everyone has their reasons for what they do."

The reassurance eased some of the tension from her shoulders. "You said there wasn't much damage?"

"Only a small burn on the rear wall. A bit of paint and it'll be good as new." He looked at Emma and Olivia. "I can come by if you need—"

"No." Her quick reply brushed away his offer of charity. "No, that won't be necessary. I am perfectly capable of applying a bit of paint."

He didn't appear put out by her abrupt claim. And it was indeed a claim. She had never wielded a paintbrush in her life. But really, how hard could painting a section of wall truly be?

Mr. Fisk smiled. "I don't doubt your ability at all, Mrs. Taylor. You strike me as the type of woman who can do anything. You're free to go on up." He adjusted his hat in her direction once more and turned back to his truck.

The neighbors who loitered on the street to witness the commotion likewise returned to their homes.

Emma held Olivia's hand as they hastened into the building, gathering the day's mail as they did so. The acrid odor of smoke burned at Emma's nostrils and seared into memories best left in the past.

A nebulous film of smoke hung in the air in the flat, making it seem as though Emma's eyes weren't adjusting properly. She tugged the ancient windows open amid their squeals of protest then examined the area near the oven while the room cleared. A pan with a charred bit of fried bread sat over one of the burners.

As Mr. Fisk had warned her, the back wall was scorched a brownish black that would indeed take several coats of paint to restore to the original soft yellow.

"I'm sorry, Mum," Olivia said in a small voice. "I didn't mean to catch the building on fire."

"I know." Emma chewed her lip.

Olivia shouldn't have been home alone, not without someone to watch her. Not for so long.

It wasn't safe.

If bombs did fall, Olivia would be alone. And if she were at school, there was only the opportunity to scatter to save her. Then there were random occurrences like this one where Olivia might have burned the building down.

After tossing the ruined food in the rubbish bin and setting the pan in the sink for a good soak, Emma sank into the chair at the dining room table and flipped through the small stack of mail. The Evacuation Office had sent another notice.

Her stomach clenched. Likely another appeal for her to return Olivia to the country. Already she had received one within a week of Olivia's return home.

Emma slid the letter free from the envelope and closed her eyes slowly against the words. There, in stark black and white, was a second citywide call for the children to evacuate on February 17.

And this time, Emma knew she wouldn't have to vacillate over the decision to send Olivia or not. This time, prudence dictated the need to send Olivia away again. For her own safety.

24

A WEEK LATER, Emma moved listlessly among the book-shelves at the Booklover's Library.

Sending Olivia away a second time hadn't been any easier. Not when her large blue eyes filled with tears and she'd begged Emma to let her stay, promising to be good. But being good wasn't the issue. The issue was safety. The issue was the government's insistence that if Olivia remained in Nottingham, she would be in danger.

If those threats became valid, the risk was not worth the cost. Emma would never forgive herself if something happened to Olivia, especially if she'd selfishly kept her daughter home.

Mrs. Pickering had been at the school with the WVS during the second evacuation, and had held Olivia's hand, leading her to the waiting bus. She had offered to secure Emma a place among the women helping with the evacuation, but Emma didn't have the heart to pull children from their mothers. Even if doing so was for the safety of those being evacuated.

Not when she knew firsthand how deeply that separation cut.

A subscriber approached Emma with a book extended, in-terrupting her thoughts. "I beg your pardon."

"Would you like to check this out?" Emma reached for the item.

"I already have." The woman offered a sheepish smile. "I love this so much, I'd hoped to buy it."

"I'm sorry, but they're only available for lending." Emma waved for her to follow. "However, we do have some books for sale, ones that have been retired from circulation. Perhaps we can find a copy."

The Booklover's Library offered books to borrow while they were in good condition. When items were returned damaged, they were immediately pulled out of rotation and placed for sale. The selection wasn't very large, but there were still gems to be found from time to time.

Rather than follow her, the woman held back. "I want this exact copy. Not one of the used ones."

Emma refrained from mentioning that technically all the books in the lending library were used, including the one in the woman's hand. "I'm sorry, but that precise book is not available for purchase. You can add your name to a list to be considered once it is no longer pristine enough for the lending shelves."

"Then it would be exceptionally used." Color touched the woman's cheeks. "I'm a Class A subscriber."

"I can help you select another book that might be similarly appealing."

"Well, if that's the way of it." The subscriber sullenly relinquished her copy of *Gone with the Wind*.

Emma scanned the popular title with a nod. "Tell me what you liked best about the story and I'll find something else you will love."

The task wasn't easy, but after nearly half an hour of rejecting most of what Emma suggested, the woman left with a new book, somewhat mollified.

How ironic that people in a lending library wanted to buy

the books. When Emma worked at her father's book shop, people had so often come in asking if they might borrow the books.

A memory flashed in Emma's mind of how Papa's gaze would flick up at the ceiling in a soul-suffering eye roll, then land back on her with a wink. The ache of his loss squeezed at her chest. But the discomfort was fleeting, replaced by warmth, and a slight note of mirth at the recollection.

In many ways, being at the Booklover's Library had brought her father back to life in her heart. The reminders hurt, yes, but they were also a comfort as buried memories rose to the surface and embraced her. She'd shoved aside thoughts of him for too long.

In so many ways, he was there with her in the lending library, coaxing her to appreciate how right returning to that community felt. One that centered on books, on being carried away by a story, and staying up far too late into the night on the wings of a tale. These were the people she connected with most in the world. And within that camaraderie was the love she had for her father and the embodiment of his spirit.

She hadn't realized how much she had missed that company of readers, how much she had needed books in her life, until now.

While Olivia's initial letter with her billeting location had come quickly the last time she'd been evacuated, any word from her now was slow to arrive. Eventually Emma finally ceded to asking Mrs. Pickering for help over tea one morning before her landlady disappeared to assist the WVS. But even Mrs. Pickering couldn't glean any information on Olivia's whereabouts, not when details were kept quiet to protect the evacuated children from attracting any attacks from Germany.

Finally, two weeks after Olivia's departure, Emma received

a postcard with an address in Kent. Yet another distant location that would have been an easy three hours by train before the war. Emma knew all too well how long train travel could run now.

But the distance wasn't what caught at Emma's concern the most. The lack of personalization was unnerving. The last time Olivia sent a postcard with her billeting address, it had been accompanied by a long letter. This postcard had not even been written by Olivia, as evidenced by the foreign hand in a swift, efficient scrawl rather than her blocky print of varying sizes that slid up and down the page.

Regardless, Emma immediately wrote Olivia a letter, asking after her new home and new life, and hoping for an expedient reply to set her troubled thoughts at ease.

Emma's fingernail worried at the cuticle on her thumb, a nervous habit she'd never been able to fully free herself of. A pearl of blood beaded where she'd been picking. Quickly, she grabbed her handkerchief before accidentally staining any of the books she'd been sorting through.

In the month that had passed, she still had not heard from Olivia despite having written several letters. Was her daughter even receiving them?

Emma had been so desperate for some kind of news, she had reached out to the people billeting Olivia, people whose names she did not even know.

Margaret came into the back room and frowned as soon as she saw Emma. "Still no word from Olivia?"

Emma shook her head. "Last time she was having such a grand time with Aunt Bess, she forgot to write. I can only hope this delay is of a similar nature."

Except that there was that worrying unease shifting and tightening low in her gut. A mother's intuition.

A feeling she couldn't ignore.

"Why don't you put these books back on the shelf." Margaret handed her a bin. "Mr. Fisk is out there. He might be a good distraction." She winked.

Emma accepted the books with a flat expression. "I'm going out there for the books, not Mr. Fisk."

Margaret gave a disbelieving hum of mild agreement and resumed Emma's task of sorting through requested books.

The handkerchief had done the trick and Emma's cuticle was no longer bleeding. She tucked it into the pocket of her green overalls and headed out to the main room of the library.

Mr. Fisk's gaze immediately went to her, holding her for a moment of suspension in the heat of those warm brown eyes. They hadn't seen one another since the fire in Emma's flat.

What if he mentioned Olivia?

A nervous flutter that had nothing to do with Mr. Fisk's appearance sent eddies cartwheeling in her stomach.

Rather than approach him, she swept in the opposite direction with the box of books. She would see to the children's section first, knowing he would likely not come to that area.

When she completed that genre, she went to the romance section.

"Good afternoon, Miss Taylor." The timbre of his deep voice was enough to make any woman stop in her tracks. "I have a book to return."

Miss Taylor.

Thank goodness.

He held out none other than the red label book with *Lady Chatterley's Lover* scrolled on the spine. A flush crept up his cheeks. "It was…" He cleared his throat. "Enlightening."

Emma had read the book just after having received it from Margaret as a Christmas gift and her cheeks blazed in shared mortification knowing *exactly* what he had read. All the while, she scrambled for something—*anything*—to say.

"How did painting go?" he asked first.

Painting? Emma frowned.

He smiled in apology. "Your kitchen."

"Oh, yes." Emma almost sighed in relief to have something else to talk about. "It's a grand streaky yellow brown." She laughed lightly. "I think a few more coats."

"Let me know if I can be of any help." He rubbed a hand over the back of his neck. "My brothers are all off fighting, so my dad and I have learned to take on all the handiwork at home."

How strange that his brothers had signed up, but he hadn't. However, that was not the subject she asked after. "Brothers? How many do you have?"

"Three." He grinned. "My poor mum has always had to deal with a household of boys."

What must growing up in such a full house be like? Emma smiled at the image that sprang to her mind—one filled with boisterous conversation and laughter.

"I can't imagine so many siblings. You must all be very close."

"We are. I'm the oldest, so I've always looked after them. Especially the youngest. He just turned eighteen and immediately signed up with the RAF. Mum was overwrought when she learned he'd be in a plane with Nazis shooting at him."

Emma briefly wondered again why Mr. Fisk hadn't signed up as well, or why he hadn't been conscripted at this point.

"I'm sure she was," Emma replied, fully understanding a mother's fears for her children. "So, what would you like for your next book?"

"I think I would like a mystery this time." He grinned and a small dimple appeared at his right cheek.

Of course a man as dashing as Mr. Fisk had a dimple.

She led him over to the mystery section and reached for a book she had recently read—*The Nine Tailors* by Dorothy Sayers. "This one had me guessing to the very end."

"Those are the best kind of books. I'll take it based on your glowing recommendation." He held out his large hand and she gave him the book.

Miss Crane appeared suddenly beside them, fidgeting with the shelf of travel books one row over. A floral scent filled the air from an application so heavy-handed, the sharp fragrance stung Emma's eyes.

Mr. Fisk did not appear to notice Miss Crane. Or her perfume. He regarded Emma with a hesitant expression.

"Are you sure that's to your liking?" Emma asked. "I can always find another."

"This is perfect." He glanced down at the book, as if surprised to find it still in his hands. "I actually wanted to see if you might be interested in meeting with me sometime for a pint." He tilted his head in consideration. "Or tea." The skin around his dark eyes tightened, assessing her. "Probably tea."

Emma froze. Was he asking her on a date? "I'm more of a tea drinker, but…"

Miss Crane glared at Emma from behind Mr. Fisk's shoulder before stomping away.

"…but I'm afraid I'm rather busy, unfortunately," Emma finished. "It's difficult to make time…I'm terribly sorry."

She'd intended to decline the offer even before Miss Crane's obvious jealousy spiked. Mr. Fisk was a handsome man to be sure, but Emma had enough to fill her time between work and the WVS. And worrying after Olivia.

Mr. Fisk nodded. "Of course, I understand." And the poignancy in his gaze said he absolutely did.

But Emma hated the sympathy in his eyes. No one regarded

her with a normal expression when they found out she was a single mother. There was often judgment, an assessing gaze resting on her ring to gauge its authenticity. With men, there was even an apparent suspicion that she had an itch in need of scratching.

She did not.

And when there was not scorn or blatant interest, there was pity. A woman on her own with a child and no husband to look after them both—however did she do it?

Not easily.

The world was not a welcoming place for a single mother. Emma had learned as much the hard way.

Her own situation was a far cry from how she'd grown up, with a single father who was praised for his efforts in continuing on without a wife to make him dinner and raise his child.

In everyone's eyes, he was a hero.

But as a single mother, she was either something to be pitied or a pariah.

"If that's all?" Emma prompted. The hurt of all those years of pity and scorn added a brittleness to her words she had not intended.

"I apologize." Mr. Fisk shook his head at himself and guilt immediately nagged at Emma for the edge to her tone.

She smiled, hoping to appear softer, warmer. "No need to apologize. I'm flattered, truly. My life is just...complicated."

He nodded, the tension easing from his face with what she hoped was understanding. "Thank you for the book." Then he turned and approached the counter where Miss Crane waited to check out his book amid a storm cloud of perfume.

"You have to wonder why a man as strapping as him hasn't signed up," a woman in the nearby fiction section said bitterly, with enough vehemence for Emma to hear. Likely loud enough for Mr. Fisk to hear as well.

"Not all our boys are brave like your George and my William, who signed up before war was even declared," another woman added.

Mr. Fisk's shoulders squared.

He had indeed heard.

After war was declared, men began to be conscripted. While it was unusual that Mr. Fisk had not signed up, Emma recalled how he handled finding out about Olivia. *Everyone has their reasons for what they do.*

Mr. Fisk had a reason, and whatever it was, that knowledge was nobody's business but his own.

"May I help you find something?" Emma asked the women, desperate to break up the discussion, and cut short the venom of their waspish attack.

They allowed her to offer Class A service despite their Class B subscription, something Emma was only too happy to provide as Mr. Fisk left in peace.

In the time Emma helped the women, Miss Crane had disappeared from the library floor and didn't reappear until after Emma finished being subjected to Mrs. Chatsworth's latest one-sided conversation. Miss Crane strode past Emma, her Cupid's bow mouth drawn tight enough to launch an arrow.

Seconds later, Miss Bainbridge entered the library, her expression serious, as she approached Emma. "Miss Taylor, I'd like a word with you."

25

EMMA'S INSIDES CONSTRICTED as she followed Miss Bainbridge to her office. Was being called to speak to the manageress ever a good thing?

Miss Bainbridge indicated the chair across from her desk as she settled into her own high-backed seat. "I am proud of the work you've been doing here."

Confusion pulled at the reins of Emma's anxiety. With the way Miss Crane had looked at her, Emma had anticipated a reprimand from their manageress. "Oh, well, thank you."

"Especially given your circumstances," Miss Bainbridge added with a smile that eased the usual sternness from her countenance. "When our employees are sufficiently trained, it is customary for them to continue their education in an alternate location to ensure they can handle anything our subscribers throw at them. It's temporary, of course. I'm thinking London."

"You're sending me away?" Emma asked. "To London?"

London was nearly halfway to Kent from Nottingham. She would be closer to Olivia.

The manageress tutted. "No need to be concerned, it would only be for a fortnight. Your daughter is in the country again, is that correct?"

"She is," Emma replied hesitantly.

The other woman leaned back in her chair with satisfaction. "Miss Crane reminded me you were likely due for training in another location. She was right and I think this is the ideal time."

"But what if Olivia tries to send me a letter…"

"It's only two weeks," Miss Bainbridge said with polished patience. "And we can forward any correspondence your way."

"I don't believe the post would arrive before I left to return home." Frustration burned a scorching path through Emma's chest.

If only motherhood were as simple as people without children assumed it to be.

There was no turning off her worries, or the fear of what could happen in those two weeks.

"We'll work something out." Miss Bainbridge adjusted a file on her desk, a clear sign the conversation was over. "You'll be leaving in a week. Details will follow shortly with your train ticket and all you'll need to pack."

Emma hesitated to rise from her chair and Miss Bainbridge lifted her eyes to regard her with sincerity. "All our girls do this, Miss Taylor."

"Of course." Emma nodded and slowly pushed herself to standing.

It was nearly April. By the time Emma was in London, Olivia's birthday would only be a month away. Perhaps Emma might take an afternoon to go to Kent and see her daughter for an early celebration. With the travel being just an hour southeast of London, surely she could make the time.

The thought helped loosen the tension squeezing at the back of her neck. A new perspective truly did make all the difference.

Heartened at the prospect of getting to enjoy an early celebration for Olivia's birthday with her in Kent, Emma returned to the main floor of the Booklover's Library. Margaret approached and glanced about at the uncommonly empty room, issuing a low whistle.

"I've never seen it this quiet," Emma said by way of agreement.

"That isn't why I'm impressed." Margaret lowered her head, her expression sly. "Mr. Fisk asked you on a date."

News traveled fast.

Before Emma could formulate a reply, Margaret continued, "I don't think I've ever seen Miss Crane in such a peevish state." Margaret laughed and looked around to ensure the other woman wasn't nearby. "Please tell me you said yes. I didn't have the opportunity to hear the rest of the story. Or rather the teller didn't care to share your response."

"I couldn't."

Margaret's face fell just as a subscriber entered the room. Emma moved to approach them, but Margaret grasped her by the arm and tugged her into the empty Bespoke Room. "You said no? He's *Mr. Fisk*, a man so deliciously tempting I might reconsider my own Jeffrey." She paused thoughtfully and a whimsical smile lifted her Firefly-red lips. "No, no, I never would. But Mr. Fisk, Emma!"

Despite Margaret's protestations, Emma simply shook her head. "My life doesn't need any more complications."

"Wouldn't life be easier with a husband?"

It would. There was no doubt about that. The very thought of being free of the scrutinizing stares, of having support to get her through hardships, or aid when it came to business dealings where women were so limited. Tasks like banking or working with any formal organization that considered women completely incapable of thought or responsibility.

Margaret folded her arms across her chest, ostensibly the victor.

Emma shook her head. "If I marry again, it won't be because I *have* to, it will be because I *want* to."

Once those words left her mouth, the idea of her marriage to Arthur changed from an amorphous thought from the past into a definable shape.

She'd never bothered to consider the reason she'd been so easily swayed into marriage, but their relationship had been entirely based on her dependence on him, her *need* for his protection, his guidance in the absence of her father, who had seen to life's day-to-day details she'd been too naïve to understand. They were all things she was adept at now—budgeting, paying bills, navigating contracts to secure flat leases. Matters women were supposed to leave to men. After Arthur's death, she'd forced herself to learn.

Maybe even then she'd known she hadn't wanted to need someone again the way she thought she'd needed Arthur.

Margaret put a hand on Emma's shoulder and blinked up at her with coal-darkened lashes. "All I'm saying is that you've been a widow for years, Emma. Your husband is no longer of this world, but you are. Don't forget to live in it."

Emma nodded and forced a smile. After all, she *was* living her life. Wasn't she?

The question rolled through her thoughts on the walk home. The late-March air was pleasantly cool against her skin, the sun fighting with the clouds overhead for purchase. Sometimes it even succeeded, casting golden warmth over the trees and burnishing the pale green budding leaves.

Did she notice such simple things enough? Or had she spent so long just barely eking by in life that she'd forgotten to savor the experience?

She entered the tenement house, stopping by Mrs. Pickering's flat to let Tubby out for a quick walk as had become her routine these days. Mrs. Pickering had fallen headfirst into her role with the WVS. No matter what the organization needed, she was ready to charge in, eyes gleaming, shoulders squared with purpose.

Using her key to Mrs. Pickering's flat, Emma let herself in to the elation of an overexcited Tubby. He leaped into the air, his torso twisting in anticipation of a walk, rendering the task of clipping his lead to his collar nearly impossible. The act took several attempts given how ferociously his body rocked with the wagging of his frantic tail.

"Ready for a walk?" she asked pointlessly.

He yipped an impatient confirmation and tugged her from the flat. As was her habit, she paused at the mailbox and lifted out the day's post to sort through as they traipsed down the sidewalk.

Tubby sped ahead, ears jauntily bouncing to his happy trot as she shifted yet another pamphlet about the Dig for Victory campaign behind a letter.

She didn't recognize the name of the sender, but did know the address.

Kent.

She stopped abruptly, tore the envelope open and yanked out the letter inside. Tubby pulled at the lead and she followed blindly, her eyes fixed on the note within, her heart dropping with each line she read as her suspicions were confirmed.

She had been right. Olivia was not doing well.

26

EMMA READ THE letter from the couple billeting Olivia, disbelieving some points made, while others left her heart in pieces.

There was the offensive claim that Olivia lacked education, suggesting she wasn't fit for the school the local children attended. True, Olivia was not an apt pupil and took some nudging toward her lessons, especially in maths, but she was hardly ignorant. And she was well-behaved with a desire to please, making her amenable to completing necessary tasks and studies.

But their claims of Olivia wetting the bed...they were entirely ridiculous. Olivia had not experienced incontinence since her toddling years.

There had always been an element of Olivia that lent itself to a desire to be as adult as possible. Bedwetting at almost eight was simply an impossibility.

The worst news, however, was of the infection that had settled into Olivia's chest. Her coughs were such that they apparently kept the household awake at night, likely due to the insufficient clothing Emma had sent—or so they'd stated. There had been clothes aplenty to get Olivia through the colder months, and warmer ones too, just in case.

The letter demanded money, more than the billeting fee the government paid them from Emma's stipend. There was the need for medication and for clothes that fit properly, as they cited Olivia had grown quickly and her garments were now too small.

Emma replied as soon as she was in her own kitchen, asking for them to notify her at once should Olivia's illness take a turn for the worse. Inside the envelope, she included more money than requested, a tidy sum pulled from the small box where she saved every halfpenny she could manage. If more medicine was needed, she didn't want them bothering with the time to write her again.

Especially if she was in London and might miss their request.

At the end of the letter, she stated her intention to visit, then she signed off and sealed the envelope.

The week following the mailing of the letter, Emma received instructions for her trip to the Aldgate branch of the Booklover's Library in London, along with a phone number for where she would be staying. The latter of which she forwarded on to Mrs. Pickering, who had recently had a phone installed in her flat and promised to call in the event of any letters from or about Olivia.

The evening before Emma's departure, she went through her usual routine of taking Tubby for his walk. In Emma's absence while in London, a younger woman with the WVS would help with Tubby.

"I'll miss you, boy." Emma ruffled Tubby's silky head.

He panted up at her, pink tongue hanging from the corner of his wide smile. She led him out and grabbed the mail.

Two envelopes immediately caught her attention: one from the couple billeting her daughter—and one from Olivia.

Once more, Emma stumbled blindly after Tubby as the dog pulled her down the sidewalk, her fingers fumbling with the envelope from Olivia.

The familiar, blocky writing drooped down the page. Emma read quickly to find the letter altogether...sterile.

That was the word that came to mind. Sterile. Clipped. Efficient, save for the misspellings and grammatical errors. But there was one final line that grabbed Emma's full attention.

I'm so sad that I wish I were with Grandma and Grandpa Williams.

Emma's maiden name was Williams. Olivia was referencing Emma's parents, wishing she was with them.

And they were both dead.

A choked sob erupted from Emma. Ahead, Tubby stopped and glanced back at her, his brows lifting in an expressive show of concern.

"Go on," Emma encouraged.

He hesitated, then carried on at a slower pace. Hands shaking, Emma opened the second letter. Within, the woman keeping Olivia in her home disparaged the amount Emma had sent, saying they could use more even as she cautioned Emma on not visiting.

When parents visit, the children become miserable upon their departure.

But Olivia was already terribly miserable.

Something cold and wet nudged at Emma's shin. She looked down to find Tubby sitting at her feet, gazing up at her with liquid brown eyes. He nudged his nose against her leg once more.

Emma's heart swelled with love for the little dog. She picked him up, tucking him against her despite his muddy paws and nuzzled his snowy fur. He settled his head on her shoulder, returning her embrace in a way that somehow did make Emma feel slightly better, despite the upset of Olivia's letter.

"You're the sweetest boy," Emma murmured into his fur.

After the walk, she brought Tubby up to her flat instead of returning him to Mrs. Pickering's and left a note stating his whereabouts. Upstairs, Emma readied her suitcase with Tubby following close at her heels. Only now, she was not packing for London. She was packing for Kent.

And no matter what, she would not return home without Olivia.

Even with only a few train delays, the journey still took a considerable amount of time. Longer than before the war, to be sure.

Miss Bainbridge had not been pleased at Emma's abrupt change of plans, but had consented under the compromise that Emma would still work at the London location in the future. Emma didn't know when that might be, but agreed nonetheless.

She would agree to anything to retreive Olivia.

And now Emma was close, steps away from the ramshackle house in the middle of a muddy field with storm clouds swelling in the distance like a warning.

A shiver prickled down her spine and she quickened her pace.

Shouting could be heard coming from inside the house and a little girl with messy blond hair emerged from the nearby barn, clutching a bucket that was half her size. Her eyes went wide in her dirty face.

"I'll get that." Emma took the bucket from the child, surprised at the weight as milk nearly sloshed over the rim.

The girl ran toward the house, silently looking back as though confirming Emma followed her.

Emma pushed through the flimsy door behind the child and was immediately hit with the damp odor of soiled laundry.

"I said you need to muck out the stalls." A woman's shrill voice cut through the thick air. "What are you doing lazing about? Go on, off with you."

"Olivia?" Emma called out.

The girl in front of her stiffened and the entire house seemed to go silent.

There was a clatter from the other room, the erratic slap of feet on the clapboard flooring. Emma rushed to the sound, through an open doorway that revealed a living area with a sagging sofa and mismatched furniture, as Olivia emerged from a door on the opposite side.

Emma's heart caught in her throat.

Olivia's once glossy waves were lank and dirty, her face smudged with filth, her clothes just as streaked as her face and appearing far too large.

A cry of rage and indignation tore from Emma. She dropped the bucket and she rushed to her daughter, capturing her in the protection of a maternal embrace.

There was a new leanness to Olivia's already slender frame. Her elbows were sharp points where they pressed against Emma's stomach and hollows showed in Olivia's normally plump cheeks.

A woman with wiry gray hair that looked to be trying to scrabble its way out of a dingy yellow headscarf emerged from the same door as Olivia. The woman glared, her eyes small and mean. "What are you doing in my house?"

Olivia flinched.

Emma rose quickly, putting her daughter behind her. "I'm her mother. What are *you* doing to these children?"

The woman thrust her fists onto her boxy hips. "I told you not to come."

"You have no right—"

"This is my home."

"And this is my child," Emma said vehemently.

The woman didn't appear at all ashamed at the state of the child entrusted to her care.

Olivia coughed, a phlegmy barking sound that tore into the most tender place in a mother's heart.

"I'm taking her with me." Emma swallowed the anger rising in her. Rage would do no good in this moment. All that mattered was rescuing Olivia. "And I'm stopping by the WVS on the way to the train station to report you."

The woman rolled her eyes at the threat and marched away. In the other room came the clatter of dishes as she loudly muttered invectives about parents who couldn't leave well enough alone.

Emma turned to Olivia, struck anew with how shrunken and filthy her daughter appeared. "Let's pack your things. You're leaving now."

Olivia's face crumpled and she reached for Emma, clutching her hand like a lifeline.

The room where Olivia slept was a small space with one other bed, if they could be called beds. Really, they were more pallets on the floor with thin blankets. There was a sour odor in the room and a chill that the rag stuffed against the bottom of the window could not ward off.

Emma's vision blurred with angry tears as she snatched up Olivia's suitcase. When she snapped it open, she found the red jumper carefully folded within.

Olivia looked up at Emma, chin quivering. "I didn't want it to get ruined."

Emma took a second to maintain control of her emotions, then handed her daughter the jumper. "You don't need to worry about that anymore."

As Olivia pulled the jumper on, Emma shoved her daughter's belongings into the battered suitcase.

The little girl Emma met earlier had followed them upstairs and watched silently from the corner.

Olivia regarded her with sympathy. "She's my mother, Gertie. You can trust her."

"Is she an evacuee as well?" Emma asked.

Olivia nodded. "Please don't leave her here."

"Gather your things," Emma said gently to the girl. "I'll bring you with me to the WVS. They'll take care of you and find a new place for you to stay. A nice place." Likely there was another woman just like Mrs. Pickering at the WVS in Kent who would gladly tuck this child under her wing.

Gertie scuttled forward and remained mute as she piled what looked like a few rags into a sheet and secured it by the corners into a large knot. Emma took the misshapen ball from her, then hefted Olivia's suitcase, and led the girls downstairs. The main area was empty, so Emma called out, "I'm taking Gertie to the WVS. I would like both their ration books, please."

Crashes sounded in the other room and both girls leaped. Emma's pulse raced along with her thoughts. If the woman was aggressive, Emma would have to do whatever necessary to keep the girls safe. She set the bags down, freeing her hands, body tensed where she stood in front of the children.

Footsteps thundered toward them and Emma spread her feet, bracing herself. The woman erupted into the room and shoved two battered ration books at Emma. "Take the bloody things."

Emma accepted them with a nod that hinted at the thanks she refused to voice, then said to Olivia and Gertie, "Come along, girls."

Once in town, Emma easily located the main office of the WVS, where a woman in a herringbone-patterned jacket identical to Mrs. Pickering's bent to welcome Gertie, tutting over her while ordering people about to prepare some milk and biscuits and bring fresh clothes.

Yes, Gertie was indeed in good hands with the WVS.

Olivia plastered herself to Emma's side on the ride back to Nottingham and continued to repeat how grateful she was to be going home. They arrived in Nottingham late in the evening with little to be had in the way of dinner.

Olivia stood in the doorway of the flat while Emma opened and closed every cabinet in the hopes of food magically appearing on the empty shelves. There had been no reason to stock up when she planned to be in London for two weeks.

"Do you think you might make me a breakfast face?" Olivia asked, her voice small and hopeful.

Emma turned and found a small smile tugging Olivia's lips upward. The first Emma had seen since she'd taken her from that awful billeting situation.

But then, breakfast faces always could bring a smile.

The special fare had originated years ago when Olivia was just on the brink of her fourth birthday. Upon waking that morning, Emma realized there was no more bread and barely any jam. Certainly nothing to make into a proper breakfast. Furthermore, it was impossible to pop out to the grocer while Olivia slept, since she was far too young to be left alone.

In a moment of desperation, Emma had gathered whatever she could find to piece together a meal, all arranged on a plate in the shape of a face, with a strip of cheese for a smile, berry eyes and nose, and a few crumbled crisps for hair. Olivia had squealed with excitement when she saw it. The following morning, she'd requested another breakfast face despite their having plenty of jam and bread.

Now Emma boiled the one remaining egg to cut in half for eyes while she searched for whatever else was available for the rest of the face. Some biscuits completed a crooked smile, a small knob of cheese made the nose and stale bits of bread made for hair that looked like it'd been set in pin curls. The breakfast face wasn't the prettiest construction, but still brought a lightness to Olivia's face that pulled at a place in Emma that felt raw and wounded.

In that moment, Emma hoped desperately that nothing would come of this war, and that Olivia could stay with her forever.

27

EMMA HELD ON to Olivia's hand as they strode a few blocks to where she'd be resuming school. Again. The back-and-forth of Olivia's education had been dizzying for them both and left Emma with a serious concern for her daughter's overall education.

Apparently, the city had convinced several teachers to return from retirement, allowing for longer school days. This meant Olivia wouldn't be home alone for very long in the afternoon, even though she now had a very strict set of rules to follow. Especially regarding the use of the oven and stovetop, and anything else that could prove flammable.

A crash sounded a few streets over and Olivia flinched.

She had been doing that a lot.

"Are you certain they never struck you?" Emma asked, inquiring for the countless time as to the hostility of Olivia's former billet.

Olivia shook her head. "They just yelled a lot and threw things around." Her hand on Emma's tightened. "They were scary."

They certainly were. Even recalling the brief interaction Emma had with the woman left her rattled.

The nearer they drew to the school, the more children appeared. Some holding their mothers' hands like Olivia, others in small clusters as siblings and neighbors walked together.

Emma led Olivia to her classroom and found an older gentleman with white hair turned away from them. There was always benefit in knowing Olivia's teachers, especially in light of the circumstances Olivia had been through. Emma approached to offer introductions.

The teacher turned around and Emma only just managed to swallow her gasp of surprise.

"Mr. Beard."

He regarded Emma, then shifted his steely gaze to Olivia before returning his focus to Emma. "Miss Taylor?"

"Mrs. Taylor," Olivia corrected him. "My father is dead." She looked up at Emma with a frown. "Everyone is so confused over what to call you, Mum."

The bewildered expression on Olivia's face nudged at Emma's guilt. She hadn't told Olivia that she couldn't work at the Booklover's Library with a child for fear her daughter would feel like a burden. Emma agreed to what was necessary for the job for Olivia, so they could have a better life that afforded necessary items and hopefully a little bit more.

"It appears I am indeed confused at her title." Mr. Beard lifted a brow at Emma in silent question.

Emma straightened a little taller. "The adjustment to my title was necessary, and the lending library is well aware of my situation."

The detail was more than he deserved and all she was willing to offer.

Despite her bravado, that telltale heat crept over her cheeks, the one that came when waiting for whatever assumptions would likely be cast about her person.

"This is Olivia." Emma put her hands on shoulders that were far too thin. "My daughter."

A sense of relief washed over Emma for another person to know she was a widow, that she had a child. She hadn't realized how much the lie weighed on her until that moment.

Mr. Beard had the presence of mind to at least offer an uncharacteristically benevolent smile as he instructed Olivia to take her seat.

"Thank you for welcoming her," Emma said. "She's been somewhat anxious about returning to school and doesn't always take well to lessons."

Mr. Beard's brows flicked up. "Only having one parent takes its toll."

If the statement was a meant as a barb, it certainly struck home.

A sharp retort caught in her throat. Now that he knew her secret, he had a semblance of power over her. A word to a few choice people and she might be sacked if anyone complained. Miss Bainbridge knew of her situation, yes, but those above her might not take as kindly to Emma's delicate predicament.

"We manage," she said defensively instead. After all, she couldn't let such a statement go without speaking up for herself.

Mr. Beard studied her for a moment. "But does Olivia thrive?" Before Emma could even bother replying, he pulled his small notebook from his pocket and flipped it open. "I'm sure I'll be seeing you again soon, *Miss* Taylor." He stressed the 'miss' in the sentence and licked his pencil to begin writing.

As Emma turned to leave, he was already furiously scribbling. No doubt about her.

Olivia gave her a nervous wave and Emma ducked into the hallway, but even as she strode away from the school, there was a pinch deep in her chest.

Was Olivia thriving?

They'd always had a home and ample food, and sufficient clothing no matter how rainy or cold a season might be. There had even been extras for going to the cinema on Saturday mornings when the children's programs ran, and presents for birthdays and Christmas.

Regardless of what Mr. Beard implied, Emma was doing her level best, and wasn't that all any parent could do—whether they were on their own or part of a team?

Olivia was indeed thriving, in every way except perhaps with her education. Surely there was a fix for that, though. Emma just had to find it. To prove Mr. Beard wrong, as well as every other person who saw her pushing through on her own and found her efforts lacking.

Preparations for the war on English soil continued despite the quiet. And the WVS was not about to fall behind in their efforts.

So, when the ARP decided to put together an exercise to showcase how very prepared they were for anything Hitler might throw their way, the fire brigade and WVS were there to help.

Emma rushed around the large kitchen of the Council House with her fellow WVS ladies, each of them in an apron with their WVS armbands and badges on full display as they prepared food for the hundreds of people who would be at the event. When she wasn't cutting the numerous vegetables they relied on to stretch food amid the ration, she was stirring several large pots or adding pinches of salt here and there.

"Have you seen the butter?" Margaret asked, her usually coiffed blond hair slightly cloud-like in the steamy kitchen.

Emma gazed askance at her friend. "Do you really think Mrs. Pickering would let such a commodity out of her sight?"

Butter was necessary for the pies, or so Mrs. Pickering had

claimed. By some miracle—or more accurately, by the haranguing on her part to some official—a small trove of precious rationed butter had been delivered to the WVS. *For the morale of the people of the Radford district* was inscribed on the tag.

"Well, she'd best hurry." Margaret glanced at the sleek watch on her wrist. "She's due to help with the ARP exercise at half past."

"I'm sure she won't be late." Emma leaned toward a younger woman who was setting some crockery in the oven. "Try cooking several items at a time to conserve energy."

The woman nodded, her cheeks flushed with the heat of the room.

"Mum," Olivia called.

Emma spun around. "I thought you were with Mrs. Pickering."

"I was, but they asked if I can help in the exercise. May I?" She grinned, revealing yet another tooth she'd lost. This time a canine.

The eagerness on her face was impossible to resist. Especially when helping Mrs. Pickering would ensure Olivia wouldn't be underfoot in the kitchen.

"Go on, but mind yourself and stay out of the way."

Olivia beamed and launched out the door. A clatter sounded from across the room as the young woman who had been at the oven earlier dropped a pan full of vegetables.

Emma turned to help, and didn't think for another second on Olivia's request.

Several hours later, the food was neatly set on foldout tables laid with clean white tablecloths. A few women stayed to swat away early arrivals and attend to last-minute details, like setting out utensils and preparing tea.

Emma had meant to remain with them to offer her assistance when Margaret pulled at her arm. "Let's go watch the exercise."

Signs in the surrounding area warned of smoke and fire and loud bangs. That alone had made Emma reluctant. But Margaret seemed to notice, and cajoled Emma from her hesitation. "You know Olivia will want you there to see how she's helped."

With a sigh, Emma let her friend drag her away from the food tables and toward the waiting audience around a cordoned-off section of the street. An icy splinter of anxiety lodged itself low in her belly and she fought off the warning in the back of her mind urging her to leave.

"We are about to begin," a voice said over a speaker. "The following explosives are not an attack, but an exercise aimed at demonstrating the preparedness of your local Nottingham rescue resources."

The voice had only just dropped away when a loud pop burst from the middle of the street. Emma jumped and clasped her arms over her chest, as if doing so might physically restrain her in place. Fire erupted from the small cylinder there, flaring higher than the fire truck behind it as a plume of black smoke belched into the sky.

The acrid odor burned into her nostrils and seared the deepest part of her that relived the nightmare of that fateful day over and over again. The bookshop on fire. The maze of flames. The blistering heat and choking, burning air. Papa lying so still. Dead.

Run.

She squeezed her arms, remaining rooted to the ground as everyone else pressed forward with awe.

Chills raked over Emma's skin.

Another explosion went off, the blast now a raging conflagration. The air was hot with smoke that left a familiar taste in the back of Emma's throat and made her heart seize.

"Fire," someone called in the distance, their voice filled with a feigned terror.

Emma.

The memory of her father's voice filled her head.

Emmaline.

That raw, primal note to her father's tone was what real terror sounded like. And it gripped her now like a vise, squeezing the breath from her lungs, catching at her heart so that it pounded, pounded, *pounded.*

Run.

The world spun and she hugged herself harder, keeping herself together, arms trembling with the effort.

Shouting continued in the distance, the sounds warbled and distorted like they were underwater.

Run.

A jet of water shot from somewhere unseen into the center of the inferno. Several men in flat metal hats with ARP stenciled in white paint rushed forward, lugging bags of sand to throw over the flames.

Their efforts tamed the wildness of the fire, which yielded with a great hiss as a sigh of steam replaced the destructive black cloud.

The sand in those bags had come from the sandstone layered beneath Nottingham, where caves were carved out like underground pockets beneath the city.

Emma drew in a steadying breath and focused on those facts to regain control of her emotions. She recalled how she and Olivia had watched great trucks grinding away at the stone to create the sand necessary for the bags that were now layered protectively around the Council House and other important buildings.

The distraction worked and her breathing slowly began to return to normal, along with her vision.

Men in layers of heavy clothing moved effortlessly to clear away the debris while the ARP wardens ran through check-lists and pulled out first aid kits.

"With every incident, casualties are to be expected," the voice over the speaker announced. "Our ARP team has been specially trained for such occurrences."

As the smoke cleared, a new scene was revealed. Rubble was cast about as if a building had collapsed. Amid the broken bricks and errant tilted furnishings were people. Some lay still; others were propped up, holding limbs with gruesome paint as they groaned theatrically.

Mrs. Pickering was one of the actors nearest Emma, with a "wound" on her leg. Whatever had been done to make the injury appear real was convincing enough that Emma had to look away. Mrs. Pickering caught her reaction and flashed a jolly little wink before giving a well-practiced cry of agony.

Several people around her lay inert, pretending to be dead.

Except they really weren't entirely without movement. One man quickly reached up to scratch at his nose. A woman shifted, self-consciously adjusting her skirt. Several people squinted an eye or two open to take in what was going on around them.

Really, the scene was almost funny as they all tried to lie perfectly motionless.

Then Emma's gaze fell on the body of a child, one who was perfectly immobile, a little girl with her wavy hair plaited into twin braids. One whose face looked as if she was merely sleeping, an expression Emma knew from the countless times she'd studied that exact visage.

Olivia.

Emma's throat caught her heart again and this time did not let go.

Olivia lay prone in the rubble, as if she were really and truly dead.

A tremble began somewhere inside Emma and rattled through her limbs, threatening to shake her apart. She couldn't be here. She couldn't stay as she shattered to pieces. Not when doing so would embarrass Olivia and ruin the entire event.

The production had been too much.

Too real. Far too real.

And this time, when the voice in the back of her head screamed at Emma to run, that's exactly what she did

28

THE CROWD PARTED around Emma, the audience as eager to see the spectacle laid before them as she was to be free of the horror of witnessing her child pretending to be a bombing victim.

Her worst nightmare come true.

If Emma thought the air would be easier to breathe once she was free from the awful scene, she was wrong. It was just as thick, just as hard to suck into her lungs.

The world was spinning, rocking her balance, darkening her vision at the edges. She reached for the building to her right, braced her weight against the solid surface and let her eyes fall closed.

Her mind displayed a picture of Olivia's still form, darkened with soot. Emma's nostrils filled once more with the sting of smoke.

Too much, too much, too much.

Her knees went soft and she started to slide down.

Strong arms grasped her shoulders, holding her upright.

Papa?

That wasn't right. She knew it wasn't him, but whatever

level of panic she'd been trapped in blurred the lines between what was real and now, and what was in the past.

"I have you, Miss Taylor."

Miss Taylor?

She blinked her eyes open in confusion and found Mr. Fisk's brown gaze regarding her with concern. Flecks of green and amber were visible in the chocolate brown of his irises. She focused on them, grounding herself enough to try to speak.

"I'm… I'm fine… I'm sorry," she gasped. But she wasn't fine. Not when the air was still too heavy to breathe, and her thoughts too wild to tame. "I don't need help."

The strength came back into her legs and she floundered for a brief second in a bid to stand on her own.

Mr. Fisk helped steady her, but did so in a way that left the firm brick wall braced at her back. "Look at me."

She let her eyes lock onto his, centering herself once more on those amber-and-green flecks.

"Breathe in slowly." He waved his hand toward himself as his chest expanded beneath his heavy fire brigade jacket in demonstration.

Emma pushed beyond the short gasps she'd been sipping and drew in a full inhale.

"Now out." Mr. Fisk swept his hand forward as he gently blew out.

She followed his instruction as he repeated the directive several times, until her vision cleared and the erratic sprint of her pulse ebbed to a regular pulsing beat.

As her body calmed, she suddenly realized exactly how close she was standing to Mr. Fisk—near enough to see the new growth of barely perceptible stubble on his jaw and how soft his mouth looked by comparison.

And how she must be staring at him like quite the idiot.

She threw her attention to the ground, where his thick boots framed the narrow toes of her loafers as he helped her remain upright. "I'm so sorry. I'm not normally so..."

"I know." The boots stepped back, giving her space, and his grip on her shoulders fell away.

Mortified, she looked up again to find him regarding her with concern.

"People can become overwhelmed at these exercises," he said. "Are you sure you're feeling well enough?"

"Yes, thanks to you." Embarrassment burned at her cheeks. "I thought just getting away might help. That I could clear my head."

"Mum always says that no one person can get by without a community of others around them." He smiled. "Think nothing of it."

"I should get back," Emma said. "My daughter was one of the—"

The casualties.

God, she couldn't even say the word.

He offered a sympathetic half smile. "She played her role perhaps a little too well, I take it."

Emma exhaled something between a scoff and a laugh. "Far too well for a mother's heart."

"May I walk you back, Miss Taylor?" He offered her his arm.

And though their arrival together was sure to raise myriad questions among those who observed, she slid her hand against the thick fabric of his jacket and found strength in the sturdiness of the man at her side.

Margaret was searching the crowd when Emma rounded the corner. Her friend's frantic gaze immediately caught on Emma and Margaret rushed toward her.

"Oh, Emma, I didn't realize, I—" Her attention snagged on Mr. Fisk, the concern in her expression going coy as she slid a glance at Emma. "Thank you for helping her, Mr. Fisk. We are truly fortunate to have men so brave as yourself to save us."

"She did well enough on her own," Mr. Fisk replied easily. "She just needed some air. But I did insist on walking her back to find you." He winked and relinquished Emma to Margaret's care.

As he strode off, Margaret's mouth fell open, putting her delighted shock on full display. "I want to hear *everything*."

"Mummy, did you see me?" Olivia raced through the crowd, her face still smudged with soot and dust with a bit of fake blood smeared at her hairline. "I was pretending to be dead and I didn't move once."

Emma knelt on the ground, not caring one bit about her stockings as she pulled her daughter into her arms. Olivia smelled of ash and char, but beneath that was the familiar clean milk-and-honey fragrance that pulled at Emma's heart.

"I did see you," she said against her daughter's hair.

"I didn't move once," Olivia repeated with pride. "I did so well."

"Yes, you did." Emma squeezed her once more before releasing her. "Now let's go see to the food. I have it on good authority the pie crusts are made with actual butter."

No matter how Emma tried over the next week, she couldn't clear her mind of Olivia lying amidst the rubble, immobile, gray with ash and the application of overly convincing cosmetics to appear dead.

Especially as the so-called "phoney war" shook off its stagnant demeanor with Hitler tearing a path through Europe. His attack launched him through Holland, Belgium, Luxembourg, and ultimately into France.

The latter invasion terrified Emma the most. If he wrested France into submission as easily as he had Poland, there would be nothing more than the strip of the Channel to keep Hitler from encroaching on British soil.

In the wake of war bleeding across Europe, the Booklover's Library was crowded with subscribers desperate for a bit of romance and mystery to wipe away their worry.

Time at the lending library swept by in a flash, blurred with new faces, a plethora of various books checked out and returned, and shelves that were impossible to keep fully stocked. On one of the quieter mornings before the rush poured in, Emma stood at the polished Class A subscriber desk, checking out a pristine copy of *Jane Eyre* to Mrs. Chatsworth. When Emma handed the book to her, the woman accepted it awkwardly with her left hand, her right engaged with the basket where Pip slept soundly on his blue velvet pillow.

"This is one of my favorites," Emma said.

"Oh, mine too." Excitement flashed in Mrs. Chatsworth's eyes and Emma knew she was in for a lengthy discussion on the merits of *Jane Eyre*. Yet this time, she found herself genuinely anticipating the prospect.

As much as the other woman liked to natter on about this and that, when she brought up books, her points were generally well thought out and intriguing. And books were a far better topic than the war, which had sent a low buzz throughout the lending library.

Mr. Beard, however, had been delighted with such fodder for his little notebook and loitered around the bookshop as soon as school was out, scribbling away with rapacious urgency.

At least the new details about the war would bury whatever he'd written about her.

He paused as she passed, offering her a slight smile. Interactions between them had been that way since he found out she was a widowed mother. Kind and respectful. Without a hint of threat, thank goodness.

And by way of thanking him, she made sure to keep him well stocked with new mysteries she knew he would enjoy despite his protestations.

Upon entering the Bespoke Room with a new delivery, Emma found Margaret already there, shifting several items about. Her lips were almost bare of lipstick, dulling her appearance in contrast to her usual brilliant red smile, and the confident lift of her shoulders drooped.

"Is everything all right?" Emma asked.

Margaret startled, her thoughts clearly interrupted. "My brother has signed up for the Air Cadets." She sighed.

"It's only a children's group," Emma offered gently.

"Yes, but you see them marching about." Margaret pulled at one of her perfect curls and coiled the spiral around her finger. "They're truly like little soldiers. Which means they're being trained to go to war and fight. How long until he signs up for the military too?"

Margaret released her hair and looked up, her eyes wide with worry.

Emma understood Margaret's concern about her younger brother. He was a sweet boy who helped around the house, from fixing whatever Margaret's father was too drunk to bother with to doing various household chores while their mother worked at the Raleigh factory, making casing shells for the Hispano guns on Spitfires.

"We can only hope this war ends in the next two years before he turns eighteen," Emma said. "Did you hear about the new canteen opening at Victoria Station?"

"Is it ready?" Margaret sat up straighter with interest, as Emma had hoped she might.

The distraction had worked.

The canteen at the train station had been in the sights of the WVS for some time, a way to help soldiers maintain morale with a hot meal, a cup of tea, and a friendly smile as they passed through Nottingham.

"I have it on good authority…" By this, Emma meant Mrs. Pickering had told her. "…it will be opening in three days. And they are looking for volunteers."

"Do you think we might be able to secure positions there? So many women were interested."

Emma smiled at Margaret, knowing Mrs. Pickering was well aware of their hopeful intentions. "I'm sure we'll both be at the canteen on the day of the grand opening."

29

EMMA SAT IN the middle of Mrs. Pickering's crowded living room the next day, with Tubby snoring at her feet as she tugged open the box in front of her. "More clothes."

Mrs. Pickering joined Emma and examined her husband's effects. "He would want this, for his belongings to go to people in need of them."

"I'm sure he would." Emma had never met Mr. Pickering, but was eager to offer her support regardless. "It's heartbreaking to think how so many people have escaped with nothing."

Refugees had been sweeping into England from the countries Hitler was still hammering, seeking succor in a land unmarred by hideous swastika flags and violence. Many had left everything behind as they fled, opting for safety for themselves and their families above all else.

What a choice they must have faced, abandoning jobs and homes and pictures tied to memories of people they might never see again. Emma hoped she would never have to face such a harrowing decision.

She sifted through the contents of the box once more to ensure there was nothing Mrs. Pickering might want buried beneath the neatly folded slacks and jumpers. "These donations will clear out several boxes as well."

Mrs. Pickering eyed the crowded living area, where an extra well-worn recliner sat between the plum-colored velvet chairs and several additional shelves created something of a maze in the formerly open space. "They will need furniture as well."

"They will," Emma agreed.

Silence followed as Mrs. Pickering chewed at her bottom lip. Tubby lifted his head from where he slept at her feet, as if sensing her unease.

Emma worried Mrs. Pickering might change her mind and keep the lot of it, remaining buried beneath memories of the past.

"There's so much," Mrs. Pickering said at last. "How can we possibly move it all? We're trying to restrict our petrol use as it is."

The bulk of what Mrs. Pickering had to donate truly was significant, and her concerns about the petrol were not invalid. But Emma refused to let such a thing as transporting the items get in the way.

"I know someone who might be able to help," she said slowly, thinking of Mr. Fisk and the large trucks and carts he worked with regularly. Surely there might be some assistance he could offer. Perhaps he could even help move some of the heavier items. "In the meantime, let's pop up and see what clothes Olivia has set aside to donate."

"I'm sure she'll have quite a bit given how quickly she's grown." Mrs. Pickering turned away from the clutter of her crowded home and patted her thigh for Tubby to join them.

Olivia had quite a bit indeed. Most items were too small for her, but at the top lay a plaid skirt worn only once, the material having been deemed too scratchy to wear again, and an ice-blue satin-and-tulle dress that had been bought on discount and was far too fancy.

Emma quashed the rise of irritation at the waste, reminding herself that these items would go to children who needed clothing more than Olivia, who had more than enough.

"We should ask Mr. Sanderson," Mrs. Pickering declared.

Emma recalled his empty flat. "I don't think that's necessary. He's a man on his own. I doubt he has extra clothes."

"Stuff and nonsense," Mrs. Pickering declared. "Everyone has items they can be rid of."

She marched toward the door.

"Mind Tubby," Emma said to Olivia as she pushed up from where she'd been boxing the donated clothes and hurried after Mrs. Pickering. When the woman had an idea in her mind, nothing could dissuade her.

Mrs. Pickering gave an efficient rap on the door as Emma caught up with her. The shuffle of feet sounded on the other side before the door opened to reveal Mr. Sanderson's familiar scowl.

"I'm here on WVS business," Mrs. Pickering announced with a formal authority. "Do you have extra clothing that can be donated?" She didn't wait for him to reply, but instead launched into the speech she had given first at the WVS meeting, and then to the grocer on the way home, as well as to the women who'd been in the rations queue alongside them.

"Refugees have come into this country, many with only the clothing on their back, sacrificing everything for safety. They need your old clothes and anything else you might donate. Can you imagine what it must be like to lose everything in one fell swoop?"

A strange expression passed over Mr. Sanderson's face. The tan jumper he wore was frayed along the hem and his slacks were almost a size too big.

Embarrassment for Mrs. Pickering's blind efficiency cut through Emma. "Only if you have anything extra," Emma added in a gentle, more genial tone. "Nothing is required, of course."

Mrs. Pickering shot her a hard look that Emma pointedly ignored.

"I'll see what I can do," Mr. Sanderson muttered.

Before another word could be said, his door snicked closed, a prompt and firm message.

That was the end of that.

Except that it wasn't.

Later that evening, Emma sat across from Mrs. Pickering with a steaming cup of tea in front of her with Olivia on the floor, slowly petting a sleeping Tubby while "We'll Meet Again" played on the wireless. No matter how busy Mrs. Pickering was with the WVS, she always insisted on at least having a cup of late-afternoon tea together—no matter that it sometimes happened at night instead.

A knock came at the door, a soft, almost hesitant rap.

Mrs. Pickering set her teacup down. "Who could that be?"

She disappeared out the kitchen. Tubby lifted his head and then lowered it with disinterest as he shifted to stretch his pink belly toward Olivia in an insistent invitation. The murmuring of voices at the front door of the flat was brief and indiscernible.

Mrs. Pickering returned to the room with a box in her hands. "That was Mr. Sanderson with some extra clothes. He barely accepted my thanks before he left. Such a strange man, that one."

Emma eyed the box. "That was kind of him to share what he has."

But Mrs. Pickering sniffed. "We're all doing our bit. It's what's expected." She set the box on the table and pulled out several items.

Curiosity drew Emma closer and she peered at the contents. "What's in there?"

"Old clothes. Mostly children's and a few women's dresses. All a bit out of fashion, I must say, but well-made nonetheless." Mrs. Pickering put the clothes back and secured the box before adding it to the stack she had by the front door, all awaiting Mr. Fisk's assistance. "They'll be put to good use."

Mrs. Pickering didn't bring up the box of items again, but Emma couldn't get them out of her mind. Whose clothes were they? And what about Mrs. Pickering's speech had so appealed to Mr. Sanderson that he'd felt compelled to bring them down at all?

Emma was off the following Saturday, which happened to be the same day Mr. Fisk said the horse-drawn carriage could be spared to collect Mr. Pickering's effects.

For her part, Mrs. Pickering fluttered around the boxes while they waited, anxiously sifting through them and pulling out various items before tutting to herself and putting them back.

After a spell, she stopped in the center of the room and cast an anxious look at Emma. "I feel like I should keep something."

"Keep anything you want," Emma said delicately, knowing how difficult this must be for the older widow.

"But there are refugees in need," Mrs. Pickering cried in plaintive distress.

A cheerful ring sounded at the front of the tenement house and Emma left Mrs. Pickering to frantically sort through the boxes one final time.

Mr. Fisk stood on the doorstep with another man behind him, an older gentleman with a shock of white hair combed neatly to the side and arms the size of tree trunks. Emma recognized him from the bombing exercise on Radford Road.

They both wore heavy trousers with suspenders, their sleeves rolled up to reveal strong forearms. An unexpected warmth swam in Emma's stomach, especially when Mr. Fisk grinned at her, flashing that dimple in his cheek.

"Thank you so much for coming, Mr. Fisk," Emma said quickly.

Too quickly?

Unease fluttered through her. She was being foolish and Olivia would likely pick up on any unusual behavior. She might even openly question it. Trepidation crept into Emma's thoughts.

This was a bad idea.

"Charles, please." Mr. Fisk grinned again. "This is my boss, Francis Fletcher. Francis, this is Miss Taylor."

"Nice to meet you, Mr. Fletcher."

The older man leaned forward and shook her hand with surprising gentleness despite his massive grip. "Just Francis."

"Then, please, Francis, right this way." Emma pushed open the door and let them enter.

She followed behind them. As she did so, Mrs. Pickering's eyes darted around her house, no doubt seeing it from their perspective. The clutter blocked the light from the tall windows, leaving the flat crowded and dark.

"Mr. Fisk." Olivia beamed up at the two of them, her eyes starry as was the way of small children at impressionable ages when it came to seeing authority figures they knew.

Emma rushed to offer the proper introductions, and to distract Mrs. Pickering from becoming embarrassed over the state of her home. After all, the reason the men were there was to clear it all away.

Hopefully.

While Emma introduced Mr. Fisk—Charles—Francis sank to his knees to pet Tubby, and gave a husky laugh as the small dog delivered jumping kisses to his hard jaw.

He got to his feet when Emma introduced him to Mrs. Pickering, towering over them all, including Charles, who was by no means diminutive in stature.

"You're the chef who made those delicious pies for the exercise." Francis shook Mrs. Pickering's hand, his ice-blue eyes locked on hers.

"Oh my, I'm hardly a chef." Mrs. Pickering's cheeks flushed. "You remember my pies?"

"Who could forget a pie like that?"

"It was the butter." Mrs. Pickering waved dismissively.

He shook his head with genuine appreciation. "A flaky crust cooked so it melts in a bloke's mouth, with just the right amount of fruit. Did you preserve the cherries yourself?"

Mrs. Pickering blinked. Or was she fluttering her lashes? "Why, yes, I did."

"Perfection."

"This chap could chat the day away." Charles patted his boss's shoulder, his tone light and playful. "What do you have for us?"

"Quite a bit," Emma said somewhat apologetically. Though given the size of Francis's arms, he likely could carry the lot of it in one go.

The smile faded from Mrs. Pickering's lips. "My late husband's belongings." She swallowed. "I've…well, I've likely held on to them for far too long. There are people in need now, and I certainly don't require so many bookshelves or all these clothes. Or any of it, really." The laugh that followed was high-pitched with taut nerves.

Francis hooked a hand on his hip. "How long has it been?"

"Ten years this autumn," Mrs. Pickering replied in a quiet tone. "He was a good man."

"I lost my Jenny around the same time." Francis nodded. "It's a hard loss to be sure. Took me almost as long to finally pull her dresses out of the wardrobe to donate. But I know she wouldn't want me pining away for her all these years. 'Put this stuff to use,' she'd say." He chuckled, his gaze distant. "I imagine your Mr. Pickering would say likewise."

Mrs. Pickering smiled softly to herself, the tension melting from her shoulders. "He'd say exactly that."

Francis folded his arms over his enormous chest and surveyed the room. "So, what are we loading up?"

"All of it," Mrs. Pickering replied with finality.

By the afternoon, exactly all of it had been swept into the waiting wagon. Even the sturdy desk had been cleared from the kitchen, the men easily carrying the monstrosity away as if it was a child's toy.

When they left sometime later, after having a glass of lemonade and agreeing to return for some pie, Mrs. Pickering finally had her flat back. And judging by the shy look lingering between her and Francis as he left, she might have come away with a little something more.

30

WHEN THE NEW canteen opened at the glorious three-story, redbrick, Renaissance-style Victoria Station, Emma and Margaret were both there, and signed up for two- and three-hour shifts throughout the week. As opulent as the train station was, the canteen was a simple tiled room filled with pots and pans so new, their surfaces gleamed like mirrors.

What's more, Mrs. Pickering had arranged for children's care for mothers so they could still assist the WVS. With so many men at war, those mothers were often finding themselves in the same position as Emma had been for years—raising children alone.

There was very little good to come out of war, but in this one small area of her life, not being ostracized as a single parent offered Emma a place in a society that previously never had room for her.

She hung up her apron after one of her volunteer shifts. "I already brewed more tea," she said over her shoulder to Margaret, then waved her farewell and swept from the room. The half mile from Victoria Station to the Council House where Olivia was being minded by the WVS was a quick, easy walk.

When Emma arrived, she found her daughter officiating a game of tag for the younger children.

Olivia grinned when she saw Emma and ran over as soon as the game concluded.

"Sorry I'm a few minutes late." Emma pressed a kiss to the top of Olivia's head. "We had a train come in at the last minute."

They were never given the train times when soldiers would be arriving, not when such information could be used by the enemy to attack their boys.

"Be like Dad, keep Mum," and all that.

So, the women at the canteen were at the mercy of when a train might come in, but always at the ready with slabs of fruitcake sliced into easy-to-grab pieces and brewed tea. The men arrived in droves, high in spirit and quick to flirt. Especially with Margaret, who always skirted around the numerous offers to go out dancing when the men were on leave.

"I don't mind that you're late." Olivia pushed her hair back from her face and grabbed her jacket, slinging it over her shoulders. "I like helping."

With Olivia being one of the older children, she'd taken on the role of assistant. Her duties were minor—helping prepare meals, coordinating and leading activities—but the responsibility had been significant to Olivia and made her stand a little taller.

The entire way home, Olivia regaled Emma with exploits from the playroom, a saga with no end yet told with such exuberance that Emma always found herself smiling.

The routine they'd fallen into was comfortable, both doing their part for the war effort, and both all the better for it. That was the thing about being one parent with one child—they were a team, able to be completely in sync with the other.

It was just the two of them against the world, as Papa had always said.

Days such as this made that tender camaraderie between

mother and daughter apparent and left Emma grateful for the special connection they shared.

"Have you seen any men coming back from France yet?" Olivia asked as the tenement house came into view. "I heard they'll be on the trains soon."

A chill skittered down Emma's back. There was news of a great defeat in France, of soldiers stranded on the shores of Dunkirk and needing to be shepherded back to British soil. Which meant France was losing the war.

Emma didn't want to think beyond France's loss. Or what the loss of a country so close to Britain might mean for England. "How do you know about that?"

"The ladies at the WVS and I were talking about it," Olivia answered with an overly mature air.

Emma hid her frown. "That isn't something to discuss around children."

"We remained out of earshot," Olivia reassured her.

But Emma hadn't only meant the smaller children. She'd also meant her own sweet girl, the one who suddenly considered herself an adult. At only eight, Olivia was very much still a child, even if she looked older than others her age.

"I haven't seen any men from France yet, but you must know that if the soldiers start to come through Victoria Station, I might have some late nights," Emma cautioned as they climbed the three short stairs to the main door. "Later than tonight."

"I don't mind. The WVS will need me then too." Olivia pulled the key from her pocket and unlocked the door to the building before Emma could fish hers from her handbag.

Tea was brewed in large vats with a pile of sparkling clean mugs to the right, and platters of simple jam and bread sandwiches were cut into neat triangles in wait of the soldiers.

Newspaper accounts had stated how British troops stranded

on the beaches in France were finally being rescued, not by large military craft, but by England's fishermen, who the government had entreated to come out with their small vessels.

Those recovered soldiers were now on trains, being transported throughout England. The WVS didn't know where those soldiers were going, or when they might come through Nottingham, but the women were prepared to provide British hospitality.

Margaret ran into the canteen's kitchen, clapping her hands. "A train is coming."

The room burst into a flurry of activity as women rushed this way and that to fill mugs with tea and ready the platters. Experience had told them that the brief train stop was too little time for the men to come up to the canteen. It was far better to bring the items downstairs with a coordinated effort in place to keep a rotation of trays coming down at a regular rate.

Emma joined the others, carefully balancing a tray of mugs full of steaming tea, her heart thumping with shared anticipation. The train pulled to a stop, the windows revealing not rows of men sitting in an orderly fashion, but packs of men, all crammed inside like sardines in a tin.

The door slid open, and the bevy of soldiers poured out, rushing toward the women for refreshments. But these weren't the clean-cut, excited men who had departed with neat kits thrown over their backs and bright smiles as they waved farewell.

These men were grizzled and filthy, some with bandages around their limbs and heads or with flecks of blood on their skin and uniforms. They carried with them the oily smell of weapons and damp wool, and the pungent odor of unwashed bodies.

One soldier approached with a skinny brown dog in tow

and pulled two sandwiches from a tray. He drew the first toward his mouth and extended the second to the dog.

"Only one," the woman holding the tray chided.

The soldier put the one he was about to eat back and gave the other to the dog. His gaze was hard as he regarded the woman. "This dog saved my life."

Before he could leave, Emma grabbed the sandwich from the tray to return to him.

He accepted it with a nod of thanks and split the sandwich with the dog, who snapped the food up without chewing.

The woman holding the tray shot Emma a chastising look, but she didn't care.

A man with a gun slung over his shoulder grabbed a cup of tea from Emma's tray. "May I take two?"

"Of course," she replied, loud enough for the woman next to her to hear. Who was she to tell a man who had risked his life for Britain that he couldn't have an extra bit of tea?

Two cups in hand, he swiftly departed.

"You're going to give away all our provisions too fast," the woman said crossly.

Emma watched the man go inside and hand the additional mug to another soldier seated in the train, who patted blindly at the mug before securing it between his palms.

"It *was* for two," Emma said, a catch in her throat. But her words were drowned out as the mugs were swiped away with nods of thanks faster than she could keep up with.

Her tray empty, she stepped back to retrieve more, only to find herself trapped in a wall of soldiers and WVS volunteers. The floor under her shoes ground and popped and only then did she realize they all still had beach sand caked on their boots that was now being scattered over the train platform.

"Coffee?" a man asked, his uniform foreign and his accent thick with what she assumed was French.

Emma shook her head. "Only tea."

One side of the man's lip pulled in and he gave a dejected nod.

Another man appeared in front of Emma, young enough that she wondered if his parents had needed to sign off on his enlistment papers, as some did for their boys who were under the age of eighteen.

His pale lashes lowered as he glanced at her empty tray and looked back up to her. "Do you have any more tea?"

"I'm sorry." She shook her head. He was replaced by another soldier with a similar question, followed by yet another.

As soon as the soldiers had arrived, they were gone, withdrawing like a wave ebbing back into the sea. The WVS women stared about in exhausted shock. Trays were scattered on the ground, and what few mugs remained lay tipped on the floor amid several crushed sandwiches.

At no point was any woman able to go upstairs to acquire more trays of sandwiches or tea, meaning some of those men left without. The woman next to Emma gave her an irritated glare, as though the entire thing was her fault for sparing an extra sandwich and mug of tea.

They would need another way. A better way.

The following evening, the ladies of the WVS were more prepared. Vats had been carried downstairs by the train station porters. Most contained tea, but several had been brewed with coffee for the French allies who were rescued alongside the British soldiers. Instead of mugs, which had all but totally disappeared by the second train, there had been a citywide collection of jam jars, which now served perfectly for tea and coffee. The soldiers did not complain.

As the trains continued to come, the condition of the soldiers worsened. These men had clothes streaked with soot and blood, their hollow eyes filling with tears at the sight of the WVS waiting for them.

The women with their trays of sandwiches, fruit cake, and tea were a glimpse of peace, or so one man said to Emma as he held his jam jar of tea and told her how surreal a contrast the welcome was to the hell of war. He said it was beautiful. And so was she.

Some of the men were full of compliments, especially for Margaret, whose smiles were tireless and without limit. But despite her outward demeanor, Emma knew worry for Jeffrey was taking its toll on her friend. Last Margaret had heard of her fiancé, he too had been in France.

One would never know her inner turmoil to look at her as she gently dodged earnest marriage proposals and offered spirited encouragements to the downtrodden troops.

It was why Emma had almost not heard the soldier calling, "I know you."

A hand settled on her shoulder. "Nice to see a familiar face."

When she spun around, she found a man she recognized, one she had to scour her memory to place.

"You traded tickets with me on Christmas Eve last year." The young man offered a charming smile, the kind men gave when they knew the effect it had on women.

"Yes," Emma replied, as the memory slammed into her. The soldier who Aunt Bess had said likely took advantage of her. Given the way he looked at Emma now, he had smooth talker written all over him.

A flash of anger shot through Emma at having missed Christmas with Olivia—more at herself than at him, for how gullible she'd been.

"You're an angel, really." The man winked.

"How is your mother?" she asked, feigning concern for a mother who likely didn't exist.

The charm bled away and he swallowed, appearing suddenly younger than the Casanova who stood before her only a fraction of a second before.

"Dead, miss." He shifted his weight as though trying to dislodge the words. "My mam was gone within an hour of my arrival. If you hadn't given me your ticket..." He looked down, briefly overcome with emotion. "I would have missed my chance to say goodbye."

He caught her hand in his and gazed at her with a sincerity that pulled deep within her chest. "You are truly my angel. Thank you."

And with that, the tide of the train's departure swept him away, leaving more French sand scattered over British soil.

31

EMMA'S THOUGHTS WERE heavy that overcast evening on the way home. Not only from her encounter with the soldier whose mother truly had been on her deathbed, but from the state of the men returning from France. There was a defeated look to them. Glassy eyes that stared at nothing, the dejected slope of their shoulders, all the blood and injuries.

No matter how the government kept up spirits with talk of how brave their boys were and how Britain would always keep fighting, Dunkirk had been an undeniable and exceptional loss.

The war was not going well.

But would France be able to hold?

Only when they were very nearly home did Emma realize that Olivia had also been markedly quiet.

"No exploits of the playroom to regale me with today?" Emma asked.

"It was quiet."

"So are you, Olive." Emma squeezed her hand in a gentle, encouraging way. "How was school?"

With Olivia, questions met with a dismissive response generally meant Emma had not asked correctly. In this particular case, Emma's query was exactly on point.

Olivia lowered her head. "Edmund was mean today."

"What did he say?"

Olivia lifted her shoulder, the same reaction she always gave.

"Is it about your performance at school?" Emma pressed.

"Mum, please." Olivia growled with irritation.

While the right questions opened doors, the wrong ones incited a wrath that shuttered the conversation altogether. When it came to Edmund's treatment of Olivia, Emma never seemed to be correct in her approach.

There was such helplessness in watching her daughter struggle through the boy's cruelty. That her tormenter was a child was especially frustrating when Emma could not let out her outrage on the boy, even if he was a bully.

Olivia gave the impression of strength with how much taller and larger she was than the other children, but inside, she was fragile as spun glass. And these interactions with Edmund had left cracks that scored deep.

"I wish he'd just leave me alone." Olivia sighed. "I always try to be nice to him, the way I know I'm supposed to, but he never lets up."

They arrived at their tenement house. Usually Olivia had her key out, ready to be the one to open the door, but tonight, she stared at the building next door where Edmund lived.

"What does he say to you?" Emma asked, trying to keep her voice as light as possible.

Olivia met Emma's gaze for a long moment, as though weighing how to answer. "Nothing." She pulled the key from her pocket and opened the door.

As Emma replayed the conversation that night, she knew there was more than one way to handle this issue. The following morning, she waited until Olivia was at school, then went next door and pressed the bell.

Mrs. Mott opened the door and smirked. "Is that dog out again?"

Emma's blood roared in her ears. She had never been one for confrontation, but she would do anything for Olivia. Even go toe-to-toe with the likes of Mrs. Mott. This bullying had gone on long enough. "I'm here to speak to you about your son's treatment of my daughter. On more than one occasion, she's returned from school upset over the things he has said to her."

Mrs. Mott folded her arms over her chest. "And what has he said?"

The roaring in Emma's ears intensified. "She refuses to tell me."

"You're coming here to complain about my son's comportment, yet you can't even relay what has been said?" Mrs. Mott shook her head. "It's always like this with mothers like you." She started to close the door, but Emma shoved her foot over the threshold, stopping the door from closing with the girth of her rubber sole.

"What do you mean, 'mothers like me'?" All the anger and the injustice that had simmered in Emma for years came out in the vehemence of her question.

Mrs. Mott's eyes widened in surprise, then narrowed. "Women who are too selfish to find a husband to help with parenting. Women who are so busy with their jobs and their own lives that they can't properly see to their children. If Olivia was close with you, she'd likely have told you whatever it is my son is saying. Unless, of course, she's just trying to get your attention, which is very likely the case. And I will not upbraid my son over your inability to properly parent."

With that, Mrs. Mott pushed her house slipper at the toe of Emma's loafer. All the fight had been stunned out of Emma at

Mrs. Mott's biting words and she yielded, clearing the threshold of her shoe in time for Mrs. Mott to slam the door in Emma's face.

The sting of her accusation followed Emma into work that day and through her shift at the WVS. As much as Emma could tell herself she was a good mother, she had to wonder at the truth of Mrs. Mott's words, especially when Olivia clearly did not trust Emma enough to share exactly what was being said.

The issues with Edmund ended a few days later, or at least were postponed, and not by his mother doing the responsible thing, but by school coming to an end. Unfortunately the summer holiday brought a new set of problems for Emma regarding Olivia.

What to do with her?

A barb of realization told Emma most mothers would be home with their children for summer, organizing activities, or sending them outdoors to play. But Olivia hesitated to go outside every time she saw Edmund from the window. And he was always there.

She spent the first week of her holiday curled up on the couch, listening to the wireless, only eating what could be had cold until the time came to help the WVS mind children while Emma worked at the canteen.

Whenever Emma departed for work, she left her daughter sleeping, though later found out through Olivia's own confession that she didn't rouse until almost noon most days. So much sleep didn't seem healthy. Especially with how much time Olivia spent listening to the wireless. Emma had grown to hate the incessant hum of a broadcast in the background after one show turned into five.

If only Olivia loved to read, she could be distracted by books rather than that infernal wireless set.

★ ★ ★

"Emma, he's safe," Margaret cried one morning as she entered the Bespoke Room.

Emma started from her thoughts. "Jeffrey?"

"Yes." Margaret's face was nearly glowing with her joy. "I heard from his mum last night. She ran over as soon as she received the letter. He's out of Dunkirk, though he cannot say where he's stationed."

"What a relief." Emma leaped up and hugged Margaret, accidentally knocking the book in her hand to the ground.

"Sorry." Emma laughed and bent to retrieve the dropped book.

Little Women. It had been one of Emma's favorites as a girl. In the absence of her own mother, she had supplemented that void with an image of what her mother would be like. And Marmee had seemed the perfect replacement.

Imagining herself caught up in the antics of sisterhood and a home rich in love has been so easy for Emma. Not that her home hadn't been rich in love. Papa had loved her endlessly and whatever void had remained in her life had been filled with books.

Yes, if only Olivia loved to read, she too might find part of what she felt was missing in the pages of a story.

"I was just putting that back," Margaret replied. "It was in the wrong place."

"I didn't put it away this morning." Emma pulled out her pocket notebook where she recorded every title she returned to the library shelves.

Emma thumbed through the pages before stopping at the day's list of books recorded from the return box. Margaret peered over her shoulder as she did so. "Who has been moving the books from their shelves?"

"I'll find out eventually," Emma vowed and picked up the

book. "I'll put this back. I was just heading out to the floor anyway." She quickly wrote *Little Women* in her notebook and returned the book to its proper place.

"That is one of my favorites," a voice said from beside her.

Emma looked up to find Mrs. Chatsworth smiling at her, a purple feather bobbing over her head where it thrust up from a blue pillbox hat affixed to her curls.

"It's one of mine too," Emma admitted with a grin.

"Did you know I didn't like books until I read that one?" The older woman laughed, disturbing the basket at her side. Pip peeked an eye open, casting an irritated glance at his mistress before nestling deeper into his pillow.

"Really?" Emma asked, incredulous. Mrs. Chatsworth was such a voracious reader, imagining her not liking books was nearly impossible.

"Really." Mrs. Chatsworth lifted her thin brows. "I'd tried several, mainly ones we were told to read in school or ones my parents had loved. Oh, I found them all so very dull, so I assumed I just wasn't much of a reader. It wasn't until I wandered into that old bookshop that was in Beeston…" Her gaze searched the air and she shook her head, unable to pull up the name. "You know, the one that burned down some years ago. Such a horrible story, that man had been so kind."

Emma's mouth went dry. "Tower Bookshop?"

Mrs. Chatsworth lit up and her feather bounced about, echoing her delight. "Yes, that was the one. I told the owner I wasn't much of a reader when he asked if he could help me, and he told me—" She tsked. "You know, it truly was so sad the shop burned down. It was such a lovely place. I couldn't walk by without at least going in to look at the stationery. They always carried the finest cardstock. And there was this cerulean-colored ink…"

Irritation crinkled Emma's usual veneer of patience for

the first time in the countless hours she'd listened to Mrs. Chatsworth. "What did he tell you?"

The older woman stopped talking, blinking in surprise at Emma's interruption. "I beg your pardon?"

Emma offered an apologetic smile. "You said the owner told you something when you said you weren't a reader. I'm so very curious as to what it was that he said."

"Oh, yes." Mrs. Chatsworth looked heavenward and chuckled, as if mocking her own inability to control her runaway dialogue. "He told me that the world is full of readers, some just haven't found the right book yet."

Warmth filled Emma's chest. Yes, that was very much something Papa would have said. And hearing those words now were as if he'd spoken them to her himself.

"Ah, but that cerulean ink, it was lovely," Mrs. Chatsworth prattled. "You know, I've never found another color quite so unique…"

But Emma was scarcely listening. Instead, she mentally combed through the catalog of books at the Booklover's Library, taking the time to fully assess her own daughter in the way she did with the Class A subscribers.

Why had Emma never thought to do this before?

Olivia just needed the right book. And Emma knew exactly which one.

32

THE COPY OF *Anne of Green Gables* had not moved from the spot on the kitchen counter where Emma placed it three days before.

"Aren't you interested in reading this?" Emma asked innocently. "I thought you would love it."

"I don't like reading." Olivia didn't even lift her head from the drawing she was working on—an image of a farm with a large house and a goat inside the barn, a wide anthropomorphic smile taking up half his face.

Another drawing of Aunt Bess's home.

Olivia's affinity for her short-lived billet wounded Emma more than she cared to admit. Likely for Olivia, her stay with Aunt Bess had felt something like a holiday, time away from home and the drudgery of day-to-day routines.

Still, her obvious love of the experience stung.

"You would like reading if you tried this book." Emma set her palm on the cover of *Anne of Green Gables*. "There is an orphan who is new to town and struggles with her classmates."

Olivia continued to color, drawing a girl with wavy brown hair who appeared extraordinarily happy where she stood in the middle of the farm.

Emma swallowed her disappointment at Olivia's obvious disinterest. If the appeal of a character enduring issues at school like Olivia didn't draw her in, there would have to be another angle. "Anne is very clever and has a bit of a temper that lands her into trouble. Like when she feels she's being teased and breaks a slate over a boy's head."

"What's a slate?" Olivia asked in a bored tone.

"Something people in school used to—"

"Oh, it's time for *The Children's Hour.*" Olivia leaped up so fast, she disrupted the table and sent pencils clattering to the floor. Oblivious, she knocked into Emma in her frenzy to snap on the wireless.

As Olivia sang the opening notes to the program in her high-pitched little girl's voice, Emma sighed, wishing she could have tossed the thing in the rubbish before Olivia ever knew of the existence of the blasted wireless set. Was there anything worse than the banal programming burbling on and on and on?

"I'm going down to Mrs. Pickering's for a cup of tea," Emma called out.

Olivia didn't respond from where she sat in front of the wireless, entirely engrossed in the program.

Mrs. Pickering opened the door just as Emma's foot landed on the bottom step. "Is Olivia not with you?"

"*The Children's Hour* is on."

Mrs. Pickering scoffed. "Wireless sets will be the downfall of the future generation, I tell you. We didn't grow up listening to programs, and we turned out perfectly fine."

Tubby rushed past Emma, clearly looking for Olivia. In her absence, he turned his focus to Emma, licking at her legs and whimpering with joy.

Though several weeks had passed since Mrs. Pickering donated her late husband's effects to the WVS, the openness of the flat was still somewhat shocking. For her part, Mrs. Pickering seemed to move better through the space. Though Emma did notice the landlady had maintained her habit of swinging her hip far to the right when she entered the kitchen, as if dodging around an imaginary desk.

"There's supposed to be an important announcement tonight," Mrs. Pickering said, clicking on her own wireless set.

Emma suppressed a smile at her friend's hypocrisy, and instead listened to the broadcast. Every night seemed to have an important announcement. Recently these had included Italy joining the war, opting to side with Germany. Then there was the declaration of no more church bells in Britain unless an attack was underway. Truth be told, Emma did miss the jolly chiming every hour.

After that had come the end of the Battle of France as the country ceded to Nazi control, followed by the official beginning of the Battle of Britain.

The phoney war appeared to be drawing to an end and they were all waiting on tenterhooks, wondering if an attack from across the Channel might finally happen.

Every day that an invasion did not come, the anticipation ratcheted tighter until it felt hard to breathe.

Mrs. Pickering set the tea in front of Emma. "I strained the leaves three times to get the most out of it."

With tea having been rationed since March, no one threw away used tea leaves anymore. Straining them several times, however, ensured the leftovers were almost as strong as the first brew.

Mrs. Pickering pushed a plate of bread toward Emma. "It's margarine," she cautioned with a wave at the greasy smear over the slices. "I've been saving my butter for a pie I plan to make for Francis this weekend."

"For Francis?" Emma gave her a friend a coy look.

Mrs. Pickering turned a brilliant shade of pink. "Well,

to thank him for his help with moving all my donations, of course. It is lovely to have the flat open again."

Emma took only one slice of bread, knowing margarine was now being rationed as well. Next time, she would bring a treat from her own stores.

In the end, the important announcement on the radio was yet another warning to keep on the lookout for German parachutists who might infiltrate British soil. No real news, at least, was good news. And the expectation of upcoming new information gave Emma an idea.

She bade good-night to Mrs. Pickering and Tubby before returning upstairs to find Olivia exactly where she'd left her, in front of the wireless.

"That's enough for one night." Emma clicked off the program as the closing notes of the show drew to an end. "I'm going to read to you."

"I'm not a baby."

True, Emma had read to Olivia when she'd been very young, and had readily stopped when Olivia became more interested in toys.

"Mums can read to their children at any age."

Olivia wrinkled her nose. "This isn't school."

"No, it's not. I'll make you some chocolate milk to drink while I read."

That was enough to sway Olivia. Minutes later, they were curled on the couch with the heated milk and a bit of chocolate powder from a tin of Bournville Cocoa in Olivia's mug.

The scent was comforting, and as familiar as the press of parent and child on the sofa with a book settled between them. This was how evenings were with Papa when Emma had been a girl. A mug of warmed chocolate milk and a story.

Emma pulled in a deep breath in an attempt to stave off the ache of her loss and opened the Booklover's Library copy of *Anne of Green Gables*.

When Papa read, he'd used a new voice for each character, pausing to offer inflection during poignant moments. There was nothing more magical in the world than the spell of a good story read by a captivating narrator.

Emma would never be as good as her father had been, but she tried her best as she began to read. Olivia fidgeted at first, sipping noisily from her mug and kicking her feet. But as the first chapter gave way to the second and Anne introduced herself to Matthew with her babbling explanation of how she'd have slept in a tree had he not come to the train station to pick her up, Olivia scooted closer with interest.

By the time Anne arrived at Green Gables and announced the farm felt like home, Olivia's drink was forgotten and she was curled against Emma's arm.

In that beautiful moment, the pain of Papa's loss had slipped away, replaced by a love so great that Emma's chest felt too small to hold it all, as if, in reading to her daughter, her father was right there with them.

Perhaps in those earlier years of reading to Olivia, she had sensed Emma's reticence and hurt. In mourning, Emma had deprived her daughter of the joy of reading.

Now was different. Now her time at the Booklover's Library had helped Emma heal, changing the pitch to her memories, from agony to the beauty of remembrance.

It was time to make amends to Olivia.

Emma kept reading, and Olivia was enraptured. One by one, the chapters fell away until the start of Chapter 8, when Marilla planned to tell Anne she could remain with them. But just as Marilla intended to confess as much to Anne, Emma suppressed a feigned yawn and closed the book.

Olivia's face snapped up to Emma. "Aren't you going to read more?"

"It's late, Olive."

"But I have to know what happens."

Emma stretched her arms over her head luxuriously. "Perhaps if we have time after we return home tomorrow from the WVS." She set aside the book and did not miss how Olivia's gaze followed it with interest.

"So, you're enjoying the story?" Emma asked casually as they settled into bed half an hour later. Olivia was able to stay up a bit later now that she was on holiday and Emma preferred to go to bed early with the blackout on.

Olivia climbed into the bed they shared, her eyes wide open, not at all sleepy. "I really like Anne. She doesn't have a Papa either. I at least have you, and I'm glad to have you." She wrapped her arms around Emma.

While Emma had expected Olivia to connect with Anne, she had anticipated the bond would be formed over the bullying Anne faced at school. Foolishly, Emma hadn't even considered that Anne being an orphan might impact Olivia.

Emma had grown up without a mother, and Papa had raised her with extra coddling as a result. Everything she wanted, she had, including her father's undivided attention.

But there was no bookshop beneath their home as there had been with Papa. Emma had to go to work far from the flat to earn a living. Mrs. Mott's words echoed in her mind, prodding at the soreness of her thoughts.

Women who are too selfish to find a husband to help with parenting. Women who are so busy with their jobs and their own lives that they can't properly see to their children.

Those words hurt because Emma saw the truth in them.

"I'm glad I have you too, Olivia." Emma hugged her daughter to her and turned out the small lamp by the bed.

Before leaving for work the next morning, she moved *Anne of Green Gables*, placing the book beside the wireless set, and hoped the power of literature would be strong enough to pull Olivia toward reading instead.

33

WHEN EMMA ARRIVED at the Booklover's Library later that morning, Miss Bainbridge called her into the office.

The manageress met her with a smile. "I'm pleased to announce you've performed with such exemplary skill and diligence within the lending library that we've been given permission to hire more widows."

Emma straightened in surprise. "I thought no one else knew."

"They didn't until the topic came up and I mentioned you and your efforts—not by name, mind you. But my manager was so impressed, he spoke to his manager and on and on, and, well, you'll be meeting Mrs. Upton today. I'd like your help in training her."

Mrs. Upton.

Apparently, Emma had done such a bang-up job that future widows were now allowed to be addressed as married women. She might have spoken up then, to fight for her right to wear the ring on her finger, to be called "Mrs." But the ring had gone cold against her skin long before she had been forced to sell it.

In her time at the Booklover's Library, she had become more than a man's wife. More than even a mother. She was a reader, a lover of books who could procure the right story for the right person at the right time. In doing so, she had begun to reclaim who she had once been, and there was a part of her that felt freed by the absence of her ring and married title.

"I look forward to meeting her," Emma replied with sincerity.

Miss Bainbridge tutted to herself. "The poor dear lost her husband at Dunkirk. Do be kind to her."

Many women had lost men to Dunkirk. Sons and husbands and fathers. The devastating news was delivered in the worst way—on the printed script of a telegram.

Emma had experienced the agony of losing a father she loved, and a husband she'd relied upon. Even though her life with Arthur had been tumultuous, his loss had still been devastating. "Oh, of course."

Miss Bainbridge paused with a gentle smile. "I ought to know better than to even ask."

Several minutes later, Emma found a woman cautiously looking about the lending library, her dark hair rolled back and pinned to reveal her pretty face. Her brows were penciled into two perfect arches and her lips were painted a similar red like the color Margaret wore.

But despite the cosmetics, the telltale bruising of a poor night's sleep showed at the delicate skin beneath her eyes. She brightened when her gaze caught on Emma. "Miss Taylor?"

Her stare was assessing, though not with shrewd criticism. In the way some women regard another, looking for kindness rather than weighing competition.

Emma offered her most welcoming smile. "Mrs. Upton, I presume."

"Please do call me Irene. Mrs. Upton is my mother-in-law." She flashed a quick grin. "She's a fine woman, watching my little William while I'm working, but I've been living in her house since Tom and I wed right before the start of the war. Well..." Her rambling petered off as she shifted her attention to the floor. "Well, I suppose I'll be there with her for a while longer, until I can afford a place of my own. I can't believe they hired me here. I heard widowed mothers could never find jobs, except at factories, but I'm too old... Anyway, I took a chance and asked and was shocked when I received notice they meant to take me on." She twisted her fingers nervously against one another.

"But I'd like to still just be Irene if that's all the same to you."

"I was in a similar position as you, and formerly went by Mrs. Taylor." Emma winked to put Irene at ease, to let her know she was not alone. After all, single parents often did feel completely alone. "And all that's well and good by me, so long as you call me Emma."

"I'd like that very much."

"Well, you won't like *me* very much when you find out how much dusting you'll be tasked with in these early days." Emma chuckled and led Irene around the library, showing her all the various spots that were hardest to dust, and instructed her on how to be mindful of book placement so she would know their location in case a subscriber asked.

There was something refreshing about not being the newest member of the Booklover's Library anymore, and knowing that there was another potential ally against Miss Crane's censure.

That night, when Emma climbed up the stairs of the tenement house after her walk home from work, she did not detect the ever-present droning of the wireless. Her breath caught with excitement and she took the stairs two at a time.

She unlocked the door and threw it open to reveal Olivia

curled up on the couch with *Anne of Green Gables* propped in her small hands.

Emma strode into the flat with a feigned nonchalance. "Is that a good book?"

Olivia startled, then lowered the book, her eyes wide with eager. "It's so good." Then she put Mrs. Chatsworth to shame as she detailed every moment Emma had missed since she stopped reading. "I can't read as fast as you, but I don't mind."

"Do you like reading on your own?" Emma carried her small shopping bag from the grocer's into the kitchen. There wasn't much to be had that day in the way of meat, but Emma would make do, especially since Mrs. Pickering's garden out front yielded so many vegetables that summer. Magazines these days were all about new recipes, creating something from nothing, but Emma had been doing that for years. The ration was just one more hurdle to tenaciously overcome.

"I do enjoy reading to myself," Olivia said. "It's like my brain drinking in something good, like warm chocolate milk."

Emma always loved the odd phrasings her daughter used to describe the world around her. That unique context gave Emma insight to life through Olivia's eyes in the most wonderful ways. "I think that sounds delightful."

As Emma prepared dinner, Olivia didn't bother with the wireless. Instead, she immediately lifted the book and slipped back onto the farm at Cuthbert place with Anne.

Emma's father had been right—every person just needed the right book to make them a reader.

Several weeks later, Emma climbed the stairs to her flat, only this time the silence in the stairwell was not uncommon. Sure enough, when she opened the door, there was Olivia, tucked into the right-hand corner of the couch, her face obscured by a green linen-bound book with a Booklover's Library badge marking its cover.

As it turned out, Olivia was not just any kind of reader. She was a voracious reader.

"Hullo, Olivia," Emma called out in a singsong voice.

Olivia lowered the book with a grin on her face, revealing the canine on the other side now missing. At least her new teeth seemed to be growing as fast as her old ones were falling out. "Good day at the Booklover's Library?"

Even as she spoke, she peered at Emma's handbag for the telltale shape of a book jutting out.

Emma coyly hid her handbag. "I did. And I might have a surprise for you if you've been well-behaved."

"I'm always well-behaved." Olivia tilted her head pensively. "Wistful, but well-behaved."

"'Wistful,' that's a good word."

Olivia straightened up where she'd been slumped against the soft back of the sofa, clearly delighted with the praise, but then, then her brow furrowed. "What does 'becoming' mean? Not in the way something turns into something else, but another meaning."

Emma swirled her mac off the coatrack and onto her shoulders like a cape and swept into the living area like an actress gliding onto the stage. "When someone, or something, is lovely." She batted her lashes.

Olivia giggled. "You are always becoming, Mum."

"As are you, darling Olive."

Nearly every day, there was a new word Olivia asked about. What did "ingenuously" mean? What color was "alabaster"? What precisely was an "epoch"? The latter of which she pronounced ee-potch, learning the very important lesson that vocabulary words read in one's mind can be used properly in speech, but may not be pronounced correctly.

It was a beautiful thing seeing Olivia, who had struggled for so long in school, embracing learning. And in the best way possible—through the enjoyment of a story.

Emma pulled out the week's rations and surveyed the freshly picked summer vegetables Mrs. Pickering harvested from their narrow garden to assemble dinner. That was the part of their evening when Olivia talked. And talked. And talked. She regaled Emma in vivid detail with everything she'd read, likely speaking more words than were written in *Anne of Avonlea*.

Truth be told, Emma had wondered if the book about Anne growing up to become a schoolmistress would hold any appeal, especially given Olivia's disinterest in school. Surprisingly, it did. She was just as riveted by the story of Anne as an adult coming into her career as Olivia had been by Anne's life as an orphaned little girl seeking a home.

That night when they went to bed, Olivia regarded Emma thoughtfully. "Since we both love books, that makes us kindred spirits."

"Indeed, it does." Emma ruffled Olivia's hair. "Your grandfather loved to read. We even had a bookshop."

"You owned a bookshop?" Olivia's mouth fell open, a reader imagining a trove of treasure.

"We lived above it," Emma replied.

"And that also burned down with your home?" Olivia surmised solemnly.

Emma nodded. She'd mentioned that she'd lived through a fire that destroyed their home when she was young, but she'd kept the worst of the details from Olivia. Mentioning the bookshop was something Emma hadn't been ready to bring up then.

"Your father loved to read too." Emma had forgotten that part of Arthur, how much he'd enjoyed talking about books with a similar enthusiasm as Olivia. But Emma had still been too raw from her father's death, and the tender, vulnerable parts of her couldn't stand even the lightest touch of memories of him.

Arthur had been left to read alone, to think about those books alone. The realization struck her then that in many ways, she had not given their marriage the chance to blossom.

It was curious how the day-to-day of life could sometimes bury the past.

Olivia perked up. "My father loved to read?"

Emma nodded.

"Do you think he'd be proud of me?" Olivia pressed her lips together as she sometimes did when she was anxious.

"I know he would be." Emma pressed a kiss to her daughter's brow and snuggled her close. "Just as I am."

Emma didn't know how long she'd been asleep when the world beneath her shuddered violently. Olivia screamed and clawed at her even as Emma tried to gather the frantic writhing limbs of her daughter into her arms.

Everything was dark, leaving them blind. Fear blared in the back of her mind. Hitler was consuming all in his path, and they were next.

There hadn't been an air raid siren.

Why hadn't there been an air raid siren?

Emma snatched up the torch she left by her bed after the first air raid siren went off last September following the declaration of war. At the press of a button, a beam of light cut through the dark.

The rumbling beneath them did not still. Something in the kitchen popped to the ground with a shatter.

"We're going to die," Olivia screamed and held on to Emma so fiercely, her skinny arms shook with effort. "I love you. I love you. I love you."

The panic in Olivia's voice set loose a primal protectiveness in Emma, fortifying her. "Shhh, it's all right," Emma soothed, her tone emollient despite the erratic thrum of her own pulse.

The floor continued to tremble and rock.

This was no bomb.

But nor was it normal.

Carrying Olivia, Emma rushed to the stairwell as Mrs. Pickering called to her amid Tubby's frantic barking.

"Mr. Sanderson," Emma cried.

Above, the sound of the door opening echoed down the corridor. "Do you need my help?"

Emma held her shivering daughter. "No, but it isn't safe."

"So I should go into those flimsy shelters?" He scoffed. "They don't even have mortar." The sound of the door being closed abruptly echoed down the stairwell.

"Outside now," Mrs. Pickering shouted.

She waited at the bottom of the stairs, as if fearful of leaving Emma and Olivia behind, then shepherded them into the summer night along with Tubby. They had agreed not to bother with the coal bin, not when the house falling in on them would kill them as surely as a bomb.

Others were already outside their tenement houses, their faces reflecting the same fear and confusion that crackled through Emma.

Though the quaking ground went still at last, they all swept into the large, blocky buildings in the middle of the street, a mishmash of pajamas, rolled hair, slippers, and bare feet. A row of narrow benches ran parallel on either side of the shelter. Emma pulled Olivia into her lap as Mrs. Pickering did likewise with her large handbag, which contained Tubby secreted inside.

No sooner had they sat down than the trembling started once more—without an air raid siren to warn them. The bricks shifted against one another, yielding a cloud of sifting dust, and Emma couldn't help but recall what Mr. Sanderson had said about the lack of mortar. Upon examination, there was some, but very little, as though the builders had been conserving the precious resource.

Perhaps at the cost of people's lives.

The paper the next evening cited an earthquake, followed by an aftershock. While knowing Nottingham hadn't been attacked brought relief, the terror had been too close for comfort. Especially in light of Olivia's reaction.

That her daughter had been so fearful told Emma the time had come to do something she'd been putting off since the start of the war. Something she didn't think she would ever do in a million years.

It was time to connect with her in-laws, to see if they would be willing to take Olivia into their home in Chester. Not now, but should evacuation become necessary.

34

EMMA WAITED FOR the Barton's bus to pull up several weeks later on her way to work after running late that morning. The strange inflated bag over the bus where the vehicle was powered by charcoal gas was nearly sagging in on itself.

"Looks like you're close to needing a refill," the man in front of Emma said to the bus driver as they climbed aboard.

"It should last several more stops." The young woman with a smart blond bob beneath the driver's cap tossed a cheeky grin. "But then I always push it to the limit."

That was another shift the city was seeing: women filling the roles men left behind. The change was refreshing for women, allowing so many doors to open to them, so many fields where they could find a career that had been barred in the past.

The other day, there had been a notice in the paper for female engineers that offered a base salary higher than had ever been seen in the career before.

Europe being at war altered everything—and in some ways, those changes were for the better.

Emma stepped off the bus, and couldn't help but notice the bag atop the vehicle was now practically flat.

Morning was one of her favorite times of day on Pelham Street, when the only people on the walkway were those with work destinations rather than shoppers lingering and filling the air with raucous chatter. The sun spilled an early golden light over the street, promising a warm August day as the yeasty scent of baking bread filled the air mingling with the fragrant temptation of fresh tea.

These were the kind of moments that promised the war would be soon behind them, that promised peace and bolstered her spirits.

Arthur's parents had responded to Emma's inquiry, stating they would happily welcome Olivia into their home should Nottingham become dangerous. Their immediate reply niggled at Emma's conscience for having waited so long to reach out. After all, Olivia was their granddaughter. Their only grandchild.

But then, Emma recalled the way they'd treated her following Arthur's death when she'd tried to live with them—the curt replies, the way they'd shared irritated looks when she spoke up, the constant demeaning remarks—and her guilt was assuaged.

Hopefully Nottingham remained at peace, and Olivia wouldn't need to go to Chester.

Emma entered the Booklover's Library to find Irene already there. The last few weeks seemed to ease her grief, as if the distraction of work had done her good.

"There was a misshelved book this morning." Panic widened Irene's eyes. "I found Charles Dickens in romance and, well…" Her demeanor shifted easily to something lighter as she giggled and held out *Oliver Twist*.

There hadn't been any misshelved books of late.

"It happens from time to time," Emma replied with more nonchalance than she felt. "Just don't ever let Miss Crane see."

That afternoon, Mr. Fisk came in for the first time in what seemed like months. Emma was already turning to help him when she caught sight of Miss Crane making a beeline across the library in his direction. Her toe caught a rug and she tripped just as Emma opened her mouth to offer Mr. Fisk—Charles—assistance.

"I've been training new recruits at the fire brigade and this last book took a while to get through." He returned his copy of Victor Hugo's *Les Misérables* to Emma.

"Long, but worth it." Emma used two hands to heft the book into the bin to be returned onto the floor.

"Absolutely. I confess, I almost came by before I was finished." He smiled, and his gaze fixed on her in a way that made the entire rest of the room disappear. "For an excuse to see you. But I couldn't do that to Victor Hugo."

"I'm certain Victor appreciates your diligence," Emma replied as a slow, welcome heat swelled in her chest.

Goodness, was she flirting?

If so, the sensation was rather enjoyable. Bubbly and effervescent, lighter than she'd felt in far too long.

"I have already read *War and Peace*," a man all but shouted across the room.

Emma glanced over and found Mr. Beard with his face as red as his hair was white, towering over a terrified Irene.

"I've also read *A Tale of Two Cities*. And *Middlemarch*. And every other classic you send my way," he continued. "I don't want to read the same books over and over."

Irene shrank back from him. "But you said mysteries are degrading Britain's literacy—"

Emma flashed an apologetic smile to Charles and rushed to intervene. "Mrs. Upton, will you please distribute the new shipment in the Bespoke Room?" Emma asked gently, then turned to Mr. Beard. "I know you don't care for mysteries, but there is one that is so dreadfully formulaic, I'm sure you'll want to explore the dull prose that many claim to be heart-stopping."

The brilliant red in his face drained away almost immediately. "I must see this book you speak of at once," he huffed, his fulmination finally at an end.

Emma made a mental note to have another talk with Irene later about Mr. Beard's affinity for mysteries despite his feigned disgust toward them. When Emma finally had Mr. Beard in a less ruffled state with a new murder mystery in hand, Miss Crane was already attending to Charles, leading him to the checkout desk.

The interruption was for the best. Emma had no time for romantic interludes.

However, as Emma approached the Bespoke Room later that day after Mr. Fisk's exit, Miss Crane's voice drifted from the cracked door.

"It's really dreadful he hasn't signed up. A strong man such as him shirking his responsibility? Especially considering the many brave men who are out there risking life and limb for Britain."

Emma wasn't one to eavesdrop, but in this circumstance, she was curious whose character Miss Crane was so thoroughly eviscerating. Surely not Mr. Fisk's.

"I'm certain the men have their reasons," Irene replied, her tone cautious, clearly uncomfortable with the conversation forced upon her. "My husband came from a long line of soldiers, so it was always in him to sign up."

"Well, Mr. Fisk truly ought to know better, or so I would assume."

Emma jerked upright as if she'd been the object of Miss Crane's scorn. Before another word could be uttered, she pushed through the door and into the Bespoke Room. "Our subscribers can hear every word you're saying."

Miss Crane usually had a sharp retort for everything. Now she sputtered in embarrassed indignation, her face red. "You shouldn't listen in on other people's conversations." Then she strode haughtily from the room, leaving a heavy silence in her wake.

"I think she was trying to befriend me," Irene said in a small voice. "She wanted to talk about what a hero my husband was and brought up the men who weren't fighting, like Mr. Fisk." She picked at a corner of her fingernail where the red varnish was chipping off. "I don't agree with her. I'm sure he has his reasons."

"I'm sure he does," Emma replied.

What she didn't elaborate on was how Mr. Fisk had clearly cast aside Miss Crane's interest and how that might well have played a part in her degrading comments. Still, the mother in Emma was disappointed with Miss Crane's pettiness, the low way she'd disparaged someone in an effort to obtain a friend.

Though the day had such an auspicious start, Emma's temples now throbbed with a headache. Thankfully she had the evening off from the canteen at Victoria Station and she planned to settle in on the sofa alongside Olivia with a re-read of *Mansfield Park*. Truly, there was nothing better than the companionable silence that fell between readers in a quiet room, each entirely lost in their own worlds.

As she walked by the small garden in front of the tenement house, a boy approached her, making her stop dead in her tracks.

Edmund.

"Mrs. Taylor?" There was a reticence to the boy, most likely a feigned meekness for the benefit of adults.

He was small for his age, certainly smaller than Olivia, and a smattering of freckles dotted the pale skin across the bridge of his nose.

Emma regarded him sharply. So many words crowded her thoughts in that moment, years of helpless frustration at the hurt he'd caused Olivia, words that Emma wanted to unleash upon him.

And yet for all his cruelty, he was still a child, and so she dammed her ire, waiting to see what he had to say.

"I want you to know that your daughter is…" He swallowed and looked down at the ground so his dark hair fell forward.

Emma tensed, the ache in her head throbbing in time with her hammering pulse.

To her surprise, when he looked up, his eyes were glossy with tears. "I teased Olivia because she don't have a father."

Emma stiffened. All the years of Olivia crying at his abuse, of the way she had refused to ever tell Emma what Edmund had said to her.

Now she knew. And what cut her deeper than Olivia being teased for not having a father was that she had taken the burden onto herself entirely to keep from hurting Emma.

"Now I don't have a father. The Germans…" Edmund snuffled and scraped his nose over his sleeve. "The Germans…" He shook his head, unable to complete what he was going to say. "When your Olivia found out, she…" His voice cracked and his lips tucked downward.

Emma braced herself, thinking of all the ways such unfairness at so much bullying might be balanced.

"She hugged me and told me it'd be all right." The boy sucked in a hard breath, his face crumpling. Before Emma could reply or even offer her sympathy, he turned and ran toward the tenement house next door.

Emma watched him go, hurting with the knowledge of the rough road of grief ahead of him. And though she didn't care for Mrs. Mott, she knew how hard the loss of a husband could be.

When Emma entered the flat, she sensed something was amiss. "Olivia?"

She was curled up on the couch, her book lying closed beside her, eyes red-rimmed from crying.

Emma sank down beside Olivia, who sat up and began to sob in earnest.

"Edmund's father is dead," she said, her words broken by hearty sobs. "I saw him crying outside and went to see what happened."

Emma had wondered when her daughter had even spoken to the boy. To know she'd actively sought him out was even more startling.

She rubbed Olivia's back in small, soothing circles. "That was kind of you."

"I know what it's like not to have a father. I don't want him to feel the way I do." Olivia's voice broke and so did Emma's heart.

Kneeling in front of her daughter, she embraced her. "I'm sorry it's been so hard, that you don't have your father when everyone else does."

Olivia held on to Emma. "I have you."

"The two of us against the world." Emma kissed the top of her daughter's head. "It was good of you to think of someone else, especially someone who has been so unkind to you."

"Anne would have done it." Olivia pulled back, her eyes big and earnest. "She always thought about people and why they do things. I know Edmund is mean to me, but I still wanted to help, like Anne."

Emma stroked her daughter's hair back from her damp forehead. She'd brought *Anne of Green Gables* to Olivia in the hopes her daughter would connect with the protagonist, to see herself there and not allow herself to be bullied.

In the end, reading had taught her an even more important lesson—one in kindness and empathy.

That late-August night, the air raid siren had them both bolting out of bed with its long, wailing cry. More efficient with practice, Emma grabbed the torch from her nightstand with one hand and Olivia with the other. Together they ran down the stairs to Mrs. Pickering, who was already waiting in a robe and loafers with Tubby tucked in a generous tote to sneak into the shelter where pets were not allowed.

They didn't bother with the ramshackle shelters in front of their tenement home. No, this time, they rushed several streets over to the entrance of the caves.

There was a network of caves beneath the city. Rumored to have once housed tanners and lepers in the medieval days, and then later bootleggers hiding alcohol, they were now used for storage and as air raid shelters.

Emma trusted the brace of centuries-old solid stone over the hastily built shelters that spit mortar with the slightest rumble.

The temperature cooled as they descended into the damp, chilly depths. Lights lined a path that spilled out into a main area where hundreds of people loitered about in their bedclothes. Some with pillows had already cradled against the rough-hewn wall toward the back, eager to return to sleep.

The room was brightly lit. No need to worry about the blackout down in a cave, after all. To one side, a wall was painted with "Ladies" with an arrow indicating one location and "Gents" with an arrow indicating the other. Likely for those in need of the necessary.

They truly had thought of everything.

"Another earthquake?" a man said irritably. His gray hair jutted from the right side of his head, clearly where he'd lain against his pillow.

"Or another false alarm," someone else groused.

All around them rose the grumblings of people who'd been roused from their sleep in the middle of the night.

Olivia remained quiet, her sweaty hand locked in Emma's as she looked around with silent fascination. "Why didn't Robin Hood use the caves instead of Sherwood Forest?"

"That is a very good quest—"

Before Emma could finish the rest of her statement, the carved room around them rumbled. Not with the elongated tremble of an earthquake, but the fast shudder of something hard and heavy striking the earth.

The room fell silent, bathed in an oily wash of fear.

A chill raised the hairs on the back of Emma's neck and had nothing to do with the temperature of the cave.

Olivia's hand tightened on Emma's. "Mum?"

Another shudder struck, this one with more force, accompanied by the muffled sound of something explosive outside. The lights flickered and several women screamed.

Emma pulled her daughter into her lap, some baser instinct recognizing the sound she'd never heard before, her gut tight with certainty.

Nottingham was being bombed.

35

THE BOMBS FELL for what seemed like hours.

Once the all-clear sounded and everyone was finally allowed out, a distinct odor of smoke tinged the night air. Fortunately there were no fires to be seen, meaning wherever the bombs had struck was not in the vicinity.

Later, newspapers reported that all of England had been peppered with explosives and incendiaries. While some fell harmlessly in the countryside and fizzled out in gardens, many of those errant hits caused damage. Casualties.

The latter remained in Emma's thoughts as she went through the motions of her shift at the Booklover's Library the following day. A little boy in Nottingham had been killed, his mother inconsolable. Emma wished she couldn't imagine such pain, but in truth, the story was all she could think about.

The new prime minister had been right—the Battle of Britain really had begun.

What if another air raid happened while Emma was at work?

She'd left Olivia with detailed instructions in the event of an air raid, to grab Tubby on his lead and rush to the caves with a tote to hide him inside. But what if there wasn't enough time? What if going to the caves instead of the shelter in front of their house took too long? A shoddily built shelter was better than nothing. Wasn't it?

Which meant that while Emma dreaded facing the truth, she knew Olivia would need to go to the country with Arthur's parents. Where she would be safe.

The suitcase on Emma's bed was on loan from Irene.

Arthur's was with Olivia in Chester, where she'd arrived safely at his parents' farm per the telegram they'd promptly sent several days ago.

The flat was unnaturally quiet again. The lifeless kind of quiet when the heartbeat of a home was rendered still by the absence of its dearest occupant.

No sooner had Miss Bainbridge found out that Olivia was being sent to the country once more than she immediately secured a place for Emma in the Aldgate branch of the Booklover's Library in London.

At least Emma wouldn't be alone. Margaret was going as well.

Emma sifted through her clothes, ensuring her smartest outfits were already packed alongside her brush and other necessary toiletries.

A sharp ring sounded from the main door of the tenement house.

Margaret, most likely, as she'd promised to collect Emma so they could travel to the train station together.

Emma snapped the suitcase closed and hefted it from the bed, grunting at the surprising weight. How could a handful of garments and a couple of toiletries be so heavy?

She shifted its bulk to her right side, as that arm had always been stronger. It was the one she'd used to carry Olivia, and the one she now defaulted to for groceries and the like.

She rushed from the flat, locking the door behind her, and hastened downstairs.

"Not my stockings," Margaret squealed from below.

Emma arrived to quite a scene where Margaret, smartly dressed in a red coat and a chic matching hat tilted jauntily over one eye, danced her legs away from Tubby. But the dog was relentless, squirming against Mrs. Pickering in a bid to get to Margaret, his neck straining as he flicked at the air with his pink tongue.

After a struggle, Mrs. Pickering pushed Tubby into her flat and closed the door. Her orderly hair was a wild mass of gray jutting out every which way and her flushed face reflected her exasperation. Behind her, Tubby scratched fiendishly at the door.

"Well." Mrs. Pickering put her hands on her hips and regarded Margaret like she'd grown a second head. "What on earth would possess you to slather your legs in gravy?"

Emma looked at Margaret's legs where her "stockings" had small tongue-sized flecks missing from the color, revealing pale skin beneath.

"Everyone does it." Margaret rubbed at her legs, as if she could distribute the color more evenly. "Especially now that Windly doesn't produce the stockings it used to." She referred to the local Windly & Co Hosiery factory that had recently stopped making stockings in light of the war effort.

"You don't have a special kind of makeup for your legs?" Emma asked, incredulous. Even she had seen the advertisements for Henry C. Miner's liquid stockings.

Margaret sighed. "The color said Gold Mist, but it looked orange when I put it on. I couldn't very well walk around with orange legs."

"Not with that red jacket," Mrs. Pickering said in such a

show of sartorial judgment as she stood there with her riotous hair and housecoat that they all laughed.

"You have the details to call the boardinghouse?" Emma asked Mrs. Pickering anxiously.

"For the tenth time, I do," she replied, patient as ever. "I'll telephone you the moment you receive a letter or telegram from Olivia or her grandparents."

Emma's shoulders eased down a notch. She'd already heard from Olivia, who mentioned she was pretending to be Anne on the farm at Green Gables. There had been an eagerness in Olivia when she left, to learn more about her father through the connection of her grandparents. Emma only hoped her daughter would not experience the coldness she herself had, lest Olivia end up disappointed and hurt.

For now, Olivia was fully embracing life in Chester and had begun to read *Little House in the Big Woods* by Laura Ingalls Wilder. A personal favorite of Emma's.

Margaret patched her "stockings" as best she could, and then she and Emma were off to the bus stop to begin their long journey to London.

The Boots' location in Aldgate boasted a pharmacy that never closed, open around the clock on all days of the week to offer medicinal aid to customers.

Emma had never heard of such a thing, but was glad the Booklover's Library didn't hold similar hours. Besides, everyone knew that a reader who stayed up beyond their bedtime to finish the book then savored its final moments as they drifted off to sleep. They did not run out at three in the morning to crack open a new adventure.

Arthur had lived in London after escaping Chester and had described the city to her. It had been too large for him, too busy, especially after the unnerving stillness of life at his parents' farm. But Emma had grown up in Nottingham, which Arthur thought to be the perfect blend of quiet and busy. To Emma, London was a wild ride she'd waited her whole life to experience.

There were theaters to attend, sprawling museums with the most fascinating artifacts to explore, and there were more shops than even Margaret could stop at in the two weeks they were to be there. And the books!

There was an entire area known as Paternoster Row lined with printers and booksellers and warehouses piled high with every book imaginable.

Truly there was no city in the world as incredible as London.

Emma and Margaret were given the first day to themselves, to become acquainted with the city. Initially Emma followed Margaret into and out of countless cosmetics shops. But there were only so many shades of red lipstick Emma could view before Persian Red, Cherry Ripe, Garnet, Firefly, and all the other enticing names began to look exactly the same.

Promising to rejoin Margaret later, Emma wound her way toward the book district, taking her time to look at the artful displays behind large sheets of plate glass marred only by diagonal strips of scrim tape.

In such ways, war had left its mark on the lovely city in addition to nearly every flat surface plastered with posters encouraging people to do one thing or another.

For now, Emma was doing as the signs instructed and walked rather than using public transportation. A misstep in her directions led to her meandering down a narrow street, happening upon a little shop that sat snug between two larger buildings, like a child pressed into the warmth of its parents' embrace.

The shop was relatively unassuming with its black-and-yellow façade, weathered by time to a pale yellow and threaded through with cracks. Glossy paint on a white sign spelled out the establishment's name in an old bookish looping script.

Primrose Hill Books.

This was precisely the kind of place she would have gone to with her father in search of rare items for their own collection.

Tape was carefully x-ed over the windows, leaving a patch in the middle to reveal an autumnal scene with paper leaves that seemed to tumble from the ceiling before settling softly on the display of books. Great care had clearly been put into crafting such an appealing aesthetic.

Something twisted in Emma's chest. She'd found solace among the fellow readers in the Booklover's Library, but she had yet to enter a bookshop on her own. This too would be part of her path to healing after Papa's death.

She entered the front door and a little bell chimed. Tower Bookshop had a bell just like it. And like Tower Bookshop, this one had rows and rows of books on offer. Neat pasteboard signs displayed the genres while tidy tables were set up smartly throughout.

Breathing in slowly, she savored the scent of thousands of books, new and old alike, of the dust that settled into cracks never able to be wiped away, of the leather that contained a million adventures between their bindings.

The knot in her chest loosened, and she knew with certainty that this was exactly the kind of place where she belonged.

A young woman with blond hair and large brown eyes approached, her smile friendly. "May I help you?"

Emma glanced up to the second floor of the bookshop where the shelves stretched up to the ceiling. "I think I'd just like to look, please."

"Of course." The woman pointed to the history section.

"I'll be right over here if you need me." On her way to the collection of shelves, she passed a glossy chestnut counter and casually plucked a balled-up bit of paper, which she bent to dispose of in a rubbish bin.

A table off to the right had several copies of Nancy Mitford's new book, *Pigeon Pie*, and a sign declaring, *Written while Chamberlain was still prime minister.* The book poking fun at the phoney war had terrible timing in its release just before France fell to the Nazis. But blaming the former prime minister who had left England irritated with his passivity was nothing short of genius.

Emma chuckled to herself.

"Miss Bennett." A gruff voice sounded behind Emma. She turned to find a man in a loose jumper with a head of white hair and eyebrows so bushy they practically rested atop his glasses. He held out a ledger to the young woman. "What the devil does this say?"

Miss Bennett appeared entirely unperturbed at his gruff demeanor and she leaned close to read, "Charles Dickens for a Christmas display."

"Christmas?" He looked at the page again. "What was I thinking?"

"Being prepared in advance," Miss Bennett suggested.

"Ah, so likely something you put in my head." Though he sounded cantankerous as he spoke, there was a glint of mirth in his eyes.

If Emma hadn't heard him call the young woman Miss Bennett, she might have thought the employee was his daughter.

Leaving them to their work, Emma slipped away to explore.

A door at the rear of the building had a small brass placard, reading *Primrose Hill Books—where readers find love.*

Emma smiled, feeling love in that moment. The love of books and the love of her father, as if his presence resided here among the fragrant aroma of books and the promise of so many stories to be discovered.

"Mr. Evans, has the post come yet?" Miss Bennett asked.

From an aisle over came the reply. "Yes, and there was nothing from your Mr. Anderson."

"And I was so hoping for a marriage proposal in today's post." Miss Bennett sighed heavily.

"I do hope that was a joke," the man answered dryly.

Miss Bennett replied with a soft laugh.

Emma grinned, recalling how she and her father had shared such banter with one another. Wandering down the classics aisle, she came upon the man who was called Mr. Evans cradling a copy of *Les Misérables* in his hands.

His tufted brows lifted. "Eh, if you need help finding a book, I suggest you ask Miss Bennett. She's far more astute at such things than me."

Emma considered his suggestion. "I think I will, thank you."

"You're better than you give yourself credit for." Miss Bennett appeared at the end of the aisle and tossed a skeptical look at Mr. Evans.

"I'm just the owner." He waved his hand dismissively and returned his focus to Victor Hugo.

"What are you looking for?" Miss Bennett asked.

"I'm willing to give anything a go," Emma replied. "What do you generally recommend?"

Miss Bennett reached for the shelf in front of Emma. "This one changed my life." She pulled a book free and handed it to Emma with a smile.

The Count of Monte Cristo.

The Aldgate location of the Booklover's Library was far busier than the Pelham Street branch back in Nottingham. Downstairs at the chemist, nurses in white caps shifted behind a stretch of counter, prepared to give first aid advice and distribute medication day or night.

The Booklover's Library was upstairs, a haven from the bustle of the chemist shop below, though by no means any less busy. The manageress there was the no-nonsense type, with her hair pulled back in a smooth bun and eyebrows that were drawn on in a surprised arch above her keen blue eyes. She was sleek and chic, even with her green overalls tied over her dress, with pearl clips at her ears and her lips a shade of red just slightly deeper and more mature than Margaret's.

"You likely won't see most of our patrons again," she explained in a slightly haughty tone. "Unlike your smaller town libraries, ours is teeming with travelers on the go. They take their book from our location and return it wherever they end up."

No sooner had they stepped onto the floor than an elderly man approached Margaret. "I'd like this one to help find me a book."

Margaret looked to the manageress, who waved her approval.

The wail of an air raid siren broke through the serene quiet of the Booklover's Library. Both Emma and Margaret flinched.

"You're welcome to go to a shelter," the manageress said in a bored tone. "I can point you in the appropriate direction."

Everything in Emma screamed at her to seek shelter, especially after the bombing in Nottingham just days ago. Ignoring the primal urge, she remained standing stoically in front of the manageress in an effort to not look as provincial as the woman had already made her feel.

"There are planes outside," a woman exclaimed and pointed at the stained-glass windows. The throb of planes reverberated through Emma's bones, pulling her toward the window.

Her pulse quickened.

There amid the red-and-orange-colored glass was a swarm of planes that seemed to blot out the late-afternoon sun.

"Those are likely our RAF." The manageress pulled a stack of books toward her and opened her mouth to speak.

Whatever she'd meant to say was overwhelmed by a powerful boom that sent the ground shuddering. The woman by the window screamed and ducked, arms coming protectively over her head. In the distance beyond the colored panes of glass, violent flames exploded.

London was being attacked.

36

EMMA AND MARGARET spent the better part of the day tucked in a nearby bomb shelter with everyone who had been in Boots'. The manageress sat mute with a distant stare, her hair slightly mussed, her naked lips even more pale in the absence of lipstick. She no longer looked chic.

When the all-clear finally sounded, Emma rose on legs that were stiff from sitting for too long, her joints creaking with movement. Margaret got slowly to her feet and together they staggered toward the exit.

There was a charred odor in the air, one that jabbed at Emma with pinpricks of alarm.

They climbed the short set of stairs from the shelter, nearly bumping into the manageress, who had exited first, and drew to an abrupt stop.

The city was on fire.

Brilliant red and orange and glowing gold lit an area of the city roughly three kilometers away. Above the massive conflagration, the sky was choked with black smoke that billowed from the flames in thick, dark plumes.

With such destruction, there would likely be many casualties.

"The Germans have finally come for us," a man beside Emma said. "After all this time, we're next."

A shiver rattled through Emma.

It couldn't be true. England falling to Hitler was unfathomable. But he had started in Poland with bombs and now he'd clearly set his sights on Britain.

Suddenly, she found herself grateful for the in-laws she'd never cared for, for their readiness to take Olivia into the quiet locale of their farm. Their home was set in the country in an area filled with stretches of farmland. The last place that Hitler would stage an attack.

Safe.

Amid the emergency vehicle sirens screaming in the distance and the murmur of concerned voices, the customer who'd first noticed the planes began to weep.

There was no electricity or water at the boardinghouse that night. The landlady had at least set a few candles and a pot of water in the room Emma and Margaret were sharing, for washing their faces and brushing their teeth. And for Margaret to swallow a couple of black pills from a tin labeled *Bile Beans*.

Emma lifted a brow. "Bile Beans?"

"Taken at bedtime to be healthy, bright-eyed, and slim." Margaret put her hand under her chin, angling her face as she gave a beatific smile, looking and sounding like a magazine ad.

"Bright-eyed?" Emma picked up the bottle with interest.

How long had it been since she'd felt bright anything? Cooking, cleaning, ironing, mending, all the household tasks made heavier by the wartime workarounds. Not to mention her work at the canteen with the WVS and the Booklover's Library.

"Does it give you energy?" Emma asked.

Margaret shrugged. "It seems to help. But they make one for mothers too." She held up a finger and rummaged about in her suitcase before straightening with a magazine in hand. The pages crinkled as she riffled through them and stopped abruptly. "Here. Beecham's Pills."

Emma leaned closer, squinting in the dim light as Margaret handed her the magazine. Pills for the "modern mother," the ad claimed, to help mothers stay slim, active, and never overtired.

The "never overtired" aspect was appealing, to be sure. While Emma could likely stand to lose a bit of weight, she didn't want to rely on a pill to be slim.

"You're so much more than your appearance." Emma handed the magazine back. "I hope you know that."

Margaret blinked in surprise.

"You're kind and compassionate, like when you gently put off the soldiers who are besotted with you at the canteen. And you are always so clever, with your witty replies and how you know what books and what cosmetics will help the women who come into the library, even the dastardly ones."

Margaret ducked her head and chuckled. "No one says dastardly anymore."

"Readers who love Austen and Brontë do." Emma grinned, aware her friend was trying to put off the compliments with humor. "And on that note, we need rest so we can offer our bookish suggestions to the patrons of Aldgate tomorrow." She fell back into bed, generating a rusty creak from the springs.

Margaret blew out the candle and the accompanying cry of springs told Emma Margaret had settled into her own bed on the other side of the room.

"Thank you," Margaret said into the dark. "For saying those things. You see me in a better way than I see myself. Like the way Jeffrey sees me. And my mum. My da…" She scoffed. "He was always more interested in ale than the likes of his own family. You should see him now, wandering about, pub to pub, 'til the taps bleed dry and they have to shove off to the next place that's still pouring."

"It's his loss," Emma replied, knowing full well the joy parenthood could bring. "And I hope your Jeffrey reassures you how much more than looks and books you really are."

"He does his level best." There was a grin in Margaret's reply that made Emma like Jeffrey all the more.

The sounds of the street outside filled the ensuing comfortable quiet with the cry of emergency sirens that had been running for hours.

"Can you still see the flames?" Margaret asked in the darkness.

Emma, whose bed was next to the window, drew back the blackout curtains. Though any light in their room was impossible with the electricity still out, the act of drawing back the curtains felt strangely wrong after over a year of keeping the windows blacked out.

In the distance, the East End glowed with flames.

She turned to look at Margaret and found her friend's face illuminated by the flickering golden light. Margaret had managed to still roll her hair into pin curls earlier by candlelight and a milky sheen of cold cream glistened on her skin.

Emma let the curtain drop. "Do you think what happened to Poland will happen to us?"

Just like pulling back the blackout curtains after constantly being told to keep them secure over the windows felt wrong, so too did voicing her fears aloud. But Emma didn't have to stay strong and positive for Olivia now. There was something freeing about putting her concerns into words, to see what they felt like when liberated from ricocheting around in her mind.

"Or Belgium, or France…" Margaret said softly. "We shouldn't expect any different."

No, they shouldn't. And that was what worried Emma most.

★ ★ ★

The following morning, the sky was still hazy with smoke, leaving the air difficult to breathe. Ash drifted around them like a fine dusting of snow and clung to their hair and coats.

"Hundreds dead, many more injured," a boy in a cap called as he held up a paper. The hooded lanterns the paperboys wore clipped to their buttonholes at night were glowing even now in the daytime to make them visible in the smoggy air. "Find out all the details about yesterday's bombing of the East End."

An ambulance drove by, attracting the attention of every person it passed, their gazes lingering longer than usual.

"Do you think hundreds really died?" Margaret asked.

Emma looked back toward the East End and the thick, unnatural clouds of smoke. Her stomach wrenched. "Yes, I do."

The manageress had assumed her polished poise once more. "I'm sure what happened yesterday was an extraordinary circumstance. You are, of course, allowed to return to Newark if you prefer."

"Nottingham," Margaret corrected her.

"And we're perfectly fine to remain," Emma lied, wishing for nothing more than to return to her small flat on Mooregate Street.

Home wasn't all Emma wanted. She longed to share a pot of tea with Mrs. Pickering again, and have Olivia there with her, snuggled into the corner of the couch with Tubby, a book in front of her face, her high-pitched giggle sounding when she read parts she found funny. Parts Emma knew Olivia would tell her all about later.

The manageress smiled tightly. "Very good. As you can see, patrons are already streaming in, ready to distract themselves with a good book from this…messy business."

"Messy business" was hardly a way to describe hundreds dead and injured and likely thousands who were now homeless. Despite her cavalier demeanor, she nearly jumped out of her skin when someone dropped a book by accident. Evidently she was not as unaffected as she claimed.

The day went on without incident until that afternoon when the air raid siren blared through the crowded library. This time, there was no condescending comment suggesting Emma and Margaret could go to a shelter if they felt they needed to. Now people shoved and pushed their way to the exit, including the manageress.

This time they were all sequestered in the shelter for only two hours, but it was enough to set everyone on edge. Most subscribers did not return to the Booklover's Library after the all-clear, likely returning home instead, and the manageress wasn't the only one jumpy now. Everyone seemed to be anxiously anticipating another air raid. Another bomb.

And still the fires in the East End raged on.

This was not how London was supposed to be. Margaret had been to the Piccadilly branch of the Booklover's Library a year before and had been eager to show Emma the parts of the city she knew. The cosmetics counters, of course, but also the theaters, the restaurants, the museums, the tea shops, and all the sights from Big Ben to Buckingham Palace.

The palace was something Emma had dreamed of seeing, to witness so grand an estate and know the king and queen resided within.

Except that exploring the grandeur London had to offer didn't feel right anymore, not when so many were suffering with loss and homelessness.

They didn't even bother going to a restaurant, opting instead to queue for fish and chips in a newsprint cone, laughing about how Emma's father used to count the meal as one of the few he could "cook." And though Margaret claimed the fried food wasn't as good as before the war, the greasy fare was delicious. And fast, affording them the opportunity to return to the boardinghouse before the blackout.

When they returned, they were grateful to find the electricity and water restored. Emma filled her bath all the way to the black line someone had taken the time to paint inside the tub and savored the luxury of the warm water she hadn't realized she'd taken for granted. When she returned to their shared room, she found Margaret with something green and wet on her face as she tamed her hair into pinned coils for perfect curls the next day.

"Feel better?" Margaret asked, having already bathed earlier that night.

"Much." Emma sighed and pulled the towel free from where she'd wrapped it around her wet hair. "Do you think they'll send us home?"

"Well, it's certainly hard to learn with everyone flinching at every little sound." Margaret separated a kirby grip with her teeth and focused on the round mirror as she pinned another twist of hair into place. "You want to go home, don't you?"

Emma secured her robe around her pajamas and sat on the edge of her bed. The springs of the mattress gave a tired groan. "I'm worried about Olivia with my in-laws. I know she's safe, but they're so...cold."

"Can they really be that bad?"

"At first I thought they were just different from my own father. Then I realized they simply didn't like me." Emma shrugged. "Not that you'll need to worry about that. I'm sure Jeffrey's parents love you and will make wonderful in-laws."

"I'm sure I'll find out."

Emma raised her brow. "Does that mean you've decided to set a date for the wedding?"

"I didn't say that." Margaret laughed. She twirled a section of her blond hair and then stared at the pin for a long moment before securing it into position. "Honestly, I'm scared. What if I don't like being a housewife? I can't go back." She turned in her seat. "Did you like it? Being a housewife?"

"I was so young…" And Emma really had been. At only seventeen, she really was still more an adolescent than an adult. "I thought it was exciting at first. And marriage gave me purpose after my father's death. Then we had Olivia and my whole world was her. I didn't have time to consider if I liked my life or not. Then Arthur died…" Emma sighed. "I was lucky he had funds set aside that I could live on for a time. And that he'd insured himself so Olivia and I could receive our pensions."

She didn't add that the money was barely anything she could live on or what a chore it was to collect. Every Tuesday, the day allotted to widows at the post office, she was able to trade in their pension orders to receive their stipends. Even then, Emma would only receive her money until she turned seventy and Olivia until she was fourteen.

"I suppose being a housewife is how I've spent most of my time as an adult." Emma shrugged. "Until I started at the Booklover's Library."

She was about to say how much she enjoyed her time working there when the shrill cry of the air raid siren filled the room.

"Again?" She groaned in exasperation.

Margaret leaped up. "I can't go out like this." Half of her hair was in curlers, and the other half was a veritable puff of un-coiffed frizz. Her blue eyes were wide in her green face and her robe hung open, revealing her pink silk nightgown beneath.

If the bombing hadn't been so terrifying the day before, the scene might have been hilarious.

Emma handed her damp towel to Margaret. "Scrub your face with this."

While she scoured at the green mask, Emma grabbed Margaret's red fedora. When her friend lifted her head from the towel, skin pink from the hard scrub, Emma dropped the hat on Margaret's head.

A sharp rap sounded on the door. "This place will go up like a tinderbox if it's struck," the landlady warned, her voice fading down the hall as she knocked on the next door.

That was all the encouragement Emma and Margaret needed as they shoved their feet into the nearest shoes they could find and ran down the stairs while drawing the belts of their robes snug round their waists.

People poured into the street in various stages of dress. Some in robes and pajamas like Emma and Margaret, others still in their attire from the day. Several people had pillows tucked under their arms, or small sacks of personal effects they wanted to keep safe.

Collectively they rushed into a brick building that was several feet thick and took the stairs down into the shelter partially submerged in the dirt. Emma couldn't help but glance at the mortar, noticing it was as thin as in Nottingham.

Everyone crowded in, filling the space quickly until the air was damp and warm with the proximity of so many people. Too many people.

Panic squeezed against Emma. The room was little more than a case of bricks scantily held together with a scrape of mortar.

If a bomb was to hit, they would all be dead.

"If they'd just open the tube stations for us, we wouldn't have to do this," a woman said with a scoff to whoever would listen.

"Wait." A man put his forefinger up, silencing the woman. In the resulting quiet came the familiar throb of plane engines.

Emma's pulse thrummed faster, harder, and the bombs began to fall.

37

THE BOMBING CONTINUED through the night. Great whumps that made the earth tremble paired with the bangs of the Royal Air Force fighting the bombers in the sky and the bone-rattling boom of the massive anti-aircraft guns distributed throughout London. The all-clear did not come until five the next morning.

Several people managed to sleep, their snores evident in the quiet breaks from explosions and gunfire, but Emma and Margaret did not sleep a wink, emerging from the shelter gritty-eyed and heavy with exhaustion.

Still, they were the lucky ones.

The East End had been struck again, the poor souls. For hours, bombers had been emptying the bellies of their planes onto the already battered section of London.

If hundreds had died before, many hundreds more had surely followed.

Back at the boardinghouse, Emma helped twist Margaret's half-curled hair into a simple chignon and Margaret artfully applied cosmetics to Emma's face, so she didn't look as thoroughly knackered as she felt. After finishing a bracing cup of tea—as bracing as one could have on the ration—the two of them entered the Booklover's Library looking presentable.

Mostly presentable, at least.

The manageress greeted them with her mouth set in a hard line. "In light of the recent bombings, it has been determined London is not safe for you at present." She pulled an envelope from behind the counter. "Here are your train tickets for your return to…" Her eyes flicked toward the tickets. "Nottingham."

They didn't have to be told twice. After packing their suitcases, they arrived at a very busy train station with what appeared to be most of London trying to flee the beleaguered city.

"The last time I saw a station this crowded was at Christmas when Olivia was at Aunt Bess's." Emma cast an anxious glance at Margaret.

They waited and waited, grabbing some tea and some nearly inedible margarine sandwiches before they could finally board the train. As they chugged out of the station, the now familiar note of caution from the air raid siren wailed after them. Margaret's face was cast in a strange pallor by the blue blackout lights of the interior, but Emma could still read the panic written plainly there.

The train wound its way from the city, following the immensely visible tracks cut into the English landscape. An ideal target for a well-timed bomb.

However, exhaustion and the lulling sway of the train won out over their fear, and both women woke with a start sometime later, realizing they were back in Nottingham.

Emma was disappointed upon her midnight arrival home to find there were no letters from Olivia. Granted, only a little more than a week had passed since her daughter went to Chester, and the post was dreadfully slow.

The rest of the mail forgotten, Emma leaned back on the counter. How had that bombing in Nottingham only been a week ago?

The tranquility of the flat, the wonderful comfort of having Olivia at her side—how had it all been within her grasp so recently?

At work the following day, Margaret showed up, looking her usual lovely self. Healthy, bright-eyed, and slim, exactly as her Bile Beans promised.

Irene greeted them both with grave concern. "You were in London during the bombing. Were you actually near the area that was hit?"

Emma and Margaret shared a look.

"You were, weren't you? Oh!" Irene clapped a hand over her chest. "Were you terribly frightened?"

"Terribly terrified," Margaret amended.

"Those poor people in the East End." Emma shuddered. "We are grateful to be home."

"It wasn't only the East End last night." Margaret pulled a newspaper from where it lay on the counter. "Apparently two hospitals were targeted as well."

Miss Crane approached. "You need to be working," she hissed.

"These two nearly died in London," Irene protested, her drawn-on brows lifting.

"And yet here they stand in good repair." Miss Crane jerked her head. "Off with the lot of you."

"She's in a mood," Margaret muttered as the other woman strode off.

"I found a misshelved book when you were gone." Irene winced. "It wasn't me as I'd only just come in that day, meaning it could only have been Miss Crane. She's been in a state ever since."

Margaret caught Emma's eye and smirked.

"Hopefully I'm absolved of some culpability now at least," Emma said, and Margaret gave an indelicate snort of laughter before returning to work.

Though being back at the Nottingham location was a relief, fatigue dragged at Emma through her shift and the whole way home until she wanted nothing more than to teeter into bed to sleep for an eternity.

But upon her arrival, Mrs. Pickering stopped her, an envelope in her hand. "I have a very special letter for you from Olivia. I tried to telephone you at the boardinghouse in London this morning, but they said you'd already left. Heavens, what the attacks must have been like." She caught Emma in a rose-scented hug and handed her the envelope. "Enjoy the letter and have a good rest, eh?"

Emma thanked her and headed up the stairs with renewed vigor. When the door closed behind her, she sank into a chair at the dining room table and slid the envelope open.

A pained exhale eased from her as she read.

Olivia was not happy.

No matter how much she pretended to be Anne at Green Gables, she found her grandparents to be "like two hard Marillas who never soften." Emma sighed. She'd found them to be precisely the same way. Any hope she had that they might be warmer to Olivia fluttered away, like moths rising from an old chest.

At least with this letter, Emma noted fewer grammatical and spelling errors. Olivia's grasp of vocabulary was stronger, with once unknown words now used correctly as she articulated the depth of her feelings.

Emma did smile at that, at the influence of books on her daughter.

But the request to return home could not be granted. Not after what Emma witnessed in London, not when such horrors could just as easily befall Nottingham.

Painful though it was, Emma responded back to Olivia explaining she must remain with her grandparents until England was safe again.

But when might that ever be?

The days slid by in the blurred way they did when Olivia was not there. Time passed in an endless whirl of trains carrying soldiers by the canteen at Victoria Station and with the influx of patrons visiting the Booklover's Library, now that people were scared into their homes at night.

Emma entered the Bespoke Room to find Irene bent over a box of books, her shoulders trembling. These days, everyone needed a moment to themselves from time to time.

Emma stepped back, intending to let her friend grieve in private, when she accidentally knocked into a shelf. A precariously resting book toppled, landing with an audible smack.

Irene snapped upright and spun around. "Emma?"

"I'm sorry, I didn't mean to intrude." Emma hesitated, unsure if she ought to leave or stay and offer comfort. "Are you all right?"

Of course Irene wasn't all right. She wouldn't be crying if she was. Why was that question the usual knee-jerk reaction when someone was clearly upset?

"It's just…all those children…" Irene wiped at her eyes with a handkerchief with the initials *TU* embroidered on it.

Emma froze. "Those…children…?"

"The *SS City of Benares*, have you heard? All those children being sent to Canada to be safe?" Irene sniffed and swiped under her lashes to clear her tears and spare her cosmetics. "My cousin said she almost put her daughter on that ship, but decided against it at the last minute, thank heavens…"

Emma had heard of the *SS City of Benares*. Didn't every mother read about the ships carting kids to Canada and wish for just a moment that their children could be sent to the far off country—where they would be entirely safe from Hitler's grasp? After all, he couldn't take over the entire world.

Could he?

"What happened to the ship?" Emma asked.

"It was attacked by a U-boat." Irene's eyes were wide, her lashes spiked with tears. "Almost all the children were killed."

Emma's thoughts reeled, imagining the parents. They had made the sacrifice to send their children to another continent, knowing months—possibly years—would pass until they would see their babies again. And they'd done it to keep them safe.

Only to have them murdered en route by a German U-boat.

Emma pressed her palm over her chest, as if the pressure could quell the pain radiating there for those poor parents.

"I know." Irene rested her hand against the front of her green overalls. "It hurts me every time I think of it."

The door creaked open and Margaret swept into the room. She looked first to Irene, then Emma. "Good heavens. What's happened?"

Before they could reply, the door opened once more and Miss Crane shoved into the room. "Was there a meeting I was not aware of?"

Irene shrank back slightly, indicating how well Miss Crane's attempt at friendship was going.

"We were just having a chat is all," Margaret answered smoothly.

But her charm only made Miss Crane glower. "Do you not have any integrity? Holing up in here like a knitting circle rather than being out on the floor to aid our patrons in their book selections?"

Her tyranny had gone on long enough.

Emma took a step toward Miss Crane. "We have plenty of integrity. And while I appreciate the lending library is of grave concern to you, there is so much more going on in the world than just this little corner of our existence."

Miss Crane drew back as if she'd been slapped. "You would think that. You have your daughter distracting you. You have the canteen to draw you from your work. You have so many moving pieces in your life." She glared around at them. "You all do. Families and children and friends and volunteer work."

"You could volunteer with us," Irene offered cautiously.

"Return to your duties or I'll have Miss Bainbridge in here." With that, Miss Crane shoved out the door, leaving a resonating silence in her wake.

It wasn't until Miss Crane's tirade that the missing pieces of figuring the other woman out finally fell into place. Miss Crane was not simply being mean. She was jealous.

Dreadfully so.

And that was a far, far more complicated emotion to handle.

38

THE COLD, LONG NIGHTS in November were marked by drums of burning oil that produced a greasy, noxious smoke lasting from dusk until dawn. The round barrels had chimneys rising up with steepled tops, like miniature roofs, issuing forth foul, choking plumes that wound through the streets, blanketing them in a wretched-smelling fog to mask the city from would-be bombers.

The precaution was not the only measure taken to spare Nottingham from being attacked. Large fires lit in distant fields outside the city, away from the homes and munitions factories, led planes to drop their explosive cargo onto empty land.

Thus far, such tactics had been effective. Enough so that Emma's resolve chipped away with each letter Olivia sent. After requests to come home failed, Olivia took to demanding, something she seldom ever did. Next came the bargaining.

Those letters were the worst.

The pleading promises for higher marks in maths, to never again try to stay home from school, to do whatever necessary to be allowed to return to Nottingham.

In the most recent letter, Olivia had plaintively asked if Emma even still loved her.

Such words were enough to break a mother's heart.

Emma stared down at that letter now, utterly torn. London was being bombed daily. Other areas of England were hit on a regular basis. So far, Nottingham had not been struck again, but for how long?

"Emma," Mrs. Pickering's voice called up the stairwell.

A glance at the clock confirmed Emma was late for their evening cup of tea. She set the letter aside, dreading writing the reply she knew Olivia would not like.

With a heavy heart, Emma descended the stairs to Mrs. Pickering's flat. But Tubby didn't greet her as he usually did. He was too busy scratching at the rear door leading to the porch area at the back of the building that they all shared.

"What's gotten into Tubby?" Emma asked.

"He's after our Christmas dinner." Mrs. Pickering waved for Emma to follow and led her through the living area, putting out the lights as she did so to remain in compliance with the black out when she opened the porch door.

"Christmas?" Emma followed, confused. "It's only mid-November."

Mrs. Pickering opened the door and edged Tubby back. "Go on, quickly, so we don't let that infernal smoke into the flat."

A distinct chill bit through Emma's jumper as she rushed outside into a night that otherwise would be crisp and fresh were it not for the haze of oily smoke.

A nearly full moon illuminated the back porch, displaying a rabbit cage, filled with straw and housing a small brown bunny with large onyx eyes.

"Got herself a rabbit, she did," Mr. Sanderson said from behind Emma.

She turned with a start to find him sitting in one of the old chairs.

"Good evening, Mr. Sanderson," the landlady said in a tone that suggested he was out there often.

He nodded to her.

Emma peered into the cage again. The rabbit gazed brazenly up at her, a wilted cabbage leaf jostling in its mouth as it ate. "Oh, Mrs. Pickering, it's too adorable to eat."

"Don't say that." Mrs. Pickering slapped at the air as if batting the words away. "I don't want a meatless Christmas this year."

"She's going to get attached." Mr. Sanderson folded his arms over his chest. "You mark my words."

"I am not." Mrs. Pickering turned to the rabbit and fished a cabbage core out of her apron pocket. "And that's why I haven't named you, isn't that right, Nameless?"

She dropped the core into the cage.

Nameless shuffled forward and sniffed at the offering, its nose twitching before taking a tentative nibble, followed by voracious munching.

"I have more where that came from," she cooed in the same voice she used when speaking to Tubby.

The scream of a teakettle sounded inside the house. "Oh, sounds like our tea is ready." Mrs. Pickering hesitated at the door. "Mr. Sanderson, will you join us?"

His focus had drifted up toward the sky. He pulled his attention back to Mrs. Pickering now and shook his head.

She disappeared inside, leaving Emma to take one last look at Nameless. The endearing little beast didn't stop chewing as it gazed up at her with those luminous eyes. "Do you really think she's going to eat it?"

"Not a chance," Mr. Sanderson replied without hesitation.

Emma straightened and smiled at Mr. Sanderson as his

focus drifted back up to the night sky. "Good evening, Mr. Sanderson."

He grunted in reply.

Emma returned inside to find an extra mug sitting on the table.

"Oh, do bring that out to Mr. Sanderson." Mrs. Pickering nodded at the mug. "I invite him to join us every evening, but he prefers to sit out there staring up at the sky. Still, it's too cold for a man to be out there in little more than house slippers and a light jacket."

"I didn't realize you invited him in the evenings." Emma carried the mug to the porch.

Mr. Sanderson didn't look away from the sky when she approached and set the tea on a table next to him.

"It would be lovely to have you join us sometime," Emma said.

Mr. Sanderson didn't reply, his gaze fixed above where the stars seemed lit with some phosphorescent paint, brilliant in the silky black sky.

"It's beautiful," Emma whispered.

"It is."

Was her mind playing with her, or was there a catch to his voice?

When she returned inside once more, Mrs. Pickering already had the tea ready. "I have business to discuss with you this evening." Her tone took the authoritative tenor she used during WVS meetings. "I noticed on your sign-up sheet, you indicated you knew how to drive."

Emma's brows lifted in surprise. A lifetime had passed since she'd filled out that form. That Mrs. Pickering either recalled it from memory or had the page readily on hand for reference did not surprise Emma in the least. "I do. Arthur taught me how to drive."

"What would you say to running our mobile canteen?"

Mrs. Pickering lifted her tea and took a long, purposeful sip, letting silence apply the pressure for her.

She really was a master at convincing people to do what she needed, which was why she was so good at leading their section of the WVS.

Emma had seen those mobile canteens in London. They were big, boxy vehicles with a window that popped open at the side to deliver food and drink to the men and women working late on their volunteer shifts.

Driving a Baby Austin was one thing. But driving that behemoth was entirely something different.

"It's a rather large vehicle, is it not?" Emma didn't bother to keep the trepidation from her voice.

Mrs. Pickering gave a little hum of delicate agreement. "Surely nothing you can't handle. You can practice a bit first. And, of course, Margaret can join you. The two of you would be quite the team, such lovely smiling faces for the exhausted men and women in need of sustenance and spirit."

Emma chuckled and set her tea aside. "Flattery will get you nowhere, Mrs. Pickering."

"That's where you're wrong." Mrs. Pickering regarded her earnestly. "Flattery gets me absolutely everywhere."

"Along with a dose of heavy-handedness…" Emma teased.

"Whatever gets the job done." Mrs. Pickering tilted her head in acknowledgment. "Well?"

There was that silence again, begging for an answer to fill the void.

Really, Churchill ought to hire the woman to press prisoners of war for information.

Emma sighed. "Very well, but not at night. I refuse to drive in the blackout."

"So, that's a yes then." Mrs. Pickering brightened, blatantly ignoring the bit about not driving in the dark. "Now that it's settled, I wanted to ask if you thought apple might go well with carrot for a pie. It's Francis's birthday next week…"

Mrs. Pickering moved quickly, as only she could do. The next day, after Emma's shift at the Booklover's Library, Mrs. Pickering was waiting at Victoria Station with Margaret and a set of keys in her hand. "Are you ready?"

Emma was absolutely not ready, but accepted the keys anyway.

"She's all loaded up with goods for you to bring to the fire brigade," Mrs. Pickering announced. "They'll be getting back from helping after a bombing raid nearby any minute now."

"Any minute?" Emma gaped at Mrs. Pickering.

The older woman was all formality and business in her double-breasted WVS coat and her green felt hat over her neat gray hair. "You'll be fine," she reassured Emma.

"I trust you not to kill us both." Margaret winked at her.

"That makes one of us." Emma descended the stairs to the parking area where a large white van waited for them.

They climbed in and Emma pressed her foot on the pedals, testing them out, before inserting the key and bringing the engine to life.

There were a couple of rough, jerking starts that rattled the contents in the back before the engine stalled out. But after a handful of attempts, they were cruising onward, striking the curb on their way out.

The entire van tilted and righted itself as something in the back clanged. "What was that?" Emma gasped.

Margaret simply laughed. "Keep your eye on the road so you don't kill us."

Her mirth was contagious and soon Emma's nerves gave way to a fit of giggles.

At least there was one benefit to the petrol ration—there were hardly any other vehicles on the road.

A frantic knocking woke Emma from her sleep later that night.

She bolted upright, blind and confused. The world wasn't shaking with an earthquake; the room was quiet, absent any air raid sirens.

The rapping continued, tugging Emma from her bed. She paused to look at her watch with the torch before rushing to the door. Seven in the morning. Nearly time to wake up.

She pulled open her door to find Mrs. Pickering in her robe and slippers. "You're needed at once."

Emma shook her head. "What on earth for? I have work today."

"I'll speak to your manageress. Oh, Emma, it's terrible." Mrs. Pickering touched a fluttering hand to her brow. "They've put out a call for anyone to help that can. You must leave at once."

"I don't understand," Emma said in a slow, patient voice. Clearly whatever vexed Mrs. Pickering was something truly awful to have her in such a state.

"Coventry," she said. "It's been bombed—almost the whole city…" She swept her hands away from one another. "Gone."

39

THE DRIVE TO Coventry took a little more than an hour, the destruction far too close to home for comfort.

Thick black smoke crowded out the morning sun, turning the start of a new day into the continuation of a nightmare. Coventry was not entirely razed, but the bombing had been considerable. Blocks and blocks of buildings were reduced to flat scars upon the earth. The dazed, blank stares of the people walking aimlessly about reminded Emma of the men who came through Victoria Station after Dunkirk. Eyes hollowed out by horrors no human should have to witness.

Margaret gave directions to the WVS station they'd been instructed to drive to, her voice small and fragile.

Makeshift medical aid stations were set up along sidewalks, where nurses bandaged who they could while the other victims waited their turn with dirty cloths held to their wounds. Those first aid efforts made Emma wish she had taken classes at the Red Cross, that she had more to offer than the provisions they carried.

Emma pulled the van to a stop in front of a building that appeared to still be intact despite missing all its windows, likely blown out by the blasts. A woman ran out to greet them, her WVS coat buttoned up despite the sweat glistening on her brow. "Park and set up here. I hope you brought a lot of food and anything else you could spare."

"Five hundred pounds of food," Margaret replied. "Several bags of clothes, all mended, clean, and ready to be worn immediately."

Disappointment flitted across the woman's lined features. "It's a start. Come on then, let's have those clothes."

Emma carried the heavy sacks of recycled clothes into the building. Men, women, and children shuffled about inside, guided by the soothing tones of the WVS volunteers.

"His name was Harold Baker," a woman with a bandage on her head said in a loud voice. "Harold Baker," she repeated, her voice breaking. "I haven't seen him since last night." Her words faded into weary sobs.

The woman leading Emma cast her a mournful look. "This might be difficult," she cautioned.

"I can take it," Emma replied, quoting Churchill's words. If Britain could take it, so could she.

When she returned to the mobile canteen, Margaret already had production underway, passing out mugs and jam jars as quickly as she could. There was a softness to her words as Emma approached, reverent and sympathetic to the countless people who lined up for their small meal of tea, a margarine sandwich and some vegetable soup.

They'd been given extra stores of sugar, knowing more than a stiff bit of tea would be needed to counter the shock of what the inhabitants of Coventry had endured. Seeing the trembling hands reaching for cups had Emma and Margaret dumping the sugar in by heavy spoonfuls.

As people received their drinks and food, they shared their stories. The neighbor's house that had caved in. The mum who ran for her daughter and never came back. The boys who stayed out to see the bombs and collect the fallen shrapnel, and who no one had heard from since.

Every person had known loss. No one was unaffected.

And neither were Emma and Margaret.

Whatever power held their composure together did so with a careful thread, one Emma knew would break as soon as she was alone. But for now, it was enough. She and Margaret could press on. They could absorb those stories that people needed unburdened, they could heal hearts as medics worked to heal bodies.

They *could* take it.

But as the queue of people did not diminish, the five hundred pounds of food that had seemed so abundant that morning was suddenly and completely insufficient. In only an hour, they were halfway through their stores with sugar running dangerously low.

"Can I get a tub of hot water?" a nurse asked.

"We can brew the tea for you if you like," Emma offered.

The nurse shook her head. "It's for the doctors. They need clean water and the mains are out."

"Of course." Emma took the empty tub from the woman. "We can boil as much as you need."

A look of relief washed over the nurse's face.

She returned several more times throughout the day, long after the food was gone.

"Go on," Emma said as she waited on the infernal pot to boil. "I'll bring it to you when it's ready."

The nurse immediately ran toward the makeshift hospital, holding her white cap in place with her hand. Emma filled the tub when the water was sufficiently boiled and carried the sloshing basin to the hospital.

Inside, the medicinal scent of carbolic mingled with other

smells she didn't want to name. All around her were cries of pain. And of loss.

She handed the nurse the tub of water and quickly tried to exit the building.

In the middle of all the chaos was a little girl wearing the dress that Olivia had donated, the one made of ice-blue satin and tulle that was far too fancy for any real use. There were no shoes on the girl's dirty feet, but that wasn't what caught Emma's attention—it was how the girl twirled so the skirt belled out around her shins, a child reveling in the simple joy of a pretty frock amid the horrors of war.

Someday Emma would share with Olivia what her dress had meant to that girl.

"My son," a woman cried. "Help him, please."

The frantic mother rushed to Emma, her son in her arms, too large to be carried, and yet limp where he hung from her grip, spilling out of her embrace. Emma froze, uncertain of what she could do, shocked to her core at the stillness of the child.

A nurse brushed past Emma before she could call for one, taking the boy from his mother and carrying him toward the hall.

Once outside, Emma staggered toward the mobile canteen, the strength that had propelled her through the day drained away to the point that her legs didn't feel capable of holding her upright for a second longer. The food was gone, the tea empty, the sugar little more than a sweet dream, and barely enough petrol in the tank to get them back to Nottingham.

There was nothing more they could offer.

Neither she nor Margaret spoke on the ride home, both processing the horrors of Coventry, fully absorbed in the stories they'd heard, the heartbreak they'd witnessed. The blackout was in effect when they arrived in Nottingham, but Emma no longer cared about her stipulations of not driving in the dark. In truth, she was grateful for something else to focus on. She dropped Margaret off at her home first, then drove to Victoria Station to park the mobile canteen.

She climbed out of the van, her legs weak, her thoughts spinning.

"Miss Taylor?"

She turned at the familiar masculine voice to find Charles Fisk in his fire brigade coat and boots, streaked black with soot. A fire truck was several meters behind him, parked at the train station as part of the citywide disbursement of emergency vehicles, to prevent them all from being taken out at once by a well-placed bomb.

"Charles." She stumbled toward him, not even feeling her feet as they moved.

He caught her when she came close, pulling her into the solidness of his body, his arms curling around her. Making her feel safe. "Emma." He breathed her name into her ear.

She clung to him, reveling in his quiet strength, not realizing how desperately she'd needed it until that moment.

"Were you at Coventry too?" His voice rumbled against her cheek where she'd laid her head against his chest.

She nodded and looked up at him. "It's so awful. This war. What's happened to those people."

His jaw flexed and his expression hardened.

"It could happen to Nottingham," Emma said, putting voice to her worst fears. "There was a woman with a son who… That could have been my daughter—"

"No." He held her gaze, his expression determined. "That will not be Nottingham. That will not be Olivia."

Emma swallowed. "How do you know?"

Charles' eyes searched hers and she tried to find the flecks of amber and green in the darkness.

"Because I will always make sure you're both safe." His brows pulled down with sincerity.

Before Emma could think about what she was doing, she pushed up onto her toes and pressed her lips to his. His arms tightened around her, equal parts gentle and firm, as his warm mouth moved against hers, capturing the kiss.

A thrill shot through her, fiery with the reminder that she was alive. That Olivia was alive. That there had been a dormant part of Emma desperately longing for this.

Charles ended the kiss with a slow, easy smile and released his hold on her. She settled back on her heels even as she felt as if she was floating away. That half grin teased up higher at the corner of his lips and made her heart flutter. "Will you *now* join me for dinner one night next week?"

Every reason she had to say no tumbled backward in her mind, pushed away by the lingering heat of his mouth on her lips, the slight burn from the rasp of his stubbled jaw at her chin. "I'm not working at the canteen after work on Wednesday."

His grin widened, showing off that dimple on his right cheek. "What a coincidence. I'm not working Wednesday afternoon either."

40

EMMA WAITED FOR Charles by the Council House that following Wednesday. The two massive stone lions in front of the building were now almost blanketed in a layer of sandbags. She stood by the left lion, the one nearest where Barton's buses with their inflated gas bags dropped people off, making it a popular meeting location.

She'd only just come to stand in front of old Leo when Charles approached, wearing a black wool coat and matching fedora, looking as striking as a cinema actor. Her heart tripped a beat.

"You look lovely." He gave her an easy smile, and offered her his arm, as debonair as he was handsome. "Shall we?"

She didn't look any different than normal, with her usual gray wool coat and no cosmetics. Though Emma had spent extra time pinning her hair back from her face that morning.

Still, heat crept up her neck and cheeks at the compliment despite the frigid November evening.

She eased her gloved hand into the crook of his arm to be cradled in the warmth there. The strength beneath her fingertips reminded her of how his arms had come around her, of just how well she'd fit in his embrace. In fact, she'd often recalled the kiss that followed. Far more than she probably should.

"I made reservations at a restaurant near the Palais," he said. "I confess, I've never been there, but thought you might enjoy it after we eat."

The Palais de Danse was a popular dance hall in Nottingham, known for bringing in great performers like Louis Armstrong and Jack Hylton, and for the special dance nights and themed parties. "I haven't been to the Palais either," she admitted.

There had been enough talk around town about it though, how the soldiers staying overnight in Nottingham went out dancing with the young women who lived in the city. There was a grand turning stage for dancing and massive chandeliers overhead that sparkled like diamonds.

"Margaret has told me about it," Emma added. "Before her fiancé was shipped out, they used to go there often."

Two women walked by and glared at Charles. "Still not out there with the rest of our boys, even as his brothers are putting their lives on the line," one woman said to the other without bothering to lower her voice.

His forearm tensed under Emma's hand, but he didn't say anything to defend himself.

Well, if he wouldn't, Emma would.

She stopped and turned toward the women, her body stiff with indignation.

But before she could offer a retort, he put a hand on hers and shook his head. "It's not important."

"It is important. They can't talk about you like that." Emma glared back at the two women huddled together, hissing their vitriol to one another.

Charles gently squeezed Emma's hand, his palm warm as he resumed leading her onward through the square. "Mrs. Emerson, on the right, is my neighbor. I've known her my whole life. Her son and I were mates growing up, but we eventually drifted apart. He liked to find ways to sneak off for a nip of this or that, which didn't interest me, and I started playing rugby, which didn't interest him. We were just different people. But Randal was Mrs. Emerson's only child and she doted on him. She never understood why we weren't chums the way we'd once been." Charles paused, and the clip of their soles on the cobblestones filled the silence. "She received a telegram this past June. Randal was killed at Dunkirk."

Emma closed her eyes, feeling the pain of the woman's loss. Even hearing the word *Dunkirk* brought to mind all those bedraggled soldiers with bandaged limbs and haunted stares.

"Mrs. Emerson is not angry at me," Charles said. "Or rather, she likely is because I'm not off fighting for Britain. But her rage comes from a place of overwhelming grief. I'm home with my mum, helping her and my father around the house. While her son...he's never coming back."

Emma studied Charles's profile, his hard, square jaw, the straight line of his nose beneath the bill of the fedora. He looked so much like the rugby player he said he was, but he had a reader's soul, one that was able to look beyond what was presented to see what lay below the surface.

"That is very considerate of you to think of her rather than yourself," Emma said softly.

"Our country is hurting right now." His throat flexed as he swallowed. "For the soldiers who won't come back, and for those who do return, but with horrible injuries. And from all the bombings. There's so much pain." He stopped speaking abruptly and shook his head. "Well, I'm a fine dinner conversationalist."

She chuckled and squeezed her hand around his strong forearm in a show of support, in the hope he wouldn't stop talking. He had been such a mystery to her for so long, one she had forbidden herself from trying to uncover. "We're not at dinner yet."

His grateful smile shifted to a more serious countenance and he slowed to a stop. "You've never asked why I'm not at war."

She didn't shy from the sudden scrutiny of his attention. "Everyone has their reasons for what they do." She quoted his own words back to him, from the day he'd realized she was a single mother. "And it's none of my business."

He considered her for a long moment. "Rugby," he said finally. "I was injured playing rugby. It's a long story and we ought to hurry, or we'll miss our reservation."

He guided them to resume walking once more, but Emma slowed and pulled gently on his arm in a nonverbal request to stop walking. "I'm not here for dinner. I'm here to get to know you, and as it turns out, tonight I have all the time in the world. Just for you."

His eyes crinkled at the corners and he smiled with such earnestness that she felt it knock into her chest like something physical, visceral. "Emma, you are an incredible woman."

"You don't know me yet," she cautioned. "You may change your mind."

"I know you better than you think. You're kind in how you always make time to listen to the subscribers at the library and the soldiers at the canteen. You're patient in the way you handle Mr. Beard no matter how irate he is or how rude he can be. You're an excellent mother in your care of Olivia, and how much I've seen you do for her in the short time I've known you. A mother's love is always apparent in the way their children look at them, and Olivia thinks you hang the moon. I *know* you, Emma, and that's why I like you so very much."

She looked away, embarrassed by all he saw in her, things she did not see in herself.

"And you're beautiful," he said softly. "The most beautiful woman I've ever seen. Not someone hiding behind cosmetics and flamboyant clothes. You're naturally, perfectly lovely."

His hand came under her chin and he tenderly guided her to look up at him. A moment passed between them, filled with quiet intimacy. Eddies fluttered in her stomach, borne of excitement, anticipation, and every glorious feeling in between.

"I think we're going to miss dinner," he said softly.

She laughed. "I saw a fish and chips stand around the corner."

"Fish and chips it is."

Several minutes later, after retracing their steps, they both held newspaper cones of sizzling fish and chips, and sat on a bench near the Council House. Despite the cold that left steam rising from their food, Emma scarcely felt the chill between the hot cone in her palm and the warm, effervescent giddiness running through her.

She broke off a piece of fish to let it cool, nearly burning her fingertips. "Will you tell me about your rugby injury?"

He grimaced. "Still want to hear that story, do you?"

"Ah, so the flattery was a distraction?" She nudged his foot with hers.

His eyes went wide. "Not at all, I—"

She winked at him, letting him know she was teasing, and he shook his head in mirth. Several people walked by, their heads tucked low into their coats against the cold evening. He watched them pass, his silence one of contemplation.

"I was playing rugby with my mates when I was eighteen and a perfectly kicked ball slammed into my face." He pointed to his left eye. "Right here."

"Your eye?" Emma asked, horrified.

He nodded. "Lost my sight in that eye for nearly a month. When it finally came back, I could only see what was right in front of me, nothing in my peripheral. There wasn't a thing to be done for it."

"Did your sight ever fully come back?" Emma asked, her food all but forgotten.

"No. I had to learn to be more cautious with things like crossing the street, and even had to learn how to read again with my impaired vision."

Emma shook her head in amazement. "That must have been difficult."

"It was worth the effort." Charles popped a chip into his mouth and chewed. "I wanted to go to university."

The fish was no longer scalding and Emma took a careful bite, warm crunchy batter with flaky, perfectly cooked fish. "And did you?"

He nodded toward a building across the square with Essex & Sutherland on a large sign above a red painted door. A local accounting firm. "I graduated with top marks and worked as an accountant for several years there. When we all knew war was coming, I tried to sign up, but was turned away. I immediately quit my job and took the position at the fire brigade, assuming I could do some good on the home front, if need be. My brothers didn't have anything to hold them back. They all signed up."

Charles looked down at the last few chips remaining in the wrapped newspaper. "I've spent my life protecting them. I can't look after them now, not when it matters most, when they're in places of incredible danger." His jaw flexed. "I've tried to sign up several times. Six to be exact. I even memorized the pasteboard eye chart. But the doctor recognized me and saw through my guise. I was told not to come back. And so my brothers are fighting Nazis, all still alive and well, thank God. And I'm here, unable to do a thing to keep them that way."

There was a sharp bitterness to his words, the kind that

emerged from the unfairness of one's lot in life, and how that most impacted those they love.

It was a taste Emma knew well.

"But you help people here," she protested. "Every person you aided in Coventry, the various villages and cities you travel to. You even helped me, that day of the ARP exercise. I know I tried to be strong, to hide how shaken I was, but had you not been there, I might well have collapsed."

He gave her a small, lopsided smile. "You were quite pale."

"I'm sure I was." Emma laughed. "I was in a bad way."

Their conversation carried on, easy and smooth, until the sky deepened from the delicate notes of dusk into the velvety blue of night and their words fogged in the frigid air.

"I hate that it gets dark so early these days," Emma lamented. But truly her disappointment wasn't that the day was slipping away. It was that their time together would soon draw to a close.

Charles crumpled the cold fish and chips cone in his hand and tossed it toward the rubbish bin where it landed perfectly inside the metal rim. "Just because it's dark doesn't mean either of us have to go home yet. We can walk about the city."

"There's nothing I'd like more," Emma replied, eager to continue their time together.

They spent the rest of the evening strolling down the blackout-darkened streets of Nottingham, avoiding the areas where the smoke screens were billowing their noxious clouds. All the while, Charles remained on the side of the pavement nearest the street, protecting her with his body from any errant cars that might miss the white paint directing them away from the curbs.

Thankfully they remained safe, and the night passed with pleasant conversations that revolved around memories of their lives in Nottingham, hilarious childhood stories of Charles and his brothers, anecdotes about Olivia—including the surprise that she and Charles shared a birthday—and, of course, discussions about books. There was even a brief mention of *Lady Chatterley's Lover* that left Emma grateful for the blackout to hide her flushed cheeks.

When Charles finally led her up the walkway to Emma's tenement house, he left her with a kiss that rivaled the one they'd shared after Coventry and promised to see her again, next time at the restaurant he'd originally reserved for their dinner that night.

Emma floated up the stairs, light with a buoyant excitement she'd never experienced. Charles awoke in her a pleasant sensation that left her with flirtatious replies and ready blushes. And after what they'd seen at Coventry, after knowing how ephemeral and uncertain life really was, she was eager to see him again and again and again.

41

EMMA REGARDED THE box on the floor with uncertainty, especially given Miss Bainbridge's obvious trepidation.

"The subscribers will hate this." The manageress sighed and lifted a pair of shears.

She'd called them all into her office that morning before they could even say a word to one another.

Margaret was there, looking not a bit out of sorts after their time in Coventry. If anything, she appeared rather jolly, with her eyes sparkling and cheeks bright with color beneath the sweep of rouge. Irene hung in the back with her arms folded over her chest, her face lined with exhaustion from a long night spent with her son, who was now cutting his teeth. Miss Crane mirrored Miss Bainbridge's concern, her mouth tucked in a sour frown.

With another great, heaving sigh, Miss Bainbridge sliced open the box, revealing the books within. The covers seemed the same as the usual stock—blue linen-bound imprinted with the neat green 'B' of the Booklover's Library seal.

"They don't look any different," Margaret said hopefully.

"It's in the paper," Miss Bainbridge replied sorrowfully. "And the print."

She reached down and opened the first book, sucking in a gasp that made them all lean forward.

Not only were the words incredibly small, but the margins were as well, with the tiny print creeping closer toward the spine than ever before.

"What will the subscribers say?" Miss Bainbridge moaned. "Especially our Class A subscribers."

"There's nothing to be done," Irene added in a practical tone, one easy to affect when truly exhausted. "We all have to make sacrifices for the war effort."

"But not our books," Miss Bainbridge cried, appearing more off-kilter than Emma had ever seen her.

Miss Crane picked up a book for herself. "It's so slight." Holding it to the side, Emma could see what she meant; the pages between the covers were not as thick as that of a usual novel. But then, wasn't that was the point? To reduce the size of print and margins in an effort to conserve as much paper as possible.

The paper ration had been announced earlier that year in July when the *Evening Post* immediately went down to only four pages, with paper too flimsy to snap upright. The restriction on paper had taken a couple of months to trickle down to books as publishers went through their reserved stock, but now they were finally feeling the impact.

"Look how thin the pages are." Miss Crane held a single page upright from the spine so light shone through the paper. "They don't even feel as smooth."

Emma lifted a book and stroked her hand over the page where the paper was somewhat coarser than usual.

Miss Bainbridge did likewise, then gave a beleaguered

whimper and tossed her book onto the pile with a wail before quitting the room.

Margaret looked at Emma. "I can't say I've ever seen her in such a state."

Irene suppressed a yawn and blinked her eyes wide like that might help her keep them open. "You know how the Class A subscribers can be."

They did indeed all know how they could be, expecting everything from everyone for the increased sum they paid for their membership. As if being Class A subscribers made them royalty.

"Even their fee doesn't exempt them from the ration." Miss Crane straightened with indignation.

Margaret examined her nails. "They won't like hearing that regardless."

"They can like it or lump it." Miss Crane shrugged and left the office.

"Now that we're alone…" Margaret cast an excited glance between Emma and Irene. "I have been so eager to share. I wrote to Jeffrey last night." She grinned. "And told him I'll marry him."

Irene squealed with delight and clapped her hands, her exhaustion cast off in her enthusiasm to share Margaret's news. Emma pulled her good friend in for a hug, knowing the sacrifice Margaret was making for love.

"I'll tell you more, but first let's grab some tea before it's gone." Margaret waved them out of Miss Bainbridge's office.

The tea Boots' provided before the ration had been plentiful and perfectly brewed. Now the concession was more of a toffee color, and if one wasn't there quickly enough, there was none to be had.

But watered-down tea was still preferable to no tea at all.

"I have to see to my dusting," Irene said. "But I want all the details later."

"We'll save you some tea," Emma promised, earning her a grateful look from Irene. "I promise things get better after your little ones stops teething."

"I hope so." Irene erupted into a fresh yawn.

"What made you make up your mind about marrying Jeffrey?" Emma asked as she and Margaret left Irene to see to the dusting, a job Emma was more than happy to relinquish.

"Coventry," Margaret answered. "Seeing what people lost, hearing the stories, and realizing that we're all in danger, but more so my Jeffrey than me. I can't wait to receive his reply."

There was a glow to her whole being, one that indicated she was truly happy with her decision, and that alone made Emma happy too.

"I'll start saving my rations for your cake," Emma promised. After all, it took a large family or a whole neighborhood's worth of savings in butter and sugar to make a decent wedding cake these days.

"I'm so grateful to have a friend like you." Margaret reached out and squeezed Emma's hand as they approached the table where the former vat of tea had been replaced by several teapots.

Margaret smiled sheepishly. "I've never had many friends. Women don't generally like me much and I've learned men often have ulterior motives."

"I've never had many friends either." Emma handed a teacup to Margaret. "It was usually just Papa and me."

Margaret poured some tea into her small cup. "And now it's you and Olivia."

Emma smiled at her friend, grateful for how well Margaret truly understood her. "Exactly. Though I confess, I have news of my own."

Margaret passed Emma the teapot and lifted a perfectly plucked brow. "Oh?"

"I saw Charles—Mr. Fisk—after I came back from Coventry...we went on a date."

Margaret's eyes widened and she clamped a hand on Emma's forearm, practically dragging her to one of the small tables where they all took tea before their shift began. "I want to hear everything."

As expected, the customers were not pleased with the new paper-rationed books, and the Class A subscribers had indeed complained. At least the Class B subscribers had a year before they were subjected to the newly released books with the subpar paper and cramped typeface.

Even Mrs. Chatsworth had been ruffled by the small print, her shrill complaints enough to wake Pip and leave him growling so ferociously that Miss Bainbridge had to intervene. They were all dealing with difficult subscribers, but poor Miss Bainbridge had the worst of it.

Emma found herself immensely glad to be home that evening. Especially when she found a letter from Olivia. It was bittersweet as always. Filled with love, but also pleading to return home.

This one declared Olivia had been receiving strong marks in school, that she had even learned to cook and could help with making meals if Emma would just let her return home. And, if nothing else, she at least wanted Emma to visit for Christmas the following month. But even as Emma wondered if her inlaws would welcome such a notion, she realized she actually had two letters. The one behind Olivia's was from Arthur's mother, her bold, slanting writing recognizable anywhere.

Olivia wishes you to come for Christmas and we would like you to join as well, knowing what it would mean to her to have you here.

Emma lowered the letter with a sinking sensation in the pit of her stomach. There was nothing for it—she was finally going to visit her in-laws.

42

CHESTER APPEARED MUCH the same as when Emma was there five years prior, with its charming downtown area of medieval whitewashed buildings artfully framed with dark wood beams. The absence of glittering Christmas lights, however, cast a fitting shadow over the city. The Taylors' farm was even more bleak, with a milky sky over a countryside blanketed in a dusting of white snow and the simple wooden house weathered to a flat, dark gray over the years.

Emma rapped on the door and the thunder of feet barreling in her direction meant Olivia had heard the knock. The door whipped back with enough force to send a waft of heated air toward Emma, carrying with it the aroma of cooking meat. Her mouth watered. The tea she'd had on the train had stopped tiding her over hours ago.

"Happy Christmas, Mum," Olivia shrieked and threw her arms around Emma.

"It's not Christmas for another two days." Emma laughed and embraced her daughter. "Have you grown again?"

"I have." Olivia stood back so Emma could look her over. Indeed, she had grown at least another inch or so in the last four long months. And all her adult teeth had come in quite neatly, making her smile even larger in her sweet face. Best of all was the healthy glow to Olivia's cheeks. There had been plenty of food for her as the farm provided an abundance of eggs, milk, vegetables, and even meat several times a week. More than she would have had access to in Nottingham.

"Soon you'll be as tall as I am," Emma declared.

Olivia giggled, her eyes bright with excitement.

"Don't keep the door open too long now," a masculine voice called, his Chester accent with a soft *k* and his *th* coming out like a *d*.

Olivia waved Emma inside, opening the door wider to a home that hadn't changed so much as a curtain since she'd last visited. The furnishings were simple and impeccably clean, including the wood-hewn table and benches along either side that Mr. Taylor boasted he'd made with Arthur. Several chairs were near the fireplace, looking as worse for the wear as ever. But on a cold evening, being near the heat of the fire made one less critical of the ancient hard-backed wooden chairs worn smooth from use. A small table by the stairs was fitted with a single framed picture of Arthur, his dark hair combed back from his young face, reminding Emma of the man she'd met all those years ago after her father's death.

Though Arthur had been gone for five years, and though their marriage had not been a happy one, she still experienced a nip at her conscience for her time with Charles. They had enjoyed several more outings together, the time spent in animated conversation as they each eagerly devoured everything the other said. As it was in a new and budding relationship.

Or at least the way Emma had read about in books in her younger years. She was only just now beginning to experience the reality.

"He's so handsome." Olivia closed the door behind Emma

and went to Arthur's picture, bending to study it with her hands reverently tucked behind her back.

Emma nodded. Because she had truly found Arthur handsome—there had been no doubt of his fine looks. If only that had been enough to make for a contented marriage.

Mr. Taylor emerged from the back room. "Emma, it's good to see you again." His hairline had receded some since her last visit, the dark strands streaked with glints of silver. His eyes were dark, like Arthur's had been, and still keen with sharp intelligence.

"Thank you for inviting me." She went to the older man and embraced him cordially.

He patted her back with his large hand, the action paternal and kind. "It's been too long."

She nodded, somewhat regretting the time she'd allowed to lapse since her last visit. But then she'd felt more welcome in these few minutes inside the Taylor residence than she ever had in the six months she and Olivia had lived there.

"City life suits you." Mr. Taylor gave a wink that was almost convivial.

"I've never been much for farming." Emma tried to mirror his friendly tone.

"Nan and Granddad told me all about it." Olivia wrinkled her nose. "Like the time you slipped on a cow patty and fell in it. Or the time that pig escaped and you had to run after it and accidentally let the lot of them out because you didn't latch the gate properly."

The smile Emma plastered on her face felt as brittle as her sudden regret for staying away so long.

Surely Mrs. Taylor hadn't mentioned how she'd made Emma scrub cow dung off her skin with snow and strip to her knickers before she could come inside. Nor would they have informed Olivia of how they'd made no effort to help her reclaim all the escaped pigs, or how hard Emma had worked to bring them all back.

Her time at the farm had been filled with constant disappointment and incessant castigation.

"Don't give your mam too hard a time." Mr. Taylor patted Emma's shoulder. "She did her best."

Emma turned to the older man, surprised at the note of support.

"Reg, I mended that part of your kecks." Mrs. Taylor descended the stairs with a pair of trousers in her hands. She stopped short when she saw Emma, her face an expressionless mask.

"My mum is here," Olivia sang out.

"I see that," Mrs. Taylor said plaintively. "And I see you're quite made up over it."

Olivia was indeed happy, her face set in a wide grin as she folded her little hand into Emma's.

"Thank you for coming." The words seemed to pain Mrs. Taylor as she spoke them, and her lips pressed together in a flat line that Emma recalled well from her time living with them. The expression was one she'd seen often.

One of obvious disappointment.

"Thank you for having me," Emma replied with more warmth than she felt.

"Why don't you show your mother your room," Mrs. Taylor said to Olivia before turning away to head back upstairs, Mr. Taylor's trousers still clutched in her hand.

Her demeanor didn't soften during Emma's stay, with any requests directed through Olivia, who cheerfully did as her Nan asked.

Christmas was quiet, with Olivia receiving another chocolate bar Mrs. Pickering had managed to procure, along with a copy of *Caddie Woodlawn* Emma purchased for her, and a new pair of sturdy shoes from her grandparents. Emma had knitted her former in-laws scarves in a show of goodwill. Mr. Taylor had put his on, modeling it with a head tilt that set Olivia giggling, while Mrs. Taylor judiciously eyed the stitching on hers before setting it aside with a slight curl of her lip.

The four days Emma spent with Olivia passed quickly, filled with puzzles and talking about books as well as Emma sharing stories of her walks with Tubby and how Mrs. Pickering had been getting on with the WVS.

"One time, Tubby dashed halfway up a tree after a squirrel before I could call him back down," Emma said.

Olivia had been in fits at that. "I know which tree you mean, the one just outside where the gate used to be."

Emma laughed. "That very one."

"I miss that tree." Olivia was suddenly solemn, her brows drawing low. "I miss Tubby and Mrs. Pickering. And I miss you." Her eyes filled with tears. "Nan and Granddad are nice, and I love hearing stories about my father, and about us when we lived here since I don't remember, but I want to go home."

If the pleading letters Olivia wrote were difficult for Emma to bear, they were nothing compared to the agonizing stab of hearing those words spoken aloud in Olivia's sweet voice. Everything inside Emma's chest blazed with hurt and regret, a visceral blow of anguish to a mother's heart.

"I wish you could come home," Emma said gently. "But you must wait just a little longer."

"How long?" Olivia demanded.

But Emma didn't have an answer.

The day of Emma's departure, Olivia wore her red jumper, the sleeves now creeping up her wrists.

"That jumper is too small for you," Mrs. Taylor chided in her ever-critical tone.

Olivia hugged herself, curling her long, slender arms around her torso. "I love this more than any other piece of clothing I've ever owned. My mum made it for me."

"Well, that explains a lot." Mrs. Taylor's cool delivery wasn't meant to be flattering.

Despite her nasty demeanor, Emma wished she could stay in Chester just a little longer. For Olivia's sake.

Those days laughing over memories in Nottingham, and hearing Olivia tell her about every book she'd read, from *Little House in the Big Woods* to Arthur's old copy of *The Swiss Family Robinson*, all those beautiful moments filled the hole in Emma's soul that had been empty in her daughter's absence.

She hugged Olivia once more and released her with great reluctance. "I love you, Olive."

Olivia nodded, eyes brimming with tears as Emma turned toward the door.

"Let me come with you," Olivia said abruptly.

The silence in the room went thick, heavy with hurt each individual felt in their own way.

"Please." There was a quiver in Olivia's voice. "Please let me come home. I promise to be good. I'll do well in maths. I'll walk Tubby every day. I'll help with making dinner. And the WVS, I can help at the children's center again." Her words were choked with sobs, her eyes a brilliant blue with her tears. "Please don't leave me, Mum. Please. I love you. Don't leave me."

Emma knelt on the ground and pulled her daughter into a solid embrace, her own throat too tight to speak.

"You have everything you need here." Mrs. Taylor's voice was calm, but her cheeks were flushed with emotion over Olivia's outburst. There was ice in her eyes as she glared down at Emma. "You coddle the child. You did before and you do it still now."

"Being away from home is difficult for children," Emma said gently.

"Yes." Mrs. Taylor bit out the word. "It's painful when a mother is separated from her child." She threw the accusation like a snake at Emma's feet, then marched away.

Olivia's sobs filled the ensuing quiet.

"You can't return home yet," Emma soothed as she rubbed slow circles over her daughter's back, fingertips gliding over each of those stitches she'd painstakingly knit with all the love she had for her daughter. "Hopefully the war ends and you can come home soon. But for now, you must be brave for me, yes?"

Olivia pressed her lips together so hard that her pointed chin jutted out, but she gave a nod, resolute and resigned.

"I'm sure your Nan can use a bit of the sugar ration for a pudding later." Mr. Taylor winked at Olivia.

But the tears didn't stop streaming down her face as she gazed imploringly up at Emma. "Please don't leave me."

The words settled on Emma like a sharp-edged stone and left her feeling as though she was abandoning her daughter. And in a way, she was—that was what hurt the most.

There had been more raids in Nottingham, including a recent one the month before that'd kept them all in the caves under the city for the entire night and left a wake of destruction in its path. With such dangers at home, how could Emma possibly allow Olivia to return?

"I love you," Emma croaked. Then she kissed the top of Olivia's head and rushed out before she lost her nerve.

Even as the door closed, Olivia's cry for Emma pierced through the solid wood and directly into Emma's heart.

"She'll be fine in a day or two." Mr. Taylor helped Emma into the cart. It did not escape her notice that he'd worn the robin's-egg blue scarf she'd knitted for him.

Her luggage was already loaded into the back of the cart,

the two horses harnessed and stomping with impatience, ears flicking at Olivia's wails.

"I wonder if I've made the right decision." Emma looked back at the house, where Olivia's face was pressed against the glass windowpane along with both her palms, as if she could touch Emma from the distance between them. The window fogged with her gasping sobs, but still Emma didn't turn away.

"As a parent, we can never know if we've made the right decisions or not." Mr. Taylor spoke slowly, as though selecting his words carefully. He made a clicking sound and the cart lurched forward.

Emma waited until Olivia's face faded into the distance and then turned back to Mr. Taylor. "I'm grateful to you for taking her in."

"It's our pleasure to do so." Mr. Taylor rubbed a hand over his cap. "I know it wasn't easy for you to write to us like you did. Or send her here for that matter." His brow furrowed as he looked out in the distance. "Especially after how you were treated during your time with us, after we lost our boy."

Emma chewed her lip, unsure of what to say.

"We were disappointed when Arthur left the farm." Mr. Taylor sniffed and adjusted his elbows on his knees. "Thought we could force him to take this place on, the way I had from my father. But he left. First to London for university, then to Nottingham to work as a solicitor. He had just begun thinking about returning to Chester, and then he met you."

Emma's stomach dipped. "He stayed because of me?"

Mr. Taylor gave a single nod.

Arthur had never told her he'd been considering returning to Chester. If he had gone back to the farm, if he hadn't married her—he would still be alive.

"It was his decision to make," Mr. Taylor said, as though reading her thoughts. He cleared his throat, a great rasping sound in the clear morning air. "We also knew you weren't happy in your marriage toward the end. Your grief was still too fresh when you married, we told Arthur that, but he didn't listen. I know he loved Olivia, that he found joy in her, and it's easy to see why. For our part, I'm ashamed to say that we blamed you. Unfairly. It wasn't your fault. Took me meeting Olivia, seeing what a caring mother you are, to understand *you* for who you really are. I'm sorry for that. And I'm sorry Mrs. Taylor is still struggling to do the same."

Emma wrapped her arms around herself, cradling a fresh ache blooming within her. How many times had she considered the mothers of soldiers who'd lost their sons? And yet she had been so scalded with hurt from the lack of welcome she'd received from Arthur's parents after her stay with them that she hadn't stepped back to consider them, the parents whose son had left home and never returned.

"I'm a mother." Emma softened with empathy for Mrs. Taylor. "I understand."

"You're a good sort." Mr. Taylor smiled at her. "Thank you for giving us this time with Olivia. I know we were likely a last resort, but we still love having her with us all the same."

Emma returned his smile, genuinely glad she had given the Taylors a chance to know their granddaughter.

Regardless of the peace she'd found with Mr. Taylor and regardless of his promise that Olivia would recover in a few days, Emma could not set her daughter's pleas from her mind. Never had she seen Olivia so heartbreakingly desperate.

Hopefully her patience would hold a little longer. After all, they were out of any other options, and Nottingham was still far too dangerous.

43

DURING THE ENTIRE journey home, Emma was haunted by Olivia's cries coming through the door of the Taylor's home, begging Emma not to leave her.

And yet she had.

Though she'd left Olivia in the care of family who loved her, Emma could not shake the unnerving sensation of abandonment.

Barbara Cartland's latest romance lay in Emma's lap, open to the same page she'd read dozens of times without ever processing a single word.

She wanted to be home. Alone.

But as she entered the tenement building, Tubby announced her entrance and the noisy chatter of voices in Mrs. Pickering's flat abruptly ceased, followed by the announcement, "She's here."

Everything inside Emma flinched. Despite their well-meaning intentions, she desperately wanted to avoid the merry well-wishes so incongruous with the oppressive darkness of her mood. She wanted to curl into bed and wallow in that sorrow, embracing and nurturing the pain until it consumed her.

Mrs. Pickering opened the door with a bright smile. "Surprise!"

Behind her stood Margaret, Charles and Charles's boss, Francis. Tubby darted from the flat and launched himself so high toward Emma he nearly touched her waist. She bent to hug the little dog, breathing in the familiar comfort of his silky fur as she gathered her wits.

These were her friends, who knew her better than most. Who loved her.

She could do this.

She straightened to face everyone, but the smile she attempted felt wobbly.

And perhaps it was indeed wobbly, for Mrs. Pickering's happy expression wilted. "Oh dear." She ushered Emma into the flat, and into a heartfelt embrace that carried the aroma of freshly baked bread and Tubby and that lovely rose fragrance she always wore.

Emma had never known a mother's embrace but imagined it to be much like this—soft and all-encompassing and smelling like home. Tears prickled in Emma's eyes and then she remembered the bag in her pocket, the small gift she'd brought from the farm. The perfect excuse to liberate herself from the comforting hug before it was her undoing. Emma withdrew from Mrs. Pickering and pulled the bag free.

Behind Mrs. Pickering, Charles winked at Emma, a welcome distraction that set her heart knocking just a bit harder in her chest.

"What is that?" Mrs. Pickering indicated the bag.

"The vegetable scraps from our Christmas meal in Chester," Emma replied. "For Nameless."

Mrs. Pickering huffed and put her fists on her hips. "And how did you know I'd still have him?"

"Because I know you." She handed the bag to Mrs. Pickering, who immediately took it outside, cooing at the small rabbit about his impending feast before the door was even closed. Francis scooped up Tubby before he could go after the rabbit and held the dog in one massive arm, making him appear little more than a stuffed bear.

Margaret immediately took Mrs. Pickering's place in front of Emma, a large glittering Christmas tree brooch on her green jumper. She put a hand on Emma's shoulder. "You're as beautiful as ever, sweet Emma, but you do look rather peaked. And who wouldn't after such a long journey?" She turned to face Charles. "Will you be a dear and take Emma's bag and help her upstairs to her flat?"

Francis nodded at Charles even as he was already stepping forward to claim Emma's suitcase by the handle, hefting the significant weight in an easy grip. Emma gave Margaret a grateful smile before following Charles out into the stairwell.

He indicated for her to lead the way and followed behind, letting the silence relax between them.

"We told Mrs. Pickering a party might not be a good idea," he said apologetically when they arrived in front of Emma's door.

"I know how she is." Trying to stand in Mrs. Pickering's way when she'd set her mind to task was a nearly impossible feat. "She means well."

"She was worried about you." Charles set the suitcase down, concern in his gaze. "I'm also worried about you."

A knot of emotion settled in the back of her throat, aching so badly she could barely speak. "I'm fine."

She was not going to let herself dissolve into tears in front of Charles. Not when she hadn't seen him in over a week. Not when everything in their blossoming relationship was going so well. Not when she was a grown woman who ought to have a firm control over her emotions.

"I know you were anxious about seeing your former in-laws." His tone was as gentle as a caress. "I hope they treated you well."

"My father-in-law was kind," she said tightly.

"And your mother-in-law?" he asked in that careful, stroking tone.

Emma offered a helpless shrug. "I understand her more now."

Charles looked down at the ground, quiet for a moment. When he looked back up, his mouth opened a couple of times, as if trying to grasp the exact words he wanted to say.

"I know that leaving Olivia was hard," he said finally. "Your love for her is obvious and saying goodbye when you don't know the next time you'll see someone you love again…" His brow twitched. "It's one of the hardest things to do."

He shifted his weight from one foot to the other. "When I'm with you, I don't just want your smiles and your good humor. I want all of you, the *real* Emma. The one who sometimes has bad days, who might not always feel like smiling. I'm here for everything you are. And if you would like me to leave you be, you have only to say the word. But if you need me, if you're hurting, know that I'm here." His hands spread out, palms up, as if he were physically giving himself over to her.

The tears she'd been ferociously restraining since she forced herself to turn her back on Olivia now stung her eyes, hot and determined.

"I abandoned her, Charles," she choked out. "She begged me not to leave, and I left her."

He opened his arms and she fell against him the way she'd done after Coventry. And once more, she basked in his solid embrace, in the warmth and comfort he offered.

Emma had spent most of Olivia's life standing on her own, being her own rock. Always strong. Never breaking.

She couldn't afford to.

Not when it was always just her.

But in this moment, she had support and strength. And she was finally no longer alone.

44

EMMA HELD A stack of blank invitations in one hand and with the other, she angled the chipped wooden edge of a large mirror to reflect Margaret's image back at her. The wedding dress needed to be taken in a smidge at the waist, but aside from that one small detail, the sweetheart neckline gown with long tapered sleeves was a perfect fit.

Several months had passed, filled with work at the lending library and with the WVS, time with Charles when they could spare it, and of course, the stream of heartbroken letters from Olivia. This was a good distraction, one that was positive and joyous.

Mrs. Avory folded her arms over her generous bosom and stared at her daughter with a smile tucking the corners of her lips. "Hard to believe I was ever that tiny. It fits you like a dream though." Margaret's mother had the same velvety brown eyes as her daughter, her hair hidden away beneath a scarf like so many factory women took to doing these days.

"I'm so glad you kept it." Margaret turned to her mother and the cream-colored silk rustled like a whisper in her quiet bedroom. There was a note of admiration in her gaze, an eagerness for approval that her mother readily gave.

"It'll bring you good luck too." Mrs. Avory winked, showcasing the same charm as her daughter. "I sucked all the bad luck out of it the day I married your father."

Margaret threw her head back and laughed. "I wonder what he might say if he heard that."

"He'd have to be home first, and earlier someone said there was beer on tap at The Bell Inn." Mrs. Avory drew out a tin of cigarettes and rattled them. "I'd be willing to bet my Woodbines he'll be there until the blackout."

"Oh, do stop, Mum." Margaret tsked. "You'd never give up your Woodbines."

They looked at each other and laughed again, a familiar, easy camaraderie shared between them.

Emma wondered about when Olivia was a grown woman preparing for her own wedding day, and what kind of relationship they might have then.

If their bond was even half as strong as that between the mother and daughter in front of Emma now, she would consider herself immensely fortunate.

She was also grateful for her timing in coming by to pick up the wedding invitations that Margaret had agreed to let her help fill out. If Emma had been any earlier, she'd have missed seeing Margaret in her dress.

They'd only just learned of Jeffrey's approved leave and there was far too much to do in such a short time to prepare for his arrival and the impending nuptials.

"I can't believe I'll be married in less than two weeks' time." Margaret turned back to the mirror, her cheeks flushed with excitement. "I know I dragged my feet for a while."

"A while." Mrs. Avory scoffed with an affectionate chuckle.

"A long while," Margaret conceded. "But I'm finally ready. Even if Miss Bainbridge will never forgive me."

It was true, the manageress had been unable to keep her

tears at bay when Margaret told her she wouldn't be able to work there any longer once she was married.

"She'll forgive you," Emma said with certainty, recalling the woman whose job Emma had stepped into. "Once she sees how happy you are with Jeffrey, she'll forgive you."

"And you promise you'll come by to see me all the time?" Margaret looked at Emma in the mirror.

"All the time," Emma vowed. "With Mrs. Pickering too, when I can pull her away from the WVS."

"Pull her away?" Margaret elbowed Emma playfully. "I'll likely be working right alongside her to keep from being bored out of my mind."

"Unless you have a babe to tend to." Mrs. Avory pressed her hands to her bosom and gave a wistful sigh. "Ah, to think of the little nippers now. I was ready to give up on ever having grands, you know?"

"I've heard that a time or ten." Margaret put the veil over her hair and threw her mother a smirk from her reflection.

Emma picked up the list of wedding guests. There was such a large crowd expected, they likely wouldn't fit into the modest church. "Are you certain I can't help with anything else?" She carefully tucked the wedding invitations and list into her handbag.

"Unless you can dream up sugar and butter, I think we're good," Mrs. Avory said.

"I can't," Emma admitted. "But I believe Mrs. Pickering is on the task."

Margaret squealed with delight and clapped her hands. "We'll have a cake the size of Buckingham Palace."

Emma could almost taste the rich confection. Several weeks with barely any sugar had her craving even the smallest taste. But the sacrifice of her rations would be worthwhile for Margaret's wedding day to be perfect.

"We'll let you know if we need anything, Emma." Margaret pulled off the veil and offered her back to her mother to undo the dozens of tiny seed pearls running down the length of her spine. "Thank you for being such a dear."

Emma closed the door, a grin on her face at Margaret's infectious joy. It was good to see her friend so genuinely happy.

Emma's own wedding had been small, an affair easily managed for an orphaned bride and a groom estranged from his parents. The day had been lovely, with gorgeous blue skies hung with puffs of clouds that looked like they'd been painted in a storybook. The auspicious start had felt like a promise of good things to come, hope that after the suffocation of her grief, she might be able to breathe again. Smile again. Live again.

But the empty pews on her side of the church had been a stark reminder of the void in her world where her father had been.

There had been no mother's dress to wear—it had been burned with the rest of Emma's life—and there had been no family to offer well-wishes and love.

There'd been only her and Arthur and the other solicitors he worked with, and their wives who tried to pretend like Emma had a place among them. And they truly had tried, coming together to style her hair, apply light cosmetics, and even lending her a lovely strand of pearls.

Perhaps someday Emma might have what Margaret did, perhaps even with Charles. She opened her friend's door to let herself out, pulling her jacket round her to stave off the bite in the early-April air, and found Charles still there waiting for her.

"I told you that you didn't have to wait," she chided playfully. But really, she was glad.

"Seeing you look at me the way you just did made the time worth it." He gave her a boyish grin. "I was thinking we could go to the cinema tonight if you're free."

Emma tapped her chin and gave him a coy look. "The ABC Cinema?"

They had been wanting to go together, especially after learning that, unbeknownst to them, they had both attended the cinema's showing of the film *Pollyanna* back when the theater first opened and was called the Elite Picture Theatre.

"Absolutely the ABC Cinema." He offered her his arm and she readily took it.

His body was so close to hers, their hips brushed as they began to walk, a quiet intimacy that sank into her soul like warm sunshine. They'd spent many of their evenings and weekends together, volunteering at events, such as Dig for Victory, and helping the WVS with their various projects. Charles was always willing to offer to lift heavier items, much to the appreciation of the ladies, in more ways than one.

The two of them had fallen into something of an easy routine in the months since she'd returned from Chester. And though being with Charles settled a part of Emma that she hadn't known was restless, she still didn't feel whole without Olivia. In fact, her relationship with Charles made her crave her daughter's presence more, a final piece to fit into the puzzle of her life, to make her gloriously, wonderfully whole.

Given the imploring tone of Olivia's letters that had only increased in desperation, she was likely feeling the pain of their separation as poignantly as Emma.

But there had been more bombs in Nottingham. More deaths.

Though the attacks were nowhere near as aggressive as in London, where bombers flew over the city like buzzards on a nearly nightly basis, but Nottingham was certainly not without its scars.

Twelve bombs had fallen on Ribblesdale Road in March, and just the week before, there had been bombs and incendiaries in Beeston.

Emma and Charles hadn't more than a dozen steps from Margaret's door when a young man with a mop of messy dark hair ran past them so quickly, he nearly crashed into Emma. Charles put his hand on her shoulder protectively and cast a hard look back.

But the dark-haired man wasn't paying them any attention as he stopped at Margaret's door and pounded at the knocker. He cast a desperate look in Emma's direction. "Is Margaret in?"

There was a pitch to his voice, a wildness in his eyes, and it set off alarm bells. Charles must have sensed the man's overly excited mood as well, and stepped forward, putting himself protectively in front of Emma.

He peered around Charles, his brows pinched together. "Please, it's urgent."

"She is," Emma replied reluctantly. "Give her a moment. She was trying on her wedding dress."

"Her wedding dress," he murmured more to himself than to Emma, then he covered his mouth with his hand and dragged in a harsh breath.

Emma walked toward him, bringing Charles with her. "What is the meaning of th—"

The door opened and Mrs. Avory lifted her brows in surprise. "His feet haven't gone cold, have they?" She jerked her thumb at him and addressed Emma. "This here is Jeffrey's brother."

The young man choked on a sob and Mrs. Avory snapped her head back to him, her playful twinkle dulled with worry. "Come in." She waved at the boy. "You too," she called to Emma and Charles. "God help me, I think my girl might need us all." She turned and shouted for Margaret over her shoulder, asking her to come down at once.

Emma and Charles entered the narrow home in time to

see Jeffrey's brother pull out a telegram, the paper trembling in the pinch of his fingers.

Telegrams seldom delivered good news. Those seemingly innocuous slips of paper struck fear into the hearts of every person in Britain with the news they brought—that a soldier had been captured, or was missing. Or worse—that he'd been killed.

It meant the man whose name was printed in the stark type would not be coming home any time soon. If at all.

The power of what that telegram meant slammed into Emma, landing directly in the center of her chest. Charles put his arm around her, holding her tight to him, as if reassuring himself she was near. And she was glad for his presence. Not only to have him at her side, but also selfishly to know she did not have to worry about ever receiving such a telegram about him.

Margaret came down the stairs, the smile bleeding from her face at the sight of the telegram. "No." Margaret shook her head, blond hair sweeping over her shoulders, eyes already welling with tears. "No, I can't read it. I won't."

Jeffrey's brother gave a hoarse sob, his voice breaking. "He's missing, Margaret. They don't know where he is."

Margaret pulled in a shaky breath and her mother was immediately at her side, drawing her daughter into her arms just as Emma had so often done with Olivia when she wanted to protect her from all the world's hurt.

"I was too late." Margaret gasped the words, as if her pain was too large to even speak around. She fell against her mother in a fit of soul-shaking sobs. "He wanted to marry me, and I was too late."

45

EMMA HANDED THE copy of *Anne of Green Gables* to a Class A subscriber. "My daughter loves this book. I'm sure yours will too."

The woman held it to her chest like a precious treasure to be guarded. "It was one of my favorites."

Despite the bombs that continued to pummel Nottingham, parents were still bringing their children home from the country. Every time Emma saw another child in the library with their mother or playing in the neighborhood, she physically ached for Olivia.

That sense of loss had manifested in other ways, however, allowing Emma to find exactly the right type of book for children who were returning home and left with too much time on their hands. Her uncanny ability to encourage any child to read had made her popular with the parents and set Miss Crane's teeth on edge.

As the subscriber walked away, Margaret breezed into the library, her lips painted in Number Seven's Firefly in a smile that made Emma's heart break.

A month had passed since Jeffrey's disappearance, a topic she refused to discuss. She'd swept away inquiries about her wedding with her beringed left hand and an airy laugh about needing just a smidge more time for preparations.

But the exhaustion darkening the area under her eyes told a different story, one of sleepless nights haunted by the pain of grief and regret, the most unforgiving of all specters.

Emma went into the Bespoke Room sometime later and found Margaret staring blankly into space, her posture slumped, lifeless, like a marionette with no puppeteer. She jumped to attention when Emma entered, animatedly brought back as if someone were pulling her strings, a smile crowding onto her face. Too wide. Too bright. Too fake.

Emma sat on the stool next to her friend. The box on the floor at Margaret's feet had not even been opened, though she'd been in the room for well over an hour.

"Talk to me." Emma opened the box and carefully began recording the name of each title they'd received.

"Whatever about?" Margaret asked, as if reading a script.

"About how you really are." Emma looked at her in time to see a flash of pain resonate in her large, dark brown eyes. She reached for Margaret's hand and found it ice-cold, her fingers more bony than slender, further evidence of the weight she'd lost in the last month.

Taking a page from Mrs. Pickering's book, Emma set her focus on the box of books and let silence coax the talking.

"He's not coming back, Emma," Margaret said softly. "Or at least I have to tell myself that because if he doesn't…" She shook her head. "His mum thinks he's coming back. She wanted to keep planning the wedding for after the war, but my heart can't bear it." Her voice cracked.

Emma hugged Margaret as she began to cry. The door opened and Miss Crane stepped inside. Emma tightened her arms around her friend, sheltering her from the other woman's wrath. But Miss Crane's hard expression unexpectedly softened and she slipped away without a word of reprimand.

There was nothing about Margaret's position to envy.

Eventually she quieted and the shuddering sobs shifted to the deep, even breathing that so often follows a solid cry.

"It's good to let it out." Emma rubbed her friend's back in small circles, the way she did with Olivia. "You can't keep that pain inside."

"I do feel better. A little, at least." Margaret pulled away from Emma and wiped at her nose with a handkerchief. "Thank you."

"You don't have to go through this alone." Emma put a hand on Margaret's thin shoulder. "We're all here with you."

She nodded, and this time the smile she gave—small and watery though it may be—was genuine.

"Take some time, I'll make your excuses if anyone asks." Emma gave her another hug, and then left her to her privacy.

Miss Crane and Irene were both occupied with subscribers when Emma exited. The only other patron in the library was Mrs. Chatsworth, who had recently borrowed *The Secret Garden*, and Emma had found herself looking forward to a good helping of loquacious feedback.

The older woman had her back to Emma, her head down so the bright blue plume of her hat pointed directly at the shelf of books in front of her.

"Good afternoon, Mrs. Chatsworth."

The woman startled and spun around so fast that Pip gave an offended growl at his mistress. "Oh, Miss Taylor." Spots of color blossomed on her cheeks.

Emma stepped back, both from the irascible little Pip and to give the startled woman space. "I didn't mean to frighten you."

"Not at all." Mrs. Chatsworth gave a nervous laugh. "Just

looking for books. You know I do love my books. I always have been the most voracious reader..."

There was a frenetic quality to her rambling as she pontificated over the finer points of reading, before finishing with a prompt good-day and hastily took her leave.

Emma remained where she stood, considering the woman's curious behavior. That's when she noticed it—a misshelved book in the mystery section. The spine stood out of place among the titles of murder mysteries and espionage, its title printed in simple lettering, reading *The Secret Garden*.

46

A STACK OF mail awaited Emma a week later as she took Tubby for a walk. The envelope on top was from Olivia.

A mix of excitement and trepidation filled Emma. Olivia's letters had become increasingly morose, no longer bothering to mention the books she'd read or the activities of the farm.

Emma had asked to visit again on many occasions, but each time Mrs. Taylor wrote back with a swift rejection, citing the melancholy that had fallen over Olivia after Emma's departure at Christmas.

A vise squeezed at Emma's chest, comprised of a mother's guilt and the perpetual longing for her child.

Emma slid open the envelope to find this time there was no preamble or begging or even sentiment. There was only one sentence.

I want to come home.

Something about the bare simplicity of the statement made the hairs prickle at the back of Emma's neck. A mother's intuition, one she had learned long ago to heed and one that sent her rushing to the train station to procure a ticket to Chester for the following day.

That night, Emma lay awake, eyes staring into the oppressive black, that single line repeating in her head on a loop.

I want to come home. I want to come home. I want to come home.

Emma squeezed her eyes against the pressing weight of the darkness, then took her own advice and set her tears free. For all the months that had passed since she'd seen her daughter, for what the rift of separation might cause in their relationship, for the depth of Olivia's hurt.

The air raid siren began its infuriating wail.

Emma put a pillow over her head, though the thin layer did little to drown out the shrill cry.

God, how tired she was of it all. The ration, the wretched sirens, the hovering threat of danger, the constant exhaustion that never abated when there were so many shifts to take on at the canteen, and scarves to knit, and food to cook, and... and...

Olivia.

Whatever stores of energy Emma had clung to these many months finally ran dry. She lay beneath the pillow, breathing her own hot, stale air, and ignored Mrs. Pickering's hammering on her door and Tubby's yelps.

They finally went away, and moments later the air raid siren stopped as well, leaving a silence behind that was as thick and tangible as the darkness surrounding her.

A hum pricked at the innermost parts of her ear, through the muffled batting of the pillow. Emma's pulse jumped even as she lifted the pillow from her head to better make out the sound.

The drone of engines—not the steady whir of British planes, but the rhythmic throb of German aircraft.

Emma jolted from bed and out of her flat, rushing down the stairs so fast, she nearly fell. Framed against the face of a nearly full moon was a formation of planes so great in mass, she could not see where they ended in the night sky.

This was no small raid.

47

THE ALL-CLEAR DIDN'T sound until past four the next morning. Emma had managed to make it to the caves, where Mrs. Pickering had Tubby in his inconspicuous tote as they sheltered along with hundreds of others. Sleep had been impossible with the earth trembling at the onslaught of an attack that continued without pause.

"We're going to need the mobile canteen." There was a slight quiver to Mrs. Pickering's authoritative voice as they shifted forward with the crowd, moving toward the exit. "It's filled with petrol and rations, fully prepared to use immediately."

Emma climbed the stairs, careful to ensure Mrs. Pickering remained in front of her to keep the older woman from being jostled. Especially with Tubby's tote cradled in her arms.

"I can't drive the mobile canteen," Emma said apologetically. "I have my train to Chester in two hours." Even as she spoke, she caught that distinct odor of smoke and destruction. A familiar prickle of cold sweat tingled across her palms and her heartbeat throbbed like a fleet of German planes.

Emma came to stand beside her friend and sucked in a breath. The nocturnal darkness of early morning was lit with fires burning in the near distance. Close enough for the heat to sear away the predawn chill and ash to sift down over them like macabre snow.

Mrs. Pickering put a hand on Emma's shoulder. "I don't think you'll be going to Chester today."

By the time Emma arrived at Victoria Station, there was already a line in front of the mobile canteen. Margaret was inside boiling water, her hair tied beneath the same kind of scarf her mother used at the munitions factory.

"The water mains are busted, and the electricity is out." She rushed around the small space, setting out mugs and jam jars for tea.

Emma helped, drawing down the stores of their sugar while calling out for one of the WVS women to bring fruitcake from the canteen in the station that they'd baked the day before.

"No water or electricity anywhere in Nottingham?" Emma asked.

Margaret gave Emma a worried look. "None. Mum wasn't at the Raleigh factory last night, but that was bombed too."

Emma hurriedly filled the mugs and jam jars and began handing them out to people crowding in front of the small window of their van. Most of those coming for tea weren't civilians, but the men and women on Nottingham's front line. ARP Wardens with their heavy tin hats dusted with ash, nurses with filthy uniforms and white aprons spotted with crimson, and firemen in their heavy gear with soot-stained faces, necks and hands.

"How are things?" Emma asked, handing a plate of fruitcake to a fireman.

"Bad. A lot dead. Even more injured." He swallowed, his Adam's apple bobbing. "Lost a few of our own."

Emma's skin prickled as if she'd been plunged into ice water.

"Who?" Her movements were automatic as she handed him a jam jar of tea.

"Dunno." The man took his drink and left.

The certainty she had in Charles's safety slipped away at that moment, like wisps of smoke gliding between her fingers. She'd known his job was dangerous, but she hadn't truly acknowledged it. Not until now.

And she had never considered that his impaired vision might put him at a fatal disadvantage in the wrong circumstances.

Her hands trembled as she distributed the refreshments, her attention fixed on those lined up, searching every face in the hope of seeing Charles. The hours dragged on in countless jars and mugs sloshing with tea, the bottoms layered in a sifting of sugar yet to be dissolved.

Whenever men from the fire brigade approached, she asked after Charles. And to each query, they simply shook their heads. Margaret kept flicking worried looks in Emma's direction, their mutual fear standing in the middle of that small mobile canteen like a dense mass.

When they'd given out the last dregs of tea and there wasn't a crumb of fruitcake to be had, Emma busied herself by doing anything possible to keep from lowering the hatch on the van.

"There's nothing left to give out," Margaret said quietly. "He's likely occupied in another part of the city."

Emma stopped shifting empty jars around. There was no purpose to her efforts when there was no tea to be dispensed. Margaret was right. The fire brigade had their hands full, and Charles was likely in another location. But somehow closing the mobile canteen seemed so final, as if doing so would cut off the possibility of any communication about Charles's whereabouts.

Emma swallowed, her mouth impossibly dry. "Can we wait a moment more?"

"I don't see why we can't keep the van open while we clean." Margaret handed her a towel.

When the last dish was washed and tucked into the locking cupboards, the time finally came to seal up the mobile canteen and return home. The late-afternoon sky was bruised with smoke and ash and Emma's lower back had begun aching several hours before. She stepped through the narrow door, following Margaret, and turned to lock it behind them.

"Emma."

She spun around at the familiar voice. "Charles." She sprinted across the parking lot of Victoria Station, her heels clacking against the asphalt, and practically slammed into his embrace. He was solid against her, real. Alive.

"Are you all right?" she gasped.

He nodded, his jaw tight. "But Francis…"

Emma's heart lurched. "Is he…?"

"He's alive, but injured." Charles twisted his mouth to the side, obviously needing a moment to compose his emotions. "I've never seen it before, being in the middle of the bombing like that. The incendiaries came down so fast, we couldn't put them out. Next thing we knew, bombs were whistling down, sending the earth erupting all around us. A dog was trapped on a second floor, and you know Francis." Charles gave a mirthless smile. "I hadn't even seen the dog, but already he was running into the burning house as it was falling to pieces. Came out with the dog wrapped in a blanket in his arms, scared but perfectly unharmed. That's when the house came down. The dog leaped away in time, but people can't move as fast, especially blokes as large as Francis. The building collapsted on top of him, broke his leg and knocked his head hard enough to leave him senseless."

"He'll recover?" Emma asked.

"Of course he will. He's Francis." But there was a shadow of doubt in Charles's deep brown gaze despite his confident reply. He took her hand in his and stared at her like he wanted to imprint her face on his memory. "Emma, when those bombs were falling, all I could think of was you. I knew Mum and Dad were in the caves, safe. But I couldn't stop worrying about you, wondering if you were safe too. I…"

Emma gazed up at him, her breath locked in her chest. "You what?"

"I want to marry you," he said in a rush. "Not now, not when I know how much you've lost in your life, and my job is so dangerous. But when this war is over, when I'm a boring accountant again, combing over ledgers and when the greatest injury I might sustain is a paper cut, Emmaline Taylor, I want to marry you if you'll have me."

"If I'll have you?" Her fear and sorrow from earlier transcended to a lightheaded joy and she found herself laughing even as warm tears wet the corners of her eyes.

"And if Olivia approves," he added.

Emma couldn't speak for a moment, so great with gratitude that he considered Olivia as much as her. "If she says yes, then so do I."

From somewhere down the street someone called to Charles. He lifted a hand up to let him know he'd be there in a moment.

Emma gripped his jacket in her hands, wishing she could tug him to her and keep him from going back. But that wasn't who he was.

She loosened her hold on him and pressed a kiss to his lips. "Be safe."

"Always." He winked and jogged away, toward the other firefighters.

Emma accompanied Margaret to the bus stop and then walked home the rest of the way. Several homes on the streets she passed had their windows blown out and one building was even missing its front door. But aside from those few instances, the remainder of the streets had been largely untouched.

The tenement house on Mooregate Street was still standing, its windows intact.

Emma opened the main door and was met with total silence. Mrs. Pickering was clearly not back yet or Tubby would be yapping in friendly welcomes. Emma was nearly to the second floor when the sound of a door opening came from Mr. Sanderson's flat.

"Mrs. Taylor." He came down the stairs in his house slippers, moving with surprising haste. "Someone came by with a telegram for you." He reached into the pocket of his jumper and withdrew the folded envelope.

Though Emma did not have anyone in the war to receive a telegram about, its presence left a warning going off in the back of her mind. She pulled the single page free and stared at the paper in her hands, disbelieving what she read.

> *Olivia has run away, likely to go home. Telegram immediately if you find her.*
> *Mr. and Mrs. Taylor*

Emma gaped at the message, her body going cold. Olivia was somewhere in England between Chester and Nottingham.

And depending on when Olivia left, she might well have been in Nottingham last night, out in the open amid the heavy bombing.

48

FIVE DAYS.

Olivia had been missing for five days.

Emma sat at the table in Mrs. Pickering's cheerful rose-patterned kitchen, feeling utterly helpless. The muscles in her thighs popped with exhaustion from having wound her way up and down what felt like every street in Nottingham. To no avail.

Maybe Olivia was somewhere between Chester and Nottingham, but she could always have become lost or taken. She could be anywhere in Britain.

A little girl on her own.

Emma put her hands to her mouth, but not soon enough to stifle her sob. There was an abyss in her chest where her heart should be, missing right alongside her daughter.

Mrs. Pickering rubbed a hand over Emma's back and put a cup of tea in front of her. Or perhaps she'd reheated the one from earlier that Emma hadn't drunk. She could hardly think to keep up with anything other than the search for Olivia and hunting down updates.

So far there had been none.

"The WVS headquarters in Chester telephoned," Mrs.

Pickering said in a delicate tone that suggested she was afraid Emma might break. "They spoke with your in-laws and Mrs. Taylor confirmed some money was missing. So at least Olivia has the means to afford train and bus tickets and food."

Emma nodded miserably.

"She won't be hungry," Mrs. Pickering added in a coaxing lilt.

Emma nodded again even as tears began to well hot in her eyes.

After this was over, when Olivia was home—and Emma refused to believe there would be any other outcome—Emma would be paying to install a telephone in her flat. No matter the cost. She refused to ever be in such a vulnerable position again. If Mrs. Pickering hadn't had hers installed recently, Emma would likely have remained camped out at the WVS headquarters.

"The whole of Britain's Women's Voluntary Service is out searching for her." Mrs. Pickering went to the window and lifted the curtain to peer out, as if scanning the street for Olivia. "I put a call out to every town and city. I gave a detailed description of her appearance and told them she'd likely be wearing a red jumper, one size too small."

Just thinking of that red jumper gouged into the emptiness in Emma's chest, tearing at the raw pain there as she remembered how proud Olivia had been when she'd received it, how she refused to get rid of the thing even though it scarcely fit.

Emma couldn't speak about this a moment longer. Talking did nothing more than make the agony of the situation even more unbearable.

"How is Francis?" Emma asked.

Mrs. Pickering had seen to his care since his injury, stopping by the hospital on several occasions with fresh vegetable soup and to read to him in the evenings.

"There's a lot more healing to do, but he's in good spirits." Mrs. Pickering flushed. "He said my vegetable soup is as good as my pie."

The phone rang, the sound shrill in the somber flat.

Mrs. Pickering ran to it so quickly she stumbled, then righted herself and lifted the receiver. "This is Mrs. Pickering."

She remained quiet as the other person spoke, their voice little more than a discordant tinny murmur from where Emma sat.

"Yes," Mrs. Pickering said before going quiet again. "Yes." The repeat of the word was a higher pitch.

Excited.

Emma straightened to attention and Mrs. Pickering gave a vigorous nod.

Hope flooded through Emma, her heart beating so fast, she felt dizzy.

"Canal Street, you say?" Mrs. Pickering nodded again, the glossy black phone receiver moving with her head. "Yes, please do try to fetch her. We'll be right there."

By the time she hung up, Emma already had her shoes and jacket on, and was pulling open the door to race outside.

"A tall girl matching Olivia's description was seen on Canal Street," Mrs. Pickering puffed, out of breath as she tried to catch up with Emma. "She was crossing the street, but by the time the woman got there to ask after her, she was gone. Likely into one of the shops, or down the street."

Mrs. Pickering paused at the bus stop.

"No time." Emma rushed on. "We can walk the two kilometers before the bus even arrives."

"Go on ahead," Mrs. Pickering called. "You'll be faster without me."

Emma picked up her pace, no longer walking at a clipped gait, but full-on running.

"Go find our girl," Mrs. Pickering shouted from behind her.

Air burned in Emma's lungs and her low-heeled shoes wobbled precariously with every heel strike, but she didn't slow down. Not when Olivia was in Nottingham, and in a location she didn't know well at that.

A spike of alarm tingled up Emma's spine a fraction of a second before she caught the sound that her body instinctively recognized. The rhythmic hum of German planes.

No.

But there hadn't been an air raid siren. How could there be planes without a warning?

Adrenaline shot through her, pumping her legs faster. Her heel caught on the pavement and twisted, sending pain shooting up her ankle. She rushed onward, her ankle growing weaker with each step.

Relying on her other foot, she limped on as quickly as possible. She would drag herself to Olivia by her fingernails if it meant finding her in time.

The throb of planes continually grew louder as Emma turned the final corner to Canal Street. They were nearly overhead now, the vibration of their engines so loud, it reverberated in the marrow of her bones.

That's when she saw it—a flash of red in the crowd down the street as people ran for shelter.

"Olivia," Emma cried. Ignoring the stabbing pain in her ankle, she sprinted as fast as her injury would allow.

But the planes were too loud. Too close.

Emma was nearer to the bit of red now, able to see the jumper plainly, how it crept up long arms, leaving lanky wrists bare, and the messy waves of chestnut hair that streamed down her back. The girl knocked hard on first one door of a private building, then ran to another, fist pounding in desperation.

Olivia.

A whistle sounded above and Emma's veins turned to ice.

She didn't need to look up to know what that sound meant. A baser, more primal part of her already knew.

The Germans were dropping their bombs.

An explosion blasted behind Emma, loud enough make her ears ring and leave her skull feeling like it was going to shatter. She bent over, covering her head, while still keeping her focus locked on the red jumper.

The door in front of Olivia opened and a pair of arms drew her hurriedly into the tenement building.

At least now Emma knew her exact location. And Olivia would be off the street, away from the bombs.

Just as she had that thought, the planes blacked out the sun overhead. The bottom of one slid open, revealing the cylindrical tube within that sailed out from the belly of the bomber, down, down, down.

Emma froze, unable to move as the bomb sailed directly toward the building Olivia had just entered.

49

THE BOMB HIT with a blast of fire that threw Emma backward in a violent wall of heat and pain. Her head cracked against the pavement and spots of white danced in her vision like drunken stars. She lay still for a moment, bewildered at the smoke rolling toward the sky, her mind mud-thick and her ears ringing.

Olivia.

The thought was instantaneous. Emma jerked up to a sitting position and the world spun around her.

She growled in frustration at her impairment, gritting her teeth in an effort to sharpen her fuzzy mind. The tenement building Olivia had gone into swam in Emma's view. Fire licked up from broken windows and part of the third floor was missing, but it was otherwise intact.

The two buildings to the right, however, were almost completely gone, with the third being little more than a patch of bald, scorched earth.

The bomb had not fallen directly where Olivia was after all.

Emma staggered to her feet, wincing as her weight landed on her bad ankle, and hobbled across the street to the building.

The first floor was on fire, evidenced by the charred curtains glowing with embers as they trailed out of the broken windows, revealing a torrent of flames within.

Olivia was in that burning building. Just as Emma had once been with Papa.

A howl of pain rose up from the emotional wound deep inside her.

She had lost her father. She would not lose her daughter too.

Her heart thundered in her ears and everything in her screamed at her to run.

Without another thought, Emma shoved down every instinct within her, and broke through the veil of smoke into an inferno of flames.

The interior of the building looked to be someone's home, with a burning sofa, scorched wallpaper, and a grandfather clock tipped on its side like something dead. The roar of the bestial blaze sent a chill down her spine despite the overwhelming heat.

The sound was one she recalled all too vividly from a decade ago. When she had been at its mercy. When that fateful fire had taken everything from her.

There was a familiar metallic taste at the back of her tongue and everything in her mind went numb with dread.

"Olivia!" Emma screamed her daughter's name, breaking through the horror of her memories and the paralysis of her terror.

The air stung her throat, burning a path down into her lungs. She pulled off her scarf to wrap around her mouth the way Papa had done with the blanket that day of the fire.

She scanned the home, searching for the jumper amid the red-and-orange flames that flicked and snapped and made invisible waves dance in her vision.

Smoke stung her eyes, and the intensity of the heat left her skin feeling as though it was blistering. But still she pressed deeper into the building, determined to find her daughter.

Olivia *was* here. Emma had seen with her own eyes. And she would not leave without her.

Emma called for her daughter again, choking on the acidic air. The sputtering gasp led to a racking cough as she sucked in lungfuls of smoke in an attempt to catch her breath.

Her head spun, aching with the fierce shuddering of her body. She inhaled, desperate to gulp in clean air, and was met only with more strangling smoke. Her limbs were suddenly too heavy and she staggered, her bad ankle collapsing beneath her. Then she was falling, crashing to the ground where the air was cooler, easier to breathe.

She drew in a deep breath. "Olivia." Her daughter's name was said on an exhale, too soft to be heard, but all she could manage. The roar of the fiery beast filled her ears, promising to finally claim her as its prize.

Her eyes fluttered closed, refusing to watch it come for her. *Olivia…*

Emma pulled in a hard breath, the air cool enough to shock her eyes open. Sunlight winked at her through a cloud of smoke.

"She's awake," someone said.

"Emma." Another voice. This one familiar.

She shifted her gaze from the sun and blinked up at Charles with a frown of confusion. Her mouth was so dry, her throat seemed to stick together. "Olivia?"

He was crouched at Emma's side, next to a nurse whose medical bag lay open. "Everyone's looking for her still," Charles replied gently. "Remember, she left your in-laws."

"No, she was in the building."

The building!

"She's in there, Charles." Emma leaped to her feet so fast, she almost fell.

Charles caught her by the arm, his hold gentle but firm. "You can't go in there, Emma, it's not safe."

The tenement building was immersed in flames now, a raging conflagration. But Olivia was in there. Right now, she could be lying amid the flames, choking on the burning air as Emma had done.

Wondering where her mother was.

That final thought had Emma pulling herself free from Charles and rushing toward the building. She went two steps before he reached for her again. When she evaded his grasp, he put his arms around her, not in an embrace, but in restraint.

"I'm sorry, Emma." His voice was laden with regret. "You can't go in there."

Something primal exploded inside her. She lashed at him like an animal, squirming and thrashing, but his grip was like steel. She didn't stop, screaming and writhing in a bid to escape his hold. A mother fighting to protect her child.

"Please don't do this," she sobbed, pleading with Charles. "Please let me go to my baby."

"Emma, you can't..." His words broke off, cracked with emotion.

There was a great, heaving howl, a sound that resonated in the depths of Emma's soul, one she'd heard only once before when Tower Bookshop crumbled in on itself.

Charles pulled her back, just as the building began to collapse.

Emma screamed and screamed and screamed, her throat raw, the sound drowned out completely by the deafening thunder as the top floor sank in on itself, burying everything within beneath a pile of blazing rubble.

"I'm sorry." Charles's grip around Emma relaxed and the fight drained out of her.

She was too late.

Emma choked on her pain. The intensity of it was so solid, so real, as if her heart had been wrenched from her breast by that savage fire beast.

And surely it had.

Olivia.

With her wild chestnut hair, and those wide blue eyes that had latched onto Emma's soul from the moment she was born. A perfect, beautiful daughter who looked up to Emma with respect. With love.

And Emma had failed her.

Olivia. With her infectious giggle, with a lovely kindness and empathy for one so young, with her enthusiasm for books, and a whole beautiful life ahead of her.

It was supposed to be the two of them against the world.

But the world had won.

Emma slid to the ground, a keening wail emanating from somewhere deep within her, a place that was irreparably broken.

Olivia was gone.

50

"EMMA." CHARLES'S VOICE called to her.

Agony rushed at her from every angle, most of all from within her heart. Emma shook her head, not wanting to be anywhere Olivia was not. Hers was a darkness from which she never wanted to wake.

"I'm sorry, Emma," Charles said in a thick voice. "I couldn't let you…"

"You did the right thing, lad." A man's deep voice resonated above Emma.

The right thing.

She blinked her eyes open to find a fireman standing over her, his hand on Charles's shoulder where he sat beside her. Charles's eyes were wet with tears, red-rimmed. He wiped at them with the back of his hand, smearing soot over his face.

A siren echoed in the air, the long, clean wail of the all-clear.

Though no air raid signal had alerted them of the attack, someone at least had the thought to let them know the onslaught was done.

If there had been an air raid warning, Olivia might have sought shelter sooner. She wouldn't be…

Emma curled around a fresh wave of pain, unable to even finish the thought.

People began to emerge from various shelters and from their homes, exclaiming with horror at the devastation wrought by the surprise daytime raid.

Emma watched them all through swollen eyes and slowly pushed up to a sitting position. "Can we..." She swallowed at the unforgiving knot in her throat. "Can we still get her out? Even after?"

"Yeah," Charles croaked. "Yeah, we can."

Crowds of people appeared in front of the burned buildings as Charles's fellow firefighters rushed to keep them at a safe distance. A couple caught her attention, an older man and woman with a little girl between them, chestnut-brown hair falling in riotous waves amid a red jumper that seemed a size too small.

Could it be...?

"Olivia," she whispered, leaning forward.

Charles grasped Emma, helping her to her feet as he looked in the direction she now stared.

"Olivia," Emma said, louder this time, desperation surging from a place deep inside her, rasping up from her very soul. "Olivia!"

The girl turned, that familiar, beautiful face that Emma had committed to memory time and time again brightening with surprise. "Mum!"

Emma rushed toward Olivia as her daughter ran toward her, meeting in the middle in a glorious clash of hugs and tears. Olivia was in her arms, all long limbs and silky hair. Not dead. Alive.

Emma cried out, an unintelligible blend of excitement and disbelief at the wonder of her daughter locked in her embrace. "You went into the building. I thought... I thought..."

Leaning back, she studied her daughter, her gaze searching to ensure Olivia was unharmed.

Olivia did the same to Emma, her eyes widening with shock. "Mum, what happened? Are you hurt?"

Charles had a supportive hand on Emma's arm. "She breathed in quite a bit of smoke, but she'll be fine."

"Smoke?" Olivia's eyes welled with tears. "Did you go into the building for me?"

"Of course I did, Olive." Then Emma hugged Olivia to her again, reassuring herself that her daughter was there, that she was truly safe.

The couple who had been with Olivia approached. "Is this your girl?"

Emma nodded, unable to find her voice.

"We were just going down into the caves beneath our home when we heard her knocking," the woman said.

"You have caves?" Emma asked stupidly. Many residents in Nottingham did. But her thoughts were reeling too fast to keep up with.

Olivia was alive. Nothing else seemed to process other than that one glorious fact.

Olivia was alive.

"Yes, we've a cave beneath the house," the man said. "Nothing too large, mind you, but a good amount of space for storage that we've been using as a shelter."

The woman looked to her home, her face lined with a sorrow Emma knew all too well. "It's a good thing the caves in the neighborhood link up together, else we might have been stuck down there."

"You saved my daughter." Emma was lightheaded with gratitude. "Thank you."

Olivia looked up at Charles, her expression one of awe. "Did you save my mum?"

"I can't take credit for it." He nodded toward a row of men shooting a jet of water into the flames from a portable cart. "One of them did, but I'm here now."

Olivia grinned at him. "I'm glad you are."

A shape in the distance jogged toward them, the movements swift but somewhat ungainly. Within seconds, that shape became Mrs. Pickering, her cheeks red, her neat gray hair flying about.

"Olivia." She came to a stop and braced her palms on her knees, huffing for breath. "Thank heavens you're safe, child. And Emma, what on earth has happened to you?" Mrs. Pickering took a WVS pamphlet from her handbag and waved it in front of her face, her skin glossy with perspiration.

Emma explained what happened, how she'd seen Olivia and been too late to stop her. How the couple who had lost their home had saved her life.

"This was your home?" Mrs. Pickering's expression went somber and she stopped waving the pamphlet.

"Was." The woman's face crumpled and the man reached for his wife, pulling her close.

"Well," Mrs. Pickering said, the self-possessed tone edging into her voice. "I'm Mrs. Pickering with the WVS, and I'll see that you have everything you need. Clothes, lodging, furnishings to get you by, a government stipend. Do you have your ration coupons?"

The man glanced around them, as though their ration books might materialize.

"It doesn't matter, we'll get replacements," Mrs. Pickering said with a confidence that suggested she could summon them out of the air. "I'll set everything to rights for you."

The overwhelming shock and profound relief of being reunited with Olivia gave way to an infuriating horror at what might have happened as Charles transported them home in the rear seat of the fire truck. Emma's ankle was bound in a wrap for support—a bad sprain that should heal in a month or so.

But Emma's ankle was the last thing on her mind as Charles helped her up the stairs and said goodbye to them both with a tousle of Olivia's hair that left her smiling. Emma waited until they were in the apartment with the door firmly closed.

"How could you have run away?" Emma asked, her words trembling with a rush of every emotion a mother could ever feel. Fear, hurt, anger, anxiety, disbelief, compassion, and love. So much love that her heart felt as though it might explode out of her chest.

Olivia faced her, straight-backed, eyes locked on Emma, stoic and absent of any guilt. "Because I missed you. I was safe in Chester, but what about you?" Her chin jutted forward with a defiance that was so rare in her daughter. "What if a bomb fell on you and you died? I'd have no one."

The anger drained from Emma and she limped to the couch, waving Olivia over to join her. "If something happened to me, your grandparents would have continued to care for you," she said softly.

Olivia slid her a look. "You know that isn't the same." But still, she joined Emma on the couch, nestling beside her, the missing piece of Emma's life fitting snugly back into place. "Please don't make me go back, Mum. Please let me stay here with you. I couldn't bear losing you."

"You were almost killed this afternoon, from the very thing I tried to protect you from." Emma's throat thickened. "How can you even ask to stay?"

"Because you know what it's like to lose your only parent."

Olivia didn't speak with spite, her words gentle, with a profound maturity that split Emma's heart in two.

"It's the two of us against the world, Mum." Olivia wrapped her hand around Emma's. "I don't want to be apart anymore."

Emma swallowed, hesitant to admit just how much she understood of what her daughter was saying. "Let me have a think on it."

While it wasn't the answer Olivia wanted and even though her lips screwed to the side of her face with quiet displeasure, she nodded. "At least that's not a no." She gave a little smile. "Can we go see Tubby?"

Emma laughed, grateful for a reprieve from the heaviness of their conversation. "After we wash up. I know he'll love to see you again. And you can meet Mrs. Pickering's rabbit."

Olivia slid off the couch, brightening. "A rabbit? What's his name?"

"Nameless."

Olivia quirked a brow, a new gesture Emma recognized as belonging to Mr. Taylor.

She stood up, careful of her ankle, and took Olivia's hand. "It's a long story."

Even as she began to tell the tale of the rabbit, her thoughts whirred on in the background, debating if she should keep Olivia home after such a near miss. And if she could even stand to send her away again after almost losing her forever.

51

LATER THAT NIGHT when all of Nottingham was asleep, Emma lay awake in bed, eyes wide open as Olivia breathed deep and even in slumber beside her.

How many hours had Emma lain awake?

She glanced at her new watch—a gift from Charles with arms that glowed with luminous paint, indicating it was just past one in the morning.

Her thoughts were too loud, replaying the fortunate events that led to her daughter's survival, as well as what could have gone wrong and tipped the scales of life precariously in the other direction.

She couldn't remain there a second longer. Careful not to wake Olivia, she slid from the bed. But even in the open living area, the flat was too stuffy, too close. She needed to get outside so she could think.

After leaving a hasty note in case Olivia woke and looked for her, Emma hurried from the flat, mindful of her injured ankle. She didn't stop until she was out into the night air, at the back of the house where a narrow strip of grass had been transformed into a thriving nest of string beans.

A shuddering exhale wrenched from her, and in the quiet solitude of the night, her tears came. Those helpless, awful tears she couldn't keep at bay a second longer. The ones that told her there was no solution that would keep Olivia both happy and safe.

When Emma's eyes were dry and the jagged hiccupping of her breathing went even, a rhythmic crunching caught her ears. She glanced to Nameless in his cage, chewing exuberantly on leafy carrot tops from that evening's dinner, an audible backdrop to an otherwise quiet setting.

The sound of a masculine throat being cleared cut through the night. She snapped upright and swiped all evidence of tears from her cheeks with the heels of her palms.

Mr. Sanderson leaned forward, emerging from where he sat in the shadows, his presence revealed in the wash of silvery moonlight.

"Sorry," she mumbled. "I didn't know you'd be out here. Not this late."

"I don't sleep well." He nodded upward. "I'd rather stare at the heavens than the flat of my ceiling."

"I apologize—I know you've had well enough of my tears."

"Your girl is home now." He gazed up at her in question.

"Yes, and she wants to stay."

He frowned. "You don't want her to?"

"Of course I want her to stay." Emma's voice pitched with incredulity. "But how can she with all the bombing? Especially after today, when I thought…when I thought she'd been killed." Her voice caught.

"But she wasn't." A fierceness lit his eyes with an uncharacteristic energy. "And she's right here. With you. Which is where a child deserves to be. With their mother."

Emma stared at him, dumbfounded by the harsh reply. Since the start of the war, people had cast their judgments, criticizing her every decision regarding Olivia. And now, Mr.

Sanderson, who didn't have children—or even a family for that matter—was glaring at her with scorn.

By God, she could take no more.

Heat blazed in Emma's cheeks. "How dare you?"

He scoffed, and looked away, unaffected by her ire. "I dare because I was in your position once."

Emma stilled, suddenly recalling the box of clothes he'd delivered to Mrs. Pickering for the refugees. They'd all been older, belonging to another time.

"Was it during the Great War?" Though Emma whispered the query, her words carried in the quiet as Nameless continued to chew.

"Just after it ended." He folded his hands together. "November 1918. The Spanish influenza."

A spell of silence fell between them, one Emma was loathe to disrupt lest the older man stop speaking. Just when she thought he might say nothing more, he continued.

"Over six thousand people died in Nottingham that November. You couldn't go down the street without seeing a funeral pass by. We had to wear these dreadful masks." He paused and looked down, shifting his feet so his slippers scuffed against the ground. "I had two boys then. Eleven and seven, they were. Your Olivia reminds me of my youngest. Just as bright and inquisitive."

Prescient anticipation squeezed at Emma's heart. She could guess where his story was going.

Mr. Sanderson cleared his throat before resuming. "He fell ill first, my youngest. Near the end of November. My wife caught it from him, then my oldest began to run a fever. The hospital was overrun, so they set up tents for those who had fallen sick. I took them there. Like all the posters and newspapers told us to do."

His chest lifted with a deep inhale that he let out in a slow, dragging exhale. "They died there. Barely even a day after I'd taken them. I kept waiting for the flu to come for me, but it didn't." He lowered his head and pinched at his eyes before looking up again. "I never should have taken them. The boys were scared. Jane was too, I could see the fear in her eyes. I wasn't there with them when they..." His words tapered off and he swallowed.

Emma put a hand on his shoulder. The gesture was simple, inadequate in the face of such agony, but it was all she could think to do.

"They died scared and alone in an unfamiliar place." Mr. Sanderson looked up, his eyes brimming with pain. "This is a war, Mrs. Taylor. Nowhere in Britain is truly safe. Don't let her be scared and alone and in an unfamiliar place. Not without you."

The words struck Emma with such poignancy that she almost winced.

"I know you work and that makes having your daughter at home difficult, especially when she has to be alone after school," he continued. "I can help. Take her to her lessons, be there when she gets out."

Emma started to shake her head. What he was offering was too much.

He settled his warm, dry hand over hers where it still rested on his shoulder in comfort. "Let this old man have a bit of purpose, eh?"

There was kindness in his words, and Emma found herself nodding. "Only if she isn't too much of a disruption."

"Quite the opposite, Mrs. Taylor." He smiled, the first real, genuine smile she'd ever seen from him.

Exactly five days later, on a sunny Monday morning, Emma and Olivia emerged from their apartment to walk to school.

True to his word, Mr. Sanderson was on the first-floor landing, waiting for them when they descended.

Emma nearly asked again if Mr. Sanderson truly minded, when Olivia bounded up to him and presented him with some bread Emma had helped her toast that morning.

"Good morning, Mr. Sanderson," Olivia chirped. "I made you fried bread in case you're hungry."

The old man beamed, his eyes bright as he accepted the food from Olivia. "That was good of you, miduk. Thank you."

Olivia held Emma's hand and reached for Mr. Sanderson's. Together, the three of them walked to the school, at a slow pace for Emma's healing ankle, as Olivia chattered on as she was wont to do. Nonstop, with barely a breath in between, as she regaled them with the most minute details about farming life in Chester.

And never had Emma heard anything more wonderful in her entire life.

When they finally arrived at school, Olivia slowed somewhat, releasing their hands as her gaze fixed anxiously on her classmates.

"Go on," Mr. Sanderson said.

Olivia shuffled forward.

Emma knew the power of her daughter's concerns and stepped forward to take her daughter's hand again, but Mr. Sanderson stopped her with a gentle touch on her forearm. He shook his head and looked pointedly at a child walking toward them. Toward Olivia.

Edmund stopped in front of her with a smile that revealed a gap between his front teeth. "We're going to race before lessons start. Want to join?"

Olivia's apprehension melted with a grin as she nodded.

Then Edmund grabbed her hand and together they ran toward the cluster of their classmates.

Emma looked at Mr. Sanderson, who simply shrugged.

In that moment, she genuinely appreciated his offer to walk Olivia to and from school so she wouldn't be lost or scared or alone. And from the smile on his face as he watched the children play, she suspected he was grateful to finally have some companionship as well.

52

"SHH, SHE'S COMING," Mrs. Pickering said, letting the curtain flick back over the window.

Emma and Charles exchanged an eager look and shifted toward the front door.

Voices sounded at the front of the tenement house, Mr. Sanderson's deep one humming in agreement, and the incessant chatter of Olivia's. Only a week had passed since Olivia returned to school, but between Mr. Sanderson's generosity in walking her to and from her lessons and the other children being so welcoming, there had been a marked change in Olivia, as though she had actually begun to enjoy her classes. Well, most of them anyway. Especially with Mr. Sanderson's patient help with her homework in the afternoons while Emma was at work.

Francis limped over and stood by Emma. They were quite a pair—him with his broken leg and Emma with her ankle still bound from her injury.

The voices were in the stairwell now, louder, and Tubby ran back and forth between everyone in Mrs. Pickering's flat, a live wire of excitement.

Charles opened the door and they all shouted, "Happy birthday!"

"And happy birthday to you too," Olivia sang out to Charles. She'd been delighted to learn he shared her birthday.

And she'd been absolutely overjoyed when Charles asked how she felt about him marrying Emma.

Olivia peered up at Charles now. "How old are you?"

"Oh, Olive," Emma chided gently. "You shouldn't ask such things."

But Charles didn't seem to mind and rubbed Olivia's head, tousling her hair. "Old enough to have cake for lunch."

"There's cake?" Olivia squealed and ran inside with an overly excited Tubby darting after her.

"Come on in, Mr. Sanderson." Mrs. Pickering waved him inside.

"Did you know Mr. Sanderson is an excellent reader?" Olivia asked, settling into a kitchen chair, her eyes fixed on the cake with a single candle thrust in the frosted center.

"Oh, is he?" Emma slid a glance at Mr. Sanderson, who simply shrugged.

"I asked him to look at the paper I'd written and he said the best way to know if it was good was to read it out loud," Olivia replied. "So he did. He was so good at it, I asked if he'd read to me sometime, the way you did with *Anne of Green Gables*, Mum."

"I told her I would as long as she had good marks in school," Mr. Sanderson added.

"Including maths." Olivia scowled and dramatically folded her arms over her chest. "But he did say he thinks I would like Shakespeare and he'd start with that."

"Shakespeare?" Emma cast a questioning glance at Mr. Sanderson, recalling tales of murder, vengeance and inappropriately licentious humor. "Isn't that a bit mature?"

Before Mr. Sanderson could speak, Olivia did so for him. "Mr. Sanderson says that we children are a tough lot because we've grown up in a war, and that Shakespeare will teach us the things we bloody well need to learn."

Emma gasped at the foul language coming out of her daughter's mouth.

But Mrs. Pickering erupted into laughter, setting them all off joining in her mirth.

All except Emma. "Olivia!"

For her part, Olivia at least had the good grace to look ashamed and slapped a hand over her mouth.

Mrs. Pickering grinned at Emma. "Oh, come now, they all do it at some point."

"And some of us need to mind what we say in front of impressionable ears." Mr. Sanderson grimaced before shooting Emma an apologetic smile.

In that past week she'd seen him more animated than in all the years she'd known him, as if he'd been brought back to life by his time with Olivia. Emma joined in the laughter, shaking her head.

"Now, what will your wish be?" she asked Olivia, intentionally swaying the topic from inappropriate words and Shakespeare.

On cue, Mrs. Pickering rushed forward with a match and lit the candle.

Olivia bit her bottom lip, her eyes lifting toward the ceiling in thought. "I'm already home," she said to herself. "And I'll have a new papa soon." She threw Charles a smile, who tossed one right back. "I think... I need a new red jumper." Then she blew out the candle, reducing the flame to a gray wisp of smoke.

"Best dust off those knitting needles, Emma," Mrs. Pickering teased.

"What about you?" Olivia asked Charles. "You need to make a wish too."

He nodded thoughtfully. "I know just what to wish for."

Mrs. Pickering lit the withered black wick once more.

Charles looked at the candle. "I wish I owned a bookshop that I could fill to the brim with every book we love, and I wish to run it with Emma as my wife so she can be married and still work with readers as she so enjoys."

Then he blew out the candle and sat upright, patting at his hip with a look of confusion on his face. "What's this?"

"Your pocket, your pocket," Olivia squealed.

Suddenly Emma realized that even though Olivia hadn't known about the surprise cake, there might have been something of a rehearsal between the two of them for this birthday wish exchange.

"There is indeed something in my pocket." Charles dug his hand into his pocket and produced a set of keys. "I guess my wish is already underway."

Emma gasped. "Did you really buy a bookshop?"

He shook his head. "Not fully yet." He got to his feet and set the keys in her palm, still warm from where they'd been cradled in his pocket. "It's just a building right now. Something to clean up and design as we like. I had some money put aside from my days at Essex & Sutherland and have been living with Mum and Dad until my brothers come home so they won't be lonely. There's nothing I'd love more than to put it to use in a venture we embark on together, one centered around the books that brought us together. Especially when I know how much you love working at the Booklover's Library and regret that you'd have to give that up to marry me. This lets you have it all."

Emma's heart swelled in her chest. For this man who knew her so completely, who went to such extremes to make her happy. "But it's your birthday. You should be receiving gifts, not me."

"Seeing how happy you are is all the gift I need." He gazed at her in the way men do when truly, deeply in love, and heat rushed in Emma's veins.

"What will we name it?" Emma asked, her mind spinning with all the possible ways they could design their bookshop.

"I thought I'd leave that to you."

Emma touched a finger to her chin. "Then I have a lot of options to consider."

A week later during her shift at the Booklover's Library, a familiar figure caught Emma's attention as Mrs. Chatsworth left the checkout desk with a book in hand. But she didn't depart the lending library with her new item and instead continued to peruse the shelves. How curious.

Emma slipped into the Bespoke Room, leaving the door cracked just wide enough to watch the woman.

Mrs. Chatsworth went to an area of the library where there was no one else and looked about surreptitiously. The only other employee on the floor was Irene, who was occupied with another subscriber.

Mrs. Chatsworth reached toward Pip, going under the little blue pillow he sat upon, and drew out a book. Still looking about, not mindful at all where she inserted it, she pushed the book into a row on the bookshelf, and grabbed another which she hastily slipped under Pip's pillow.

The swap happened in only a few seconds.

Clearly, this had been going on for some time.

Emma had at last uncovered the mystery of the misshelved books. She quickly entered the library floor and approached Mrs. Chatsworth.

402   MADELINE MARTIN

"Oh, goodness, you startled me with how quiet you are."
Mrs. Chatsworth put a hand to her chest and chuckled.

"I know."

Mrs. Chatsworth blinked her stubby little lashes. "I beg your pardon?"

"What's under Pip's pillow?" Emma indicated the dog, earning her an indignant growl from the ever-irascible Pip. "I know what's there. And I know you've been doing this for some time now."

"I…well…erm…that is…"

For once, Mrs. Chatsworth was entirely out of words.

She paused, sighed, then started again. "A subscription for two books is beyond my means, but I read them so fast, I need a fresh book for when I'm done with the first." Concern pulled her brows together. "I won't be losing my membership over this, will I?"

Her words took Emma aback. In truth, she hadn't considered what would happen with Mrs. Chatsworth, only that the mystery of the misshelved books—and occasional missing books—had finally been solved.

Mrs. Chatsworth took Emma's silence as confirmation of her terminated membership. "Please." Her shoulders sagged. "My husband left me several years ago. I don't have anyone else in my life but Pip." She looked down at the little dog, who had readily fallen asleep once more on his pillow. "I take two books at once because, well, because I know coming here takes you from other subscribers because…" She shifted from one foot to the other. "Well, I talk too much. I know I do. I heard Miss Crane mention it once to another subscriber, saying I needed my own employee just to listen to my stories. I don't mean to be so voluable, truly. I just…that is… I'm lonely." She swallowed, her expression pained. "I suppose that's terribly pathetic."

Suddenly Emma was grateful for the many times she'd listened to Mrs. Chatsworth rather than trying to rush her from the library. "I enjoy hearing what you think of books you've read," Emma said.

Mrs. Chatsworth blinked in apparent surprise. "I'm sorry?"

"You always have such lovely insights into what the author wrote." Emma smiled at her. "We're happy to have you here, Mrs. Chatsworth. Please know you needn't worry about coming in too often to select new books. We would rather see you and Pip more often than have you feel like you need to secret an extra book home."

Mrs. Chatsworth gave a tentative smile in return. "Truly?"

"Yes, of course. And I think if you're willing to simply come in more often, and not subject Pip to the discomfort of hidden books, then perhaps we can forget this ever happened."

"I would like that very much." Mrs. Chatsworth tilted her head graciously.

Emma held out her hand for the book.

Mrs. Chatsworth withdrew *The Mask of Dimitrios* from beneath Pip's bedding with a sheepish grin. "Do you mind holding this for me?"

Emma accepted the book. "Not at all."

"Then I'll see you in two days." And with a jaunty swirl of her hat's feather, Mrs. Chatsworth turned to exit the library with only one book—properly checked out—in hand.

As she departed, she shifted around someone. A soldier.

He strode into the library with a slight limp and looked around the room, as if searching for someone. There was an unnatural leanness to his face and his uniform hung loose on his thin frame.

Emma approached him, intending to help, when recognition dawned and she gaped in shock.

"Is Margaret here?" He glanced around the library. "Miss Avory, I mean. I…"

Just then, the Bespoke Room door opened and Margaret emerged then abruptly stopped.

The book in her hands thudded to the floor and she put her hands over her mouth. "Jeffrey?"

"Margaret." His voice was husky with emotion, and he reached her in three long strides, pulling her into his arms.

Margaret touched his face, her eyes searching his, and Emma knew she was afraid to trust that this was real. That *he* was real.

"I thought you were dead," Margaret whispered. "That I'd never see you again."

"Captured." Jeffrey stroked her hair, her cheek. "I thought of you every day. I think it's what kept me alive until I could escape."

Irene stood beside Emma, dabbing her eyes with a handkerchief as Miss Crane approached with Miss Bainbridge following behind her.

Jeffrey pulled Margaret to him and kissed her. It was a hungry, desperate kiss, the kind one reads about in books, filled with passion and promise and love amid the harrowing landscape of war.

Like what Emma had shared with Charles after Coventry.

"This is unacceptable," Miss Crane hissed. "In the middle of the library."

"Oh, do hush, Miss Crane," Miss Bainbridge snapped. "We could all use a little joy these days. Even you."

And they truly did all need a little joy in the darkness of war. Whether through the return of a loved one, like Olivia and Jeffrey, or finding a new love, like with Charles. Or even in the discovery of an unexpected friend or a riveting new novel, both of which were to be found within the Booklover's Library.

For so long, Emma had resisted the urge to ask others for help, or even to accept it when offered. For so long, she had always told herself it was just her and Olivia, the two of them against the world.

But really, they weren't alone at all. There was also Mr. Sanderson, and Mrs. Pickering, and Charles, and Margaret, and the women of the WVS, and the subscribers and employees of the Booklover's Library. Theirs was a community built on love and respect and a willingness to help.

That would be how they would all get through this war.

That, and, of course, the occasional distraction of a good book.

EPILOGUE

June 1946
Five years later

THERE WAS A familiar comfort in the short walk downstairs from their flat to the two-story bookshop below. Emma went about her routine, turning the lights on, and straightening this and that in preparation of opening. A hot cup of tea waited for her on the countertop by the cash register, a ribbon of steam curling from the dark liquid.

A smile touched her face as she wrapped her chilled hands around the hot mug. Charles always brewed her a cup before leaving to fetch the morning paper.

She looked around at the quiet shop, similar to the classic dark wood-and-leather interior of her father's bookshop, but with more feminine touches, like the stained-glass windows, the carpets on the hardwood floors, and fresh flowers in vases. Attributes that reminded her of the Booklover's Library.

The renovation of the old building had been intense, and carefully done around the ration on materials, through hard work and cost efficiency.

A rumble of footsteps clattered down the stairs and Olivia strode toward the large front desk, her gait confident. At fourteen, she was nearly as tall as Emma, her wavy hair now tamed into soft curls that framed a face that had lost the plumpness of youth. She was elegantly beautiful, with high cheekbones and a lovely smile that always made the boys at school follow her about like besotted puppies.

"Morning, Mum." Olivia set her suitcase on the floor—that same battered thing that had once belonged to Arthur—and reached for Emma's tea, stealing a sip as she'd recently begun to do.

"Do you have everything you need?" Emma asked, mentally going over everything Olivia might require for a trip to visit with her grandparents in Chester.

"Almost." Olivia slipped down one of the aisles, her gaze skimming the neat row of spines.

"Are you sure you're comfortable traveling on your own?" Emma tried to keep the nervousness out of her voice.

Olivia had gone to her grandparents every summer since the year she ran away. After all, the intent to run away hadn't been because she didn't like them, but how desperately she longed for home. She'd traveled on her own already once before, the previous year—at her insistence—and been perfectly fine. But was there ever a time in a mother's life when she didn't worry about her children?

"I'll be fine." There was a note of impatience in Olivia's tone. One that seemed to say *I'm an adult now.*

But she wasn't an adult despite how much she tried to be. At fourteen, she still had a few years to go. Not that anyone could tell her as much.

"Promise you'll ring once you arrive at your grandparents'?" Emma asked.

The Taylors underwent the expense of a phone being installed the first summer Olivia went back to visit, to ensure she could call Emma should she begin to feel homesick. It had helped tremendously and made for an easier time for all involved.

"I'll call as soon as I arrive." Olivia set a book on the counter as she fidgeted with the long bag slung over her shoulder.

"Anne of Green Gables?" Emma lifted a brow.

"Nana says she doesn't like to read. I thought I might try to get her interested the way you did with me."

Such words were music to Emma's ears.

All of Olivia's life, Emma worried if she was doing the right thing with each decision made. In this particular case—regarding books and reading—she was glad to know she had indeed done well by her daughter.

"And what book are you bringing to read?" Emma peered into the large tote Olivia used like a handbag.

Olivia pulled out a copy of *Hamlet.* She'd been an ardent Shakespeare enthusiast since Emma finally conceded to allow Mr. Sanderson read *Macbeth* to her several months before. He'd performed it for all of them, down in the tenement house on Mooregate Street, and read so beautifully that there was not a one of them who hadn't been moved. Even Tubby had remained in silent awe where he'd sat at Mrs. Pickering's feet.

Although, she wasn't Mrs. Pickering anymore. Not since 1943, when she'd married Francis and become Mrs. Fletcher. Their wedding was supposed to be a quiet affair, but the full force of the Nottingham WVS and the fire brigade had turned out, making the event the talk of the season. And while there'd been cake, there had also been pie, which Mrs. Pickering had been insistent on making herself, much to Francis's delight.

"Has Charles come back yet?" Olivia glanced at her watch and bounced on the balls of her feet with the impatience of youth. "I want to say goodbye before I leave."

"Give him a moment." Emma unlocked the door and flipped

the sign to Open. Several women were already walking toward the shop, holding the hands of their children.

Story time on Saturday mornings was one of the most popular events at the bookshop.

A jaunty whistling tune came from the back of the shop, followed the by hard close of a door that too often stuck on damp mornings.

"Ah, here he is now." Emma smoothed her hair in anticipation of seeing her husband.

They had been married nearly a full year, though in some ways, Emma couldn't remember a time when he hadn't been in their lives.

Their wedding had been everything she'd wanted, with Olivia and all their dearest friends to witness the joyous occasion and the man she'd fallen in love with waiting for her at the end of the aisle. Margaret had found a lovely blue dress at a WVS clothing exchange with small beads on the skirt that winked and sparkled like gemstones when Emma moved. And though Charles had said he'd marry her in a potato sack, she loved the way his eyes widened when he saw her in that dress.

"You're always whistling," Olivia teased as Charles approached the front desk.

"I'm always happy when I see you two." He set the newspaper on the countertop and gave Emma a kiss on the cheek, his face still cool from the morning air. "Is it time already?" He glanced at his watch.

"Now that I can say goodbye properly it is." Olivia embraced Charles and released him with a smile before going to Emma for one last hug and kiss.

"I'll walk you to the station," Charles said.

Olivia folded her arms over her chest. "I can do it on my own."

There was that whine to her voice again, the desire to be an adult even as she was acting like a child.

But Charles wasn't put off by her attitude. He never was. "I only meant so I could carry your suitcase. It looks heavy..." He reached for it and gave an exaggerated grunt.

Olivia laughed. "It isn't that bad."

"Isn't it?" He staggered, putting a hand to his lower back as if in pain before meeting Emma's gaze with a playful grin.

"Maybe it's a little heavy," Olivia conceded.

Charles straightened, still holding the suitcase.

And just like that, he'd done it again. He'd managed to watch over Olivia in a way that didn't make her feel like she was a child who had to be looked after.

They shared a bond between them, as sure and fast as if Olivia had truly been Charles's daughter by birth. And while he had no intention of ever erasing the memory of her father, he'd taken on his role as a paternal figure in her life with an earnestness that warmed Emma's heart.

She waved as the two set out for the train station, knowing Charles wouldn't return until he'd seen the train safely off. But then he'd always protected them. Especially so after his youngest brother's death in '44. The devastating news had left him with a streak of white in his hair and a determination to protect everyone else in his life.

Several women entered the shop with their children, waving good morning as they passed. In a single-file line, they took their seats at a cleared area near the back of the shop where large stained-glass windows cast shades of pink and yellow and green over a thick pile rug.

Seeing all the children back in Nottingham again was such a lovely thing. Some had found reuniting hard, the stretch of nearly six years yawning between them as children returned entirely different than who they'd been when they left. Emma was grateful she'd allowed Olivia to remain home after that fateful day when she'd almost lost her.

But as joyously as they'd celebrated the end of the war, there had been such great sadness as well. The devastation to the families of the many men who did not come home. The horrors of the camps revealed, as well as the atrocious persecution and murder of so many innocent souls. The destruction of what was left behind, where once great cities had been reduced to rubble and dwindling populations.

The war was over, and Hitler was dead. The time had come to rebuild in any way they could. To recover amid so much pain.

That rehabilitation of their lives was what Charles and Emma kept in mind when they finally opened their bookshop several months back. A way to heal, to bring joy to a world that felt too dark and bleak.

Mrs. Chatsworth entered with a bright yellow hat and an equally cheerful singsong of a good-morning to match. She glanced around a bookshelf, peeking at the cluster of mothers and children sitting on the carpet.

"It's Mrs. Chatsworth," a little girl called.

An eruption of cheers rose up from the floor.

"And Pip," someone added.

Mrs. Chatsworth lifted Pip's basket a little higher and was rewarded with a chorus of delighted squeals and coos.

"Have fun." Emma handed her the copy of *Peter Pan and Wendy*, marked at the location Mrs. Chatsworth had left off the Saturday before.

"Always." She thanked Emma, not that it was needed. The radiant joy on her face every Saturday as she read to the children was thanks enough.

Emma had gotten the idea to ask Mrs. Chatsworth to be their story time reader from the happiness Mr. Sanderson derived from his friendship with her and Olivia. As though being around the exuberance of children eased the grip of loneliness and loss.

Just as working at the Booklover's Library had helped heal Emma.

The door chimed again. "Sorry I'm late." Margaret swept into the shop, glowing with good health.

"You know they're all here for Mrs. Chatsworth anyway." Emma scooted out of the way so Margaret could put her things behind the desk.

Handbag and jacket properly stowed, she came back around the desk, and leaned against the edge with a hand on her round stomach. Jeffrey's grandmother's diamond ring glittered on her hand, paired with a wedding band.

She'd been lovely in her mother's wedding dress, and there hadn't been a dry eye in the church when she and Jeffrey finally wed. He hadn't returned to the war after he reunited with Margaret that day in the Booklover's Library. The injuries he'd sustained when he was captured were too great.

Emma wasn't privy to all the details, but she knew Jeffrey found strength in Margaret and that she had enough love, kindness, and patience for them both.

"This wee one has been active this morning." Margaret rubbed her stomach with an affectionate smile. "I can't wait to meet her—or him—to have the kind of relationship I've seen you have with Olivia."

That Margaret saw Emma's relationship with her daughter as something to aspire to was truly one of the best compliments she could ever receive.

"Oh," Margaret said abruptly, as though having just recalled something important. "You'll never guess who I saw on my way over here."

"Mr. Beard?"

Margaret laughed. "No, but we are set to receive a new batch of mysteries next Wednesday. I suspect we'll see him then." She opened her mouth to answer when the door chimed open, and Miss Bainbridge entered.

Of all the people who might have entered the shop, Emma had not expected the manageress of the Booklover's Library. But then, there was really no competition between a bookshop and a lending library.

"Miss Bainbridge, how wonderful to see you."

The older woman reached for Emma's hand with an affectionate squeeze. "I meant to come when you opened, but I've been so busy. I left Miss Crane in charge of the library this morning, which you know she doesn't mind." She glanced between Emma and Margaret. "Oh, it is so good to see you both working together again."

Then she turned to the bookshop with a soft intake of breath.

"What do you think?" Emma asked, suddenly very eager to please her former manageress, the way she'd been when she worked for her those many years.

Miss Bainbridge sniffed and put her hand to her chest.

"Are you quite all right?" Emma asked.

Miss Bainbridge blinked rapidly in an obvious attempt to compose herself. "Forgive me, Miss Tay—" She stopped and smiled as she continued, "Mrs. Fisk. It's only…"

Emma regarded the other woman with concern. "What is it?"

Miss Bainbridge gave an embarrassed shake of her head. "You see, your father and I, we dated some time ago."

Whatever Emma had been expecting, it was not that. "I beg your pardon?"

"Oh, nothing terribly serious." Miss Bainbridge waved her hand dismissively. "Several dinners, a few outings at the cinema, an evening at the Goose Fair." The wistful expression on her face didn't speak of "nothing terribly serious." And judging from the rosy hue creeping up the older woman's cheeks, their relationship had been far more than all that.

Emma thought back to those days before the fire, all her father's appointments that had taken him away on evenings. She'd relished the freedom of those nights. Not that she hadn't missed his company, but she'd embraced the responsibility of running the shop on her own, tasting those first few notes of adulthood and savoring the feel of being grown-up.

"You cared for him," Emma surmised gently.

"Yes." Miss Bainbridge offered an embarrassed little laugh. "I wanted more from the relationship than he was able to give. He had loved your mother so very much." There was a note of sadness to her voice. "I don't think he could ever have felt for me what I felt for him."

The sorrow to her tone made Emma ache for Miss Bainbridge, who'd had the terrible misfortune of unrequited love. "You never told me you knew him."

"It was too painful." Miss Bainbridge clutched her hands together. "After his death..." She gave a resigned sigh. "I thought of going to you many times, but didn't know if doing so might be overstepping. After all, he had never mentioned introducing me to you. Oh, but he loved you so very much." Her eyes sparkled. "When we weren't chatting about books, he was talking about you. How kind a young lady you were, how lovely, how very clever, how the bookshop would flourish under your care one day."

When he was alive, Papa had told Emma all those things. But to hear the words spoken from someone else, to find that he hadn't been able to stop talking about her, was truly precious.

"He would have been so proud of you, my dear." Miss Bainbridge wiped the corner of her eye with a handkerchief. "How hard you worked at the Booklover's Library, how your efforts paved the way for the other widows we've hired. And now this…" She gestured to the grand bookshop. "What you've done, what you've created here…he would have been so proud." She nodded to herself. "So enormously proud."

Emma dabbed at her own eyes now, thoroughly moved by Miss Bainbridge's words.

"And what do you think of the shop's name?" Margaret asked.

"The Booklover's Bookshop?" Miss Bainbridge gave a cheeky lift of her brows. "It couldn't be more perfect."

And Emma had to agree. After all, the Booklover's Library had been something of a sanctuary for her and the other readers of Nottingham, providing succor from the war and the painful separation of so many loved ones. For Emma, the lending library had given her a chance to come to terms with her father's death, to open her heart to reading again, and to bring Olivia into a bookish world that had once been everything to Emma and her father.

During her time at the Booklover's Library, Emma had found herself without ever realizing she'd been lost in the first place.

She hoped that the Booklover's Bookshop might offer the same for people, a community built around healing and love, and an appreciation for the power of a good story.

The children on the carpet laughed collectively and Mrs. Chatsworth spoke in a high voice for one of the characters, sending them all into fits of giggles. It was the sound of joy, the sound of a nation healing.

But perhaps most lovely of all, it was the sound of a room full of future book lovers.

★ ★ ★ ★ ★

AUTHOR'S NOTE

WHILE THERE AREN'T too many lending libraries around now, they used to be popular in England in the late nineteen century and early twentieth century when books were less affordable than they are now.

Public libraries tended to carry more literary classics and research books with fewer contemporary novels that the general public wanted. This and many other reasons created a need for lending libraries that could offer a subscription for borrowing books priced a little more than the cost of a brand-new book.

While the Booklover's Library no longer exists, I did have the opportunity to visit Bromley House Library in Nottingham, England, on my research trip. Bromley House dates back to 1816 and is a fully functioning lending library that charges a subscription fee and offers an array of incredible books and archives. There is a gorgeous spiral staircase, rare books available for subscribers to peruse, reading rooms that are so numerous I got lost going through them all, and even a children's reading area that has a secret Narnia closet. The staff was immensely kind and answered all my questions, gave me a tour, and allowed me to study there for a day. Seeing a lending library in action was so helpful in my research.

So, yes, Boots' Booklover's Library was a real lending library that started in Nottingham and eventually had multiple locations in many Boots' chemists throughout England. These lending libraries were held to a high standard to provide an elevated level of service to their subscribers. Where most other lending libraries were relegated to basements and windowless areas, the Booklover's Library offered comfort and elegance with carpets, fresh-cut flowers, and stained-glass windows. The location of the Booklover's Libraries in the Boots' chemist shops was often on the second floor or at the back of the shop to create an experience where patrons could be immersed in the joy of selecting their next read away from the hustle and bustle of the chemist.

What's more, their employees were incredibly well cared for. Not only did Mrs. Boots insist early on that "her girls" be given hot chocolate or tea in the mornings, but prior to her retirement, she also personally visited her employees when they were sick, she helped created a school in Nottingham for their higher education, and she gifted a Bible to those who got married and had to leave their positions at the Booklover's Library.

Which leads me to why I found the lending library to be an inspiring setting. The women who worked for the Booklover's Library loved their jobs and were disinclined to leave, even if that meant holding off on getting married. They were known to have notoriously long engagements to avoid having to sacrifice the jobs they loved so much.

Many companies incorporated a marriage bar, meaning that when women were married, they were required to leave their jobs to become full-time wives. Boots' continued this practice into the 1950s, and the marriage bar became illegal in the UK in 1975 under the Sex Discrimination Act of 1975. While not all companies enlisted a marriage bar, most did, especially those with a higher-end clientele, like the Booklover's Library, which catered to the upper middle class.

Sadly, the marriage bar extended to widows with children, even though the widow was no longer married. This bar for widows was a large part of the inspiration for this story.

I'm divorced and spent several years as a single mother of my two beautiful girls. Even in these modern times when divorce for couples with kids is estimated to be as high as 40 percent, there are stigmas attached to being a single parent. Those stigmas were even more pronounced in the 1930s and 1940s. I won't go into a lot of detail on this, but I will say that many of my own experiences were shared in this story. Not only the bad, but also the good. Because as grateful as I am for my current wonderful husband, who is truly my own Mr. Fisk, those years when it was just me and my girls are still precious and left me with many fond memories.

One of those is the advent of breakfast faces. They started one morning when I realized we were out of milk—a necessary staple for my cereal-loving girls. In a pinch, I had to think of a way to entice them toward what we did have: eggs, bananas, grapes, and dry cereal. The breakfast face was born and still makes them smile a decade later.

Another memory that I wanted to share through Emma's eyes was how much gifts meant to her when going back to an empty home. Not even a month after my separation from my ex-husband, I attended a conference and was dreading returning home to an empty house while my girls were with their dad. As it happened, I won a massive gift basket full of books the last day of the conference (assembled by a romance book blogger who is now a friend, PJ Ausdenmore with *The Romance Dish*). Going home to a sad, empty house that had once been full of joy and laughter is something I would not wish on anyone. But that basket was a light in the debilitating dark. I think I took two hours to go through every item. It was a gift that was so meaningful to me at a time when I needed it most that I knew I had to incorporate it into Emma's story.

My girls are now teenagers (where did the time go?), so to recall some of those earlier days, I looked up pictures of when they were seven to nine years old to ensure I had Olivia's behavior just right at that age. All it took was a glimpse at those moments and the memories came rushing back. Olivia is a cross between both my girls: the artistic, sensitive nature of my oldest and the quiet, contemplative traits of my youngest. Reliving those aspects of my daughters through writing Olivia left my heart full and happy, and truly made me ache over Emma's plight in having to send her away.

When I first wrote about England at war in *The Last Bookshop in London*, I was horrified to learn about the children's evacuation. I cannot imagine having to choose between putting my girls in danger or sending them away to live with a stranger. Immediately I knew I wanted to write a book about the evacuation at some point. This interest was further piqued when a woman named Joyce Harvey reached out to me with an incredible evacuation story of her own. She had been so desperate to return home that she ran away from where she was billeted along the coast and managed to get all the way to South London, where her parents and police officers were waiting anxiously for any news on her. With such incredible real-life inspiration, I had to write this story. Thank you for sharing your amazing story, Joyce—you are plucky and fearless!

On the note of *The Last Bookshop in London*, I confess, I love the characters from that book dearly. They are lodged in my heart so thoroughly that when I realized I intended to bring Emma to London for her training, I had to include a cameo.

I hope everyone enjoyed the small visit with Grace and Mr. Evans at Primrose Hill Books as much as I did.

As with all my books, I did extensive research to ensure this story is as accurate as possible. One key element of this research was one I used also when writing *The Last Bookshop in London*: the Mass Observation. This initiative began in 1937 when hundreds of people were asked to record their daily thoughts and went on for almost thirty more years. The recorded thoughts were meant to capture the overall public feel for King Edward VIII's abdication and coincidentally segued into the start of WWII and captured the mood, reaction, and general daily life details of the population before, during, and after the war. Not everyone was in support of the Mass Observation, with some people finding it an invasion of privacy to friends, family, and neighbors who were being discussed in these diaries. However, the thoroughness of people's recordings through the Mass Observation has been invaluable to me as an author. And if you're wondering why Emma confronts Mr. Beard about what he's writing and learns he's working with Mass Observation—that was entirely meant to be tongue in cheek.

I always try to stay true to every historical detail I can with very little exceptions. In this particular book, the air raid that struck while Emma was chasing Olivia on Canal Street did actually have an air raid siren that went off. However, not all air raids had accompanying sirens to warn the populace beforehand. This was my one small tweak not only to heighten the danger of Emma seeing Olivia before the bombs fell, but also as a means of demonstrating what some people did endure with surprise air raids.

A reader's guide and list of titles mentioned in this book will be available upon the release of *The Booklover's Library* on September 10, 2024, on my website, www.madelinemartin.com.

ACKNOWLEDGMENTS

WHILE WRITING IS often seen as a solitary endeavor, it takes a community to bring a book into the world. I'm so immensely grateful for the team of friends, family, and colleagues who have helped *The Booklover's Library* become what it is today. Thank you to the stellar team at Hanover Square Press: to Peter Joseph and Grace Towery for your diligent edits to make my novel shine, to Leah Morse and Dayna Boyer for your immense marketing and publicity efforts to help spread the word about *The Booklover's Library*, and to Eden Railsback for always being so helpful with everything I need—no matter how big or small. Thank you also to the cover design team for yet another gorgeous cover and for always being so patient with me. And a huge thank you to Kathleen Carter for loving this book so much and for putting the publicity behind that passion to help launch *The Booklover's Library* out into the world. It is such a pleasure to work with every one of you.

None of this would be at all possible without my agent—the incomparable Kevan Lyon. Thank you for always believing in me and for your constant diligence and support with this book and all my books. I'm grateful for you every day.

Thank you to Felicity Whittle for taking time out of your day to join me in Nottingham and chat about *The Booklover's Library*. I'm also so grateful to the kind and generous staff at Bromley House Library who gave me a tour of their gorgeous lending library and allowed me to work there for the day.

I'm so fortunate to be surrounded with love and support from my family and friends. Thank you to my parents for always being so proud of me and for reading my books, and to my mother, who is always one of the last people to read my books before they go to print. Thank you to my husband, who helps with my plot for every story and is thus subjected to more history than he ever thought he'd hear in one lifetime—you truly are my very own Mr. Fisk and I'm forever grateful to have you in my life. And thank you to my sweet girls, who were such an inspiration for this story as well as being such an integral part of the creation of Olivia's character as she is made up of so many memories from both your childhoods. Thank you to my bestie, Eliza Knight, for being my sounding board, lifeline, and constant comapnion through our careers. Thank you to my dear friend Tracy Emro, who is the first person to read every one of my books as I'm writing them—your suggestions and ideas are always so helpful, as is your endless support. And thank you to Susan Seligman for taking the time to read through this book when it was in a rough state and provide such helpful feedback.

Thank you to the Lyonesses—my agent sisters—who are as close to real sisters as I've ever had and whose counsel and support are always so welcome. To my reader group, thank you for always being so excited along with me as I share details of my book ideas and for always being my best cheerleaders.

Thank you to the librarians and booksellers who carry my books and recommend them to their patrons. Additionally, thank you for all the years you have fed my love of reading by supplying me with endless amounts of books to love.

To all the book bloggers, reviewers, and bookstagrammers, thank you for your passion for books and your talent to share that passion with others. You are so integral to the book community and your efforts are so appreciated by readers and writers alike.

An enormous thank you to my readers. Thank you for always being so excited for the next book, for the power of your support, for all the time you have spent reading my books, sharing with friends, and writing reviews. You carry my characters in your hearts the same way I do and that means more to me than words could ever say. Thank you.